TREE SLAYER

TREE MAGIC BOOK TWO

HARRIET SPRINGBETT

TREE SLAYER

Published 2020 by Impress Books

13-14 Crook Business Centre, New Road, Crook, County Durham, DL15 8QX

Cover design by Molly Phipps

ISBN 13: 978-1-911293-39-2

To Sally, whose idea sparked this story.

Praise for Tree Magic

'Very well-written and well-constructed ... here is an author who has the skill of an accomplished novelist.'

Curtis Bausse, author of *One Green Bottle*

'Rainbow's journey was a wonder to read; Tree Magic is utterly stunning from start to finish.'

Rachel Bell, #SundayYA host

'This book is full of emotions ... a book that will be enjoyed by both young and older adult readers.'

Jacqui Brown, blogger at The French Village Diaries

'This is an original and complex story that kept me engaged. Highly recommended.'

Susan Elizabeth Hale, author of
Emma Oliver and the Song of Creation

'The writing is poised and elegant with many moments of lyricism.'

Atthys J. Gage, author of *Spark*

TABLE OF CONTENTS

PART I

HALF

CHAPTER 1

Rainbow put down the phone and raced upstairs to her bedroom. Christophe had a surprise for her and he sounded excited about it.

She pulled on shorts and a t-shirt, scraped her long brown hair into a ponytail and clattered back downstairs. She paused at the bathroom to brush her teeth. She didn't want morning breath to interfere with kissing.

Mum was in the kitchen, humming her new song as she made tea for the commune adults.

"Can I borrow the Mini?" Rainbow asked. "I'm going over to Christophe's."

Mum yawned. "I thought you were revising all weekend?"

"I've got the rest of the day to revise. And tomorrow. I won't be long."

Mum nodded, sat down with her tea and started scribbling musical notes on her manuscript. Rainbow dropped a kiss on her cheek, scooped up the keys and dashed outside into the sunny June morning.

She hadn't seen Christophe all week. He'd been training a

new motorbike apprentice at work and persuaded Rainbow to spend the final evenings before her Baccalaureate exams revising instead of hanging out with him. So she had. She'd ignored the call of the woods and sat in her loft, her school books open, gazing out of the windows at the enticing leaves.

Christophe. A smile spread across her face as she drove towards his flat in Cognac. They'd been together for nine months – the nine best months of her life. They'd also been the strangest, but that wasn't because of Chris. It was because of Mary.

When she and Mary hugged the silver maple tree last September, it had somehow absorbed Mary's body. Rainbow absorbed Mary's mind, which supposedly healed the split that should never have happened. All Mary's memories and emotions, from the moment she and Mary split into two parallels, had lodged themselves inside Rainbow.

Rainbow didn't feel healed. Mary continued to live on: to think and react to everything in Rainbow's life, making Rainbow feel overstuffed with bizarre feelings that conflicted with her own. Mary's negativity and her rebelliousness, her irreverent humour, her courage and her uncertainties all battled with Rainbow's own, simpler worldview. Mary was so strong that Rainbow could almost hear her voice, and she experienced yearnings for places she'd never seen and people she'd never known.

After nine months, she still felt as if she'd swallowed Mary whole, like a dose of unpleasant medicine, and was unable to digest her. All she could do was to keep the thoughts and feelings that emerged from Mary in a separate part of her mind, a small part that didn't interfere with her true self. Between her and Mary was a mental wall, a wall of bricks.

The only good part of sharing her mind and body with Mary was the love for Christophe she'd brought with her. There was no keeping *that* behind the wall. It seeped through the gaps and filled her with a heady scent that made life more joyful than ever before.

Luckily, Christophe understood her Mary problems. He understood everything about her – except, perhaps, that she didn't like revising. Or her obsession with Amrita Devi.

She parked Mum's Mini in front of the motorbike shop in Cognac and jumped out, hoping the surprise wasn't anything to do with motorbikes. Christophe's flat was above the shop where he worked, though he didn't work on Saturdays. She rang the doorbell to his flat and waited.

Amrita Devi was the girl in the Bishnoi legend who had saved a tree and lived – or saved a tree and died, according to Mary. Rainbow firmly believed Amrita had lived.

Although she hadn't seen Amrita since her vision last September, she'd had incessant dreams about her. At the beginning, the dreams showed her and Amrita as the closest of sisters, running through woodland together, holding hands, sharing secrets and laughing. But the dreams were becoming darker. The last few times they'd been nightmares, with Amrita pleading for help and begging Rainbow to understand something that Rainbow could never grasp. When Rainbow told Christophe about her dreams, his brown eyes would begin to glaze and she'd have to tickle him until he listened properly.

Christophe buzzed open the front door for her and waited

at the top of the stairs. She looked at him carefully as she walked up, in case the surprise was something boring like a new haircut. His thick hair was standing up at odd angles, which was normal for the morning, and there were no signs of piercings or tattoos. He did look worried, though. She glided into his bear hug and he held her tight.

"Is everything OK?" she asked.

"I missed you this week."

His warm lips met hers, and she responded to the softness of a kiss that was theirs and theirs alone. The colony of butterflies that had alighted in her belly last September awoke and fluttered around her whole body.

Rainbow ended the kiss and looked over his shoulder. He'd shut his flat door, which was unusual, so she couldn't see any enticing packages.

"What's all this about a surprise?" she asked.

He ran a hand through his hair. "I've got a present for you. Kind of. I hope I haven't done something stupid. You will tell me, won't you, if you think it's a mistake?"

"It won't be a mistake. You know I love your presents. Well, most of them."

She still hadn't learnt to ride the motorbike he'd given her for her eighteenth birthday – partly because Mary sent pangs of longing through her body whenever she saw it. Rainbow didn't see why Mary's wishes should take precedence over her own. Anyway, life was too busy for motorbike lessons. At weekends they partied with Christophe's friends, raced to the sea or jumped on a train and visited Bordeaux, Toulouse, Poitiers or La Rochelle. She'd never laughed as much or felt as light-hearted as she had done since September. Life was easy and fun – apart from schoolwork, Mary and the Amrita nightmares.

Christophe held her hand and carefully pushed open his door.

The flat smelt acrid, different from the usual mix of coffee and engine oil. She looked around. There was no wrapped present on his table.

He was grinning. She followed his gaze to the old velvet sofa they'd heaved upstairs from the shop reception together. He stepped behind it and crouched down.

A head appeared from under the sofa: a small, black head with white patches on its pointed ears.

"Ohhh!" She dropped to her knees and held out her hands. The kitten disappeared back under the sofa. She pursed her lips and made a squeaky call. The velvet edging lifted. She saw a pink nose, whiskers, and then another head. This one was tabby.

"Chris! They're gorgeous. How many are there?"

She scratched on the rug and two kittens crept out to investigate the noise. The black one batted her fingers while the tabby one hung back and watched with wide green eyes.

"Just the two of them," he said. "Though last night it sounded as if they'd multiplied by ten."

"Last night? How long have they been here?"

"I picked them up from the rescue centre yesterday evening. The new apprentice does voluntary work there and told me about them. I only meant to get you one, but they looked so sad in the cage that I couldn't help taking them both."

"You big softie!"

"I'd have brought home all the animals if I could," he

said. He sat down on the floor and leant against the sofa. The tabby kitten bounded onto his lap and pressed itself against his belly. Rainbow watched him stroke the length of its back and then tickle its ears. The way his hands moved as they caressed the kitten was bewitching. She almost felt jealous. As if reading her thoughts, the purring kitten turned and looked at her with love-drugged eyes, claiming Christophe for itself.

"Do you like them?" Christophe asked. "Is it a good present?"

"Are you kidding? I love them."

"Cool! I remember how much you missed Acrobat when you arrived at the commune, and how Domi would never let you get another cat in case his clients were allergic. We'll have to keep the kittens here but they'll still be yours."

"They're ours," she said. "What shall we call them?"

"How about Apple and Acorn?" said Christophe.

Rainbow spoke the names out loud and watched the kittens' ears twitch in response. "Perfect!" she said.

The black one, Apple, found a cork ball from Christophe's table football collection and chased it across the floor. Acorn leapt from Christophe's lap and joined it in a mad scatter of paws and tails. Rainbow laughed. When she glanced at Christophe she saw he was smiling: at her, not at the kittens. She slithered across the floor into his arms and kissed him.

Later – once Rainbow had coaxed Apple and Acorn into her lap and they'd fallen asleep there – Christophe suggested she bring her revision to the flat. Delighted with the idea, she was attempting to slide the kittens into their basket without waking them when the phone rang. The kittens woke and stretched.

Christophe held out the phone receiver. "It's Thierry for you," he said.

She sat up straight and took the phone.

Thierry was Christophe's motorbiking friend and, more importantly, a tree surgeon. Last October, Christophe had introduced them to each other in the hope Thierry would employ her. None of the other tree surgeons she'd contacted would give her work, not once they'd seen her use her gift to shape branches rather than cut them off.

Thierry had agreed to give her a week's work experience during the Christmas holidays, and then he'd employed her in the February and Easter holidays too. As long as his clients didn't see her using her gift, he didn't mind.

The Mary part of her wanted to fight for her right to be different from other people. She wanted Rainbow to ignore people's prejudices and defy them by demonstrating her gift. Rainbow was able to keep Mary's thoughts in check, because although Mary was strong in her mind, she couldn't enforce anything. And Rainbow disagreed with her. She would never talk about her gift or show it to anyone, even though she continued to use it, because being different was more of a hindrance than a help. She longed to work full-time with Thierry, who gave her so much more than payment. No way would she risk upsetting him.

"I've got a problem," said Thierry on the phone. "Can you come and help me with some tree work?"

"Right now?"

"Yes. The radio has forecast gale warnings in the west of France. My phone hasn't stopped ringing since the announcement and I can't deal with all the requests alone."

"Well …" She watched Christophe stroking the kittens. Mary projected an enticing image of herself lounging in Christophe's flat all afternoon while he helped her revise and the kittens played around them.

"Please, Rainbow? It's an emergency."

She pictured the trees in his clients' gardens, unbalanced, their lives put at risk by the people who'd pruned them badly. Many of his clients had built their houses too close to trees, and wanted him to hack off the branches that threatened their precious homes. They blamed the trees for growing too close to their houses. But it wasn't the trees' fault. No one ever defended trees. If she didn't help them, who would?

"OK," she said. "I'll have to change my clothes though. Can you pick me up at the commune?"

Thierry agreed. She hung up and faced Christophe. He had Acorn in his hands and was cradling her like a baby, tickling her tummy. He smiled at Rainbow, though his brown eyes were sad.

"Don't worry about me," he said. "I've got my hands full here. Thierry needs you. And they say last-minute revision is useless anyway. Go on."

She petted Apple and Acorn one last time, kissed Christophe and thanked him. There was no doubt he was the best boyfriend in the world.

CHAPTER 2

Eole stood on his front door step and undid his muddy walking boots, making sure the lace ends were the same length. It was June, but the field behind the barn was always muddy until the sheep left on their transhumance to the summer pastures.

Eole didn't mind the mud, but it belonged *outside* the house. He, Maman, Papa and Hestia belonged inside. In a Venn diagram of what belonged inside and outside, there would be an intersection of the two sets. This intersection was the hall, where everyone left their muddy boots.

He opened the front door and took off his headphones. Darwie followed him into the hall, shook himself, and then nosed open the kitchen door and checked his dog bowl. A cocktail whiffed through the goat-cheesy air: lemon, sugar, crusty pastry, strawberry and mould. The first three smells meant Maman had baked lemon meringue pie, which had been Tintin's favourite tart. But Eole couldn't identify the mouldy smell, despite the power of his olfactory receptors. He followed Darwie into the kitchen. The lemon pie was cooling on the worktop and he traced the mould to an open jar of jam.

Maman looked up from wrapping sandwiches. She was wearing black trousers and a black jacket under her apron, which was right. Her blouse was green, which wasn't right.

"Bang on time," she said. "Has Papa finished mending the fence?"

"No."

"I mean, has he finished for the morning?"

"Yes. He said he'd come indoors to change in two minutes." Eole looked at his watch. "In thirty seconds' time."

"Good. You'd better change too. Dark colours, remember."

"I know. You already said."

Sometimes Maman treated him as if he were cognitively impaired; as if he were Paul Coutances, his classmate who couldn't even understand the maths questions in their Baccalaureate practice papers, let alone find the answers. Not that Maman would use the term 'cognitively impaired'. Her favourite word was 'special'. Eole was special: his physics marks were the highest the *lycée* in Argelès-Gazost had ever seen. But Maman used 'special' in a way that was starting to strangle him, which was strange because when he was younger the same word used to feel as comforting as a hot water bottle.

In any case, her word was wrong. He was logical, not special. Most people he knew were illogical, including Maman. For example, what was the point of making Tintin's favourite dessert when he wouldn't even be there to eat it? She should have made Brigitte's favourite – chocolate cake – since Brigitte was Tintin's wife. Or quiz cake, which was

Eole's own favourite, since he would miss Tintin more than anyone else.

Their farm, which used to belong to Tintin and Brigitte, lay in the Val d'Azun part of the Pyrenees mountains, above the village of Arras-en-Lavedan. Eole remembered arriving at the farm from Paris, nearly seven years ago, when he was eleven. He remembered the way Maman had driven relentlessly upwards and how happy (and wrong) he'd been to think they were going to live on top of a mountain.

🌱 🍃 🌱

He and his family walked down the track towards the village, like four black beetles (one with a green chest). They were going to say goodbye to Tintin, even though it was too late to say goodbye because he was dead – and even though Eole should be revising for his remaining Baccalaureate exams tomorrow and on Friday. At the bottom of the track was the lane; at the end of the lane was the street; after the street was the main road and, beyond that, at the end of Rue du Clocher, was the church.

Although it was Wednesday and not Sunday, the whole village would be waiting there. Dozens of eyes would look and not-look at him.

He blocked the picture from his mind and thought about ups and downs instead. He definitely preferred ups. The way the communities got smaller as they went upwards was logical. It was like the mountains themselves: from their wide bottoms, full of people bustling to and fro, to their pointed peaks, which were empty of human life. The vegetation was the same: big trees (assassins) surrounded the farm, but the woods thinned out as the mountains rose in altitude, and there were only the smallest mosses and lichens growing on their bare tops.

He planned to live near the top of the mountains once he'd learnt everything Toulouse university could teach him about meteorology. He would build an extension to Tintin's hut up on the summer pastures, equip it with a scientific laboratory and workshop, and live in it with Darwie. Tintin had taught him everything he needed to know about survival in the mountains. He would only come down once a month, on a Thursday, to visit the library, buy provisions and sell his inventions.

He knew his plan wasn't realistic: it was an ambition. It was good to plan ambitions. Papa hadn't planned his ambition properly, and had burnt out. He'd stayed in bed for a year and then changed from a city trader into a farmer. Eole didn't know if it was Papa's ambition to talk only a strict minimum with him and Hestia, or whether it was the fault of the burnout. In any case, Eole's ambition was all ready. Tintin had said it was a good one. Girls liked boys to have ambitions, he'd told him, so Eole was fully equipped for the moment a girlfriend appeared.

When they reached the bottom of the track, where it joined the lane, Eole stopped at the chestnut tree stump and kicked it. Hestia left Papa's side, hawked up a noisy mouthful of snot and spat it onto the stump, where it lay, a shining jewel on the wood chippings left by the villagers' chainsaws.

"Hestia! That's disgusting," said Maman.

"I'm hardly going to ruin my new shoes by kicking it, am I?"

"It wasn't the tree's fault. It was God's will," said Maman.

"Poor Tintin."

She made Eole the love-hug sign: starting with both hands in the middle of her chest, she traced a heart shape over her breasts and down to her navel.

He turned away before she'd finished.

Hestia caught and held his gaze. When she did that, it meant she was on his side. He nodded back to show he'd understood her sign. God had nothing to do with it. They both knew it was the chestnut tree's fault.

The boys at the *lycée* complained about their sisters but Eole never joined in. Although Hestia was only in her first year and he was in his third and final year, everyone knew her. She was always in the right place at the right time, a moment before everyone else arrived. They called her a ringleader. He'd heard people call them Beauty and the Beast, too, which was illogical because Beauty and the Beast weren't brother and sister. And Maman and Hestia both said he wasn't ugly: he was tall, broad and fair, like Papa's side of the family, whereas Hestia was short and dark, like Maman. In any case, since Hestia had arrived at the *lycée*, life was much easier because the others left him alone.

They crossed the main road and walked along Rue du Clocher. If he and his family were black beetles (one with a green chest), then the people swarming around the church were black bees. Despite the shield of his headphones, the volume of their buzzing increased as Eole approached. His legs slowed down. He usually took off his headphones once he was safely inside buildings, but today they felt like a protection from bee stings.

His fingers fiddled with the folded-up paper in his pocket.

He'd prepared his words for Tintin during yesterday's exam, but now he was here he didn't think he could speak in front of the whole congregation. Maybe he would wait until everyone had left and then say the words to Tintin's coffin. It was pointless, in any case, since Tintin wouldn't hear them. It would be far more logical to give eulogies while people were alive instead of waiting until they were dead.

When they reached the crowd, Eole hung back. Hestia slipped through the side gateway into the churchyard and Papa stopped to greet Monsieur Delage. Eole never knew what to say to people, even though Maman had helped him practise. He knew he wasn't supposed to talk about science or the sheep or Darwie or himself. He was supposed to comment on the weather, agree with whatever the person said, and get into an alternating rhythm with one line of conversation each. "Think of it like the instruments in that classical music you're always listening to," Maman had explained. "Don't they take it in turns to play the melody?" But her metaphor wasn't very good. A duet would be a better metaphor, though it still didn't help him master the art of conversation with anyone outside his entourage.

He couldn't handle conversation today, not with all the buzzing. He fixed his eyes on an 'S' of white thread stuck to the back of Maman's jacket and followed it.

Instead of waiting at the edge of the swarm, she headed straight towards the centre. He'd made a bad choice: the church was the other place where Maman belonged, along with the barn, cheese room and house. It was too late to change his mind. He followed the white thread as it weaved a path through the people towards the entrance, where Brigitte stood in a black cardigan, bent over her walking stick. She looked strange without her blue-and-white apron, like an older sister of the Brigitte who helped Maman make cheese. She didn't blow him her usual kiss.

The bells began to chime. He took his eyes off the white thread to listen to the series of dongs. It was the funeral death knell. "Birth, life, death," the bells seemed to chant.

When he looked for the white thread again, it had gone.

He was alone in the middle of a surge of bees squeezing into their hive. He must remain calm. He was one of them. A bee, not a beetle. Bees didn't have feet, so his own feet couldn't itch, start to shuffle and then walk him away. There was nothing to panic about.

"Bzzz," he said.

No, that wasn't right. The people were only bees in his mind. He had to concentrate on the reality, not on the metaphors his mind tricked him with. He hunched his shoulders against the movement and reached down for Darwie's muzzle. No, that wasn't right either. Maman never let him bring Darwie to church. It didn't matter. He was a human like the other bees. They wouldn't sting him.

He ignored the itch at the bottom of his legs and searched the bees' backs for Maman's white thread. She had dematerialised. Spontaneously combusted. Ascended, like Jesus.

"Bzzz. Bzzz." His voice sounded higher than normal. Where was she?

He looked at the faces, searching for hers. The faces looked back at him. Their buzzing stopped. He arranged his features to reflect theirs, like in the mirror expressions game Maman made him play. They looked away.

He spotted her black hair and then her face, a few steps in front of him. The white thread had fallen off. She was talking with Père Laurent, the priest.

"Maman!"

She turned around. Her mouth made an 'O' shape. She pushed out her arms, excusing herself to the buzzing faces, and made an empty space between him and her. It was her crowd ruse, the one she used for opening time at the science museum in Paris. The crowd parted and, like Moses, he stepped into the gap. He looked at the ground, which was safe. His black trainers edged forward over the worn stone slabs at the same rate as her black lace-ups until they turned their noses towards him, and Maman said he could sit down.

They were inside the church. He sat at the end of their pew, the one nearest the exit, and watched Maman's shoes go towards the altar. He'd done it! Sweat had gathered in his armpits and the cold cotton of his shirt clung to them. His feet hadn't betrayed him with their *itch, shuffle and escape*. He eased off his headphones and put them in his jacket pocket.

"Budge up," came Hestia's voice. She smelt of cigarette smoke.

"No. This is my place."

"Let me through then." She squeezed past and sat in her place, next to the wall, where she used to carve blasphemies into the stone while everyone else was praying. That was before Eole had deduced God's non-existence and they'd stopped coming to church.

The crowd ordered itself into lines of people's backs, which was far better than milling bodies. Eole raised his eyes higher. Nothing had changed in the church. It used to be one of his favourite places because it was easy: it smelt of damp stone and wood polish, was full of cool air and had sparse decoration. If he only heard the voices inside church he might have thought, like Maman, that they belonged to God. But they didn't talk to him here. It was a pity. He'd like to have been a Believer, like Maman, because she had an answer for everything.

Instead, he'd found Darwin. Now he was one-hundred-percent sure God didn't exist and, like Darwin, he looked to science for answers. Darwin had used empirical science to prove evolution by natural selection. Eole tried to explain this to Maman, but she stuck to her belief that God had created everything, which was illogical. She called Charles Darwin "the source of today's evil". Eole hadn't known this until after Hestia had named their puppy. If he'd known, he'd never have agreed to her suggestion. He'd quickly nicknamed him Darwie, but Hestia liked to use Darwie's full name, especially when she and Maman were going through a stormy, cumulonimbus phase.

Here, in the church today, it didn't matter that he believed in Darwin's theory and not in God, because they weren't here for God. They were here for Tintin, even though he was no more present than God.

Tintin's coffin rode up the aisle on the shoulders of men who weren't from the village. They must be his professor colleagues from Toulouse university. Eole watched the wooden box pass. Tintin's death didn't seem real. Ever since they'd heard the news on Saturday in Brittany, he'd been expecting someone to tell him it was a mistake. He hadn't cried like Maman, Hestia and Papa. They'd cut short their visit to Aunt Isabelle, who was ill, and had rushed home early on Sunday because Brigitte couldn't feed and milk the sheep and goats on her own.

Much as he tried, he couldn't associate the wooden coffin with his mental image of Tintin. There was a compatibility problem. How could Tintin be in that box?

Eole was glad he had a mind for dealing with compatibility problems, as well as a brain. His brain dealt with logical thinking, whereas his mind came up with metaphors and creative solutions to problems. This was a typical situation where he needed his mind, and it soon presented him with a solution: Tintin wasn't in the box. He was up on the summer pastures, beside the hut, studying cloud formations and examining insects. Eole could easily visualise him there. Compatibility problem solved.

Maman and Papa came and sat between him and Hestia, and then Père Laurent began to talk about Tintin. It was easy to concentrate because it was the only big aural event in the church. The sniffs, coughs and murmurs around him were little aural events.

He listened to the details of Tintin's career as a physicist and university lecturer. Unfortunately, Père Laurent skimmed over the interesting parts and began describing the peace Tintin had felt when he'd returned to his roots here in Arras-en-Lavedan. It was boring compared to his career. Eole wanted to put up his hand and ask questions about Tintin's work, like at school, but questions weren't allowed in church.

He stopped listening and visualised Tintin in the summer

pastures, milking the goats and placing the churns in the carved hollows beside the stream, where Papa would drive up on the quad and collect them. That's where Tintin was now: the ewes were still in the valley, but Tintin had gone up to the pastures to prepare the hut for summer. That's why he wasn't here. Any minute now he would arrive and ask what all the fuss was about. Maybe he was already waiting outside. The congregation would leave and then Eole would smell Tintin's billy-goat odour and know he'd arrived. Tintin would come and sit beside him and they'd discuss quantum entanglement or Aristotle's treatise on *Meteorologica*.

"... his later years. And that's when he met young Eole, who brightened his retirement and allowed him to share his passion for physics. Now, I hear Eole has prepared a few words to share with us. Would you like to come forward, Eole?"

Eole had the usual shiver-shock when he heard his name being spoken by an official person in front of an audience. It sounded wrong. *The Virgin Mary, Noah, Adam and Eve*: they were right. *Eole* was wrong. And now people were turning to look at him. He must stand up, walk to the front, stop at the lectern, take out his paper and read the words.

He couldn't do it.

If he couldn't talk in front of the villagers, how would he ever manage university, where there were amphitheatres full of strangers? Tintin had promised he'd help, that he'd introduce him to his colleagues before term started. But Tintin had gone. Now the idea of university loomed like a black hole. It attracted him but maybe it would destroy him too. He couldn't think about it. Not yet.

"Eole?" whispered Maman. "Your speech."

The congregation started buzzing again. *Itch*. He fingered the paper in his pocket.

"The words are for Tintin," he said.

"I'm sure Tintin would have wanted you to be brave and share them. Shall I come with you?"

Eole shook his head. Maman wouldn't be able to come with him once he was in Toulouse. In any case, she was wrong about Tintin. He would have understood. He'd have seen Eole's feet start to shuffle. He'd have let him go and then followed him up, up, up – until Eole's feet stopped at the top of the ridge. Then he'd have sat beside him and talked about scientific theories until everything felt safe and logical again.

But Tintin wasn't here. God wasn't here. What was Eole doing here? *Shuffle*.

"Eole –"

"Maman, leave him alone," said Hestia, her voice a ferocious whisper.

She pushed past Maman and Papa, fixed Eole with her look, and then stepped into the aisle and walked towards Père Laurent. The congregation's eyes unlatched from Eole and followed her instead. She didn't have any paper in her hands.

Nobody was looking at Eole anymore. He stood up.

"That's my boy," said Maman. "Go and join your sister."

Eole scrunched up the paper in his pocket. There was no point saying any words at all, neither here nor anywhere. His feet retraced the path out of the church.

And escape. He was going to join Tintin.

CHAPTER 3

Rainbow had never experienced such a wind. It was freaky for June. She squinted at the thrashing canopies of leaves around Madame Poulain's house, searching for Thierry.

He was gliding down his rope from the top of a creaking sycamore tree. He shouted at her, his chainsaw held aloft in one hand, but the wind ripped his words away and scattered them into an incoherent jumble of urgent voice. She held out her arms for protection from whirling debris and stumbled towards him. Amputated branches littered the foot of the sycamore tree. She stepped carefully around them, wishing she could transmit her gift to him and prevent this massacre.

"It's too dangerous to continue!" he shouted.

"But we haven't finished. The walnut will blow down if we don't do something."

"Not a priority. It's nowhere near the house."

He undid his harness and they threw the tree surgery equipment into the back of his van. Then he told her to get in while he fetched Madame Poulain's cheque.

Rainbow watched him stride towards the house, his grey

overalls filled with air like a dirty version of the Michelin Man. Mary hated being told what to do, and although Rainbow didn't mind following Thierry's instructions, she couldn't bear to see the walnut tree suffering. As soon as he'd gone inside, she scrambled into its whipping branches. Placing her hands on its communication spots, she reassured the shivering tree that she'd help it find its balance again. Then, using her energy and the tree's knowledge, she shaped the branches outwards, like a tightrope walker's arms.

The tree wouldn't relax into its new shape. It was brimming with fear. She laid her ear against its trunk and emptied her mind so she could better absorb its feelings. It was terrified: not for itself, but for an old oak tree.

The gale howled, breaking her concentration. The walnut tree's feelings were jumbled from its fear of the wind and it didn't make sense. She patted the trunk and jumped down, bidding the tree to hold strong.

The wind should have propelled her back to the van, but now it pushed in the opposite direction, like the suck and drag of waves on a beach. Thierry hadn't returned with his payment yet. She opened the van door, holding tight with both hands to stop it blowing off its hinges, and collapsed inside. Gusts whistled around the contours of the van, jostling it, and she willed Thierry to hurry so they could save as many trees as possible before dark.

She picked up the clipboard to see where the final job of the day was scheduled, thinking about all the oak trees she knew and wondering which one the walnut tree had meant. The oldest was in François I park, in Cognac. It was tall and strong, capable of withstanding any storm.

While she waited for Thierry, she took out her sketch pad and started to draw the painful angles of the sycamore tree's tortured branches. At last, the driver's door swung open. The papers on the clipboard rattled and thrashed, and Thierry thumped into the driver's seat.

"Holy Moses! It's worse than ever. That wind isn't far off the hundred mark."

"Maybe it's the end of the world," said Rainbow. "Like those crazy people are predicting for the year 2000, except it's four years early."

Thierry shot her a sideways look as he reversed out of Madame Poulain's drive. She grinned back at him. He was still nervous about her spiritual commune home and its influence on her. She put her sketch pad away and asked if they could stop at François I park before the next job on the schedule.

"Forget the schedule," he said. "It's late and we're going home to safety."

"But we can't abandon the trees!"

"Haven't I taught you anything? We won't be able to help any trees if we're injured. Or dead. That wind is lethal."

Rainbow reluctantly agreed, and Thierry drove back towards Cognac through a rain of whirling twigs and small branches. Beside the River Charente, a row of half-uprooted ash trees raised their branches to the sky like prayers for mercy. Empathetic pain washed along Rainbow's arms. She would come back tomorrow and try to heal them.

"I can't understand how the forecasters didn't see the gale coming," said Thierry. "They should study the clouds instead of their computers. Still, the clearing up will be good for business. I might even be able to give you a job after your exams."

"Really? I'd love that. Though let's hope there's not enough damage to warrant it."

Thierry grunted. "Are you seeing Christophe this evening? I can drop you off in town if you like."

She hesitated. She wanted to see Apple and Acorn, but she was wet and dirty. And Christophe had planned to help the new apprentice with paperwork this evening. She loved Christophe's kindness, and wasn't surprised that, as a sucker for lost causes, he was keen to help the boy. Rainbow had been busy revising since the apprentice's arrival, so she hadn't met him. When she'd pressed Christophe to talk about him, he described him as "young, shy and a natural with motorbike engines", and she wondered how it was possible to be 'natural' with something as unnatural as machinery.

"Rainbow?"

"Sorry," she said. "No, he's busy. Can you drop me off at the commune?"

"Sure."

They bumped along the track to Le Logis de Châtres. Her mum had brought her here from Dorset five years ago, to consult her friend Domi about Rainbow's gift. Domi had become her tree guru, and when he and Mum had got together, Le Logis became Rainbow's home.

"Mind that half-dead *Acer Saccharinum* doesn't blow down on you," Thierry said, when they arrived. "You really should fell it."

"No way. It means far too much to me," said Rainbow. She kissed his cheek and braced herself to face the gale.

"And stay indoors tonight. That wind is still rising!" he shouted as she slammed the van door.

Rainbow bent forwards and walked towards the house. Dusk was falling early, camouflaging the racing black clouds in darkness and silhouetting the swaying branches in the wood around Le Logis. The roar from the wind rushing through millions of leaves sounded like anger.

Her special tree, the silver maple, was still standing. "*Acer Saccharinum*," she murmured. She'd have to learn the Latin names for trees if Thierry gave her a job. It was half-dead, though there was beauty in the rough nudity of Mary's leafless branch. She wouldn't cut it off until she really had to.

No! What was she thinking? Mary's indignant voice rose like nausea inside her: she mustn't *ever* cut it off.

But Rainbow was in charge, not Mary, and she alone would decide if and when the tree needed attention. She hugged it and breathed in its familiar woody scent. It was trembling. Silver maples weren't an indigenous species, and few grew in the Charente. She wished she could ask it questions and receive clear answers, but her communication with trees only ever amounted to understanding their feelings and weaknesses. The one exception had been the oak tree beside the Drunken House in Dorset. When she'd asked it to shrink so that she could climb into Michael's garden and retrieve a keepsake, it had spoken to her in images and filled her with tree history.

The maple shivered violently under her hands. Like Madame Poulain's walnut tree, it was afraid of the gale. The second reiki course Rainbow recently completed had improved her technique for gathering universal energy and, as she stroked the maple's bark, she channelled this energy through her hands to calm it.

The maple wouldn't absorb her energy. A deep feeling was emerging from further than the maple's roots. She pressed her ear harder against the trunk. Was it Amrita? Rainbow had been hugging this very tree when Amrita had spoken to her in a vision last September: "*Rest for now and be ready. Our future lies together,*" she'd said – though the only signs of Amrita since that moment had been the dreams.

The wind dropped momentarily. Amrita didn't appear, but Rainbow sensed that an ancient, motherly oak tree in the king's forest needed her help.

Mary's disapproval swelled inside her: it would be crazy to enter a forest in conditions like this. For once, Rainbow agreed with Mary. She didn't have the power to help a tree in a gale. She would think about the meaning of the message and find the motherly oak tree tomorrow. Could it be the oak tree in François I park? Domi would say that if her intuition suggested this, she must trust it.

There was a sudden loud crack: the sound of a splitting trunk. A gust balled into her, knocking her sideways. She dug in her heels and strained her eyes towards the noise.

The beech tree in the garden toppled to the ground in slow motion, snapping the swing's ropes and taking a chunk of earth with it.

"No!" she screamed.

There was another bang. This time it came from the house. Mum appeared, holding her flailing black hair tight to her head with both hands. "Rainbow! It's no weather to be tree-hugging."

"Look! The swing beech!" cried Rainbow.

"It's Armageddon out here. Come indoors."

Rainbow willed the silver maple to stay strong and, wishing her gift allowed her to bring trees back to life, followed Mum inside.

The silence was deafening after the racket outside. She showered and then went down to the kitchen. It was full of visiting children and their parents, on the point of leaving. They were the clients that Domi – convinced he could save the world by healing one child at a time – had invited to his 'Listen to Your Inner Voice' workshop.

Rainbow took a plateful of pasta into the sitting room, where Sandrine was doing her primary-school homework. She looked up as Rainbow entered.

"So, here it is," she said.

"Here what is?" asked Rainbow.

"The gale I saw in my daydream. Don't you remember?"

The hairs on Rainbow's neck and arms rose. Domi had told her about Sandrine's clairvoyant prediction on the day she'd discovered that Michael, the friend in Dorset she'd accidentally killed, had actually been her father. The prediction had seemed insignificant beside the shocking revelation and she'd forgotten Sandrine's words. Until now.

"You mentioned something about a gale," she said. "But it was on the eve of the year 2000, not in 1996."

"If you're a tree, you live such a long time that 1996 *is* the eve of 2000," said Sandrine.

"You think this is it? Remind me what you predicted."

"The gale will be the start of your destiny," said Sandrine. "A new life. With English tree friends." She bent back over her homework.

One of Mary's memories permeated Rainbow's mind: Mary's best friend, Trish Bellamy, had lived in trees with a group of protesting ecologists. But Mary's memories came from a different world: some kind of parallel world. Rainbow had no idea how parallel worlds worked.

"Can you remember any more?" she asked Sandrine. "Like a clue about what I'm supposed to do?"

Sandrine shook her head.

Rainbow finished her meal. The problem with clairvoyants – if you could count an eleven-year-old as a clairvoyant – was that they were so vague. She didn't want to return to the dissatisfaction that came from wondering about her destiny. Christophe was the centre of her life now, Mary reminded her. She intended to train with Thierry to become the best tree surgeon in the world, not to chase a spiritual destiny. Anyway, there were gales every year.

On the other hand, Amrita *had* told her to be ready.

No. She banished her childish fantasy of a starring role in a tree revolution that would save the planet. What mattered was her life here.

A particularly strong gust buffeted the shutters. She hummed Mum's new melody to block out the sound of the wind tumbling gardening tools, buckets and chairs around the garden.

"Shut up!" said Sandrine. "I can't concentrate with your tuneless droning."

Rainbow stuck out her tongue at Sandrine and took her empty plate into the kitchen. Outside, the gusts were sporadic lulls and shrieks, like an ogre taking deep breaths and then blowing out. She was safe indoors. As Thierry said, it would be stupid to risk her life, even for an ancient oak tree.

It was no good. She couldn't settle until she'd had a look.

CHAPTER 4

Rainbow suppressed Mary's protests and brushed off Mum's objection to her driving in such dangerous weather. The meteorologists had named the gale 'Martin'. It seemed strange to name storms: surely by naming something, you gave it more power?

She stepped into the night and forged her way to Mum's Mini. It was too dark to make out the silhouette of the woods and she couldn't see her silver maple properly, though she could hear the frantic rustle of its leaves.

Keep strong, she willed, holding her hand against its trunk as she passed.

There were no cars on the road to Cognac, though she saw plenty of airborne traffic: plastic bags pulsed like flying jellyfish and a piece of cardboard wheeled and flapped. She drove slowly, looking into roadside copses at the fallen trees. It was too dark to see the full scope of the damage, but if the glimpses she caught were anything to go by, Martin was one hell of a storm.

She stopped in François I park. The wind channelled along

the river valley and had already ripped up a line of poplars from the timber plantation on the opposite bank. She could see them in her headlights, lying in disarray like a giant's box of emptied matches. She turned off the lights and got out. The gale howled, louder than ever, and a branch crashed to the ground behind her. She spun around. It blocked the road. She pushed all thoughts of home to the back of her mind, fixed her torch to her head, and hurried along the path to the old oak tree in the middle of the wood.

The wind was quieter among the trees. Twigs and leaves whirled in eddies, but she could see no fallen trunks. At the foot of the oak tree, she stopped and examined its lower branches, which were all she could see in the torchlight. It appeared to be solid and in no need of any help. Perhaps the silver maple hadn't been referring to this oak. Or perhaps she'd imagined the message. There was only one way to find out. She stepped over the brambles and laid her hands on its trunk.

She'd never touched this kingly tree, and couldn't find its communication spots. She stretched her arms as high as possible and groped for a sign of sensitivity, cursing herself for her shortness. Still nothing. She hauled herself onto the lowest branch and eventually found a way in. She emptied her mind, ready to be saturated by the tree's feelings.

An image of herself, clinging to its trunk, rippled into her mind. No tree, apart from the Drunken House oak, had ever communicated in such a way. But this oak tree's images were weak. She understood that it was a mother tree, a sentinel, protector of the forest and guardian of the trees' history. She could see roots pumping knowledge through underground networks of silver filaments. And it was spiritually linked to something higher, like a church is linked to God. It was linked to Amrita.

If only she'd known how special this tree was, she could have come and made contact with Amrita every day. Was this what her nightmares were telling her?

She concentrated on the images, trying to understand. But the pictures of saplings, acorns, snow-lined branches and landslides were vague and disjointed. She couldn't perceive an overall message. It reminded her of Arlette, Domi's Alzheimer's client, whose sentences jumped from one subject to another with no apparent logic.

Can't – hold – on.

The words were there, suddenly, in her mind. The oak tree's words. She hugged the trunk, sending encouragement.

The trunk twitched. Something was moving inside it.

It was the wind. Stormy air rattled within the oak's heartwood like an angry child shut in a box and banging to get out. No wonder the oak had no energy to spare for communicating with her: it was absorbing the wind to protect the trees around it.

HelpUsRainbowMary.

The oak's pronunciation of her name was a mournful song, an unwelcome reminder that she was no longer just Rainbow, but Mary as well. She wasn't sure she wanted to share her name with Mary. Mary, equally insulted, urged Rainbow to return to safety.

Rainbow willed her to shut up. The oak needed her: she couldn't abandon it. She grasped the trunk and let the wind enter her too, sharing the blows and pushing them down through the oak's trunk to its roots, where they dissipated deep in the earth.

Her effort helped stabilise the shuddering branches. Gradually, murmurs of thanks, like prayers, filtered up from beyond the oak's roots. She was inside the oak. She *was* the oak. The murmurs were emanating from a silver web that connected the roots of all the trees in the forest. She was part of a huge network of tree thoughts. It was magical!

But the wind's force was still rising. She pressed hard against the trunk, her arms circling it, the fingers of each hand wedged into a bark wrinkle to hold her tight in place. Mary seethed with frustration, her desire to escape undermining Rainbow's efforts.

Don't – let – go, said François I oak.

Mary's objection was almost as strong as the wind, which was edging down Rainbow's chest and trying to peel her from the trunk. Rainbow's fingers lost their grip and slipped by a few bark wrinkles. She was no match for the gale, not with Mary fighting her within. She berated Mary for weakening her.

Mary raged in protest. She expanded in Rainbow's mind, pushed at the mental wall separating them, and demanded that Rainbow flee. The pressure was unbearable. Rainbow's head was going to explode. She had to release Mary's frustration. She drew a breath deep into her lungs and threw back her head.

"I HATE YOU, Martin!" she screamed. "STOP!"

There was a lull. Maybe it was a good idea to name a gale, after all. Her stiff fingers regained the bark wrinkles they'd lost. Then a ferocious gust, stronger than any before, bowled into the oak tree. Rainbow gasped. What had she done?

The oak tree groaned. Branches began to splinter. Rainbow

held on tight, begging the oak tree to forgive her outburst. But before the oak could respond, the wind wrenched her from the trunk and dashed her to the ground.

She lay, stunned, her torch broken, the scent of decaying leaves heavy in her nose. The darkness was full of dim, swaying shapes, and a deluge of woody fibres hailed down on her. She covered her face with her arms while she stretched each leg in turn. Her body still worked.

Her head was thumping from Mary's demands to crawl away. But she couldn't abandon the oak. This was her fault. She shouldn't have yielded to Mary. She crawled back towards the tree.

The ground beneath her started to shudder. No! The oak mustn't give up. She'd only just found it. It couldn't die. The earth crumbled and began to lift. The tree teetered, a branch cracked and she felt the wrenching of roots under her knees.

She pushed herself backwards, struggled to her feet and stumbled away.

The oak fell with a crash. Another tree slumped onto it. Without the mother oak, the trees were deprived of their strength. Like a pack of unruly dominos, they toppled onto one another, taking brothers and sisters with them as they fell. Beneath Rainbow's feet, the underground web of silver that connected the trees' roots must be ripping to shreds.

Rainbow groped forwards. Her path was blocked. She heard a whimper and realised it came from herself. She turned around and floundered between diagonal branches, trying to keep her memory of the forest paths clear in her head. But the paths had gone. She tripped on a bramble bush and fell to her knees. Her head knocked against familiar bark. The oak tree.

Horizontal. Dead.

Sobbing, she pulled herself up and hugged its trunk.

Amrita appeared.

Rainbow blinked and rubbed the tears from her eyes. It was dark, but she could see Amrita in the same sari of pinks and reds she always wore, her long black hair untouched by the wind. This time she was real. She was actually here, sitting on the oak's trunk, a few metres away. Unlike the Amrita in Rainbow's nightmares, she was calm, her smile benevolent.

"The wind–" Rainbow started to say.

"Come." Amrita reached out and took Rainbow's hand. Her touch was misty damp.

A series of images flashed through Rainbow's mind: Amrita was speaking in the same way as the Drunken House and François I oaks. First came a picture of hundreds of bubbles: different worlds hanging in space. Then her view zoomed onto one bubble. She was thirteen years old and in hospital. Mum sat beside her bed. There was a flash of white light and the bubble split into two. The two new bubbles spun, close together, cupped between Amrita's hands. In one, she could see herself. In the other, she saw Mary.

Amrita's image focused onto a cedar tree in one bubble, the Eiffel Tower in the other. Then Christophe filled both bubbles. There was a momentary collision, like a kiss. She saw Christophe, Mary and herself in the same bubble. Her and Mary, hugging the silver maple – and then she and Mary blurred together, and the two bubbles wafted apart.

Amrita let go of Rainbow's hand and floated down from the trunk.

"I have given my life force to reunite you as RainbowMary,

and now I am weak in your world. Yet while a little strength remains, I must guide you. Come."

Rainbow stumbled after her, along an invisible path that twisted between the trembling trees. She tried to understand exactly what Amrita was. More than a tree spirit, she seemed to control parallel worlds – at least, her and Mary's worlds. It was crazy to think that an external being could control whole worlds – as crazy as believing in God. Did scientists have theories to explain parallel worlds and how they worked? It was too big an idea to absorb, and she had more immediate worries. She concentrated on keeping up with Amrita.

All around, trunks creaked and crashed – but Amrita glided through a tunnel in the wind, her fingers caressing each tree she passed. Within minutes they arrived at the Mini. Rainbow pushed the lashing ends of her ponytail out of her eyes and faced Amrita.

"I failed the oak tree," she said. "I shouldn't have let Mary provoke me. I'm so, so sorry."

"No longer are you Two, RainbowMary. You are One. You must recognise this and accommodate each other if you are to become truly whole and help me."

Although Mary was inside Rainbow, she felt distinctly separate. How could Rainbow possibly reconcile herself to Mary's thoughts and treat them as her own when Mary was so alien and had lived such different experiences? Before she could express her doubts, Amrita continued:

"This oak tree's death, along with many other One Trees' deaths, has exhausted my life force. I am not of your world, as you know: I am of the trees and cannot intervene except to advise you, for a part of me lives in your heartwood.

47

"Now I wane and may guide you no more. But hear me while I still may speak: this evil wind has wreaked its vengeance and slain my trees, and I am diminished. You alone can restore my life force. To accomplish this, you must vanquish the Tree Slayer, who threatens us both. But you will need to learn patience and humility if you are to succeed.

"Seek your other half in the sheep pastures of High Azun, and bring home this shepherd who possesses a gift equal to your own. Thereupon will your other half lead you to Koad to rescue the last One Tree and thus restore the remnants of my life force.

"Succeed, and we shall spend halcyon days revelling, hand in hand, in the dappled sunlight of spring-green woodlands. Fail, and we shall all perish. Remember, you are RainbowMary. Trust yourself, trust the trees, and learn to accept your other half."

"But – I don't understand."

"You will, when the time comes. My strength fades and I cannot explain further. Go with haste."

Amrita rippled like a reflection in water.

"Amrita! Don't leave me!"

But Amrita was snatched by the wind and shredded into a thousand petals of red and pink.

"Amrita!"

Darkness closed around Rainbow. Where Amrita's ethereal voice had prevailed, the triumphant wind now howled. Rainbow rubbed her throbbing head. Her hand came away sticky with blood.

Had she understood correctly? Amrita needed her to accomplish a mission. But it was all so vague. How could she, armed only with a gift for shaping branches and healing sick trees, vanquish this Tree Slayer and restore Amrita's life force? Amrita was expecting too much. Rainbow hadn't even managed to save the François I oak tree, so what help could she possibly be to a tree spirit who controlled parallel worlds?

CHAPTER 5

The snow on the mountain pass above Tintin's hut had melted and the tiny stone building looked undamaged from the outside.

Eole unlocked it. On his way here from the church, he'd picked up the key and his photos of Tintin, and then he and Darwie had left before the rest of his family returned from the funeral. He'd have to go back home this evening because he had more exams tomorrow, but right now he needed to get as close to Tintin as he could. His family would know where he was. It was the only place he ever went alone, apart from the library.

Tintin's grandfather had built the hut from mountain stone to make a shelter for the summer months, when he looked after the sheep. It stood above the treeline, beside a lake at the foot of the summer pastures. As soon as Tintin retired from Toulouse he'd continued his grandfather's tradition with Patou, the young Pyrenean mountain dog who'd grown up with the flock. And he'd carried on when Eole's parents bought the farm from him. Patou still lived with the flock and was as white as a sheep. Eole was convinced that Patou thought he was a special sheep.

Every summer, as soon as school finished, Eole would join Tintin here. Together, they'd milk the ewes and goats, check the flock's feet for rot, treat injuries and go for long walks. Empty mountains were the best places for thoughts about physics, but what Eole liked most were the conversations with Tintin. Winter was for inventions and experiments in Tintin's laboratory in the valley, but summer was discussion time. While they cut brambles out of fleeces or sprayed antiseptic on maggot-infested cuts, Tintin explained scientific theories to him, such as the differences between level III and level IV parallel universes and how Schrödinger's cat could be simultaneously alive and dead.

Apart from Eole's family, Tintin had been the only person he could talk to without having to concentrate on saying the right things in the right order and making the right expressions with his face. In Paris, before he'd known Tintin, his world centred on Maman, Hestia and the library: they were still his nucleus, but he needed something bigger. Tintin was bigger. But Tintin had gone.

Eole opened the hut door. It smelt damp but there were no puddles. The silence inside wasn't right. It should be filled with Tintin's snores from the bottom bunk. He shook the silence out of his head and fixed the photos to the wall, following Hestia's decoration rules for putting them at different heights and angles.

Hestia had avoided the hut since last summer, when she'd had the vodka vomit experience. She'd just split up with one of her boyfriends, and had hitched a lift to the car park a few hundred feet below so she could tell Eole how much she hated the boy – even though she'd declared she loved him only the day before. She hadn't brought anything sensible with her, like a sleeping bag or food, but inside her jacket she'd secreted an opened bottle of vodka. She'd tried to share it with him, but he refused, explaining she was killing her neurones with each sip, and that she would end up as cognitively impaired as Paul Coutances. As usual, she'd ignored his advice and finished the bottle. He had to help her down the path, stopping for her to be sick several times. Some trekkers insisted on giving them a lift, which Maman had said was lucky. Eole wasn't sure it was lucky to have his silence clouding the car and Hestia's vomit all over the back seat.

He finished attaching the photos, left the hut and walked up to the pass, where he sat in his favourite patch of heather. Here, he was free from people and all the sensory complications of the valley. And free of the voices. The macro-silence was complete. The micro-silence of water, insects and wild animals wove together with mountain aromas of flora and fauna like the threads in a familiar blanket.

He'd had a blanket, years ago in Paris. Lying in the heather was the closest he could get to the comfort he'd felt from that tatty rag with silk edges and red embroidered lumps. He belonged here, like Maman belonged in church, even if Tintin wasn't beside him. The only movement around him came from Darwie and the birds of prey above. And the clouds, of course. He was alone with his cloud secret now. Only Tintin had known about his special skill. They'd pored over books together in the library and talked about it right here. The mountains were full of Tintin memories. On top of the ridge, Tintin taught him about glaciation. Beside the lake, he'd demonstrated wave theory.

Tintin's face wouldn't form properly in Eole's mind. When he tried to focus on a detail, it blurred. Was he forgetting him? He didn't want to forget him. He must find a way to remember him and his scientific theories forever. He needed to map everything and make an encyclopedia of it.

He lay down and let his mind think about maps and encyclopedias. He would cross-reference each part of the mountain with the scientific concept Tintin had explained to him in that spot. He would call the result a mapopedia, and store it in the section of his brain that illogical people used for remembering pointless data like song lyrics and fashions.

He would begin right now.

He sat up. Darwie raised his head and wagged his tail. Eole looked around, searching for a good place to begin.

Someone was sitting in Maman's place on the stone bench that ran along the side of the hut, though he couldn't see who it was. He took a deep breath and analysed the smells with his olfactory receptors. It was useful to have such a sensitive nose, and he quickly detected a familiar lilac-goaty smell.

The person was Maman.

He felt lighter now he had his mapopedia plan. It wasn't as good as being with Tintin, but it was the closest he could get. He would begin on Saturday, right after his exams, and stay here all summer making his mapopedia and reading while he tended the sheep and goats.

He whistled Darwie to heel and walked down to meet Maman. She made the love-hug sign, fussed over him, and said everyone had missed him at the funeral wake. He told her he'd needed to get as far away as possible from the not-Tintin in church.

"God is everywhere," she replied. "But it's true that the higher we go, the closer we feel to Him."

She linked everything to God. He decided not to tell her about his mapopedia. It would be another secret, like his special skill.

"If God exists, why did he kill Tintin and make us all unhappy?" he said.

"It's not our place to question His decisions. But if you pray hard, He may make his designs known to you."

She was talking about the voices. As a kid in Paris, he'd presumed everyone heard the voices. It was only when he'd mentioned how he preferred being indoors to outdoors because of the voices that Maman had told him it was unusual. She thought it was God speaking to him, of course. For years he'd thought this was what made him special.

"You *know* I don't hear the voices up here," said Eole, as Maman passed him a slice of lemon meringue pie. "Which is more evidence that they're not him. Anyway, if it was him, he'd be intelligent enough to let me understand what they say."

"God works in mysterious ways, darling. Now, are you ready to come home? You should get back to your revision."

He locked the hut and they walked down towards the trekkers' car park, where Maman always left the pickup.

"Papa's going to need your help now Tintin's with God," she said. "You'll have to stay at the farm this summer instead of coming up here. We're going to keep the goats in the valley so it's easy to milk them and only bring up the ewes once they're out of milk."

Eole stopped walking. "I can't."

"The sheep won't need milking up here, darling. And Patou will keep them safe."

"But I have a project to do here. For Tintin," he added.

Maman sighed. "I see."

She made another love-hug sign and they continued down to the pickup. She understood. He wasn't so sure that Papa would.

Back at the house, Maman took Papa into the kitchen and sent Eole to prepare the goats for milking. He and Darwie gathered the goats on the runway that led to the milking room, then he unwound the swiss-roll bale of hay along the feeder platform. Once the water troughs were full, he went to get Maman.

She was coming out of the kitchen with an orange folder under her arm. The orange folders were out of bounds to Eole and Hestia, though Hestia had told him they contained boring bills and accounts.

"Papa says he'll manage while you do your project," Maman told him. "But before you go, we'd like you to re-fence the field beside the house."

He loved fencing, and he'd finish the field in a few days. After that, he'd have all summer to work on his mapopedia.

"OK. Are you going to employ a farm hand to help Papa?" he asked, pointing at the orange folder.

Maman snapped the elastic over its corners. "We'll see. Now, go and catch up on your revision."

At dinner that evening Papa announced they would do the transhumance on Saturday, in three days' time.

"We can't," said Eole. "It's my birthday."

"We can and we will," said Papa. "The sheep need fresh grass and I need everyone's help to get them up to the summer pastures now Tintin is gone. Ours is the last flock still in the valley."

Eole's birthday normally meant a visit to a museum of his choice and then home for quiz cake and the measure. He tugged at his lip and started to recalculate this change: would that mean no quiz cake, or would they have it before or after the transhumance, and how would Maman have time to cook it if it was after, and if it was before, he'd have to get up early to leave the house so that he didn't accidentally smell the ingredients and cheat, and how would they fit a museum visit into the day, and …?

"We'll have a late birthday tea and do the measure afterwards, and then we can take the sheep up," said Maman. "It'll be cooler for them in the evening. You can stay the night at the hut, darling, to make sure Patou and the sheep settle, then come down on Sunday morning to begin the fencing. We'll visit a museum the weekend after."

Eole nodded. Papa nodded. Hestia burped. Maman told her off, then smiled at everyone and said grace.

CHAPTER 6

In François I park, the gale was stronger than ever. Rainbow got back into the Mini, fighting the wind to close the door. Her whole body ached from the fall, especially her bleeding head, and she wanted to go home to treat her injuries.

An overwhelming desire arose from Mary, urging her to seek comfort in Christophe's arms. Amrita had said that Rainbow must accommodate Mary in order to become truly whole. And, anyway, a fallen branch blocked the road back to Le Logis. She set off towards Christophe's flat, driving slowly. He'd have finished with the apprentice and would be feeding Apple and Acorn before going to bed. He'd help her decide what to do about the mission.

Amrita had made a serious misjudgement. Discontent radiated from Mary, who wanted to stay at home with Christophe. Rainbow wasn't keen on the idea of facing this Tree Slayer, whatever it was, either. She had no idea how to vanquish it or restore Amrita's life force. She replayed Amrita's words in her mind. High Azun sounded mountainous, and the closest mountain ranges were hours away from Cognac. She couldn't exactly pop into High Azun on her way home from school. And what about her exams, the kittens, Christophe? She couldn't simply leave everything and drive into the unknown alone.

But neither could she forget what had just happened. Amrita needed her. Rainbow was the only one who could help. She was important.

It would have to wait for the holidays. She didn't have anything planned for the summer, other than mouldering in the commune giving reiki and reading palms. Perhaps Christophe would go with her – except that he'd be at work until mid-July. Amrita had told her to be quick. She might be dead by July. If Rainbow was to help her in time, she'd have to go straight after her exams. On her own.

She couldn't do it. Not alone.

She wished she could ignore her vision: it wasn't as if Amrita was real. If she did nothing and let Amrita die, perhaps her nightmares would stop.

She drove along the deserted Cognac streets towards the motorbike shop. A dustbin overturned. She swerved as the wind rolled it into the road and tin cans rattled out.

It had been difficult enough to forget Amrita even before this mission. The Tree Slayer was daunting, but the shepherd 'other half' with a gift like hers sounded intriguing, even if it didn't make sense. She'd thought that Mary was supposed to be her other half, since two halves make a whole. Amrita must mean that RainbowMary had another half, a kind of guide, someone who'd know more about this Koad place and how to vanquish the Tree Slayer. Someone who was as close to trees as herself. It sounded as if she and Mary had a soulmate.

She wondered whether her soulmate was male or female. She liked the idea of him being big and strong, able to fight the Tree Slayer. Disgust permeated her mental wall: Mary disapproved of her stereotyped assumption that her soulmate must be a man in order to fight the Tree Slayer. How was Rainbow supposed to integrate Mary when everything she thought and felt opposed her?

She ignored Mary's disapproval and imagined her soulmate as a wise shepherd with a staff, like in the photo Michael had once shown her of his great-grandfather. The old man would know what to do and where to go, and he'd be dead efficient. Perhaps her whole mission could be accomplished in a weekend. Yes! Christophe would be free at the weekends. Everything would be easier if he were with her – though it might be more tactful to refer to her soulmate as a shepherd. The last thing she wanted was to alienate Christophe.

Her priority was to help Amrita, despite Mary's unwillingness to leave home and the fact that she and Mary were supposed to unify. It was Mary's turn to adapt. Rainbow would find High Azun on a map and then she and Christophe would look for the shepherd next weekend, after her exams. It would be a first step, even if they had to return the weekend after to vanquish the Tree Slayer and bring home her shepherd.

🌢 🌿 🌢

When she arrived in Christophe's street, she saw him pacing up and down under a flickering street light, running his fingers through his hair.

He opened her car door. "At last! Your mum phoned and

told me you'd dashed off in a frenzy. I was about to come looking for you."

She climbed out and crumpled into his arms.

"Merde! You're hurt," he said, touching her sticky hair. "Shall I take you to Casualty?"

"I think it's only cuts and bruises. How are Apple and Acorn?"

They went upstairs to his flat, where he sprayed antiseptic onto her head while she petted the kittens. She tried to call Le Logis to tell Mum she was safe, but the number was unobtainable. The gale must have blown down the telephone lines. She lay on the sofa with an ice pack on the bump and Acorn on her belly, and told Christophe about her encounter with Amrita.

He looked more concerned than excited, even though she was careful to use the word 'shepherd'.

"How far did you fall?" he asked.

"A couple of metres. Why?"

"Hmm. You're always talking about those weird Amrita dreams and that bump on your head is pretty big. Maybe you blacked out and imagined her."

"What? *Imagined* her?"

"Maybe. Isn't that what happens with concussion?"

Had it all been a hallucination? Surely not. It was too vivid. Christophe shouldn't doubt her: he'd been present when Mary had disappeared into the silver maple.

"I didn't imagine her. She was real."

"If you say so," he said.

She glared at him. He wouldn't come to High Azun if he didn't believe her. But now she'd made up her mind, she wanted to go. She owed it to Amrita to atone for her error with the oak tree. If Christophe wouldn't support her, she'd find someone who would. Her soulmate, for example. She'd go on her own and find her shepherd and together they'd vanquish the Tree Slayer. Then Christophe would have to believe her.

"She was real and I'm going to prove it," she said.

"Hey, Rainette. I'm not saying you're making it up. I'm just concerned about that bump."

He leant forward to check her wound. She pushed him away and sat up. The ice pack fell to the floor, making Acorn jump.

"I'm fine. I'd better get back to Le Logis before they start to worry."

"I guess so. Do you want me to drive you?"

She shook her head, stroked Apple and Acorn one last time, and then kissed Christophe briefly.

He held onto her. "Come back tomorrow morning, yeah? We can spend the day together."

He looked sad. Maybe she was being too hard on him. After all, he hadn't actually seen Amrita. She relented and agreed to bring her revision with her the next day.

She drove the long way back towards the commune. It would be cool to meet someone totally on her own wavelength, as a soulmate with a gift like hers was bound to be. A soulmate would believe in Amrita. They'd be able to heal trees together, and share their knowledge. He might even be young and attractive.

Mary's displeasure cut into her daydreaming, reminding her that Christophe was everything she could ever need. Rainbow conceded that Mary was right. She must imagine her soulmate as a wise, old shepherd.

❧ ❦ ❧

Back home at Le Logis, which was plunged into darkness from a power cut, she asked Domi if she could consult him. He took one look at her face and agreed. He was her guru, her confidante in everything that concerned trees, and she told him all about the vision.

"Don't take this lightly," he said. "The fact that you've got a part of Amrita inside you explains where your gift comes from, but if her life force disappears, your own life is at risk. As for Mary, I don't think you should give her too much space. Keep her separate with that mental wall I suggested you build, and be careful her personality doesn't take over."

Rainbow decided never to let Mary's feelings overcome her again. She'd only allow her to make minor decisions: that way, she'd recognise and accept Mary, as Amrita wanted, and still follow Domi's advice.

Domi made her write down Amrita's message on a page of her sketch pad, and then, while she held up a candle, he took a road map from the commune bookcase. They couldn't find Koad, and she wondered whether it was an object or a person rather than a place. But Koad and the last One Tree were secondary. First, she must deal with her shepherd in High Azun.

They discovered that Azun was the name of a valley in the Pyrenees mountains, renowned for its green pastures. There would be plenty of sheep in the Val d'Azun. The seed of doubt Christophe had sown in her mind withered. She'd hardly have imagined such an unusual place name. Amrita's message was real. She may not be part of this world, but Rainbow knew she existed somewhere. She existed, and she needed Rainbow's help.

When Domi calculated it would take five hours to drive to the Val d'Azun, and that she'd have to negotiate Bordeaux, Rainbow's bravado about going alone faltered. It was a long way to drive and she was useless at map reading. She'd have to persuade Christophe to come with her, even if he didn't believe in the vision. They could leave on Friday evening, as soon as Christophe finished work for the weekend. Her final exam ended at midday, and Thierry had promised her a restaurant lunch as a late birthday present. She'd be able to pack her mum's camping equipment afterwards, in the afternoon. They'd return to Cognac on Sunday evening so Christophe could be back at work on Monday morning. It was a perfect plan.

If they found her shepherd and vanquished the Tree Slayer, Christophe would have no choice but to accept her mission was real. If they didn't find him – well, she preferred not to consider that option.

♣ ♥ ♣

At dawn the next day, after a dream-free night, Rainbow took a deep breath and then opened her bedroom shutters. Yesterday it had been too dark to see all the damage from the gale and she dreaded what daylight might reveal.

It was a thousand times worse than she'd imagined.

She stumbled downstairs, her whole body stiff and bruised, and opened the front door. The air was calm but the woods around Le Logis were a wasteland of debris. Her legs gave way and she slid to the ground, her back against the wall. It took a lifetime for a tree to grow. She'd never again see the wood as it used to be. A few hours of ferocious wind had been enough to destroy the trees she'd loved and healed, climbed and shaped. They'd been her friends.

She struggled up on wobbly legs and walked around the house to her silver maple. It was still standing, thank goodness. Had Amrita made sure it was protected? She sent her a silent message of thanks and hugged the tree. She didn't know what power she had to help Amrita, but she would do her best to find out.

In François I park more than half the trees had fallen, according to the radio report she heard as she ate a quick breakfast. The gale had swept the whole of western France, from the northwest coast to the foot of the Pyrenees mountains. It was the most catastrophic French storm in living memory.

She slung her revision notes into the Mini and drove towards Christophe's flat. The view as she drove past François I park made her gasp. The radio statistics were nothing compared to the sight of solid-trunked oaks and beeches skewed across each other. Those that remained upright had lost their crowns. The wind had ripped off their leafy branches and now their bare trunks speared the sky.

The sap inside her body rose to boiling point. The wind had indeed been an evil one, as Amrita had said. No other gale she'd known had done so much damage. Amrita hadn't been clear about the form of the Tree Slayer, but she had talked about the evil wind slaying her trees. The Tree Slayer could be the wind. Rainbow remembered how it had reacted when she'd shouted that she hated it. It had heard her! Would it recognise her as Amrita's ally and try to kill her too? Her shepherd had better devise a good way to destroy it, because she had no idea how to fight the wind.

At Christophe's flat she scooped up Apple and Acorn and smothered them with kisses, then she tearfully described the gale's devastation to Christophe.

"The Tree Slayer's storm has even hurt ancient trees that seemed too solid to be affected," she said. "I bet the last One Tree Amrita mentioned is one of them. Imagine if it's another mother tree like the François I and Drunken House oaks. I must find it quickly and heal it before it dies." She added that she'd discovered Azun was in the Pyrenees mountains, and asked if he'd come with her.

"Now?"

"I wish we could, but it's too far for a day trip." She tickled Acorn's ears. "We can't go until next weekend. You will come with me, won't you?"

He sighed and emptied the grounds from his coffee maker.

"Please?" she pleaded. "Then I can prove that Amrita wasn't a hallucination. It'll be fun with you."

"Sometimes I don't understand you, Rainette," he said. "For years you've been desperate to find a way to help trees. And now you can truly help the trees that suffered in the storm, you want to go to the mountains. Thierry will probably offer you some clearing-up work next weekend. If you don't help him, he'll find someone else. If you do, there'll be more chance of him giving you a proper job. Isn't that what you want?"

It hadn't occurred to her that Thierry might find someone else. "Of course. You know it is."

"Then forget this Amrita business," continued Christophe.

"Have you even thought how you'll find this stranger in a whole valley of strangers? Are you going to ask everyone if they've got a gift like yours?"

Put like that, her plan sounded naïve. She could feel Mary gathering her strength to side with Christophe.

Rainbow looked out of the window. The road a little further along was closed because a cedar tree had blown down. It was the tree she'd climbed to rescue Sylvia's cat, three years ago. The tree in which she'd had an out-of-body experience. The tree Amrita had shown her in yesterday's vision.

"All I can do is try," she said. "Are you coming or not?"

CHAPTER 7

Before Christophe could answer her question, the doorbell buzzed and Thierry appeared. He wanted Rainbow to help him clear the storm debris today, even though it was a Sunday.

"I'll pay you double time, of course," he said.

Christophe passed him an espresso coffee, which he swallowed in one go, while Rainbow tried to catch Christophe's eye to see what he thought. He wouldn't look at her.

"I'd planned to spend the day revising with Chris," she said. She didn't add "and the kittens" because that was hardly a reason to turn down tree work.

"Fair enough. I just asked on the off chance," said Thierry. "Those exams are important."

Christophe cleared his throat, but still wouldn't look at her.

"Though I suppose it's too late to learn anything more for tomorrow," she added.

Christophe took back Thierry's empty cup. "If you go with Thierry I guess I could call the apprentice to help me do some work on my bike," he said to Rainbow.

She stepped in front of him so he was forced to look at her. "Are you sure you don't mind?"

His eyes slid away. "Of course not."

He did mind, even though he'd just told her she should make herself available to Thierry. It was impossible to please everyone. She had a whole day in front of her, and helping the trees would be more useful than going over her revision notes again.

"Let's go," she said to Thierry. She gave Christophe a quick kiss and pulled away to follow Thierry downstairs.

He grasped her hand. "Rainette—"

"I've got to go," she said. Thierry was already in the street.

Christophe held on. "You know I'd do anything for you," he said. "If you're serious about going to the Pyrenees next weekend, of course I'll come with you."

She stopped resisting him. "Really?"

"I'm not leaving you to drive all that way alone and get lost in the mountains."

She hugged him. "Thanks loads. You're the best, Chris. I'd be useless on my own."

"You'd better think up a good plan to find this shepherd," he said.

"Don't worry. I've got all day to work it out while I'm clearing up the poor trees."

She kissed him, properly this time, and then hurried after Thierry.

As Thierry drove them towards his client's house she studied his weatherbeaten face, creased with laughter lines, under the baseball cap he wore in winter and summer. She knew better than to tell him about her vision: he wasn't open to spiritual experiences, and wouldn't understand its importance. If he asked her to work with him next weekend, she'd say that she and Christophe had booked a mini-break. It sounded so grown-up!

The more time she spent with Thierry, the more she wanted to be his assistant. His wife Claudette had invited her and Christophe for a meal the week before, and the evening passed in an instant because she was so absorbed in Thierry's tales about the trees in Massane forest, where he'd worked for thirty years. Who'd have thought that trees were capable of migrating when the climate got too hot or cold? Or that forests created so much transpiration from their leaves that they made clouds, which carried rain inland? She'd told him he should write a book about his knowledge, but he laughed, claimed he hardly knew how to hold a pen, and added that he was counting on a Canadian scientist to catch the world's attention once she'd got some solid results from her research.

He stopped the van near Cognac golf course, where his client's garden resembled the aftermath of a tornado. Tears pricked Rainbow's eyes and she struggled not to break down in front of Thierry.

"You'll have to use the chainsaw today," he warned.

She straightened her shoulders and ignored her bruises. He needed a workmate, not a blubbering kid.

"OK. As long as it's only for dead branches."

They sawed up wood and piled the logs in stacks. The client soon lost interest in watching them, and went indoors. In normal circumstances, this was the point Rainbow anticipated. Once the client had gone, Thierry would let her climb into the trees and do her healing and rebalancing work. Today, however, he needed her to clear the ground.

Isolated by her ear defenders, she started to think about a plan to find her shepherd the following weekend. She remained convinced he was a man and hoped to prove Mary wrong, even though Domi had advised her not to imagine her other half's age, gender or physical features because it would blind her to recognising the person. Domi added that she might see an aura around her other half, and that she must keep her eyes open for signs.

She had no idea what an aura looked like, but she imagined it as a golden light. It would illuminate her shepherd as he sat hugging a mountain pine tree with his sheep at his feet, infusing both tree and human with glowing light. She and Christophe just had to find the sheep pastures and walk around them until they saw the golden glow.

She wished she had a better idea of how long the mission would take. It was impossible to plan anything and difficult to speculate on how to vanquish the Tree Slayer until she met her shepherd.

She continued cutting up dismembered branches and lugging logs until she could no longer lift the chainsaw. She made a T-sign to Thierry, who nodded. Once she'd taken off her ear defenders, she climbed into an injured beech tree, which she soothed, rebalancing its branches and stroking its trunk. She could sense damage in its roots, but she couldn't do anything for them except send energy downwards.

Thierry joined her a few minutes later.

"I always forget to take a break. Claudette is right: you're good for me."

"I'm actually working," she reminded him.

"I know. And even if I don't understand what you do, I can see it's fundamentally right. There's so much we don't know about trees. We've picked up fragments of information but we need scientists to do more studies. Most of them aren't interested or can't get funding to do extended research."

"Tell me one of the fragments."

"This is just a short break, right?"

"Of course," she said, grinning.

"OK. You know trees communicate with each other?"

"*I* know," she said. How else could the beech tree near Le Logis have known about the beech tree she'd maimed in Dorset? "But I get sideways looks when I tell other people. How do *you* know?"

"It hasn't been scientifically proven yet, though that Canadian researcher I told you about is working on it. But my experience has convinced me. In Massane forest, some of the beech trees had far less light than the other trees around them. In theory, less light means less sugar from photosynthesis, and so these beech trees should have had problems growing. But – get this – they actually grew just as well as those in full sunlight. I reckon those trees share their nutrients. I'm sure something connects the root systems to each other. Perhaps they work in symbiosis with the mycelium network under the forest floor. That would explain why some of our Massane tree stumps continued to live, despite having no leaves."

"What's mycelium?"

"The vegetative part of fungus. It's made up of millions of

threads called hyphae, which absorb nutrients from the soil."

Rainbow thought back to the oak tree in François I park. She recalled the murmured thanks from the other trees pulsing upwards from a silver underground network. It could have been these mycelium hyphae threads.

Thierry continued. "In ancient forests, trees grow close together. Survival comes down to teamwork, you see – you'd do well to remember that, by the way. You're a bit too much of a loner."

"It's not my fault. No one ever wants to be on my team," said Rainbow. Even Mary, who had no choice, didn't want to be on her team.

"Perhaps you should learn to trust other people the way you trust trees. Anyway, this Canadian scientist suspects there are hub trees with connections to all the trees in their forests."

"It's true! There are," she said, thinking of the François I oak tree again. "They're mother trees." He wasn't talking about the spiritual kind of communication she had experienced. But it was fascinating, even if he did reduce everything to science. "Can you tell me more about mycelium?"

He stood up and grunted. "You ought to do an arboriculture course after your Baccalaureate. That would teach you all the basic facts – and how to work in a team."

"Couldn't *you* teach me? I've already learnt loads from working with you."

"I could. But you need a qualification. Come on, back to the chainsaws."

She'd had enough of books and classrooms, but if Thierry gave her a job afterwards, it would be worth it. Manual courses were much shorter than academic ones. It would be useful to be able to talk about trees like Thierry did, in words people would accept more easily. She'd have to investigate courses and hope her literary Baccalaureate – if she passed next week's exams – would be sufficient to get her a place on one.

She put aside all thoughts of her mission and mentally revised the different philosophers' ideas in preparation for her first exam the next day.

CHAPTER 8

On Friday, Thierry and Claudette picked up Rainbow from the *lycée* to take her to lunch. Thierry had chosen the restaurant in François I park. Although Rainbow thought it heartless to celebrate her birthday among the orphaned trees, she lacked the courage to act on Mary's desire to tell him.

As they drove to the park, she answered Claudette's questions about her exams, which had been neither disastrous nor easy, and told her the results would arrive in mid-July. Now her exams were over, she could concentrate on her mission.

Since the vision, her Amrita nightmares had stopped. Rainbow hoped it was because she'd decided to take action and not because Amrita's life force had already expired. She'd come up with a plan, which she would explain to Christophe at the restaurant, once he'd dropped off the apprentice at the supermarket.

First, she and Christophe would find a woody campsite in the Val d'Azun. Then they'd ask the villagers to direct them to the sheep pastures. Well, Christophe would. He was far better with people than she was. Much as the idea of going there alone had alarmed her, being with him would make it fun. If she could get him to enter into the spirit of finding her shepherd, it would be an adventure. It would have been even better with Apple and Acorn, but it made more sense for the apprentice to look after them for the weekend.

Thierry was talking about trees, as usual. Rainbow put her anticipation for the weekend to one side and listened.

"… so they concluded that the giraffes stopped eating the leaves because the acacia trees upwind had sent a warning message to the other acacias," he said.

Rainbow imagined prickly acacias in the savannah sending invisible messages to each other.

"Did they communicate through their roots and mycelium, then, like the trees in Massane forest?" she asked.

"No. That's the interesting bit. The researchers reckon that when an acacia tree senses a giraffe eating its leaves, it gives out a warning gas. The wind carries the gas to the other trees, and they produce an unpleasant taste in their leaves. Clever, eh? That way, the giraffes don't eat the leaves of the acacias downwind of the one attacked by the giraffe."

Rainbow gazed out of the van window and thought about how the wind could both help and hurt trees. Maybe there were helpful winds and unhelpful ones: tree-slaying winds and tree-saving winds. She'd have to make sure she vanquished the right one.

There was a biker at the traffic lights opposite. He looked like Christophe. The helmet was the same as his and the bike was the same colour as the bike he'd given her, which he always rode. But a girl was riding pillion. A girl with long, blonde hair curling from under her helmet.

It was Rainbow's helmet. The boy was Christophe, and the girl had her arms around him, even though they were stationary and she didn't need to hold on.

She stared. Christophe was supposed to be with the apprentice. Was he using the apprentice as an excuse to see this girl? The apprentice always needed him for something or other.

Mary urged her to wind down the window and shout at him. But she couldn't. What would she say? Her Christophe. Her reliable, honest Christophe.

"Trees react the same way when caterpillars bite their leaves," came Thierry's voice through the red mist in her mind. "The researchers say the signals are electrical, though. Everything is slow with trees, so it takes a long time until the leaves all produce a substance that's toxic to that particular caterpillar. I've seen this kind of thing myself, though I knew nothing about the signals. I just saw caterpillars attack and then, an hour later, they stopped eating. How about that? Rainbow?"

The lights changed and Christophe whizzed past. The helmet covered the girl's face, but judging by her long legs in tight leather trousers, she was tall. Tall and blonde: the complete opposite of Rainbow. Mary's frustration boiled, demanding that Rainbow get Thierry to turn around and follow him. But last time she'd let Mary's anger spill out, the oak tree had been killed. She must only listen to Mary when she was calm.

There had to be another explanation for the girl. Mary was always quick to believe the worst. Christophe wouldn't have given Rainbow the kittens – their kittens – if he planned to run off with another girl. In a few minutes she would see him at the restaurant, where he would explain everything and tease her for over-reacting.

"Everything all right, sweetie?" asked Claudette.

"I'm fine," croaked Rainbow. "Just tired after my exams."

"A good meal is what you need. Stop rabbiting on about trees, Titi, and give the poor girl some peace."

They parked and walked towards the riverside restaurant. There was a splash, probably from a coypu, and a group of wild ducks squawked. Rainbow hardly noticed them, nor the desecrated woodland. She followed Thierry and Claudette to their table on the terrace and sat down, facing the entrance. They ordered their meals, and then Thierry cleared his throat.

"Let's get down to business," he said. "I've got a proposal for you."

"A proposal?"

"Yes. How long have we been working together now?"

Rainbow's eyes slid back to the entrance. Still no Christophe. He was late. Was he lingering over a last kiss?

"Since December. Six months," she said. It was three months shorter than the time she'd been going out with Christophe.

"That's right. And during those six months you've never let me down. You've worked as hard as me, and you're always ready to learn – unless I'm trying to show you chainsaw techniques, of course. There's still some room for improvement there."

His voice seemed to register several seconds after he'd spoken. Now he was chuckling. She fought off the image of Christophe and the girl kissing, and concentrated on Thierry.

"So I'd like to sponsor you for an arboriculture course," he said. "There are some excellent sandwich courses locally, so you could do your work placements with me and study at the same time."

All thoughts of Christophe fell away. "Really? You mean it?"

"I most certainly do," he said. "I'm not promising you a job afterwards, mind. We'll have to see what the market's like in a year's time."

"That's so cool! Thanks, Thierry." She jumped up from her chair and kissed both him and Claudette.

"There'll be no slacking off, though. You'll have to study hard. And you'll work for me this summer too, of course. I've got a project that I think you'll like, starting on Monday."

"A summer job and sponsorship? You've made my day." She grinned at them both. She'd be back from the mountains on Sunday evening, having found her shepherd and vanquished the Tree Slayer. They could deal with Koad the weekend after. "So what's the project?"

"I'll tell you on Monday. Eight o'clock sharp, OK?"

"You bet!"

"I think champagne is in order, don't you?" said Claudette. "Just as soon as ... Ah, here he is."

Christophe walked across the terrace, unzipping his leather jacket. Mary's anger surged, almost knocking Rainbow off balance with the force of her desire to demand an explanation. Rainbow's joy evaporated. She could hardly make a scene here, right in front of Thierry and Claudette. Not after they'd just shown their confidence in her.

"Hey, Rainette." Christophe leant forward to kiss her.

"How was the exam?"

"Fine," she said, tilting her face away. She couldn't kiss him on the lips that had just kissed another girl. "Did you deliver your apprentice?"

"Of course. Only fine? Didn't you finish all the exam questions?"

He was lying. "I said it was fine, OK?"

She frowned at the crownless spikes of trees behind the restaurant, struggling to keep Mary's fury in check. If she were honest, the anger didn't only come from Mary.

Thierry passed Christophe a glass of champagne. He looked surprised, and when she said nothing, Thierry explained why they were celebrating. Christophe exclaimed and enthused, over-compensating for Rainbow's silence. They toasted her future as an arborist as well as her nineteenth birthday, and sipped. She couldn't force a single drop down her dry throat.

Thierry turned to Christophe and winked. "How's that young apprentice getting on?"

Rainbow frowned. Why the wink? Did he know Christophe was using the apprentice as a cover to see Blondie?

"Fine," said Christophe.

He was blushing.

Rainbow choked and spat out her champagne. She wasn't the fool they believed her to be. She didn't have to take this. It would be easy to give in to Mary's rage and shout at him, slap him, storm off.

Christophe patted her on the back. She flinched but he didn't even notice. He was asking Thierry about his new motorbike.

She stood up and pushed back her chair. It fell over.

Thierry's words tailed off and all three of them stared at her. She mustn't scream or shout, as Mary wanted. She had to leave before she gave in or burst. She stumbled across the terrace.

A chair scraped and she heard quick footsteps. She walked faster, leaving the sickening smell of grilled steak behind as she hurried into the leafy shelter of the woodland.

Christophe ran up beside her and clasped her arm. "Rainette! What's going on?"

She shook off his hand and carried on walking.

"Rainbow?"

"You tell me," she said.

"Tell you what?"

She stopped and glared at him. "Are you kidding me? Do you really have nothing to say? About that girl?"

"What girl?" His voice was uncertain.

"The blonde girl. On your motorbike just now."

"You mean Emilie? What about her? I told you I was taking her to the supermarket."

The river, trees and path all slanted to one side. She was slipping off the world.

"Her?" She swallowed. "The apprentice is a girl?"

He nodded, his cheeks still pink.

"You told me she was a boy," she said.

"I didn't."

She ran his comments about the apprentice through her mind. She couldn't find an example to contradict him. How could she have been so stupid, so sexist? Maybe Mary was right in accusing her of being stereotyped in her assumptions.

"OK, I presumed she was a boy," she said. "But you never

corrected me. Why not, Chris?"

He ran his fingers through his hair. "I don't know. I'm sorry."

She thought about all the lifts he'd given the apprentice. The times he'd stayed late to help her in the workshop. The way he never talked about her in detail. She wasn't sure if this was better or worse.

"So there's nothing between you?"

"Well … No."

That single second of silence, in which he had to think whether the girl meant more to him than she should, stabbed her heart. It was definitely worse.

He took her hands. "We haven't done anything, Rainbow. Honestly."

Another stab: that "we", which meant him and her, Christophe and Emilie. Not Christophe and Rainbow.

She swallowed. "But you want to?"

His brown eyes avoided hers. He took his hands away and shoved them in his pockets.

"I don't know."

"What do you mean, you don't know?" A sob caught in her throat. "What about the kittens? Our kittens? Why did you get them if you want us to split up?"

"I love you, Rainbow. It's just that–"

She covered her ears. "Don't say that. You're not allowed to say that anymore."

"It's just that there's this thing happening inside me." He reached towards her, then dropped his hands and sighed. "So what do we do now?"

"You do what you like. I'm off. I've got stuff to do. In the Val d'Azun."

"On your own? You can't go alone."

She wasn't alone, technically. Difficult though Mary could be, she was with her, boosting her confidence right now and encouraging her to go through with this. Mary wouldn't fall in love with someone else and abandon her. Together, she and Mary could do this. They had to do this. Nothing else made any sense.

"Well, I can't stay here," she said. "Not when I might bump into you and her. I guess this is goodbye."

"Wait! Rainbow!"

She turned and ran into the forest. He didn't follow.

CHAPTER 9

Eole's exams had finished yesterday, and today was his eighteenth birthday. Inside the barn, he checked his watch and then whistled to Darwie. Patou and the sheep that no longer had any milk were ready: fed, wormed, painted with a blue stripe on their rumps (except Patou), and separated from the goats. In two minutes and forty seconds he'd be allowed into the house for tea, and then they'd do the transhumance.

He crossed the yard. Four of their seven cats were miaowing at the door. Darwie snapped at them and they exploded in different directions, where they sulked from the wall, the tractor, the roof of the cheese room and the wood shed. Maman never turned away strays. She took them all in and fed them. She didn't know about the kittens, which Papa dealt with in the stream. Maman took in stray people, too, and Christmas meals were complicated because there was always an archaic villager sitting at their table and asking Eole illogical questions about school. Unfortunately, Papa didn't deal with them in the stream.

Eole went indoors, took a deep, steady breath and

concentrated on the smells. Maman made the best, most difficult quiz cakes for his birthdays. The air flowed past his olfactory receptors and down into the giant labyrinth of his lungs. Darwie whined. The overriding smell – besides the normal mix of curdled milk, cat piss and lilac – was one of burnt sugar.

The quiz cake sat on the worktop beside a pile of five (no longer six) plates. It wasn't even iced, and looked as disappointing as it smelt. Maman was leafing through an orange folder. She smiled at Eole and then shouted at Hestia to wake up and come downstairs for tea.

"Papa's gone to get Brigitte," she said. "OK for a birthday kiss?"

He nodded and bent down so she could kiss his cheek. It was no worse than Darwie sliding his wet nose into his hand, and it was the birthday tea tradition. Even so, he couldn't help straightening up immediately afterwards.

Maman cleared her throat. "While we're alone, I've got something to say. Now you're eighteen." She scrunched her mouth to one side and tapped her chin, looking at the folder. It was the same expression as when she'd had a bad phone call from the headmaster.

He waited.

"Well, you're eighteen now. An adult," she said.

"I know."

"Which, in theory, means we're no longer responsible for you. But that's just the law. In practice, nothing changes. We're still here for you, whatever you may need, darling. OK?"

"OK. Is that all?"

The door opened and Hestia appeared, yawning.

Maman closed the folder and turned to Hestia. "What time do you call this? Don't forget we're taking the sheep up after tea."

"Uh-huh." She looked hard at Eole as they bumped fists. "Happy birthday. You look pale."

"Yes, you do," said Maman. "Exam fatigue, I suppose."

He did feel pale today, even though he wasn't tired and the exams hadn't been particularly demanding. He felt even paler with them both staring at him.

Papa and Brigitte arrived. Eole took a step back from the sudden bustle and slid into his chair by the wall. Hestia opened the fridge and took out a bottle. It was Moët & Chandon champagne, just like the bottles from the Paris days.

Maman took it from her. "There's Champomy for you."

"I'm sixteen, not six!"

Maman opened the fizzy apple juice and served Hestia a champagne glassful while Papa poured the real champagne. Eole took the glass with the least in it, thinking of his neurones and his mapopedia.

Everyone sat and held up their glasses to chink, except for Papa. He'd picked up the orange folder and his lips were pursed. Maman was watching him.

"Pa-a-a-trick!" sang Brigitte in her nanny-goat bleat. "We're waiting for you."

Papa slid the folder across the worktop to the far corner and chinked glasses. Maman had a sip and then left the room to get Eole's present. Papa turned to pick up the cake.

Eole felt a kick on his foot. This was one of Hestia's signs, so he quickly looked at her face. She winked at him and exchanged their glasses, then smiled at Brigitte and put her finger to her lips. Brigitte giggled. Eole nodded. He wouldn't need to destroy any neurones now. His mapopedia would remain intact.

Maman returned and they each attempted to guess the contents of the quiz cake before eating it. The ingredients had never been so easy. Eole unwrapped his presents, which were always books, and nodded his approval at the titles: *A History of Aviation*, *Multiverse Theories* and *Electronics & Computing*. The computing book reminded him how he and Tintin had taken apart Tintin's old Amstrad computer, tested everything, and then rebuilt it.

Brigitte explained that Tintin had chosen the multiverse book for Eole before he died. Instead of being a portal to new knowledge, *Multiverse Theories* now looked more like a gravestone.

The final part of his birthday was the measure, which required him to stand against the door frame while Maman climbed onto a stool and marked his height.

"It's official," she said. "You've stopped growing. You're the same height as last year."

And that was the end of his birthday.

Brigitte and Maman went to the cheese room and Papa left with Darwie to get the shepherd crooks. Eole cleared the table while Hestia swallowed the champagne dregs.

"Is Maman OK?" he asked her.

"Oh. My. God. You've actually noticed something."

"Two facts indicate a problem," he said. "Her quiz cake was too easy. And she burnt it."

"Yeah, something's up. She's all agitated. Maybe she's

realised I'm right about you needing to get a job with other people this summer rather than staying here on your own. Or she's worried about how you'll cope alone at uni." She broke off. "What?"

"La, la, la, la, la," droned Eole, his hands covering his ears. The idea of going to university had to ease gently into his mind. It had to make a space and turn around a few times, like Darwie in his basket, before it settled down. Once it was comfortable, he would face it.

"You've got to prepare for uni," Hestia continued. "We need to find you a friend in Toulouse this summer, someone who'll stick by you."

"La, la, la, la."

Hestia shook her head. "Come on. We've got to work. Some birthday, huh?"

"It's not my birthday anymore. It's transhumance."

It wasn't a proper transhumance without Tintin to lead them, but Maman, Papa, Hestia and Darwie were still here. They'd follow the same routine. It would be fine.

He slung his rucksack onto his back and put on his headphones. Darwie yelped in excitement and circled the pen, and Eole had to order him to calm down. Papa handed out the crooks and told Eole to walk in front of the sheep.

The front was Tintin's place.

Eole hesitated, recalculating: he'd presumed Papa would lead. He couldn't do it. Not without Tintin. Unless … His mind searched for a creative solution … Unless he pretended Tintin was beside him.

There was a scrape of metal hurdle on stone and then a rush of bobbing heads charged towards him. He and Tintin held out their crooks and led the way. Maman and Papa followed the flock, shooing the sheep onwards and smacking them when they stopped to snatch at the long grass on the verges. Darwie ran in excited curves around the flock, his ears pricked, nipping at the sheep's hocks to make them move faster. Hestia lagged behind, grumbling that she detested the stink of sheep, hated the mountains and was missing the best party of the year.

Several hours after leaving the farm they passed the cattle grid. The trees thinned and the pastures opened out before them in the twilight. Eole took off his headphones.

"I'll take them on from here," he said, as Tintin had always done.

"At last," said Hestia. She turned around and started to walk home at twice her previous pace.

"OK, darling. Have a nice evening and see you tomorrow for lunch," said Maman.

Papa patted Darwie and reminded Eole to put the sheep in the pen for tonight, and to check their feet before letting them out the next day.

Eole watched his family fade into the darkness, Maman and Papa walking together and Hestia far in front. He liked knowing his family were in the valley below him, that he belonged with them but that he could belong here as well. They were like an anchor. He was a boat with an anchor, though the wind had died so he couldn't set sail and leave.

He, Darwie and an invisible Tintin folded the sheep into the pen, leaving Patou outside to guard them, and then he stretched out on the grass beside the hut and gazed at the night sky. It was good to have made a new transhumance routine without any sign of *itch, shuffle and escape*. Maman said it was important to be flexible about routines when you were grown up. Hestia said he should stop hanging off Maman's every word and get himself a life, because he was perfectly capable if only he'd trust himself.

He didn't have to think about them or their advice now. He could relax and pretend Tintin was asleep in his bunk bed. Other flocks, streaked in different-coloured paints, roamed on the slopes above him, but most farmers no longer stayed with their sheep. He was probably the only human here on the mountain. The sky of starry satellites stretched above him and he let Tintin and his mapopedia fill his mind.

The morning dew had dried and Eole's flock of fifty sheep were spread across the smooth flank of the mountain, free in the midday air. It was time for him and Darwie to return home.

He shouldered his rucksack and whistled to Patou, who left the flock and came trotting to the outcrop of granite above them.

"Darwie and I are off. We'll be back for the summer as soon as we've finished fencing in the valley," he said.

Patou stood still, his tail lifted. Tintin had told Eole that animals understood human voices, even if they didn't understand the actual words. Eole could see his point. He didn't understand the words of the voices he heard, but there was an overriding tone and even a smell to them. He'd kept a mental catalogue of the smells for years in Paris, though he didn't write them down. It wasn't easy to find words to describe them.

He put on his headphones and walked towards the valley with Darwie. When he glanced back, Patou was still watching them. Nothing would dare attack the sheep, apart from the Slovenian bears the government had released into the mountains. But they were three valleys away.

When he arrived home, the farmyard smelt and looked different. The goaty odour was thin without the woolly undertone of fifty fleeces, and Papa had made a pile of fencing tools and posts outside the barn. It would be good to use his hands again after all the studying. Brigitte had told him he could continue to tinker in Tintin's laboratory, but he hadn't managed to get any further than opening the door.

Maman waved at him from the window and gestured to him to come indoors. She was back early from church. In the kitchen, the spicy smell of chilli emanated from the slow cooker. The clock ticked. A goat bleated on the far side of the yard. Maman and Papa were sitting at the table, unusually silent. An orange folder lay in front of them.

Eole reached out for Darwie, who slid his wet nose into his cupped hand.

"It's all right, darling," said Maman in a not-all-right voice. "Come and sit down."

Eole stepped back to the door.

"It's OK. Everything's fine. We've got something to tell you, but it won't change anything," said Maman. "It's like I told you yesterday about being eighteen: there's no actual difference, it's just a piece of paper."

Papa pulled out Eole's chair and pushed Scatty Cat off it. Eole crossed the room and sat down. Darwie put his head on his lap. The fridge broke into a menacing hum. A tractor rumbled closer.

"You know how we go to Brittany in the holidays to see Aunt Isabelle?" said Maman. "Well, when Papa and I were younger, we spent a lot of time there–"

"Just tell him, Alexandra," said Papa.

Maman frowned at him. "I'm doing this my way."

"Tell me what?" Eole couldn't see any link between the orange folder, Aunt Isabelle and himself.

"It was before you came along," continued Maman, "and God hadn't yet decided to give us a baby."

Papa muttered but Maman ignored him.

"We learnt that a baby from a village in Brittany was looking for a home," she said. "We prayed–"

"*You* prayed," said Papa.

"And God told me it was his will for us to adopt this baby," said Maman.

Eole looked at her face and then down at the document she was holding. "So?"

"So we adopted him."

"We adopted *you*," said Papa. "You were the baby, and now you're eighteen Alexandra thought it was time to tell you."

"Do you understand, darling? We're still your parents – we'll always be your parents – and we love you. Now you're an adult you should know the truth because the truth is important, even if it doesn't change anything."

She said his name and made her love-hug sign.

The words flew at him but they wouldn't enter his brain. They raced over and under his head like the diagram of the air flowing around the cross-section of the aeroplane wing on the cover of his new book.

"Darling?"

He nodded, because when Maman used her worried voice, Hestia said it was because he was looking blank and forgetting to use facial expressions.

"We don't know who your biological parents were," said Papa. "All we know is that you came from a village near Paimpont in Brittany. If you want to know more, you're allowed to investigate."

Eole put his hands over his ears. There was too much information. Out of all the words they were speaking, only one would stick: adopted. *Adopted*. ADOPTED. Where did it fit on his scale from minor modification to major change? The scale wasn't big enough anymore.

He was adopted. *Itch.*

Therefore, Maman and Papa weren't his parents.

Therefore, Hestia wasn't his sister.

They weren't his real family.

He didn't belong with them. *Shuffle.* So where did he belong?

A black hole opened up in his mind and he was falling into it. More words attacked him. Hands reached for him. Maman was crying. But she wasn't Maman anymore.

And escape. He fought off the hands, burst out of the house and let his feet take him away.

CHAPTER 10

Rainbow had seen photos of the craggy Pyrenees mountains in library books: snowy winter ski slopes; spring prairies dotted with pink, blue and yellow wildflowers; dour villages of houses with steep slate roofs mounted on low walls. In a television documentary she'd seen marmots and she'd heard the roar of waterfalls, the cries of raptors in the silent sky and the tinkling of cow bells. She'd even tasted Pyrenean tome cheese bought from a little man in a black beret at Cognac market.

None of this, however, prepared her for the reality of the mountains.

She first saw their hazy outlines on the horizon when she reached the heights of a plateau in the Gers countryside, where she mistook them for clouds. Gradually, the shapes became more solid. Her misery at the battered woodlands she'd driven past all afternoon turned into fascination for what lay ahead until, just before Lourdes, she was struck by the startling enormity of the rocky, snow-capped mass.

Look! she wanted to say. But there was no one in the

passenger seat to hear her.

She couldn't think about Christophe. She'd closed his name into a box since yesterday lunchtime at the restaurant, thanks to Mary's suggestion: Mary had kept a *before* box sealed for years.

The only thing that mattered now was her mission. Mary agreed, since staying at home in safety with Christophe was no longer an option. Her assent had eased the pressure on the internal wall inside Rainbow's head. Somewhere, squeezed between two crags, was a pasture, and in that pasture was her soulmate. He – or she, Rainbow conceded to Mary, given her stupidity over presuming Christophe's apprentice was a boy – would help her vanquish the Tree Slayer. She had to believe in this. There was nothing else left.

The Val d'Azun was a few kilometres up a snaky road beyond the market town of Argelès-Gazost. A tourist road sign announced it and then, around the corner, a wide, green valley appeared. She'd done it! If someone had told her before yesterday's catastrophe that she would drive to the Pyrenees on her own, she'd never have believed it.

Yesterday, she'd raced home from the restaurant and sobbed her anguish about Christophe into Mum's shoulder. Mary's anger with him subsided into silence, which, unexpectedly, made Rainbow feel lonely. She couldn't face driving to the Pyrenees alone. But Mum encouraged her to follow her spiritual calling, and Domi planned the car journey with her. Though they helped enormously, she'd navigated the journey alone.

The Val d'Azun was long and U-shaped, with wooded slopes leading up to rounded hilltops in the foreground and rocky peaks behind. Tiny villages dotted the valley bottom and sides. The view, in the golden light of the Saturday evening sun, was worthy of a picture postcard. But the valley was much bigger than she'd imagined.

She passed several villages – Arras-en-Lavedan, Arcizans, Aucun – and snatched glances at the acres of pastureland, pretty in long grass and wild flowers, as she drove. There were no sheep or shepherds in sight. This wasn't going to be as easy as she'd anticipated.

She stopped at the first campsite she spotted, in a village called Arrens-Marsous. This was the bit she was dreading. Christophe normally did the talking when they went out. She must trust Amrita's belief in her and take one step at a time.

The owner was in his office and she checked in without getting any sideways looks or questions about why a young girl was camping alone. She wanted to pitch her tent and hide in it before she said something weird, but Mary reassured her she was doing fine. She compelled Rainbow to focus on her goals, so Rainbow asked the owner where she could find the sheep pastures of High Azun.

He stared at her and she lowered her eyes. She could just leave.

"Oh, you mean the summer pastures?" he said.

"Maybe. Where are they?"

"It depends. Each village has its own pastures up on the heights." He took out a tourist map of the Val d'Azun and circled a series of plateaux and passes along both sides of the valley. "But if it's the transhumance you're after, you've missed it," he added.

"Transhumance?" she asked. The word sounded like a

gender identity, or the name for a human who had changed into something else. But the campsite owner explained it was the annual movement of sheep and cattle up to the summer pastures and back. It was an occasion for celebration and attracted journalists and tourists from all over western France.

"Are all the shepherds up there?" she asked.

"There aren't many shepherds left, these days. Are you a trainee journalist or something?" He nodded towards her sketch pad, which she'd taken out of her bag while she scrabbled for her proof of identity.

She knew better than to talk about soulmates and tree gifts to strangers. "It's for school. I'm doing a project on shepherds," she said.

She'd made a good start, and the talking was easier than she'd expected, thanks to Mary's encouragement to forget the past and concentrate on looking to the future. She was almost enjoying her conversation with the man, who accepted everything she said without surprise. It made her feel like a true adult rather than the skinny weirdo from the spiritual commune.

"If I were you, I'd start at the pastures above Arras-en-Lavedan," the owner continued. "There used to be an old shepherd there all summer. Keep an eye out for bears, though."

She searched his face for signs that the bears were a joke. But he was serious, and told her about the recent introduction of two wild brown bears into the mountains. Christophe would have known how to handle a bear. The prospect of facing one alone made her feel vulnerable again and she quickly left to pitch her tent.

She settled in the far corner of the campsite, beside a

comforting oak tree. Then she studied the map and its promising circles before preparing for bed. Tomorrow she would find the old shepherd, who may well be her soulmate. Together, they'd get revenge on the Tree Slayer for all the trees it had killed, and for hurting the One Tree she must heal in order to save Amrita.

PART II

TWO HALVES

CHAPTER 11

Tintin's hut was far below Eole. He had walked upwards without stopping in the hours since ~~Maman~~ Alexandra had told him he was adopted, and now he was balanced on the ridge. He couldn't go any higher. There was a steep drop on both sides and in the distance he could see Mount Balaïtous and the permanent glacier on Vignemale.

He knew exactly where he stood in the physical world, but the physical world and his mental world were now two different places. Where once they'd matched and meshed, like gear wheels, their relation to each other had now shifted. It was as if one of Newton's laws of physics had been proved wrong and all the ensuing scientific theories were built on a false foundation. They'd crashed to the ground and tumbled down the mountainside into the valley below.

He didn't belong with his family.

Why hadn't Patrick and Alexandra told him sooner?

He took a deep breath. Darwie whined and sidled towards him. Darwie never came right to the edge of the drop and was uncomfortable when Eole stood like this, one step from death. Normally Eole came here to practise his special cloud skill. But today it was too dangerous to practise. He'd learnt his lesson last time he'd been unsettled, and now he knew he must divert his thoughts. He reached out and stroked Darwie's head. He must fix his mind on something solid while he let his brain recalculate the eighteen years of his life.

His mapopedia held parts of his physical and mental world together. Here, on the height of the ridge, Tintin had explained how glaciation worked. Eole concentrated. He imagined Tintin beside him and sculpted the words 'firn', 'calving', 'moraines' and 'ablation' into the curve of the ridge. With each mapopedia entry, his bewilderment subsided a little. At last, he sat down on the rocky ridge, studied the clouds and allowed himself to practise his art a little. It was fine. He was back in control.

His stomach rumbled. He hadn't had the chance to eat any of the lunchtime chilli. In Tintin's hut there were emergency rations of dried sausage, savoury biscuits and fruit-and-nut mix. He made his way down towards the food, stopping from time to time to add to his mapopedia.

Rainbow slept late on Sunday. After lunch she parked in Arras-en-Lavedan, put on her walking boots and set off from the village towards the forest that cloaked the mountain's rocky shoulders. Luckily, the campsite owner had given her directions: she'd never have found the path from the map. To her relief, his directions matched the terrain around her. She was doing this alone – and succeeding!

While she kept her eyes open for shepherds with golden auras, she absorbed the atmosphere of the trees. They seemed tougher than those in the Charente, from the deciduous trees on the valley floor to the multi-trunked mountain pines clinging to the steep slopes. The mountain pines reminded her of Thierry. During their work breaks, he'd talked about those in Massane forest, and how walking in woodland – which he called 'forest bathing' – could increase or decrease people's blood pressure, according to whether the trees were suffering or not. Her blood pressure was definitely high. Her heart was beating fast, though that may have been because of the steep climb. Or the prospect of meeting her soulmate. Or the bears.

She wasn't in a hurry. There was no longer anything to go home for. She'd ruined her whole future with Thierry when she left the restaurant without any explanation. He wouldn't appreciate her behaviour, even though the Mary side of her insisted it was Christophe's fault rather than hers. It was one more reason why she had to accomplish her mission. The lid of the box in her mind opened and she shoved Thierry inside with Christophe. Instead of thinking about them, she concentrated on her surroundings.

The wood above the village ended and she stepped into a green prairie humming with crickets, bees and horseflies. The grass was long and seedy and there were pockets of wild flowers. Some, a purple-blue colour, were irises, but she couldn't identify the others. She stopped and took some photos to show Mum. There were no sheep, and the prairie soon gave way to steep slopes.

She thought the summit of the mountain was just ahead

of her, but when she arrived she realised it was only a bump, and that the top was a little higher. When she reached it, there was yet another peak ahead of her. There was also a car park, which she hadn't noticed on her map.

The mountainside was dotted with boulders. She caught a movement on top of a flat one and took out Domi's binoculars. A marmot was sitting in the sun. It looked like a cross between a rabbit and a fluffy cat. Missing Apple and Acorn, she crept off the path towards it. It scampered a few metres higher. She climbed. But then she heard a sharp whistle, like an eagle's cry, and it disappeared into a round hole under a rock.

She continued up a steep, zigzagging path until she arrived, breathless and with aching legs, at a small plateau. It had slopes around it and looked like a giant's seat. A tiny stone cabin stood to the right, beside a metal gate enclosure. In a dell behind the cabin was a lake, and a pencil-line waterfall cascaded into the far end. A path led around it and up to a pass between two ridges, with rocky peaks visible beyond.

She took out her camera. The scene would have been perfect, had there been fewer sheep droppings and some trees. But there weren't even any stunted bushes; just bare, grassy slopes sprinkled with scree. She was hardly going to find her soulmate in a treeless pasture.

Actually, the slopes weren't bare. A flock of sheep straggled in a loose group below the pass. She picked up her binoculars and searched for the shepherd. The sheep were grazing and moving slowly downwards. Some joker had graffitied their fleeces with blue stripes, which spoilt the natural beauty of the view. All except one, on the far right, which had escaped the paint can. She let her binoculars drift from right to left.

There was no shepherd. A long way to the left, closer to her, one white-and-blue fleece was separated from the others. The sheep was struggling. It was caught in something.

She walked up the path towards the sheep, skirting the lake and admiring the reflection of the mountain peaks and blue sky in the water. The air was almost still, with no sign of any tree-slaying wind, and it wouldn't be dark until ten o'clock.

The stranded sheep wasn't on the path, and it was hard work picking through the rocks and squishy heather. She collapsed onto a rounded boulder, panting. Cloud fragments wisped like mist just above the pass, changing shape constantly. She'd never been so close to clouds before, and she watched, fascinated. They seemed to have a life of their own and were transclouding – if such a word existed. She fancied she saw a dog, which changed into a boat. She closed her eyes, and when she opened them again, the clouds had evaporated.

Back on her feet, she approached the sheep. It was lying on its side, its fleece and leg snagged in barbed wire. It was bigger than Dorset sheep, and had a huge hooked nose, long legs and curly horns like broken pasta twists. It bleated: a long, plaintive cry.

A low, threatening bark answered the bleat.

On the hillside, between the flock and herself, stood a large white dog, its feathery tail raised. It barked again and trotted towards her.

She drew back from the sheep.

There was a different bark, short and sharp, and she saw a border collie sheepdog silhouetted on the pass. Beside it, the head and shoulders of a person appeared, suddenly, as if he'd been lying down.

The shepherd.

Rainbow waved and made pointing gestures to the sheep. The shepherd stood up. He was too young to be the old shepherd the campsite owner had mentioned. There was no golden glow around him – but why would she see an aura when she'd never seen one in her life before? Auras were Domi's domain, not hers. And Amrita hadn't actually said her shepherd would be old.

She gestured to the shepherd again. He sat back down and disappeared from sight, as did the collie.

"There's a problem with a sheep!" she shouted, her hands cupped around her mouth.

There was no reaction.

The white dog crossed the scree and approached the sheep, which struggled even more. Rainbow prepared to shout at it and throw her rucksack if it attacked, but the dog sniffed the sheep and then nudged it, encouraging it to stand up. Then it looked at Rainbow again, as if accusing her of the sheep's misfortune. Rainbow backed away.

The dog turned and loped up the slope towards the shepherd. The trapped sheep stopped struggling. It panted, its sides heaving. Rainbow sat down and waited for the shepherd, rooting herself into the earth, as her reiki master had taught her, to calm her mounting excitement.

🌱 🍃 🌱

Patou only bothered Eole if there was a problem, so when Eole saw him trot over the crest of the hill, he stood up again and looked back down towards the tourist.

He didn't spot her immediately. She wasn't wearing the brightly coloured clothing that made most tourists visible from far away, and which gave him plenty of time to hide. This one blended into the hillside in her dark green and brown clothes. He breathed in and smelt lichen and goat cheese – and blood, which was probably why Patou had come to get him. There was another smell too, a rare one, which seemed nevertheless familiar.

He followed Patou down the slope, Darwie at his heel, and riffled through his mental catalogue of smells for something close to the familiar woody-musty-green odour coming from the tourist. There was nothing in his memory bank.

He rounded a bend in the path and saw the source of the blood: Dizzy. She was caught in a trap. He'd been concentrating on his mapopedia and his cloud practice, and hadn't noticed the flock was one sheep short. Luckily, the green girl wasn't between him and Dizzy. He wouldn't have to acknowledge her.

Dizzy was the worst one for this kind of situation: she panicked, which is how Hestia had chosen her name. If one sheep ran the wrong way when Darwie was rounding them up, it would be Dizzy. She probably suffered from *itch, shuffle and escape* too. Eole hadn't named any of the animals. He had no idea how to find a name for something, and Tintin's nickname had only arisen because he hadn't been concentrating when they first met.

The girl didn't say anything to him. Normally people tried to talk, especially if he was with the sheep. Women were the worst. He would nod at them, as Alexandra had taught him to do. If they kept talking he kept nodding. They soon stopped talking and walked on.

Dizzy's rear haunch was oozing blood from wire barbs entangled in her wool and buried in her flesh. He knelt down and put one hand on her head and the other on her back. She struggled against him, showing the whites of her eyes.

"Keep still, idiot sheep," he muttered.

"I think I can help."

The girl was right behind him. Patou hadn't growled. In fact, both Darwie and Patou stood close beside her.

Eole doubted she could help. She was just like the other tourists, after all. He nodded, hoping his silence would send her away. Then Dizzy kicked him in the stomach. The movement made more blood seep from her flank. He swore.

Instead of leaving, the girl crouched in front of Dizzy, murmured to her, and then stretched out her hands and brought them close to Dizzy's head.

Eole watched her suspiciously. She still didn't say anything, but ignored him and closed her eyes. He would give her one minute and then tell her to go away.

Dizzy bleated and lowered the leg that had been kicking. Forty-seven seconds later, she relaxed her head onto the ground. The girl shifted closer and laid her hands on Dizzy's neck. A shudder ran down Dizzy's spine but she didn't move. The girl opened her eyes – which were green – and nodded to Eole, keeping her hands in place. He didn't need to question what she meant: somehow, his brain knew it was the moment to disentangle Dizzy. He unwound the wire, looped it into a circle, and bent it away from her flank.

His Swiss army knife wasn't adequate for the next job. "Wait here," he said to Darwie and Dizzy.

He jogged down to the hut, glancing up at Dizzy while he unlocked the padlock. The girl was still there, doing her magic thing. No, not magic. There had to be a logical explanation, a technique she might teach him if he was careful not to scare her away.

Back at Dizzy's side, he cut the wool from around the wounds and sprayed them with antiseptic. The girl gave Dizzy a final stroke and then rubbed her hands together and shook them hard, like he did when he wanted to get rid of a stench on his fingers.

"Will she be OK?" asked the girl.

"I don't know."

She raised her eyebrows and then smiled, though he couldn't see anything humorous.

"Good point," she said. "What I mean is, do you think she can stand up and go back to the flock?"

"Yes."

He dug into the ground where the barbed wire was buried, snipped it off below the surface with his wirecutters and put it in his pocket. He looked at the girl's face again. She was staring at him and had forgotten to put on a polite expression. Maybe she was special too; though did he still qualify as special, now he was adopted?

He whistled to Patou, who nudged Dizzy. Dizzy gathered her feet under herself and heaved herself up, and then Patou accompanied her back to the flock.

Eole's stomach rumbled again. The girl was silent as she watched Dizzy and Patou. She was different from the girls at school with their red lips and pointless conversations, their giggles, mysterious pauses and 'don't-touch-my-hair' shrieks.

She was more like an extra dog than a girl.

"I'm going to eat my emergency rations from the hut and then you can show me how to do that thing with your hands on the sheep, and we'll practise when I go to check on Dizzy in one hour," he said. He checked his watch. It was five forty-two p.m.

Rainbow opened her mouth to tell the shepherd she'd used reiki to calm the sheep, and that she couldn't just show him how to do it. But the boy, having spooled out his string of words in a monotone, turned and walked down towards his hut.

He may be a shepherd but he didn't match her idea of a soulmate. Besides, he was nowhere near a tree and didn't have a golden aura. She took out her sketch pad. He was an interesting subject to draw, even so, because although his face was expressionless, his movements were full of emotion. She perched on a boulder and sketched his tall, bulky frame and blond hair. His shoulders sagged as if he carried the weight of the world on them, and he was compressed around the edges like a drawing contoured with a heavy black line. Maybe it was because he was ill: after all, he'd rattled out something about feeling dizzy and needing emergency rations, and he was much paler than the weatherbeaten shepherd she'd imagined.

He entered his hut without looking back at her. She added his sneaky little border collie to her sketch, picturing the way it had sneered at the sheep. She couldn't quite get it right. Nor could she capture the shape of the sheep's head and its wild eyes. She shaded the shepherd's face, disappointed that she couldn't nail his awkwardness. Her sketch showed an ordinary, good-looking, sad boy. She needed to do some serious drawing practice.

The boy came out of his hut with a plastic bag, looked in her direction, and waited. Was he staring at his flock, counting them or something? She glanced behind her. There was nothing there. Anyway, he'd need binoculars to count them. He was looking at her.`

She waved. He waited.

She stood up and put her sketch pad away. He was still standing there, so she slung her rucksack on and walked down to the hut.

"Are you waiting for me?"

"Yes. I already told you. I'm going to eat my emergency rations and then you're going to teach me to calm sheep."

"Oh. Actually–"

He walked to the lake with his dog, sat on a flat rock and took a little book and a dried sausage out of the bag. He cut the sausage into slices and stuffed a handful into his mouth as if he were ravenous.

She followed him. "Do you want some bread to go with that?"

"Yes, but I haven't got any."

"I have. Here."

She gave him half of the baguette in her rucksack and he made a sandwich. His hands were coarse, workmen's hands with bitten nails, though his fingers were long and artistic. He didn't have bark-roughened palms from communicating with trees.

As soon as he'd made his sandwich, he opened his book. It

was a first aid guide, which seemed to be a strange choice for a leisurely read. She was obviously far less interesting to him than first aid. She considered leaving, but Mary pushed her to make conversation with him and ask about shepherds. It was all right for Mary: she was safe inside and didn't have to overcome her shyness to speak to the unfriendly boy.

"My name's Rainbow," she began.

He glanced up. "That's not a name."

At least he hadn't given her a sideways look, like most people did. "It's because my mum's a hippie. So what's yours?"

"Eole."

She laughed. "*That's* not a name."

He snapped his book shut. "It is. It comes from a mythological Greek god. The day I arrived, my – " He hesitated, and seemed to struggle to find his words. "Alexandra, heard God whisper the name 'Eole' to her, so that's what she called me. It was totally illogical because if God exists, why would he choose the name of a mythological god? And isn't it blasphemy to name me after a different god, even if Alexandra is Greek? If God existed, surely he would have punished her?"

Rainbow hesitated, unsure of how to respond to the splurge of personal information and philosophical questions. She didn't believe in God – not a conventional god, anyway – but she liked Domi's suggestion that people's souls fused with universal energy when they died. She still wasn't sure how Amrita, with her ability to control parallel worlds, fitted into this scheme.

"Those are rhetorical questions," Eole added, "so you don't have to answer them."

She smiled. "That's a relief. Faith is a complicated subject."
There was no reaction from Eole.

"Never mind," she said. "Tell me, are there many of you shepherds up here?"

His face was inscrutable. He reminded her of Guillaume, an intense boy whose parents had left him with Domi for spiritual healing. It was impossible to have a proper conversation with Guillaume or predict how he would react, so most of the commune avoided him. She remembered how isolated she'd felt at Le Logis when she first arrived, and had spent her spare time sitting with him and sketching. Domi told Guillaume's parents that he needed no healing: he was perfect as he was.

She changed her question: "What I mean is: are you the only person who looks after the flocks on these summer pastures?"

"No. All the farmers look after their flocks but I'm the only person who sleeps here now Tintin has gone. I've finished my sandwich, so it's time for you to explain how you calmed Dizzy."

Rainbow had to play back Eole's words and insert pauses before she understood that Dizzy was the sheep's name.

"Hang on. Who's Tintin?" she asked.

"He was my friend."

"And where's he gone?"

"He died."

He didn't give her any more information about Tintin and she wondered if, by waiting a week before coming here, she'd missed her soulmate.

"Oh. I'm sorry," she said. It felt wrong to ask if Tintin had healed trees. But she could ask if Eole had a tree gift.

She hesitated, wondering how to form the question. Mary's frustration rose: she wanted Rainbow to ask straight out. So Rainbow did.

"Have you got a gift for communicating with trees?"

He shook his head. Rainbow was pleased with Mary's advice. Now she'd ruled out Eole, she could continue her search for her soulmate.

"What about the other shepherds?" she asked. "Can any of them do weird stuff with trees?"

He shook his head again. "It's my turn now. What did you do to Dizzy?"

"Oh, just some reiki," said Rainbow. She looked up towards the mountain pass, where the high pastures awaited her. It would take the rest of the day to explore them.

"What's reiki?" asked Eole.

"An energy healing technique. I was taught by a reiki master and I can't teach you."

"How does it work?"

"Well, there's energy in all living things. Reiki is a technique for channelling that energy through your–"

"Mass-energy or motion-energy?"

She hesitated. "Universal energy. Life-force energy. When we do reiki, we raise the vibrations of whatever we're treating. You have to be attuned–"

"How do you raise the vibrations?"

His habit of interrupting was starting to annoy her. "You tune into the earth's natural vibration–"

"How?"

"Well, that's why you need a reiki master."

"Is it just in people's heads? Like God and voices?"

"No. Yes. I'm not sure. But there's scientific proof that it works, if that's what you want. You'll have to look it up. Anyway, the point is, I can't teach you to do it." She paused. "Did you say 'voices'?"

"Yes. But reiki can't be that difficult if it's only in your head."

Mary was urging her to negotiate. Rainbow couldn't teach him reiki, but she could show him a breathing technique that would help calm him and therefore his sheep. She suggested this and he agreed.

"In exchange, will you take me to the other shepherds?" she asked.

He nodded.

"Cool! Let's go."

He looked at his watch and then picked up his first aid book. "We can leave in nine and a half minutes."

She wanted to ask him why but he was already absorbed in his book. He stroked his dog, whose chin rested on his lap, as he read. Seeing him and his dog reminded her of Apple and Acorn, and her hands ached to have a ball of purring fur to caress.

She started a new drawing of him. It was much easier to capture his partly focused, partly oblivious air now they'd talked together.

CHAPTER 12

Eole stood beside Tintin's hut and looked at Rainbow's drawing. He had no idea whether it was good or not. She'd made Darwie look snide, so maybe that meant it was bad. He folded it and tucked it into his pocket. He would ask Hestia. Then, next time he saw Rainbow drawing, he'd be able to say, "That's good" or "That's bad" and she'd continue to find him normal and want to stay with him.

He had quite a lot of things to ask Hestia. He was looking forward to telling her how well he'd managed his conversations with Rainbow, who had just left to return to her campsite.

Rainbow. Her name reflected what she was: a colourful arc that brightened the sky. He knew that rainbows were actually illusions caused by the refraction and dispersion of the sun's rays by water droplets in the atmosphere. That's what his brain told him. His mind told him she was no illusion. It wanted to forget the facts and simply relax in the arc of her familiar woody-mossy fragrance.

A movement on the path below caught his eye. He breathed

in odours of lilac and goat, which brought the word 'adopted' to the front of his mind. It was Alexandra.

It wasn't right to sit on the stone bench where they'd sat together as mother and son. He went to the lake and waited for her on his flat rock, where he counted the tadpoles wriggling along the muddy bottom of the lake.

"Eole."

It was the voice she used when he'd done something wrong but she wasn't going to tell him off because it wasn't really his fault. She sat down beside him.

"That's not my real name," he said.

"Of course it is, darling. Have you had a think about our conversation at lunchtime?" She passed him a ham sandwich. "You missed the chilli. You must be starving, poor thing. And you're still pale. Are you ready to come home?"

He shrugged and pushed the sandwich back into her hands.

"The adoption issue doesn't change anything," she said. "And the field needs fencing. You were looking forward to that."

The fencing. He couldn't start it tomorrow because he'd eclipsed the valley from his mind while he'd been with Rainbow and had promised to meet her here in the morning. But he'd promised Maman too – except she was Alexandra now. His promise didn't count.

"Darling? Come home with me. Nothing needs to change. It's just a piece of paper."

"Why didn't you tell me before? I have to recalculate everything now."

"I thought you might. That's why I left you alone all afternoon."

He watched the families of tadpoles swimming happily

around in their simple world. It was easy for Alexandra: she'd always known he was adopted.

"I didn't tell you before because I didn't think it was necessary," she continued. "We're still your family. I'm your mother, Papa's your father, Hestia's your sister."

"Is she adopted too?"

"No, once we stopped trying–"

"And my real name?"

"Darling, Eole is your real name. You didn't have a name before. We're your family."

Itch. He put his hands over his ears.

She carried on talking. *Shuffle*.

"You're not my real family," he interrupted. "Stop saying you are."

But she continued, repeating words that sliced between his fingers and pierced his head: words about love and truth, about tracing biological parents, dossiers, his eighteenth birthday, a village in Brittany.

"I don't want to hear!" he shouted. "Leave me alone!"

The next thing he knew, the stars were out and he was lying on wet grass at the top of the ridge with Darwie beside him. He looked at his watch: it was two o'clock in the morning. Alexandra would have gone. He stroked Darwie and then stretched out his stiff legs and walked down towards the hut in the moonlight. He could smell spicy meat, ham, ewe cheese and crackers. There must be campers in the area.

When he reached the hut he saw his sleeping bag and rucksack outside the door. The rucksack was topped with a note signed 'Maman'. He screwed it up, unrolled his sleeping bag and mat, and checked the contents of his rucksack.

Alexandra had packed his birthday books as well as plenty of food. He wolfed down half the tub of chilli and rice and then stretched out on his top bunk. Tintin's snores would normally be coming from below. He concentrated on the memory of them and drifted into sleep.

Rainbow saved herself hours of walking this morning by parking in the car park she'd passed yesterday. It was just as well because her rucksack was heavy on her back.

Eole had agreed to let her pitch her tent beside his hut. By camping at the summer pastures she'd have more chance of seeing the shepherds, who brought up food and water for Eole in exchange for news of their flocks. Also, Christophe had called the campsite while she'd been out yesterday. If she stayed here, she wouldn't be tempted to call him back.

She erected her tent close to the hut and then followed Eole and Darwie up the grassy slopes to look for shepherds.

Eole stopped to wait for her at the mountain pass and when she arrived, puffing, she saw three grazing flocks on the slopes above, each with different colour paint on their fleeces. There were no shepherds.

They started walking along a narrow ridge. It was windy and desolate up here, despite the sun, and she felt exposed. All it would take was one gust of wind and she'd be blown into oblivion. It was the perfect place for the Tree Slayer to attack, and she didn't intend to fall foul of it before she met her soulmate. She told Eole she'd wait lower down while he checked for shepherds, and retraced her steps to the safety of the pass.

She was photographing some tiny flowers and thinking about her mission when Eole returned. He told her there were no shepherds on the ridge and then gave her the names of the flowers, like he'd done with the birds they'd seen yesterday and the beetles earlier that morning. He was a living encyclopedia!

She asked how he knew so much, and he started to tell her about his best friend Tintin. It was like a dam bursting. All thoughts of her mission slid away as she pictured his life with the retired physicist, learning about science and tending the sheep. The poor old man had died when a chestnut tree fell on him last Saturday, on the day of the gale. No wonder Eole was sad – she felt sad too, not only for Eole's loss, but also because Tintin sounded like the shepherd soulmate she'd imagined. He'd obviously meant a lot to Eole. She reached out to touch him but he edged away.

"I lost someone I loved," she said instead. "He was killed by a tree, too."

"Assassins," he muttered, and kicked a rock.

"Actually, it wasn't the tree's fault. It was mine."

Eole looked at her directly, though his expression was as unreadable as ever. She wondered how he would react to hearing about her gift. When she found her soulmate, she'd have to mention it. She should practise making it sound as ordinary as possible.

"You see, I've got an unusual relationship with trees," she continued. "They let me heal them and shape their branches."

"You've got a special skill," he said, nodding.

The concept of what was normal didn't seem to affect him: things just were or weren't. He was a treasure. She wished everyone could be so accepting.

"Domi calls it a spiritual gift," she said. She lay back in the heather and told him about Michael's accident and then – because he still seemed interested – all about the spiritual commune.

"There's a scientific explanation for spiritual phenomena," he said. "It's just that no one's found it yet. That's what Tintin used to say. It's like thunder and lightning, which people used to think came from Zeus and Athena, and like my anomaly, which science can't explain yet, either."

She sat up. "What anomaly?"

He shook his head violently, as if denying his words. What did he mean by his anomaly? She could feel Mary's disdain, her conviction that by 'anomaly' he meant his obvious difficulty with human interaction. But Mary wasn't necessarily right. He could have an anomaly that made him akin to trees in some way. He might have a gift that was equal to hers, but different. Was he her soulmate, after all? Amrita had told her to be patient and Eole definitely demanded patience.

"Do you mean you've got a gift?" she asked, slowly. "You told me you didn't have one."

Eole stared at the sky as if he hadn't heard her question.

"Eole? Have you got a gift too?"

"No," he said. He stared at her, and then looked down at his feet and mumbled, "I've got a special skill."

Mary was sending out waves of scorn, suggesting he was probably good at shearing sheep or something irrelevant like that. Rainbow ignored her.

"Cool! So what can you do with your special skill?" she asked.

"Tintin told me not to tell anyone about it. Your face looks completely different. It's all bright and sparkly."

"It's because I'm excited," she said. "You see I'm looking for my soulmate. I'm told he's a shepherd up here in the pastures and he has a gift. I think it might be you. Tell me about your gift – I mean, your special skill. Is it something to do with the voices you mentioned yesterday? We may have a mission together. Can you shape and heal trees too?"

Eole opened and shut his mouth and shook his head, but no words came out. She reformulated her questions.

"I promised Tintin I wouldn't tell anyone," he said. "It's nothing to do with the voices: they're just annoying. Alexandra says it's God speaking to me. She says I'll understand when the time is right, which will be never because God doesn't exist."

Rainbow thought about Amrita's godlike manipulation of her and Mary's parallel worlds, but she didn't want to start a theological discussion – and Eole's voices didn't matter. It was more important to find out if his special skill made him her soulmate.

She didn't want to force him to break his promise to Tintin but she needed to know if his gift was "equal to her own" as Amrita had put it. She'd never seen auras before, so the gift was the only way to be sure of her other half. Wasn't her need more important than him keeping his promise to Tintin, however dear he'd been to Eole? Mary certainly thought so.

"If you tell me, I won't say anything to anyone," said Rainbow. "Tintin will never know. It'll hardly be breaking your promise."

But Eole stood up and started walking up the flank on the other side of the pass.

This pasture didn't look as dangerous as the ridge, so Rainbow followed. She had to find a way to persuade him to confide in her.

CHAPTER 13

Eole sat down at the fork in the path and ate yesterday's ham sandwich while he waited for Rainbow. *Soulmate*, she'd said. He turned the word around in his head. He didn't like the word 'soul' because he hadn't found a satisfactory explanation for the concept: though, as Tintin used to say, the unknown is just the queue to the known. *A mission*, she'd said. He liked that word a little more. It was a bridge. It spanned the black hole of adoption and led somewhere.

She'd also said *together*, and this was the word that frightened and excited him most. Together had been him and Tintin, him and Hestia, him and the people he'd thought were his family. Together was all the bests but also all the worsts. Together was having to explain things and disrupt his routines. But as long as she didn't harass him to find out about his special skill, *together* with Rainbow might feel good.

He took his new *Multiverse Theories* book out of his rucksack. If this summer had been like previous summers, he and Tintin would now be discussing each section as he read it.

Instead, he had to learn about Hubble volumes, gravitational clustering and multiverse levels on his own. Tintin had wanted them to share the book. Reading it alone felt like betrayal. It felt as wrong as it would be to tell Rainbow about his special skill. If he couldn't share science with Tintin, he wasn't sure he wanted to read about it. He didn't open the book but simply examined the cosmic pictures on the cover.

Rainbow flung down her bag and collapsed onto the grass beside him.

"This is going to kill me," she said.

"I doubt it. The majority of deaths in the mountains are caused by lightning strikes."

She smiled, though it was no smiling matter, and asked what he was reading. He showed her the title.

"Can I have a look?"

He passed her his book and watched her flick through it while she ate her sandwich. He liked seeing her face change as she read. He copied her expressions, wondering if Hestia would class her as a total babe. He didn't think she was an ugly bitch, which was the other term Hestia used for girls.

"Wow!" Rainbow exclaimed. "They say here that scientists aren't asking the question of *whether* there are parallel universes, but of how many *levels* of universe exist. I wish I could show Domi this. How much do you know about parallel worlds?"

He calculated where to begin and then recited everything he'd learnt, starting from Tintin's initial explanation four years ago. He hadn't even completed this when Rainbow put her hands into a T-shape. Hestia had taught him the 'time out' sign. He stopped talking.

"There's no need to give me all the details," said Rainbow. "I've had a bit of experience with parallel worlds myself, and I think my theory might be relevant to you." She talked about someone called Mary, and then an Amrita, and added that her whole mission was due to an unexpected split into two parallels. He quickly realised her experience was only spiritual. He was considering using the T-sign on her when she reached her conclusion:

"The point is that I can almost hear Mary's voice in my head. Maybe the voices you hear come from an alter ego in a different parallel," she said.

It was all very well having theories based on fanciful ideas, but unless it could be backed up by science it was no more credible than Zeus and Athena's thunder and lightning. He shook his head and took back his book. The pages were heavy with new ideas, and gave him a pain in his chest. He couldn't do more than skim a couple of pages. Under the heading 'Level III Multiverses', however, he spotted a paragraph about merging and splitting branches, and folded down the corner of the page. He would read it when the pain had lessened. He closed the book and thought about Rainbow's suggestion. Had she found a theory to explain the source of the voices? Tintin would have wanted him to explore this path.

"Domi interprets voices," said Rainbow when she'd finished her sandwich. "You should come to our commune and consult him."

A commune meant a group of people and it meant travelling to get there, which Alexandra wouldn't want him to do. Just the thought of leaving the mountains made him feel shaky, though that could be because he was still famished. He stood up, told her he couldn't leave the pastures, and then took the right fork in the path.

There was only one flock left to check. It was unlikely that Jacques would be there, but Rainbow had said she wanted to check them all and, despite her terrible physical condition, she hadn't changed her mind.

He soon left her far behind. He crossed the scree slope and arrived at the dell where Tintin had explained the grand unification theory. Jacques' flock was there, shepherdless. Eole checked the sheep and then lay down with his eyes closed and added the grand unification theory to his mapopedia. This was the only way he could be with Tintin now.

Before long he heard puffing and smelt Rainbow's woody-mossy odour. He opened his eyes as she appeared, red-faced, between the boulders – which was when he noticed the imminent danger.

"Don't tell me there's no shepherd, after all that walking," she said.

So he didn't. "We have a problem," he said instead.

She edged closer to him and looked around. "What is it?"

Cumulus congestus clouds towered behind the peak in the next valley. He took a deep breath and inhaled the frosty electric smell of them. They were buzzing with ice pellets and ice crystals, all colliding and picking up positive and negative charges. The mountain air had been heating up all day, and now there was going to be a storm. He'd seen the signs from the wisps of cirrus cloud on the ridge but had been so focused on Rainbow that he'd forgotten about them.

He pointed to the clouds and told her they had to get

the flocks to the hut before the storm broke. He whistled to Darwie, who raced around the sheep and sent them down towards the pass.

"Please don't leave me behind again," said Rainbow, trotting after him like a sheep. He slowed down and tried his best to stay within a couple of steps of her. She would probably be frightened in the coming storm. They'd need to shelter in the hut. It would be a good opportunity to test the tourist role play he'd practised with Alexandra.

❧ ❧ ❧

Thunder cracked as Rainbow hurried downhill behind Eole. Its echoes sounded like underground trolls grumbling inside the mountain. She loved the excitement of storms at home but there was a raw violence in the rising wind. What if it was the Tree Slayer coming to kill her before she could vanquish it? She needed to get Eole to tell her about his gift. If only she could find out without him telling her, he wouldn't break his promise to Tintin.

She stopped. That was it! She had the perfect solution.

"Eole!" she called. He was watching Darwie drive the sheep across the scree slope. She joined him as fat raindrops began to fall.

"You don't have to tell me about your special skill. You can just show me," she said.

He shook his head and moved on, whistling to Darwie.

She sighed. Amrita had told her to be patient, but she'd also said to make haste. If he wouldn't tell her freely, she'd have to be smart like Mary and trick him into showing her. For that she'd need a tree, and there weren't any nearby.

The aroma of rain on dry ground rose all around her. Darkness was falling, even though it was only late afternoon and they should have hours of daylight ahead of them. The slopes around the lake were decorated with multicoloured sheep, and the hut – which had been dour in the sunshine – now looked welcoming compared to her flimsy, flapping tent. She checked the tent pegs were all firmly wedged into the ground and then carried her rucksack of dry clothes towards the hut.

There was a sharp crack followed by a rumble. Deafening retorts reverberated around them, and she clapped her hands to her ears.

Eole cocked his head to one side. "Rockfall."

The rain intensified, causing both ridge and mountain pass to disappear into misty dusk. Eole hovered beside the door, looking nervous.

"Can we go inside?" she shouted above another rumble. "I'm getting drenched!"

"Would you like a cup of tea?"

His invitation sounded like a line from an eighteenth-century play. It couldn't be a joke, because his face was blank. He was serious. Of course he was serious.

"That would be lovely," she said.

He motioned her inside. She edged past him and dumped her rucksack on the floor. Darwie snuck in behind her, shook himself – which soaked the few parts of her legs that were still dry – and curled up on a hessian sack in the corner. When Eole came inside, there was just enough room for the two of them in the space beside the bunk beds.

"Please have a seat," said Eole.

She sat on the planks of the lower bunk and watched him light a gas burner and heat some water. Gusts of air filtered through the cracks in the walls, causing the photos of an old man, presumably Tintin, to flap and jostle. The echoing thunderclaps made conversation impossible. She listened to the wind howling around the hut, and shivered. At least there were no trees for the Tree Slayer to kill: only Rainbow herself.

Eole passed her a mug of black tea, lit some candles, and sat down on the far end of the bunk, where he took out his multiverse book and looked at the back cover. The candles guttered and cast devilish shadows on the walls. It was a little cosier now, but Amrita's words about the Tree Slayer haunted her. Would the hut withstand its force?

"How long will the storm last?" she asked.

"I don't know. The average time is twenty-eight minutes. The normal distribution spreads from ten minutes at its lower limit to three hours at the upper limit. Are you frightened? Hestia gets frightened."

Rainbow asked who Hestia was and learnt she was a 'kind of' sister. She tried to understand if she was a sister-in-law or step-sister, or even a religious sister. But Eole studied the cover of his book and wouldn't explain.

When she'd imagined being with her soulmate, she'd pictured them sharing their deepest feelings without restraint. She'd expected to learn from him, to share the same worldview, and for them to explore the magic of trees together. She hadn't envisaged this difficult exchange of basic information. She was probably wrong about him being her soulmate. What was she even doing here on this treeless mountain? She'd forgone a job with Thierry and she'd given Christophe to Emilie without even fighting for him.

Inside her head, Mary rapped on the mental box and told her off for looking backwards instead of forwards. Saving Amrita was their only future, now that life at home had been ruled out. Rainbow conceded that Mary was right. She must concentrate on her mission and think how to persuade Eole to show her his gift. She sipped her tea and watched him.

He looked up. "Because if you're frightened, tell me."

A tingle of excitement rippled up Rainbow's spine.

"I *am* frightened, actually," she said.

He closed his book and took a folded yellow anorak out of his rucksack. He put it on, closed the zip and all the poppers, and then opened the door. Darwie raised his head, whined and stood up.

"Where are you going?"

"Outside," he said.

"Can I come?"

"No."

Mary's rebellious trait flared up inside her but Rainbow didn't need any encouragement. As soon as he and Darwie had left the hut, she yanked jumpers, flip-flops and underwear out of her rucksack. Her raincoat was at the bottom. She put it on and followed him out into the storm.

CHAPTER 14

The wind had changed direction and was rushing up towards the pass, reminding Rainbow of the suck and drag in last week's tree-slaying gale. Eole had told her that storms sometimes caught in a valley and spun round and round, gathering strength until they could escape – but was this actually the Tree Slayer coiling like a snake in preparation for attack?

She retreated to the safety of the hut doorway and squinted through the rain. Something moved beside the lake. It was Darwie, galloping towards her with his tail between his legs. He was alone. Had Eole had an accident?

A flash of yellow caught her eye. Eole was high on the lakeside slope, near the pass. It took her a while to find him with Domi's binoculars, but eventually her rain-blurred circle of rock and grass showed a yellow figure with his back to her. It was difficult to keep the binoculars still, and he didn't seem to be doing anything. She lowered her aching arms.

The storm was passing and she could see blue sky in the valley below the hut. She raised the binoculars again. Eole was facing her now, his lips pursed, his chest thrown out as if he was about to launch into a song. Something weird was going on here, something that had sent Darwie racing to safety. Was he calming the storm by singing to it? This must be his special skill. Why else would he have forbidden her to watch?

The gale in Cognac had redoubled in force when she'd shouted that she hated it. If the wind reacted to shouting, it may also react to singing. It made sense. Eole had the physique of a singer, with his barrel chest and broad shoulders. By singing to the wind he could control it, like a snake charmer controlled snakes with music. He had a wind gift, not a tree gift. This was amazing!

Amrita hadn't actually said her soulmate could communicate with trees, just that he had a gift that was equal to hers. Eole had to be her soulmate, the person who would help her vanquish the Tree Slayer. It was obvious, now she'd seen the effect of his singing.

Amrita, I'm coming to save you, she thought.

Should she join Eole and get him to destroy the Tree Slayer immediately? Mary resisted the idea, pointing out the danger of exposing herself to it. And Rainbow didn't know if the wind outside actually was the Tree Slayer. It could be a helpful wind, or just a normal one.

Eole would know. As soon as he returned, she'd tell him he didn't need to break his promise to Tintin because she'd guessed his special skill. They would devise a way to vanquish the Tree Slayer and then she'd get him to take her to Koad. With a bit of luck, they could go there without stopping at Cognac, where they risked seeing Christophe and Emilie.

She watched Eole turn his back again and strained her ears for song, but the whistling wind masked any other sound. It didn't matter. She wouldn't have to trudge up any more mountains in search of shepherds. Eole might not be the wise old shepherd she'd expected, but she rather liked him. All she had to do was convince him to help her and coax him away from his pastures.

The last black clouds floated past and a blue sky, dotted with fluffy white clouds, prevailed. She may have to be patient, but it shouldn't be too difficult to enlist his help.

Eole bent over and breathed normally while he waited for the thumping in his head to cease. Wielding his special skill had never given him a headache before. He was always careful to allow enough oxygen for his brain to function correctly when he breathed in for a big task. He didn't want to black out.

Something had changed inside his lungs. Their capacity was exactly the same, but they felt weaker. Was he losing his skill? Perhaps God did exist and this was his punishment. But no: there was no God, only the queue of unknowns waiting to be explained by science.

He walked back down to the hut, planning the evening ahead. Tintin had said he shouldn't tell anyone about his special skill but, despite his promise to Tintin, he wanted to tell Rainbow. He wanted to share everything with her because that's what soulmates did. She'd made a good, logical point about not breaking his promise if he showed her rather than telling her. He could compromise and let her see his art. It might keep her with him, keep them *together*. Once the grass had dried, he would show her and then, when darkness fell, he would share the names of all the stars he knew.

Rainbow was shaking the rain off her tent when he arrived at the hut. Darwie stood beside her. Tintin said animals didn't need to be intelligent like humans because they trusted their instincts. Eole didn't think he had many instincts, but if Darwie liked Rainbow, she must be a good person.

She smiled at him, looking sparkly. "So, you're a singer," she said.

He didn't know why she was talking about singing, but it wasn't a question so he didn't answer it.

"It's time for dinner," he said. "Then I'll show you my art and after that I'll tell you the names of the stars."

"OK, but we need to talk."

He paused. "I'll make dinner, then we'll talk, then I'll show you my art before it gets dark, and then I'll tell you the names of the stars. And then we'll sleep, and tomorrow we'll look for shepherds again."

"I don't need to see the other shepherds anymore," she said.

He recalculated. "OK: I'll make dinner – "

She made the T-sign and took a bag of packaged food from her rucksack. He explained the harmful effect of additives and excessive salt and sugar on the human body and told her he'd already organised dinner. He brought the gas cooker outside onto the stone bench, cooked the box of pasta Alexandra had left him, and mixed it with the rest of the chilli and rice. Rainbow opened a bag of crisps and offered them to him, but he refused. For dessert, she took out a cake.

"Quiz cake!" he exclaimed.

"Sorry? It's fruit cake. Want some?"

He nodded, smelt it and then listed the ingredients, certain he'd guessed them all. But Rainbow said she had no idea what was in it. She asked what he meant by quiz cake and so, because she'd said they had to talk, he explained.

They washed up in the stream, and then Rainbow told him they had to talk.

"But we've just done that! I must show you my art." He checked his watch. "It'll be too late in forty-six minutes."

Her mouth made a downward shape. "Does it involve walking? Because I don't think my legs will take me anywhere else today."

He looked down at her short little legs and up at the sky. "No. I can show you right here."

🌿 🍃 🌿

Rainbow put on her fleece, sat on her raincoat and followed Eole's instructions to lean back against a rock. She looked up at the clouds and thought about his gift as she waited for him to get out his art. What kind of songs did he sing, and what kind of voice did the wind respond to? Nothing would ever respond to her own tuneless voice – apart from cats, perhaps.

The clouds were flocculent and higher than the wispy ones she'd noticed transclouding yesterday morning, before she spotted Dizzy and met Eole. They looked solid, like cotton wool.

Eole stood up and breathed in. He was going to show her his special skill, not his art. Perfect! She sat up straight. Darwie obviously didn't like his singing, because he whined. She waited for Eole to burst into song, but he simply leant his head back. He breathed out a long, slow breath directed towards the sky. A very long breath. At the same time he moved his head around, as if he had stiff neck muscles and was stretching them.

She looked up. The shapeless cloud had become the letter 'R', and the one beside it was transclouding into the other letters of her name.

"Wow! You're a cloud artist. How cool is that?" He hadn't sung to the storm: he'd blown it away. "You must have massive lungs."

"I do. It feels like I have a world of wind in them," said Eole.

"Let me try," she said.

She took a deep breath and blew up at the 'R'. Nothing happened. She laughed and turned back to him. "Is this your special skill? To be able to blow really hard?"

Panic flashed in his eyes and his feet shuffled as if he were struggling not to walk away.

"You don't have to answer," she said. "You needn't break your promise to Tintin because I know this is the special skill that makes you my soulmate."

His feet stopped shuffling.

"I'm really happy to meet someone else like me," she said.

He smiled. It was the first time she'd seen him smile and it transformed his face. She let her eyes linger on his illuminated features, wondering if this was his aura, and memorising the change so she'd be able to draw him like this.

"Does anyone else know about your skill?" she asked.

"No. I would have told Hestia, except that sometimes I tell her secret things and then Alexandra knows about them. Ninety per cent of the time they either argue or ignore each other. But occasionally when I go into the kitchen they're sitting with their heads close together and giggling, and they stop and it's like when I don't understand a facial expression. Tintin said that if I told people–"

"You'd be exploited," she finished. Michael had said exactly the same thing to her when she'd revealed her tree gift in his garden at the Drunken House. The ache of losing him burned inside her heart.

Eole hesitated and then resumed as if she hadn't spoken. "I'd be exploited. But I didn't tell you, I showed you."

"Don't worry. I won't exploit you. But cloud art is risky. What if someone sees?"

"Hardly anyone notices clouds. And if they do see a shape, they think it's their imagination and congratulate themselves on their pareidolia – that's what it's called when you make patterns out of random shapes."

"Can you make me a tree cloud?" she asked.

"Yes. What kind of tree?"

"Any tree."

He looked consternated.

"A silver maple?" she suggested.

"I don't know what that looks like."

She listed a few trees – avoiding 'chestnut' in case it made him sad about Tintin again – until he nodded at the suggestion of an oak tree. He breathed in for ages, and then started carving.

His cloud art was quite similar to her branch-shaping art, which made his gift 'equal to her own' – though, luckily for her, his wind control was much more powerful than her healing gift. And it didn't impinge on her territory as the tree specialist. Would she have been jealous if his gift had proved more powerful with trees than her own? No, of course not: she loved trees. Any gift that could help them would have been a cause for celebration, not jealousy. Still, she preferred it this way.

She needed to broach the subject of the Tree Slayer, but she didn't want him to panic at the idea of having to use his skill to destroy something. It didn't seem to be in his nature to be destructive. Mary wanted her to get on with it, but Amrita had said she must be patient.

"When you're ready, I've got something to tell you," she said.

He didn't answer. He was standing doing absolutely nothing. She'd never seen anyone do nothing. She took out her sketch pad and sketched his figure, contoured with its heavy black lines, and tried to recapture the radiance of his smile.

❧ ❧ ❧

Eole had only discovered his special skill when his voice broke. He didn't know if he'd always had it, if it had simply appeared, or if his lungs had just kept growing when all his other organs had stopped.

He'd started blowing away wisps of condensing water particles while he was minding the sheep. When Tintin had noticed, he'd said Eole was doing something special. Eole already knew he was special, thanks to Alexandra, but this was different because it was a skill, and skills had to be maintained and developed. Tintin had helped him understand the anomaly in his lungs and nose. He'd explained his theory of how they allowed him to gather and store so much air.

It was plausible, he said: plausible, but unusual. This meant it was scientific and not a present from God, which is how Alexandra would interpret it if he told her.

He heard Rainbow's voice from a distance, floating towards him on the breeze like a promise. It blew away the cobwebs of the times he and Tintin had sprawled in the heather, him practising cloud art while Tintin talked about meteorology. His brain reached out and grasped her words. She had something to tell him. The sun was low, but he'd left a time-buffer before showing her the stars because part of being *together* was allowing space for the other person to be illogical and disorganised.

She put away her coloured pencils and he glimpsed a picture of a boy holding hands with a small Indian girl dressed in pinks and reds. Pink and red didn't go together, which was a clue that her drawing wasn't any good, but he needed to ask Hestia before he commented on it. He'd have liked to discuss Rainbow's special skill with Hestia as well, but Rainbow didn't want him to mention it. Either it was in her head, like reiki, or she had an anomaly too.

The best scientists keep an open mind, Tintin had said, so he put aside the feasibility of Rainbow's special skill. He told her he was ready, sat down opposite her and concentrated on achieving a perfect him-her-him-her rhythm to their conversation.

She repeated what she'd said about a soulmate, except this time she wasn't speaking in conditionals. She said that now she'd seen his special skill she was convinced they were soulmates. Their future lay together, and they had an evil force to fight.

He imagined black holes, spacecraft and laser beams. His heart beat faster. She talked about him guiding her, though he didn't understand where he was supposed to guide her: perhaps around his mapopedia? She talked about trees and spirits, and mentioned that strange name 'Amrita' again. And then she said she needed his special skill. She needed him! The evil force was a wind, and without his help it might kill her.

He didn't want her to die too. He didn't know if there was an evil wind or not, but he did know that he wanted to stay with her. He wanted her to be his new *together*, and to share her mission. He wanted to protect her with his special skill, blow the storms away and keep her safe under blue skies. He wanted to be everything she needed. He would guide her anywhere she wanted to go (within reason), because he was ace with maps and everything would be all right because they'd be together and she made him feel good.

"OK," he said.

Rainbow was a little disappointed by Eole's lack of enthusiasm. "Thanks, Eole," she said. "So, first we should deal with the evil wind. I'll tell you the details about the rest of the mission later. All I know about this wind is that it kills trees. Amrita called it the Tree Slayer. Do you have any ideas how we could fight it?"

"I can protect you from all the winds. I can counteract them."

"Good. We need to set a trap to attract the Tree Slayer. Then you must blow it into a box or something so it can't escape. Are you strong enough to control a gale?"

He nodded.

"Are you sure? What about the gale last week? Gale Martin. The one that blew the chestnut tree onto Tintin. *That* was the Tree Slayer. Could you have counteracted it?"

He looked confused. She calmed Mary's wish to shake him, and rephrased her question: "Didn't you say the gale made a chestnut tree fall onto Tintin?"

"No."

"But you said a tree fell on him. The same day. Didn't you?"

He nodded, but wouldn't look up from his feet. There was something he wasn't telling her. She thought about how she'd accidentally killed Michael when the branch she was shaping fell onto him.

"Did *you* blow it down on him by accident?" she said.

"No!"

"OK, but I don't understand. Did the tree fall on him before or after the gale?"

"Before." His feet were squirming against each other. He stood up.

Her mouth was dry. Mary wanted Eole to explain himself. Rainbow's head hurt from the pressure of Mary trying to exert her will.

"Let me get this straight," she said. "A tree fell on Tintin. And then a huge gale blew down loads of trees?"

"Yes."

Rainbow swallowed. "Tell me what happened. Tell me everything."

"OK. We were in Brittany seeing Aunt Isabelle, because she's ill, when Brigitte phoned and told us that Tintin had .. . that an assassin tree had fallen on him. I got *itch, shuffle and escape*, and the next thing I knew I was on top of a hill and I was shouting his name, his real name and not the nickname I gave him, and I didn't realise what I was doing, and then I did realise and I didn't care and then I did care so much, and I wanted all the trees to die, and I blew harder and for longer than I'd ever done in my life, and my breath created a low pressure and the air rushed to fill it, and it was as if the air agreed with me and followed where I'd led, and then I saw the fallen trees from the top of the hill and I stopped but the wind kept going, of course, and I sat on the hill and cried and then Alexandra arrived and told me to come indoors out of the storm, and the next morning we returned home because of my exams."

"Jesus, Eole!" whispered Rainbow.

She'd got everything wrong. He wasn't her soulmate: he was the Tree Slayer.

And that meant she had to kill him.

CHAPTER 15

If Eole had had a tail, it would now be between his legs, which is where Darwie's tail went when Eole was cross with him.

Rainbow was cross. She'd lost her sparkles and hadn't spoken a word at breakfast this morning, except to say that she'd changed her mind about the shepherds and wanted to see them all before going home. She was much nicer than any other girl but she was still illogical.

She was full of questions too. Yesterday evening, after he'd told her about his gale and she'd blasphemed, he'd asked her if she thought he was the Tree Slayer. She hadn't answered immediately, probably because her face was hidden in her hands. He repeated his question and then she broke a conversation rule because she answered with another question, saying, "Do *you* think you are?"

That had thrown him for a while, like an unexpected chess move. So instead of telling her that he wasn't evil, he answered her question with: "I can't be, because I'm your soulmate, aren't I?" But his move hadn't paid off, because she countered his question with "Are you?", which was a question but it felt like an answer, and he was confused. He began to point out the names of the constellations that were becoming visible in the sky instead. She'd sighed and didn't ask any more questions nor give him any answers.

He heard the tent zip and then Rainbow appeared in the hut doorway, dressed and ready to set off on another tour of the pastures. He suggested they wait at the hut for the farmers to come up from the village, or go down to meet them in the valley, but she said she needed to walk.

"Can you stay beside me today, instead of racing ahead?" she asked.

He agreed, even though it meant that Darwie kept running back to him and winding himself around his legs. It was a sign she still thought he was her soulmate and not the evil Tree Slayer.

She didn't stop and look at any flowers or take any photos, even when he pointed out five griffon vultures spiralling down to feed on a corpse.

"I hope the dead animal isn't Dizzy," he added.

She didn't answer.

When they checked his sheep he was relieved to see Dizzy hobbling along in the flock. Rainbow calmed Dizzy so he could spray the wounds. While she concentrated, Eole studied her face. She had dark rings under her eyes, like Hestia when she'd had a sleepover at Caroline's house.

They continued up to the pass, where Rainbow recovered her breath and told him she wanted to walk along the ridge. A cloud shadow hovered over it, darkening it into a menacing cliff.

"There won't be anyone up there," he said. "The sheep are all here."

"It doesn't matter. I want to take a photo."

He led the way up the slope and they started along the narrow ridge path in single file. He was about to warn her to concentrate on where she put her feet when she cried out. He spun around. She'd slipped on a tuft of grass and her arms were spiralling like windmills. He stepped between her and the steep slope, and held out his arms so she wouldn't fall. Darwie barked.

"You must be careful on this part," he said. "Do you want to take my arm?"

She shook her head. "Actually, yes," she said.

He crooked his elbow like he did with Alexandra. After a second's hesitation, she put her arm through it. He didn't mind feeling the soft skin of her arm against his, though her palm was rough and cracked. She wasn't touching him, he told himself; their skins were simply in contact. And now he was the same height as her, since she was on the ridge path and he was on the tufty grass beside it.

He had to concentrate on his feet as well as on keeping Rainbow safe. Darwie stayed close behind him, to heel, even though Eole hadn't whistled him there. He laughed and let Darwie slip his muzzle into his free hand.

Rainbow stopped. "What's funny?"

"It's Darwie. He's rounding me up like a sheep to protect me."

Rainbow didn't even smile. It seemed that her sparkles had gone for good.

Suddenly, she jostled him. She immediately grabbed him

again, but he staggered and stepped on Darwie's paw. Darwie yelped.

"Hey!" he said, and disengaged his arm.

"It was a joke," she said. "Just testing Darwie's skill."

"Well, don't. It's dangerous here."

She carried on walking and he stayed close beside her. He didn't want her to trip again. When he was tired he tripped all the time, the toe of his boots catching on raised stones and making him break out in cold sweats.

Her face was red and her expressions kept changing, like during a conversation. It would be good to understand what each of them meant. He'd like to catalogue them alongside their definitions and make an expressionopedia, now that his mapopedia was almost finished.

At the highest point of the ridge, she asked him to take a photo of her with the mountains behind. He pointed the camera at her, his eye pressed to the viewfinder. She wasn't smiling. Alexandra always put on a fake smile for photos and Hestia made silly faces.

"You're too close," she said. "I'd like the peaks in the photo. Take a step back."

He moved back towards the rocky ledge above the precipice. Darwie cowered beside Rainbow with his tail between his legs. Eole framed her once again. She was frowning and biting her lip.

"Cheese!" he said. "That's camera language for smile."

"Just do it, Eole. Actually, go back a bit further. As far as you can."

He did as she said. He was right on the edge now.

Darwie whined and Eole told him to be quiet. He raised the

camera, closed an eye and squinted through the viewfinder. Her head and shoulders were bang in the middle, which is what made the best photos, though there was too much blue sky and not enough Rainbow for his liking.

Just as he was about to press the button, she pitched sideways, screamed and disappeared from the frame. He dropped the camera and threw himself into her as she rolled towards the edge. There was a thud of contact, a cry, and then stillness.

He disentangled himself and stood up. Darwie was on the path where Rainbow had been, his head jutting towards her and his lips drawn back into a snarl. Blood seeped through Rainbow's trousers below her knee.

She turned away from him and buried her face in a tuft of grass. Her shoulders heaved and she made little whimpering noises.

"Darwie! Bad dog," he said. He crouched down beside Rainbow. "I'm sorry he bit you. It's because he's always nervous up here. I've got a first aid kit at the hut, so we can go back if you like. Please don't cry."

He knew he wasn't very good at comforting people, so he wasn't surprised when her whimpering turned into proper crying. He retrieved the camera and took a photo of the peaks for her.

🌹 🌹 🌹

Rainbow cursed her weakness. She was a failure. People in films and books did this kind of thing all the time but it was much harder in real life. The conditions were perfect – they hadn't seen a single person since she'd been up on the pastures

– and yet she'd aborted her mission at the first hurdle.

Mary was scornful of her half-hearted attempts to vanquish the Tree Slayer. But Rainbow couldn't bring herself to push him off the mountain. She wasn't strong enough to be Amrita's saviour. The problem was that Eole was so trusting. She liked him. Even if he was the Tree Slayer, he didn't deserve to die. Well, he did, given what he'd done and what he may do in the future, but she couldn't murder a real person. Not even to save Amrita.

Darwie's bite was bloody though not deep. She pressed a tissue to the wound until it stopped bleeding, keeping an eye on Darwie, who crept towards Eole and begged forgiveness with his brown eyes. Eole ordered him to get away.

"It's not Darwie's fault," she said.

"Yes, it is."

His voice was cold. She hadn't seen this judgemental side of him before, and she felt guilty that Darwie was being punished when, in fact, he'd saved his master's life.

Eole stayed close beside her as they backtracked along the ridge. Her resolve gradually filtered back. She'd messed up, but perhaps her true soulmate, once she found him, would deal with Eole. Could she betray Eole, though? She was too pathetic even for that, she was sure. There must be another way to vanquish the Tree Slayer.

When they reached the safety of the pass, she faced him.

"About last night: you know, when you told me how you'd killed all those trees?"

He looked at her and waited, so she continued. "Do you feel bad about it?"

"No." He kicked a rock.

Although it was clear he was the cause of the evil, tree-slaying gale, he claimed not to be the Tree Slayer. And she felt no fear of him. Something wasn't right.

"If you're not the Tree Slayer, how do you explain Amrita's talk of the evil wind during your gale?" she asked.

"Easy!" he said. "I'm glad you've asked. If we assume that your Amrita can be trusted, we know the evil wind killed the trees. I didn't actually kill any trees. I just blew hard and wished the trees would all die. That doesn't make me the Tree Slayer. My theory, assuming the evil wind exists, is that it's a form of energy yet to be proved by science – you would say a kind of spirit, I expect. This energy form is attracted by high winds, so when I created the corridor of low pressure, the energy form rushed in with the winds to fill it. I presume Amrita detects the presence of this 'spirit' and blames it for blowing down trees. In any case, whatever the theory, I know I'm not the Tree Slayer. I'm your soulmate, and I'm going to protect you from anything that tries to kill you."

"Wow, that's some theory," she said. He could be right about the Tree Slayer being a wind spirit. Amrita was a tree spirit, so there could well be a wind spirit too. Rainbow's whole mission could be part of a spiritual battle between the trees and the wind. It explained why she didn't feel threatened by Eole. He wasn't the Tree Slayer, but the Tree Slayer took advantage of his special skill. He was unwittingly on the Tree Slayer's side.

"So, do you agree with it?" asked Eole.

"It does make sense."

But what the Tree Slayer had done once, it could do again. Whatever the theory, it didn't change the problem: as soon as

Eole created another gale, the Tree Slayer would use it to kill Amrita's last One Tree. Rainbow still had to vanquish Eole.

Did vanquishing necessarily mean killing, though? She had an idea. Although she now knew Eole was associated with the Tree Slayer, it wouldn't do any harm for him to think he was her soulmate. In fact, it might help.

"You mustn't make any more gales," she said. "Then the Tree Slayer can't take advantage of them and it won't kill me. Do you promise never to blow up a storm again?"

He looked up at the sky, obviously thinking before he made his promise.

"Can I still do cloud art?"

"Yes," she said.

"OK. I promise."

"Good." She smiled and then shivered: she'd almost made him fall off the ridge. Thank goodness she hadn't succeeded. She hadn't really meant to kill him. Mary might have been capable of that, but Rainbow wasn't a murderer. It was one thing to have the idea, another to seriously carry it out.

She watched Eole tip back his head, take a long, deep breath, and carve a shape from one of the clouds above them. It was a tree.

"That's beautiful! Can you sculpt a rose?"

She watched a flower form above her head and clapped. Her mission was progressing. In her own way, she had neutralised the Tree Slayer even if she hadn't actually vanquished it. She was glad she hadn't mentioned Koad to Eole, since he had no further role in her mission. He would stay here, believing he was her soulmate, which should be enough to stop him from breaking his promise.

Meanwhile she could continue her search for her true soulmate: the shepherd with a golden aura and tree gift; the person she'd be able to share everything with and who would guide her to Koad. The one who might fill the void Christophe had left.

❧ ❧ ❧

They walked down from the pass, Eole studying Rainbow's face. She looked sparkly again, and as he made her a cloud scallop, a star and a marmot, his chest filled with something lighter and sweeter than air. He was her soulmate, she was his *together* and they had a mission. He would never let her down.

Back at the hut, she said she was leaving and started to pack her rucksack.

"But why?" he asked. This wasn't the plan. *Itch*. He was supposed to guide her.

"Because I need to talk to the other shepherds. We haven't seen any here. It'll be easier if I go back to the campsite and use it as a base to check the other pastures in the Val d'Azun."

His feet relaxed. He could guide her around the pastures. He didn't know what information she wanted from the shepherds but she'd said she would explain the mission details later.

"OK," he said. "So where shall I meet you tomorrow?"

She stared at him. He realised he'd got something wrong or that she hadn't understood him properly.

"To guide you," he added. "To show you the other pastures and protect you from the Tree Slayer in case there's another storm and it uses the wind to try to kill you."

"Oh. Right. Good idea. But will your sheep be OK? I didn't think you wanted to leave your pasture."

"The sheep will be fine with Patou. We're staying in the valley, aren't we?"

"Ye-es," she said, untying a guy line.

"So I can take you to meet the other farmers."

"OK. Yes, why not? I'll see you at the campsite tomorrow morning at eight," she said, and continued taking down her camp.

He was sculpting her a griffon vulture when she called his name. He stopped carving.

"Are they shepherds?" she asked, pointing to two people coming up the hill.

It was Hestia and Alexandra. He explained who they were and the corners of her mouth turned down. He was getting good at reading her expressions. She didn't want them here, and if she didn't, he didn't either.

When they arrived on the plateau, Darwie – the traitor – wagged his tail and made a fuss of them. Eole stood closer to Rainbow.

🌿🍃🌿

It was too late for Rainbow to escape small talk with Eole's family. His mum was skinny, only a little taller than Rainbow, and his sister looked nothing like Eole: she was black-haired, like his mum, and petite. The way she walked, with an insouciant swing to her step, gave her the air of an extrovert. She probably had a gang of noisy friends at school. Hestia's confidence made Rainbow want to hide behind Eole. Mary reminded her that Hestia was only a kid, but Mary's disdain didn't help.

"Hello darling!" Eole's mum said to him, and traced a heart shape over her chest.

Eole growled at Darwie to lie down and didn't respond.

Eole's mum introduced herself as Alexandra. Rainbow mumbled her own name and then Alexandra nudged Eole's sister.

Hestia ignored the nudge. "What are you doing with my brother?" she asked.

"Hestia! Don't be so rude," said Alexandra. She looked Rainbow up and down and then threw her hands in the air. "Oh, my word, you're hurt."

Rainbow looked down at her leg, where the blood had dried in a patch.

"Darwie bit her," said Eole.

"It's only a little nip," said Rainbow.

"I'm so sorry," said Alexandra. "Eole, go and get the first aid kit."

Despite Rainbow's protests that she would treat her wound at the campsite, Alexandra hustled her to the stone bench. Rainbow sat down. Hestia stood right in front of her, her arms folded.

Rainbow would have felt intimidated, but Mary compared Hestia to a mini-warrior princess and made Rainbow giggle. She quickly turned her laugh into a cough, at which point Eole appeared with the first aid kit and Alexandra started to clean the injury.

"I'm Rainbow's soulmate," said Eole.

Alexandra stopped dabbing at the wound. When she resumed, her touch was rougher.

Eole pulled out a folded piece of paper from his pocket and gave it to Hestia. "Is it good or bad?"

"Did *she* do it? Your 'soulmate'?" Hestia made air quotes as she pronounced the word.

Eole nodded and Rainbow realised they were studying her drawing of him.

"It's all right, I suppose." Hestia passed it back. "So what's this soulmate business?"

"It's nonsense, that's what it is," said Alexandra. She slapped a plaster onto Rainbow's leg and stood up. "There's no such thing as a soulmate, darling. God looks after your soul. What you mean is that you're her special friend."

Hestia turned away from Alexandra, caught Eole's eye and mimicked sticking two fingers down her throat. Rainbow grinned. Eole was lucky to have a sister.

"I'm not her special friend," said Eole to his mum. "I'm her soulmate. Like I'm not your special son, I'm your adopted son."

There was a silence.

"Now you *are* talking nonsense," said Hestia. But her eyes were wide, and she looked uncertain. She glanced from Alexandra to Eole and back again.

"I have to go," mumbled Rainbow. She picked up her packed rucksack. "See you tomorrow, Eole."

CHAPTER 16

"I don't believe it! You've lied to us for all these years!" shouted Hestia.

Eole closed his eyes and rocked from the balls of his feet to his heels and back again. With Rainbow's departure, his joy at finding a new place to belong had evaporated like a low-altitude cumulus cloud.

"It's not like that," retorted Alexandra. "Stop being so stubborn and listen to me. Hestia! Come back here this minute."

Eole heard footsteps retreating, more shouts from further away and then, at last, calm. He opened his eyes. Alexandra's lilac fragrance and Hestia's pomegranate deodorant lingered as sour reminders of their visit. He didn't want to be here when Alexandra came back, so he strode up to the pass with Darwie at his heels.

Now Rainbow had gone, his thoughts returned to Tintin. He wanted to finalise his mapopedia but he couldn't conjure up his friend with the same strength as before he'd met Rainbow. Tintin's deep voice kept morphing into Rainbow's clear laugh, and he found himself planning the most efficient routes between the summer pastures for tomorrow's mission rather than concentrating on his memories. It felt wrong to be thinking about Rainbow when he should be mourning Tintin.

Before nightfall, he returned to the hut. There was no sign of Alexandra. He packed his rucksack, put on his headphones and walked down to his former home in the valley.

Hestia's boots, platform shoes and flip-flops were sprawled over his floor tile, as well as over her own. He put his walking boots on the spare tile, the one reserved for visitors' footwear. In the kitchen, Patrick was sitting in the rocking chair in a pair of shorts, drinking a glass of – Eole breathed in to check – Hoegaarden beer. Alexandra made a half-smile at Eole. It didn't match her red eyes.

"Darling, you're back! Come and sit down. Your sister has gone to spend the night with Caroline."

"If that's an invitation to dinner, I accept," he said.

"What nonsense! You don't have to be invited."

He sat down in the chair she pulled out for him and folded his hands in his lap.

"Sheep OK?" asked Patrick.

Eole nodded and told him about Dizzy's wound.

Alexandra bustled around, passing him the mixed salad, heating up moussaka in the microwave and asking questions about Rainbow. He didn't know any of the answers, except where Rainbow lived, so he told her about the spiritual commune.

"She sounds rather weird," said Patrick.

Alexandra jabbed him in the ribs. "She's Eole's special

friend. Where are you going with her tomorrow, darling?"

"I'm showing her around the summer pastures," said Eole.

"What about the fencing?" said Patrick.

"Let him spend some time with his friend," said Alexandra. "He'll do the fencing when she's left."

"Which is when?" asked Patrick.

Eole shrugged. He didn't want her to go home. Ever. Once they'd finished her mission in the pastures, he hoped she would stay for the rest of the summer. She could draw while he made cloud art for her and tried to actually read his birthday books instead of just staring at the pages and missing Tintin.

After dinner, he had a shower and listened to Bach's Brandenburg concertos while he changed his clothes for a clean set of grey shorts and black T-shirt. He found his lightweight tent and repacked his rucksack, zipping his wallet of savings into the top pocket. Alexandra tried to stop him leaving when he told her where he was going, but he thanked her for her hospitality and walked out with Darwie, saying he'd be back in four days.

At the campsite, he found Rainbow's tent – he could smell her woody fragrance – and pitched his tent next to it, his guy lines crossing hers. He couldn't get any closer. He crawled inside and fell asleep with Darwie beside him.

🌱 🌿 🌱

For the next few days, Rainbow followed Eole through cool woodlands, into shrubby prairies and up to each village's summer pasture. Eole hovered in the background and didn't ask her why she was still searching. Perhaps he believed the school project excuse she gave the shepherds as she studied them out of the corner of her eye, looking for a golden glow, and asked tactful questions about tree gifts.

She drew pictures of everyone she met, as well as sketching sleepy marmots, an injured stoat and a Pyrenean chamois. In the evenings she visited the farms in the valley while Eole remained beside his tent, wearing his headphones, his nose in a book. He was even less confident about talking to people than her, so she had to take the lead. Gradually, her self-assurance increased and Mary's voice grew quiet. Rainbow didn't mention her gift or Amrita or the Tree Slayer to anyone, and as a result nobody treated her like a weirdo. It was refreshing. She felt like a different person, as if doing things alone made her a whole person in her own right. And she was touched by the farmers' interest – though none of them, so far, were remotely golden or gifted.

By the end of the third day her legs no longer ached. On the fourth day, after she'd healed a Scots pine suffering from dothistroma disease, Eole asked her to demonstrate her gift. Seeing no harm in it, she shaped the branches of a healthy pine for him.

"Can anyone else do that?" asked Eole.

"No. I think I'm the only one. For some reason Amrita chose *me* to bear this gift. Sometimes it feels like a weight, but mostly I feel lucky. It's part of me – in fact, it *is* me. It's who I am. If I didn't have this, I'd be nothing. But it would be great to find someone who's as close to trees as me. At least, I think it would, though actually it's nice to be unique." She stopped talking, wondering why she was sharing this with the very person who might inadvertently kill the One Tree and cause her and Amrita's deaths. "Is that how you feel about your special skill?"

"No," he said.

He didn't offer anything more and she didn't pry. He was the easiest person to get on with, never questioning her decisions and showing no need for conversation. He didn't seem to need anything apart from huge amounts of food and to keep his distance from other campers. He closed in on himself when he came down from the mountains, and would put on his headphones and sit outside his tent, staring at his books or leafing through them. She didn't get the impression he was actually reading them.

On Sunday evening, as she stirred their sausage and lentil dinner, he told her they'd finished their tour of the summer pastures and that she'd met all the farmers.

"No! Surely there must be one we've missed?"

He shook his head. "So what's the next part of our mission?"

She sat back on her heels. She'd trusted that she'd find her soulmate. She'd never given up hope, even in the difficult moments when she missed Christophe and wished she were working with Thierry. Now there was no hope left. She must have done something wrong or ignored a sign. Or had her soulmate been Tintin? Surely not, because he was already dead when Amrita had appeared and given her the mission. There was no point staying here without her soulmate, yet she couldn't bear to return to Cognac and risk bumping into Christophe and Emilie.

"I don't know what to do now," she said.

"We could go back to Tintin's hut," said Eole. "You could carry on your project research and drawings there, and help me look after the sheep. I could shape clouds for you and we could read my books together and discuss multiverses."

"It's not as easy as that," she said. She needed a sign. "I'm going to hug a tree. Do you want to come?"

"No," he said.

He didn't have the slightest affinity for trees but at least he'd stopped kicking them and calling them assassins. She ate her meal, then left him with his boring books and walked to the deciduous trees on the edge of the campsite. She hugged an old beech tree and an oak, and then healed a few ashes that were suffering from pest infestations. She was searching for a mother tree like the François I oak: one that would show her images, talk to her and give her advice.

The valley trees breathed deeply and slowly as if, like Eole, they held a world of air inside them. They were clean and relaxed compared to the Charente trees, and she suspected it was because they suffered less from human interference. As with all trees, she could sense their feelings when she placed her hands on their bark, but none spoke to her. Amrita had told her to trust the trees but the trees weren't helping her find her soulmate.

Help me, Amrita, she pleaded as she hugged one tree after another.

There was no response. Had her vision been a hallucination, after all? Had she lost Christophe and Thierry for nothing? Her Amrita dreams had stopped, which must mean something. And she'd neutralised the Tree Slayer by getting Eole to promise never to make a gale again. Only her soulmate was missing. Perhaps it was time to go home and think about what to do next.

When darkness fell, she returned to the campsite. As she

passed the office, the owner came out and greeted her.

"That Christophe called for you again," he said. "It's none of my business, but I'd appreciate you calling him back and telling him to stop pestering me."

She apologised. It was the fourth time he'd given her the same message: the fourth time Mary threatened an explosion of anger if she dared give in and call him back. The first time she'd put it off because she didn't want to think about Christophe. The second time she'd wondered whether it was urgent, and decided Mum or Domi would have called if it had been important. The third time she'd expected it. Last night he hadn't rung, which should have been a relief, though she'd actually felt disappointed. It was time to prioritise the poor campsite owner above Mary's threats.

She fetched her purse, picked up the telephone receiver of the public phone in the campsite office and dialled Christophe's number. The owner went outside onto the terrace.

Christophe answered and she fed her coins into the phone. It was bittersweet to hear his voice again. She understood why Mary hadn't wanted her to phone him.

"Please stop harassing me," she said. "The campsite owner is sick of taking messages and I don't want to talk to you."

She pressed her fingers onto the plastic prongs that held the receiver, cutting off the call. Her hand was shaking.

The phone rang, making her jump. Mary implored her to leave it. Rainbow looked outside the office and saw the campsite owner gesturing at her to answer. The call could be for another camper. She reluctantly picked up the receiver.

"Rainbow? Please listen. I need to talk to you. Are you there?"

"I said to stop calling me."

"Rainette. I miss you so much. I didn't realise how much I'd miss you. I made a terrible mistake. I should never have let you go. Please come home. Please forgive me. Rainbow?"

She imagined Christophe sitting on his sofa, his head in his hands as he spoke to her, motorbike oil under his bitten nails. She pictured the way he swung his head back when he laughed and how he slotted his fingers between hers when he teased her. She imagined Apple and Acorn playing together at his feet.

"What about ... that girl?"

"I can't even think about her. My head and heart are full of you. I'm lost without you," he said. "Nothing makes sense."

She visualised his warm brown eyes, his hand running through his hair and tugging at its ends.

"Rainbow? Are you OK? Have you found your shepherd?"

"Not exactly. I've pretty much failed at everything."

"Oh, Rainette. I'm so sorry. What happened?"

Rainbow hesitated, waiting for a reaction from Mary. At the very point she needed Mary's resolve, Mary was silent.

"I'll tell you about it tomorrow," she said. "It'll be easier face to face."

※ ❧ ※

Eole didn't like Lucien Latapie's campsite. He'd much rather have been free in the peace of the mountains than hemmed in by people and voices. But Rainbow was here. The headphones worked well, and nobody approached him and Darwie. He hoped they would work as well at university – and that he'd be able to read again before the new school year started.

It was dark when Rainbow came back from tree-hugging.

She smelt of crushed leaves, sticky sap and something sleepy from the trees. He studied her face, trying to analyse the smell. She wasn't looking sparkly but she wasn't frowning either.

"It's time to go home," she said.

He reached into his tent, pulled out his sleeping bag and began rolling it up.

"Not now, Eole. Tomorrow morning."

"Oh. To the spiritual commune with Domi, Jasmine, Sandrine, Alain, Aziz–?"

She made the T-sign before he could finish the list of twenty people and said, "Yes." He had lots of questions about what they would do there – whether he could sleep in his tent, away from the commune so he didn't have to meet the people but not too far so that he would be close to her; whether it was near the sea because he liked long empty beaches but not the sea itself; whether Domi would tell him where the voices came from; and what the next part of their mission involved. But the questions were all rushing and tripping over each other, like the farmyard stream when the glacier melted and the white water gushed and swirled in eddies. He couldn't get the words out.

His feet started to itch. He concentrated on them and played part one of the trick Rainbow had shown him when he'd described *itch, shuffle and escape* to her: he imagined his feet growing wiggly little roots down into the earth, spreading through layers of strata in a delta shape from his feet and holding him tight in place. Now his feet couldn't take him anywhere.

Rainbow went to brush her teeth and he played part two

of her trick, which was to let all his thoughts slide down his body, through his legs and his roots into the earth, where the sand and stones absorbed them.

While his thoughts travelled, he studied the stars until the names of the constellations filled the vacuum in his mind where his questions had been. When he'd finished, he rubbed his stiff neck and found he was in control of his feet again. It was enough to trust that Rainbow knew where they were going and what they were doing. His place was with her because soulmates belonged together. He climbed into his sleeping bag and stroked Darwie until he fell asleep.

At seven o'clock the next morning they took down their tents and Rainbow threw all her kit into the yellow Mini. He packed his rucksack, gave her a 200-franc note to pay Lucien for his pitch and then sat in the passenger seat with Darwie at his feet. He was ready.

They left Arrens-Marsous and he opened the map book. But when they reached Arras-en-Lavedan, Rainbow turned left.

"Where are we going?" he asked.

"I'm taking you home. Where exactly do you live? You said it was up here somewhere."

He reached for the door handle and pulled it open. Darwie yelped. Rainbow swerved into a gateway.

"Close the door! What's the matter with you? I told you yesterday that we were going home today."

The words wouldn't come. He shook his head violently and slammed the door shut.

She pulled on the handbrake and sighed. "Did you think you were coming home with me?"

He nodded.

"Look, your part in the mission is over. I've had a nice time with you and I need you to keep your promise about the Tree Slayer. I'm going home, back to my boyfriend and hopefully my summer job, and you've got your sheep to look after."

"The sheep don't need me. They've got Patou. I'm coming with you," he said.

The word 'boyfriend' kept popping up in his mind, distracting him from arguing his case. Of course she had a boyfriend, even though she'd never mentioned him. But he, Eole, was her soulmate. A soulmate was more important than a boyfriend. He belonged with her, because if he didn't, where else could he belong, apart from on the top of the mountains where he wasn't needed? Not at home, and not at university yet.

She demanded directions to his house and he reluctantly explained. He wouldn't get out of the car there. She couldn't force him.

They stopped in the yard. Rainbow jumped out and opened his door. Darwie escaped with a yelp, ran around sniffing places and then came back, wagging his tail. The fencing equipment was still piled beside the barn. Alexandra came out of the cheese room and said hello to Rainbow, who explained she'd brought Eole home.

He sat in the car.

Alexandra came to his door and talked at him. Rainbow explained that he'd got it into his head that he was coming home with her. Alexandra put on her surprised face, followed quickly by her disapproving face.

"Eole can't travel. He's–" she paused. "Special. He's not

ready to go anywhere he doesn't know. Come on, darling, out you get."

He stayed where he was.

"Listen, Eole," said Rainbow. "We can talk on the phone. I can come back to visit you. We'll see each other again."

He looked at his twitchy feet. He could feel imaginary roots curled up under the soles. They started to uncurl and creep towards the earth.

"Just look at those fencing posts," said Alexandra. "They're dying for you to deal with them."

"I'm going with Rainbow to her commune," he said. "I'm her soulmate. I must stay with her."

"Darling, you live here. You wouldn't be happy with people like that. It's ungodly."

"Very ungodly," said Rainbow. "And totally unscientific."

Alexandra continued: "Not to mention that you'd have to live with a group of people you don't know. You'd be lost without your routines. We'd worry about you. And I'm sure they couldn't take Charles."

"Who?" asked Rainbow.

"Charles. His dog," said Alexandra. Darwie had come back to the car and was sitting on the ground with his head on Eole's lap.

Eole didn't care if the commune was ungodly and unscientific and full of strange people. His place was with Rainbow, like Darwie's place was with him. Alexandra opened her mouth to pile on more reasons for him to feel sweaty, so he quickly intervened:

"They have lots of animals so Darwie will be fine, and I'll stay in my tent so I won't have to live with strangers, and

Domi will tell me where the voices come from and I don't need to ask your permission anyway because I'm eighteen and I'm adopted, now you've finally told me the truth, so I don't belong here, and anyway you don't have any legal authority over me, which means you can't stop me – so, Rainbow, get back in the car because we need to go, and–"

Rainbow was making the T-sign but he'd been staring at Darwie's grainy black nose while she spoke and he only noticed when he looked up.

Alexandra's mouth was an 'O' shape.

"Darling, the voices come from God and this is your home. You belong here. Stop being silly. That's enough, now. You must let this young lady go."

Rainbow drummed her fingers on her chin.

"It's true that Domi could hypnotise you and find out why you hear voices," she said. She glanced at Alexandra and added: "Maybe he would confirm that it *is* God."

She gave a long speech about Domi's 'inner voice' courses, took a flyer from the glove box and gave it to Alexandra. Alexandra shoved it into her apron pocket without reading it.

"This is ridiculous, Eole. You were perfectly happy here until this girl came along. Now get out the car."

She nudged Darwie away with her leg, reached forward and put her hand firmly on his arm.

He didn't mean to do it.

He didn't do it.

It was his arm that shook her off and made her sprawl backwards onto the ground. He knew his arm had done a bad thing but he didn't care. He heard Rainbow gasp and he heard her help Alexandra up, but he couldn't see anything because his eyes were squeezed closed and he was trying to pull up the roots and trying to send them deeper into the earth at the same time, and it was too difficult to do both, and Rainbow was talking about someone called Guillaume who'd stayed in the commune, and Alexandra went quiet and Rainbow told Alexandra that she'd look after him and that she'd call when they arrived and that Alexandra could come and collect him in a few days, and Alexandra used her steamroller voice and argued and said nasty things about influence and taking advantage and soulmates and hypnotism and spiritual people, and she called Rainbow bad names, and Rainbow's voice was like an icicle down his back, and Darwie jumped into the car and sat on his feet and licked his hand, and Alexandra shouted and then Rainbow sat beside him again and muttered swear words under her breath and she leant across and shut his door and the engine started and his roots were wrenched up by the movement of the car as it screeched out of the yard, and he felt too tired to continue monitoring everything, and ...

CHAPTER 17

Rainbow drove gently around the Val d'Azun bends so as not to wake Eole. She was still trembling. She hadn't expected Eole to be so violent, especially with his own mother – even if Alexandra was a narrow-minded, interfering busybody. She felt sorry for Alexandra: the adoption was obviously a thorny subject, though part of her – the Mary part – thought it served Alexandra right for lying.

It wasn't a bad idea to take Eole with her for a few days. She could make sure he kept his promise not to conjure up a storm. At Le Logis he wouldn't suffer from the stupid stares he'd received from people on the campsite. And Domi might help him understand the source of his voices.

Eole slept for most of the journey northwards past the increasingly devastated woodlands, which gave Rainbow time to open the box in her mind and peep at Christophe and Thierry. Chris had made a mistake. Anyone could make a mistake. The important thing was that he still loved her. Their ten-day break may even have been good for them. Now he knew he didn't love Emilie, their relationship could go back to normal.

This was less likely to be the case with Thierry, who'd probably found someone to replace her. She left Thierry in the box and let Christophe creep out. Everything would be fine and in a few hours she would see her gorgeous Apple and Acorn.

They arrived in Cognac at lunchtime. The sight of the storm-ravaged trees shocked her once again, especially now she knew the source of the storm. She pointed out the damage his gale had done but Eole didn't respond. It was appalling to think that all this destruction had been caused because one boy lost his temper with a chestnut tree that hadn't even chosen to fall on Tintin. Such huge power shouldn't be allowed in one person, even if it was the Tree Slayer and not Eole who'd caused the damage. He mustn't ever lose his temper like that again.

Christophe's motorbike was parked at the commune, which meant he hadn't brought the kittens. Now she was so close to seeing him, she was nervous – as was Mary. The apprentice's shadow hung over them. Even if Christophe regretted his decision, he'd still chosen Emilie over her. Could things ever be the same as before?

She waited while Eole unfolded his long legs and ventured out of the Mini. He immediately dived back inside. She was about to encourage him out when she realised he was simply getting his headphones.

"OK?" she asked.

"A bit better."

He dragged out his rucksack and held it close to his chest. She suggested he take off the headphones to meet her family but he refused and put on his rucksack. Darwie looked happier than Eole, running backwards and forwards, cocking his leg in the hedgerows and then trotting back to Eole. They walked around the building towards the back door, stopping for Rainbow to stroke the silver maple and tell Eole that Mary had disappeared here.

It was Monday and the children, except a sick-looking Sandrine, were at school. The adults had finished lunch and were sitting around the outside table, under the parasols, drinking coffee. Christophe jumped up, sat down, stood up slowly and finally came towards her and Eole, his hands shoved into his pockets. He looked as awkward as she felt. He was probably surprised to see her with another boy.

"This is Eole. I've brought him to consult Domi," she said quickly.

Christophe relaxed his hunched shoulders, said hello and held out a hand to shake Eole's.

Eole ignored it.

Rainbow wasn't sure how to greet Christophe. Should she kiss him on the lips as if nothing had changed? Or just on the cheeks, like with any friend?

He ran his hand through his hair. He was probably asking himself the same question. She took a step towards him to kiss his cheek.

He touched her arm, murmured an apology about his stupid choice and then looked into her eyes. She couldn't resist the heat of his gaze. She didn't want to resist. She told him they'd talk about it later, slid her arms around his neck and kissed him on the lips. He held her tight. Mary's happiness saturated her. Things felt exactly the same as before.

By the time he released her, the other commune members had arrived – and Eole had retreated. She let go of Christophe, joined Eole and whispered that everything would be fine.

"Hi, everyone," she said. "This is Eole and his dog, Darwie. They're going to camp in the garden for a few days and want to be left in peace. Eole will come and say hello to you in his own time."

There was a chorus of greetings. They returned to the table and Rainbow told Eole to wait there while she said hello to everyone individually.

Mum hugged her and told her she was looking more confident and complete.

"What do you mean?" asked Rainbow.

Mum shrugged. "It's just an air about you," she said.

Rainbow smiled. She did feel more confident. Mum looked different too, as if Rainbow hadn't seen her for years, not days. She seemed older and yet more childlike, and Rainbow had a flash of premonition in which she saw Mum as an old woman.

Christophe took her arm before she could return to Eole's side. "Is Eole the shepherd you went looking for?"

She hesitated. If she told him she hadn't found her soulmate, he would presume the whole vision had been a hallucination and try to discourage her from returning to the Val d'Azun to continue her search. And she'd promised not to tell anyone about Eole's special skill.

"Not exactly," she said. "He's kind of involved with the Tree Slayer. I'll explain once he's settled, OK?"

She led Eole into the kitchen, where she poured him a drink and filled a dog bowl with water for Darwie. He still wouldn't put down his rucksack. She showed him around and when they went past Alain's workshop he stopped and stared.

"Can I go in?" he asked.

"If you really want to. It's just oily machine bits and mechanical stuff."

She hovered in the doorway with Darwie while Eole walked around touching the dirty tools and examining the chemistry equipment. He obviously liked the dingy workshop. She would introduce him to Alain and then she could leave them together here while she went to see the kittens and Thierry.

Christophe sat with her and Eole while they ate the leftovers from lunch. She told him about her trip. Domi joined them while she was raving about the beauty of the mountains. He welcomed Eole to the commune and when he asked if he could shake hands with him, Eole accepted. They looked into each other's eyes. Rainbow remembered the moment she'd first met Domi and how safe his hand had felt. Did Eole sense this too? Neither of them said anything.

Rainbow briefed Domi about the voices Eole heard and then Domi asked Eole a few easy questions about his home, his studies and his age. Eole answered with single words.

"I'm free this afternoon, Eole, so come and see me when you've pitched your tent and had a rest," said Domi. "Rainbow, can I have a word?"

Eole watched Rainbow go into the house with Domi. His feet wanted to follow her but she'd told him to stay and talk to Christophe. It wasn't a suggestion, like for his headphones earlier on. It was an order.

He hugged his rucksack between his knees and looked at the squat boy with dirty fingernails who smelt of metal and grease, and who stroked Rainbow as if she were his dog. He wished this boyfriend would stop touching his soulmate.

"I'm Rainbow's soulmate," he said.

Christophe laughed, then stopped and frowned.

Eole felt as if he'd made an unexpectedly good chess move.

"That's not what she told me," Christophe said. He flexed his biceps and stretched. "So, you've left your sheep to come and consult Domi, have you?"

"Yes."

This Christophe obviously wasn't very bright, because he'd listened the whole time Rainbow had explained to Domi why she'd brought him here. Rainbow was as illogical as Hestia in her choice of boyfriend. Eole considered explaining everything again, but decided against it. The more you said to the boys at school, the more ammunition you gave them to mock you. Obviously Christophe didn't know Eole was her soulmate, because Rainbow wouldn't tell a boyfriend something so important until she knew him well. Boyfriends only lasted for a few weeks, whereas soulmates lasted forever. And soulmates didn't touch each other all the time, like Christophe kept doing with Rainbow.

"Rainbow isn't a dog, you know," he said.

"Um ... Yes, I do know that," said Christophe. "So what makes you think you're her soulmate?"

"Because I am. She told me."

Christophe smiled. "She did, did she?"

"Yes."

Eole was pleased with his flexibility in getting into such a good conversation rhythm with a stranger. But it was pitiful to see how Christophe had to have everything repeated.

"Look: she drew me," he added.

He took out her drawings from inside his *Multiverse Theories* book and handed them to Christophe. They showed him lying on his back, shaping clouds; directing Darwie around the flock; spraying Dizzy with antiseptic. The last drawing was an imagined one, because it showed him standing on the mountain pass blowing away storm clouds and she hadn't seen him do that.

Christophe's smile disappeared.

Checkmate, thought Eole. His chest swelled, even though he wasn't breathing in.

"The drawings are all right, I suppose," he added, pleased he'd managed to consult Hestia about them.

Christophe's eyebrows shot up. "They're a lot more than all right." He dropped the drawings onto the table and strode towards the house.

🌱 🌱 🌱

Rainbow wondered why Domi wanted to talk to her alone. Was he angry that she'd brought Eole without warning him first? The Mary side of her protested that they didn't need Domi to tell them off. Rainbow ignored her grumbling: Mary was bound to dislike the person whose advice was to keep tight control of her. Domi was Rainbow's guru. She trusted him.

She followed him into his room, closed the door behind her and asked what he wanted.

"I'd like to know how you got on. And how you're connected to Eole," he said.

She told him everything about her trip, apart from Eole's secret wind gift. She didn't mention how she'd considered pushing Eole off the mountain, either. She was too ashamed. Instead, she told him Eole's theory about the Tree Slayer being a wind spirit that had taken advantage of the gale.

"I can't explain more because I promised Eole I'd keep his secret," she said. "But I *can* tell you that he's linked to the Tree Slayer."

Domi nodded, even though there was no way he could understand without knowing about Eole's incredible lungs.

"He has a powerful aura around him," he said. "It's so compressed that it's black."

Rainbow gasped. "Is that an aura? I saw it. I even drew it. But I didn't know what it was. Do you think it's the Tree Slayer's mark?"

"It could be," said Domi.

Rainbow clasped the arms of her chair, struck by a horrific thought. Her tree gift was due to a part of Amrita being inside her: could a part of the Tree Slayer be inside Eole? Instead of being an external wind spirit, the Tree Slayer could be internal. It would explain the black aura.

This was far worse than she'd imagined. The Tree Slayer might be lying dormant inside him, waiting for the right moment to destroy the One Tree. As soon as she found it, the Tree Slayer would strike.

"His inner voices might be the Tree Slayer," she whispered.

"Perhaps," said Domi.

Thank goodness she hadn't told Eole about Koad or the

rest of her mission. From now onwards she must be careful not to reveal anything. Or she could try to entice the Tree Slayer out and then kill it. Was it a malevolent spirit that possessed people, like the ones Aziz exorcised for the commune clients?

"We must purge it from Eole's body," she said. "Then I'd truly vanquish the Tree Slayer without hurting Eole. I bet my soulmate will only appear once it's gone. Yes! We'll ask Aziz to exorcise it and then I can go back to the Val d'Azun and find my other half."

Domi was shaking his head.

"One thing at a time, Rainbow. I'll know more when I've examined him but I won't be able to tell you anything about my discoveries. I have to keep my sessions confidential, remember? Whatever happens, it's important that you trust your intuition. If you keep your mission in mind and remain open to signs, you'll make the right decisions. Talking of which, how are things with Mary?"

If Rainbow's suspicions about the Tree Slayer were true, she and Eole had more in common than she'd thought. She had Mary inside her whereas he had the Tree Slayer.

She suppressed Mary's feeling of disgust at being compared to the Tree Slayer, and told Domi nothing had changed: she was still influenced by Mary's emotions but could control them, thanks to the wall in her mind.

"Good," said Domi. "Let me know if things get out of hand."

She agreed – though she could sense Mary's resistance to telling Domi anything – and left the room.

Christophe was waiting for her in the corridor. She grinned

and took his hand, glad that he was still hers, and asked where Eole was. He frowned and jerked his head to indicate Eole was outside.

"We need to talk," he said.

"Is Eole OK? I'm not sure I can leave him. What's he doing?"

"He's fine. Forget about him for a minute and come with me."

He went upstairs towards her bedroom. Rainbow peeked outside and saw Eole sitting at the table with Darwie. She was tempted to share her discovery about his aura with him and ask if he could feel the Tree Slayer inside. But the Tree Slayer was her enemy. She was Amrita's saviour: she was going to revive Amrita's life force. If the Tree Slayer was there, it would know she'd guessed its secret. It might try to eliminate her before she could save the One Tree. She'd better pretend nothing had changed.

Eole looked settled. He was good at doing nothing and would be fine for a few minutes. She raced upstairs after Christophe.

On the second flight of stairs she slowed down. Maybe he wanted to talk about Emilie. She didn't want to think about the apprentice: about her blonde hair and long legs, which Christophe must have caressed; about them exchanging kisses as they took motorbikes apart. She couldn't do this.

She stopped.

Christophe took her hand, drew her inside her bedroom and closed the door.

"I've got this huge lump inside my chest, Rainette. I don't think it'll go until I've explained what happened with Emilie."

Rainbow sat down rigidly on her bed. This was going to hurt.

He pulled up a chair, sat opposite her and started to explain how he'd mistaken his feelings, how he'd confused wanting to look after Emilie with being in love with her. He'd realised this as soon as Rainbow left and Emilie put her arms around him to console him. She felt wrong. She smelt wrong. All he could think about was his Rainette.

"She's pretty," he said. "But so are you. And you're ... well, you're you. That's special. I'd forgotten it because we've been together for so many months. Emilie could never replace you. You're the girl I love, not her."

Rainbow relaxed her clenched fists. It wasn't as if he and Emilie had actually been out together, or that Emilie had rejected him and he'd come back to Rainbow by default. He'd never truly loved Emilie. He'd just been his usual softie self and had wanted to help a lonely girl.

"Can you forgive me?" he asked.

Rainbow quelled Mary's joyful surge of agreement. Could she bear to go through this pain again if the same thing happened in the future?

"How do I know you won't fall for the next helpless girl you see?" she asked.

"I've learnt my lesson. You're the only one who counts. You've always been the only one," he said.

"Then I forgive you." She leant into him and they kissed. The butterflies, which had been asleep in Azun, woke in a flutter. She surrendered to their tingling pleasure.

After a few minutes she broke away. It didn't feel right to have a kissing session.

"I have to get back to Eole," she said.

"But you haven't told me anything about him. You haven't explained why you brought him back with you."

"He's a kind of host for the Tree Slayer. I think I've got him sorted, but I need to keep an eye on him because he may be dangerous."

"You're not in love with him?"

"Chris!"

"We need to be honest with each other."

"OK. I'm definitely not in love with him."

"So he's not your soulmate or anything?"

"No."

She stared at his strange expression. His eyes were closed, as if he were praying.

"He showed me the drawings you did," he said.

"And? Are they awful? I couldn't quite nail him. Domi says the black line around him is an aura. Chris?"

He looked at his watch. "I have to get back to work. Can you come over this evening? Or don't you want to see Apple and Acorn?"

"Of course I do! But it's difficult to get away from Eole."

Christophe stood up. His jaw was set, making him look callous.

"Chris?"

"It's your decision. Just let me know so I don't go out."

He jogged down the stairs before she could answer. He hadn't even kissed her goodbye. Was he jealous? Of Eole? She could feel Mary's indignation. How dare he be jealous after dropping her for Emilie!

Eole looked around the commune garden. It smelt of green, of animal ammonia and sun tan lotion, and was a lot more chaotic than the farmyard in Arras-en-Lavedan. There weren't any neighbours, only untidy trees at all angles. He didn't like the way they huddled together like an intimidating crowd of gossiping people.

A group of women were sitting under a weeping willow with a girl of about eleven years old. She was staring at him. He stared back. She stood up and came towards him, which kids didn't normally do. He quickly stopped staring and cradled Darwie's head on his lap.

"Hello. I'm Sandrine," she said. "Can I stroke Darwie?"

Darwie was pushing hard against Eole's legs, so he refused.

She stood watching him. He explained that Darwie was shy and that she must let him sniff her hand first. She held it out. Darwie licked her fingers and wagged his tail. She stroked his head and then patted him.

"He likes me. It'll be hard for you to leave him behind."

"I won't leave him behind," he said.

She gave him another long stare. He thought she was going to speak but she said nothing more.

Christophe came out of the house, slammed the door and strode towards the car park. A motorbike engine roared into life and then faded away. When Rainbow emerged, a few minutes later, she looked unsparkly.

"Are you sure you want to camp?" she asked. "There's a spare bed in the boys' dormitory."

He was sure. He chose a spot beside the house, at the opposite end of the path to the car park and as far away from the animal pens and woods as possible. When his camp was ready, he sent Darwie on a walk with Sandrine and followed Rainbow indoors, wiping the sweat from his brow.

He was going to be hypnotised, which was a medical procedure and therefore not a problem for his brain to accept. His mind, however, started to peel away from his brain's logic and worry about the new experience. It felt like the time he hadn't revised for an oral English exam. But Rainbow was with him, and Domi was rather like Tintin. If his mind pretended Domi was Tintin, he would avoid *itch, shuffle and escape*. Problem solved.

It was a relief to be indoors. He took off his headphones. Domi's room was neither a scientific laboratory, nor a cheesemaking laboratory: it was a spiritualist's laboratory. Smelling of lavender, it contained a desk and armchairs, a table for bodies, a basin and a sideboard with candles on it. Piano music came from a cassette player but it wasn't orchestral. Hestia would call it 'music for healing warts'. The melody made him think of the farmyard stream in summer. He visualised his former home as he sat down and took the 'Listen to Your Inner Voice' leaflet Domi gave him.

CHAPTER 18

When Eole stepped out of Domi's French windows after his hypnotherapy session, the world seemed dimmer than before. He blinked, put on his headphones and looked for Darwie and Rainbow.

School must have finished for the day because there were children everywhere: playing with the goats in the pen, swinging on the climbing frame and crouching in the vegetable patch. He could smell raspberries, fresh baguettes, orange juice and schoolbooks. Sandrine was sitting at the outside table, brushing Darwie with a pink brush like the one Hestia used to have in her doll box.

Eole whistled and Darwie danced towards him, wagging his tail, his tongue lolling. Eole couldn't see or smell Rainbow. He waited with Darwie at his heel until, three minutes and twenty seconds later, she came out of the front door.

"Domi says you don't need any more sessions. How was it?"

He shrugged. The hypnotherapy had been like lying down for a siesta, when you don't actually sleep but your mind drifts out of earthly reasoning and into clouds of colours.

"Did you learn what your voices are?" she asked.

"No."

Domi had told him that the voices were external. When Eole asked if it was God, Domi said he didn't know because he couldn't explore external sources. He kept asking in different ways where Eole came from and eventually Eole told him he was adopted. Domi said this might explain why he had the impression that Eole didn't belong. Eole decided to find a library and look up the scientific research on hypnotherapy, since it was so accurate. If he looked at a book with no link to Tintin and the mountains, perhaps he would manage to read again.

Rainbow was waiting for an answer to a question he hadn't heard. "Pardon?" he said.

"If you turned off your music, you'd hear what I was saying," said Rainbow. "Did Domi mention whether you'd split into two parallel worlds, like me, and then come together again? Does it feel as if you've got a conjoined twin inside you? That's what it's like for me with Mary."

"No." He imagined cutting open Rainbow's head and finding two linked brains inside. What would it be like to have Hestia's brain in his head? In some ways she was already there, her voice advising him what to do. But he knew this was his own inner voice remembering her words, not actually Hestia. If she were really there, she would make him drink vodka, run away from home, kiss boys and tell Alexandra lies.

"What about the Tree Slayer? Did you learn anything about its whereabouts?"

"No." Her question was totally illogical. There was no reason for the Tree Slayer to be anywhere nearby, since he hadn't started a gale.

"Well, keep it all to yourself if you must," said Rainbow, looking cross. "Oh, and don't forget to ring your mum."

Before he could tell her Alexandra wasn't his mother and that he didn't want to talk to her, a loud bell began to clang. It kept clanging. He slammed his hands to his ears, on top of his headphones, and ran.

The ringing ceased and he stopped running. He let his hands drop and felt Darwie's comforting muzzle beside him. People appeared in the garden, spilling out of the front door and the sets of French windows, and headed to the table. He was reminded of the bees at Tintin's funeral, though these weren't buzzing. They went backwards and forwards with crockery and glasses, bowls of salad and baguettes. They were ants.

Rainbow caught up with him and explained that the clanging was the dinner bell. His feet had grown roots, even though he hadn't activated part one of Rainbow's trick. Faces turned to him. While those of the adults quickly looked away again, the little ones stared. He stared back. They sidled up to an adult and reached for a hand or clasped their arms around a thigh.

Rainbow was talking to him in her quiet voice, the one she'd used on Dizzy. She was telling him that she would get him some food and bring it to his tent and they could eat together. She kept talking, forgetting to stop and let him have his turn, which was just as well because none of his thoughts would make words and if she'd left a gap he wouldn't have been able to speak, and his one-hundred-percent perfect record of normal conversation rhythms with her would be broken, and she'd not want him as her soulmate.

She left him and went to the table to collect their meals.

He dug up his feet – the imaginary roots dangling and then curling up and dissolving – and walked in a straight line over the vegetable plot fence and between two rows of tomato plants to his camp.

His tent was familiar, as were his sleeping bag, mat, rucksack and books. As long as his belongings were here, he knew he was in the right place, even if it wasn't home. That must be why people called possessions their 'belongings'. He pulled out his mat and sat down to think about where he belonged.

Now that he didn't have the excuse of Domi and the voices to keep him here, Alexandra would insist on taking him home. He'd be separated from Rainbow and wouldn't be able to protect her from the Tree Slayer. No one would keep her safe – certainly not cognitively impaired Christophe – and she'd die.

He had to find a way to stay. He must prove to Alexandra that he fitted in here, that he was learning people-skills in preparation for Toulouse.

🌢 🌿 🌢

Domi told Rainbow that exorcism was out of the question. Eole's hypnotherapy experience hadn't resolved the voice mystery but it had given Domi an idea he wanted to follow up.

Domi was always following up ideas. It sounded to Rainbow like a poor excuse to avoid saying that hypnotherapy was useless – and it didn't help in her search for her soulmate. He suggested she continue life as normal and keep her eyes open for signs. Two weeks had passed since her vision and she still had no idea where to find Koad or the last One Tree. But what else could she do?

After dinner, Eole still refused to phone his mum but he agreed to let Rainbow call her. He seemed more at ease this evening and responded when people talked to him. Alain took him into the workshop and persuaded him to help distill lavender into essence for the consulting rooms. While he was busy she went into the hall and rang the number Alexandra had given her that morning.

"So. You kidnapped my brother," came Hestia's voice.

"Well, it wasn't–" Rainbow began.

"And made Maman cry. Even Papa came out of his bubble and said it was out of order."

"I didn't kidnap him. He wanted to come. The voices in his head bother him and–"

"Shut up and listen to me!" snapped Hestia. "If anything happens to him – if you hurt him or break his heart or abandon him – I will personally come after you and kill you. Or worse. OK?"

Eole didn't realise how lucky he was to have a sister like this. "I won't hurt him," she said. "And the commune takes really good care of people."

She explained that Eole had finished his hypnotherapy and was resting. Hestia had a shouted conversation with her mum and then told Rainbow that Alexandra would pick him up in two days' time.

"You'd better be wearing armour when she arrives," added Hestia.

"I get the message. And, Hestia …"

"What?"

"You're a great sister."

Rainbow hung up quickly, tears welling in her eyes. Mary told her not to blubber, pointing out that an internally conjoined twin was far better than a sister. Mary did sometimes reassure Rainbow – on the rare occasions they agreed on an issue – but it wasn't like having a sister. Amrita might be more of a sister, if Rainbow managed to restore her life force: a knowledgeable older sister she could confide in and learn from.

At breakfast the next morning, Rainbow explained to Eole that she had an appointment to see Thierry at eleven o'clock, and was then having lunch with Christophe. She suggested he stay in the workshop with Alain.

"No. I'm coming with you."

"You can't," she said.

"I'll go to the library. There must be one in Cognac. I've got some research to do."

Surprised, she agreed. They left Darwie with Sandrine and she dropped Eole off at the street that led to the library, explaining where he'd find the building. He stood beside the car and waited, his feet shuffling. She sighed, parked the car and walked him there, pointing out a shop where he could buy a sandwich for lunch. Then she told him she'd pick him up at two o'clock and left.

She was free, at last! But she was late and had to race to Thierry and Claudette's house.

"Sorted things out with Christophe?" Thierry asked when he opened the door.

"I think so. I'm sorry for disappearing like that."

He sat back down at his desk, where he was typing invoices, and Rainbow took a seat opposite him.

"These things happen," he said. "Once is acceptable. Just don't let it happen again." He wagged a finger at her. "It's a shame you missed the climate change conference. You could have learnt a lot."

"Was that the special project you had in mind for me?"

"Yes. The organisers were looking for volunteers to create a database of trees so we can track the effect of climate change on them. But there's good news too."

He wiggled his bushy eyebrows. Rainbow smiled. "Go on. Tell me the good news," she said.

"I'm off to Massane on Thursday for a week of biodiversity conferences. I could take you with me, show you the forest and introduce you to my former colleagues. There's nothing like networking for a young student. Interested?"

Thursday: in two days' time. Eole would have left and Domi had advised her to continue life as usual. The timing was perfect.

"You bet!"

"Think you can leave loverboy so soon?"

"Of course." This trip would make a break from her mission. When she returned she might have some fresh ideas for finding her soulmate and could go back to the Val d'Azun. Meanwhile, she'd have to work hard to prove to Thierry that she was serious.

"Tell me more about the conferences," she said.

Thierry pulled out a folder and for the rest of the morning she studied the biodiversity of Massane forest, which had been set aside as a nature reserve a hundred years ago. It wasn't until Claudette told her lunch was ready that she remembered Christophe. She jumped up and explained she had to go.

"I'm leaving at eight o'clock on Thursday," Thierry called as she rushed away. "Don't forget."

"No worries, you can count on me," she said.

CHAPTER 19

After leaving Thierry's house, Rainbow raced to Christophe's flat and rang the bell. Christophe had said he'd mistaken his feelings for Emilie, but would his jealousy of Eole make him reconsider them?

She heard him jog down the stairs in his metal-capped safety shoes, which meant the intercom was broken again. He opened the door and peered behind her.

"No shadow today?"

"I've left him at the library."

"Good." He kissed her briefly. "Let's eat. I have to get back to work soon."

He was still in a strange mood. She apologised for being late and told him about Thierry's offer. His demeanour softened and they went upstairs to his flat, where lunch was congealing on the table. Apple and Acorn scampered to the door and she grabbed Apple before he could dash downstairs.

"We didn't finish talking about Eole yesterday," said Christophe as they ate.

"Well, you went all jealous on me and stomped off."

"Can you blame me? Eole's a bit strange, but he's good-looking."

"Come on, you know I don't care about appearances," she said.

"It's more than his looks. There's something in the way you drew him, something intimate. A kind of longing."

Rainbow stopped chewing. She'd believed him to be her soulmate when she'd done some of the drawings. Were her feelings so obvious in her art?

"When I saw you arrive together," he continued, "I got this heavy feeling in my heart. Something almost tangible seemed to link you. A bit like with you and Mary before you hugged the silver maple. It hurts because I love you."

"Oh, Chris." She took his hand. "I'm not in the least bit attracted to Eole. You probably just picked up on the vibes of us being together for a week. There's nothing at all between us."

"So why did you tell him he's your soulmate?"

She frowned. "He told you that?"

"It was the first thing he said."

"Oh."

"Yes: *Oh*. You say he's dangerous, but you still hang around with him. You tell *him* he's your soulmate but won't admit it to me. I don't understand, Rainbow."

She realised that trying to protect Chris from being jealous actually made things worse. The only solution for them to find their former trust in each other was to be completely honest.

"It's complicated," she sighed. "Basically, he's got a gift that I promised to keep secret. At first I thought he was my shepherd. I was a bit hasty and told him he was a kind of soulmate to me. Then I discovered that he's not the shepherd I'm looking for. He's the Tree Slayer – or, rather, the Tree Slayer takes advantage of his gift. But Eole is attached to the idea of being my soulmate. I've got to keep him happy because if he gets upset, the Tree Slayer will use him to destroy this One Tree I must save. And meanwhile I still haven't found my Val d'Azun shepherd."

"I see. Kind of. But it's not fair to pretend Eole's your soulmate. You should tell him the truth."

"I've tried but he's got the soulmate thing stuck in his head. He knows I'm with you."

"Does he? He's pretty possessive. But I suppose that's not your fault. Anyway, I'm going to give you a chance to prove you're not in love with him."

"How?" she asked.

He grinned. "Come on holiday with me."

A slow smile spread across her face, which was nothing compared to Mary's explosion of elation. "Cool! When?"

"After your conferences in Massane. I've booked the July bank holiday week off work, remember?"

Thierry also took his holiday around Bastille Day, which meant he wouldn't need her. This was the sign she'd been hoping for. "Can we go back to the Val d'Azun?" she asked.

"That's exactly what I was going to suggest, since you've fallen under the charm of the Pyrenees. We could try paragliding and go mountain biking and potholing. And canyoning. We could climb a peak and sleep under the stars."

She thought of wildflower prairies, marmots and rocky peaks. It would be romantic. And she'd be able to hunt for her shepherd with Christophe beside her, as she'd originally intended.

"What do you think?" asked Christophe.

Emilie wouldn't dare interfere in her and Christophe's relationship when she heard about this.

"You bet!" she said. "Don't count on me for the paragliding, though."

"Chicken! It'll be even better than dune-jumping. Let's send off for some brochures right now."

Rainbow hummed as she drove to the library after lunch, not caring if anyone heard her through the open Mini windows. Thierry still wanted her. She and Chris had overcome their problems and were back on track. She had plans for the next step of her mission and Eole had promised not to unleash a gale again. As long as he kept his word, everything would be fine.

She hoped he fully understood the destructive power of his special skill. If *she* lost her temper, her gift would only allow her to knot a few branches. But when Eole got angry, he flattened whole forests. No wonder the Tree Slayer had chosen him.

It was horrible to think it was inside Eole right now, biding its time, waiting for him to lose his temper or have an episode and lose control. It may even be feeding on poor Eole, gathering force until it could take full possession of him and command him to create a storm. The thought made her blanch. If naming a gale gave it more strength, then warning Eole he risked being possessed by an evil spirit – one already lodged inside him – would make him even more susceptible to its power.

She couldn't tell him. She wouldn't be able to influence him or calm him once he'd gone home, but the success of her mission depended on him resisting the Tree Slayer. There was one more thing she could do before he left.

🌹 🥀 🌹

Eole didn't manage to buy a sandwich on his own, even though he could buy one perfectly well in Argelès-Gazost. If he hadn't started imagining all the possibilities of what the shopkeeper might say, the questions she might ask and the decisions he would have to make, it might have been fine. As it was, he'd preferred to stay hungry when the library closed at midday. He waited for two hours and five minutes on the bench before Rainbow arrived.

She was looking all sparkly again.

"Hey, Eole! Did you do lots of research?"

He nodded. Reading hypnotherapy books in Cognac library had felt less like betrayal than reading his birthday books. His brain told him that Tintin didn't belong here and therefore Eole wasn't forsaking his memory by learning something new and not sharing it. This had thawed his frozen mind and he'd managed to read everything he'd taken from the library shelves.

Rainbow looked him up and down as they walked back to the car. "Have you forgotten your headphones?"

"No." He pulled them out of his pocket to show her. "I don't need them in towns."

The lead unwound and dropped to the floor, the jack making a metallic 'clink' on the stone cobbles.

"Careful. Don't drop your Walkman," she said.

He rolled up the lead and put it back in his pocket. "I haven't got a Walkman."

She wore a confused expression, even though he couldn't find anything ambiguous in his sentence. Then she made a lightbulb-moment face.

"Clever tactic. Maybe I should wear headphones when *I* want some peace."

She drove them back towards the commune but stopped unexpectedly at a car park on the edge of a wood.

"What are you doing?" he asked.

"Out you get."

He put on his headphones and followed her reluctantly along a path.

"You see these dead and damaged trees?" said Rainbow. "This is your fault. You and the Tree Slayer did this."

They were hundreds of miles from Brittany. He hadn't realised he had so much force, though of course he'd only started the gale. The Tree Slayer had intervened and blown down these trees, not him. He couldn't remember how many hours he'd blown for but he knew it was the middle of the night when he'd come down from the hill, exhausted and hurting from the loss of Tintin.

Many of the trees here were uprooted and others leaned drunkenly against each other. Rainbow stroked them as she passed, like he stroked Darwie. She looked sad as she pointed out sawn-off, horizontal tree trunks on each side of the path. He didn't like her to look sad.

A tree beside him creaked. It was dangerous to walk here. One might fall on them at any minute, like one had fallen on Tintin. He stopped and told her they should go back to the car.

"Come on. We're nearly there," said Rainbow.

He dragged his feet as they fought through undergrowth, squeezed under toppled trees and weaved through thickets. At last she stopped at a fallen trunk. She put her arms around it, like she did with Christophe. Eole wrapped his arms around himself and asked her if they could go now.

"Why don't you touch the tree?"

He shook his head. He didn't want tree-stink on his hands.

"Go on, Eole. Touch it. Here." She pointed to a spot.

He sighed and put the tip of his index finger on the mossy bark. He would wash it three times with soap when he got back to the commune.

Rainbow stared at him. Was he supposed to be doing something?

She hugged the tree again and put her cheek against it. Her eyes were closed so he took his finger away. After thirty seconds, she opened her eyes.

"Nothing," she said. "Poor oak."

She made him do the same on an upright tree too and then looked disappointed, as if she'd expected something to happen, as if she still thought he was the Tree Slayer. He shook his hand and wiped it on his shorts to get rid of some of the smell. Rainbow sat down, her back against the trunk, and told him to sit down too. He did so, making sure he wasn't touching any trees.

"You caused all this destruction to avenge one person, Eole. What would Tintin have said about that?"

He hadn't thought about his gale from that perspective. Would Tintin have been disappointed in him for losing his control over his special skill?

"I'm going to tell you something important," she continued. "Why don't you take off your headphones?"

He shook his head. If he took them off, he wouldn't be able to concentrate on what she was saying.

"Never mind. Can you hear me properly?"

He nodded.

"When you have a special skill, you have a responsibility to be careful how you use it," she said. "The more powerful the skill, the bigger the responsibility."

He and Tintin had never talked about the ethics of his special skill. They'd focused on making cloud art and doing experiments to measure the capacity of his lungs, not on his responsibilities.

"You're going home tomorrow, so I want you to remember this," she said.

"I'm not going home. I'm your soulmate."

"Listen: you have an important role to play in the mission and you don't have to stay with me to do it. You've already promised never to blow up a storm again; but actually your role should be bigger than that, since you've got so much power. Whenever there's a gale, you must counteract it so the Tree Slayer doesn't use it to harm more trees. If you protect trees, you'll save my life. And Amrita's. Your role is vital, Eole. Can you promise to do that?"

He didn't care about the trees or Amrita. But if that's what it took to be Rainbow's soulmate and save her life, he would do it. He'd have to chart the movements of the winds, which would be interesting, and he'd need to know where she was all the time. But would it be enough? He'd only be able to protect her approximately eighty per cent. To give her one hundred per cent protection he'd have to stay close to her.

"Eole?"

She'd told him he *didn't have to* stay with her, not that he *mustn't* stay with her. Whether he settled for one hundred per cent or eighty per cent depended on how things went with Alexandra tomorrow.

"I promise," he said.

CHAPTER 20

Rainbow watched Eole take off his headphones as she started the Mini's engine. He was always putting them on and taking them off. Until her discovery at the library this afternoon she'd thought he was listening to classical music. She reversed out of the parking space and asked him why he bothered wearing them in her company.

"It's not because I don't want you to talk to me," he said. "It's because they block out the voices."

Headphones wouldn't work for Mary's voice – not that she noticed it so much these days. Was she getting used to Mary, at last, and becoming truly whole? It was strange to think that headphones would stop an inner voice. The act of wearing them must have a psychological effect on Eole. She wondered if the voices did belong to the Tree Slayer, and what they sounded like. She couldn't ask him directly, of course.

"What kind of things do your voices say?" she asked, as they drove towards the commune.

"I don't know."

"Can't you understand them?"

He shook his head.

"So they're in a foreign language?" The Tree Slayer wasn't that clever if it had chosen the wrong language for Eole.

"No. I listened to recordings of all the foreign languages in the Paris library and it didn't match any of them. It's not a language."

"I bet your mum thinks it's God speaking to you in tongues."

"It's noises. And she's not my mum."

"Noises? In your head?"

"No. Outside my head. The voices make it complicated to concentrate on what people are saying because they go on and on all the time and distract me."

"Hang on: you mean the voices are external? They're real voices?" That didn't sound as if it could be the Tree Slayer.

He nodded. "I don't hear them when I'm indoors. Or in town. Or on the mountain tops. They come when I'm too close to plants and trees, and–"

"Trees? This is crazy! It's the trees. You can hear the trees talking."

"No I can't. Trees don't talk."

She swerved into a lay-by and stopped the car. This was incredible. The Tree Slayer's voice would be internal. Eole's voices had to be the trees. It explained why he'd never worn his headphones on the bare summer pastures but had kept them on in the wooded valley. And why he wore them here.

"How do you know trees don't talk?" she said. "They don't bend their branches when someone puts their hands on them, either."

"Yes they do. I've seen you do that to them."

"Exactly! So why shouldn't the trees be talking to each other? Or even to you?"

"You're starting your theory in the wrong place," said Eole. "You should collect the evidence first, then deduce a theory from your empirical proof. I don't have enough evidence yet. All I know is that the voices speak through nature and are accompanied by smells."

"It's the trees' voices, I'm sure," she said. To think that trees talked – and that Eole could hear them! "But what do you mean about smells?"

"Part of the anomaly that gives me my special skill is the overdeveloped sense of smell in my olfactory receptors. I can smell things in more detail than most people. Trees stink, for example. Tintin and I did a battery of tests ..."

He continued explaining his experiments but Rainbow hardly heard him. The smells could be the chemicals Thierry had told her about, like the gas the acacia trees give off as warnings when giraffes browse on them. But if he could hear the trees and smell their chemicals – which probably wasn't very pleasant, come to think of it – was he her soulmate after all? Her soulmate *and* the Tree Slayer's host?

"Why didn't you tell me?" she said.

"You didn't ask."

This changed everything. He was her other half, her guide to Koad. But his gift wasn't equal to hers: it was far superior. She wasn't sure she liked this new development. She didn't want Eole to be closer to trees than she was. He didn't deserve it.

"I *told* you I was connected to trees," said Rainbow. "I showed you. I even said how I'd love to find someone who was as close to trees as me. Why didn't you say anything about the voices coming from them or through them?"

"It didn't occur to me. Anyway, everyone always has their own opinion on what the voices are. No one ever asks me what I think."

He had a point. She'd assumed he heard a voice like Mary's or that it was the Tree Slayer's voice; his mum was convinced it was God; and whatever Domi had thought was confidential. Domi. This must be what Domi had suspected after the hypnotherapy. But wouldn't he have told her something so important to her mission? Perhaps she was jumping to conclusions in believing the voices he heard were the trees. Or – came Mary's suspicious thoughts – could Eole be making this up so she didn't send him home? It might even be the Tree Slayer prompting Eole to invent this pretence.

How could she tell what came from Eole and what came from the Tree Slayer? She was sure no one could tell which reactions were hers and which were Mary's – even *she* had difficulty at times. Not often, but occasionally.

There was one way to be sure: she could ask Eole if he could guide her to Koad. On the other hand, she mustn't let the Tree Slayer know the details of her mission. No wonder Amrita had implied she should vanquish it before setting off for Koad. How would she get out of this conundrum? She needed time to think about what to do. He could hear the trees' voices but he didn't understand them. He was her other half but she couldn't ask him to guide her to Koad. What was the point of him being able to hear the trees he resented? It was so unfair. Why hadn't Amrita given *her* the gift of hearing trees talk instead of her stupid branch-shaping gift?

"Anyway, the voices are irrelevant," she said, "since you don't understand what they're saying. You'd better go home and concentrate on counteracting the winds and not making any more gales. Leave the trees to me. Some of them speak to me too, through images. And I can sense their feelings. I don't need to hear their language or smell them or whatever other disgusting thing your gift lets you do."

Eole made the T-sign three times in quick succession.

"What?" she said, crossly.

"You didn't tell me you understood trees' feelings. It's given me an idea. We can do a scientific study to see if we can interpret the voices. You can tell me what the trees feel and I'll make a dictionary to associate each feeling to a noise and smell combination. We can stay together and I can protect you one hundred per cent from the Tree Slayer. We'll soon see if it's the trees or not. Shall we start now?"

Mary was chiming warning bells inside Rainbow: it was too much of a coincidence. She was convinced it was a needy Eole trick or a Tree Slayer ruse. Rainbow didn't know about tricks or ruses, but she did know that Eole didn't care about trees. He called them assassins and kicked them and said they stank, whereas she knew trees and loved them. She would do anything to help them. She'd have worked on understanding their voices, not put on headphones and ignored them. Or killed so many of them.

"No, we can't start now," she said. "I've got more important things to do."

She didn't want to see him having friendly chats to trees while she stood by, powerless to understand. She didn't need to know more about the voices that he could hear and she couldn't. And she didn't need his protection. She would find Koad on her own.

She revved the engine hard and accelerated out of the lay-by, glaring at him when he told her that nine thousand people were killed on the road each year and that she should drive more slowly.

🍂 🌿 🍂

If the voices hadn't stopped him being able to concentrate on what people were saying, Eole might have continued the voice research he'd started in Paris. But a key had been missing, a key to break the code. If the voices did come from the trees themselves, which he doubted with Tintin's healthy-scientific-doubt-but-open-minded attitude, Rainbow could be the key.

Tintin had told him that scientists follow up many false trails before finding the right one. In the interest of science he had to test whether Rainbow was the key. Therefore he must stay with her. He was eighteen and didn't belong to Alexandra. He didn't have to obey her.

He practised reciting these reasons as he walked from the workshop across the grass to the commune table, where Alexandra was shaking hands with Rainbow, Domi and Jasmine, Rainbow's mum. Alexandra had her back to him. His feet wanted him to go faster and get close to her but his brain told them to slow down.

Rainbow had only spoken seventeen words to him since his code-breaking suggestion yesterday. None of the seventeen had been in agreement with his idea. Her near-silence was like cumulonimbus clouds overhead.

Alexandra looked up and saw him.

"Darling!" She made the love-hug sign and checked him over, like Tintin used to check over lambs before he bought them at the market. "Are you all right? You look thin. Haven't they been feeding you?"

He told her he'd eaten every meal and was fine. "I'm so fine that I've decided to stay here with Rainbow," he added.

"But darling, the hypnotherapy is over. I've driven all this way–"

"Which is why you must stay to lunch," said Domi. "Come and join us."

"Anyway," said Rainbow, "Eole can't stay here with me because I'm leaving."

Eole stepped back from the group. There were too many illogical sequences and unsaid words. He looked at Rainbow's frown, at Domi's hand on Alexandra's arm and at Alexandra's face, which made her surprised expression before giving Rainbow a purposeful smile. Where was Rainbow going?

"You see, Eole?" said Alexandra. "Rainbow's going away too. We'll have a quick lunch, then you can pack up and come home with me. Charles must be missing his sheep."

She patted Darwie and accompanied Domi and Jasmine to the table.

Eole stood, rooted, as the arrangements for his life spun out of his control. Whenever other people were involved in his plans, they always went awry. It was so much easier to live with the sheep up on the pastures. The thought of long summer days, free of confusing confrontations, made him ache. He wanted to go to the hut and think about Tintin and science. But he wanted to be with Rainbow too. He wanted to go back in time to last week, when she'd camped beside his hut and everything had been easy. In a parallel universe, that's exactly what he was doing.

"It'll be fine, Eole," whispered Rainbow. "Remember: you have the winds to manage."

He sat on Alexandra's right side, from where the commune group seemed much less intimidating than before. He answered her questions about the voices, telling her that Domi hadn't found a solution and then explaining Rainbow's theory. Nobody else was listening to them at the beginning, but as he got to the part where Rainbow was convinced the voices were the trees, he realised that everyone else was quiet. He stopped, mid-sentence, and stared at the lettuce leaf on his plate. *Itch*. His brain sent messages to his feet, telling them to uncurl their roots.

"Well, that's extraordinary," said Alexandra. She was good at filling the silences after his monologues. "It makes me think of the oak trees in the Dodona wood at home in Greece, where priests used to go to a sanctuary and listen to Zeus giving his oracles. That was before they understood there was only one God. They heard his words via the whisper of the wind in the leaves. I told you it was God speaking through nature, darling. Rainbow's almost right."

Eole wondered how to turn Alexandra's story to his advantage so she would let him stay. If he'd had Hestia in his brain, like Rainbow had Mary, she would tell him to use Alexandra's belief in God.

"That's why I need to stay here," he said. "Because Rainbow has a special tree skill and she can help me understand the voices. Between us, she and I will be able to decipher God's message. And spread God's Word," he added, as an afterthought, since it made him sound more like Père Laurent.

He felt a kick on his ankle. It couldn't be a sign because Hestia wasn't present.

"I doubt Rainbow wants to spread His word," said Alexandra.

"I *don't*," said Rainbow. "I'm far too busy."

"There you are, darling," said Alexandra. She finished her salad.

"I wonder," said Domi. He glanced from Eole to Rainbow and back again, but didn't explain what he was wondering.

Eole saw Rainbow's cumulonimbus clouds darken over Domi. It was as if she and Domi were talking together without saying any words. He thought back to what he'd read about telepathy in the Cognac library book.

"No, Domi," Rainbow said out loud. "I'm going to Massane forest with Thierry tomorrow."

"Then you have all afternoon," he replied.

"No, I don't. I'm seeing Apple and Acorn."

Domi folded his arms, looked at her and sent another telepathic message.

"It's pointless," she replied. "It couldn't possibly work."

Eole decided they were arguing about his plan to interpret the voices. "It could," he said. He stood up and pushed back his chair.

Domi told Rainbow to go on.

Alexandra told Eole to stay put.

Eole watched Rainbow roll her eyes up to the sky as if looking for help from God, which was good acting and would surely help convince Alexandra. He turned and walked towards the woods.

CHAPTER 21

Rainbow wanted to ignore Domi but, deep down, under the layers of resentment and suspicion about Eole's voices, she was curious to know what the trees were saying.

His idea probably wouldn't work, and she'd have preferred to hear the trees' voices herself. But if she did this test with him, and it succeeded, he could share their words with her. They might give her some advice, though of course the Tree Slayer would hear it too. But all this presumed his far-fetched plan was feasible. She would spare him a few minutes. Only then, if it worked, would she think about what to do next.

She sighed, stood up and joined Eole beside an alder tree in the woods.

"So what's your plan? I've only got five minutes," she said.

He checked his watch and pressed a couple of buttons before he answered: "You hug a tree and tell me what it's feeling, and I'll listen and breathe in the smell. Then you hug another tree and we do the same. Each time, I'll note the results as a correlation between the tree's feelings and the noise-smell combination I detect. After a certain number of trees

– I can't estimate how many, yet – a pattern should emerge, which will permit us to make a kind of dictionary. Let's call it a treeopedia. We don't have to analyse the source of the voices for this part of our study because we're just collecting data."

"That'll take more than five minutes."

"We'll start with a five-minute pilot test."

It sounded horribly scientific … and yet: imagine if his dictionary would allow her to understand what the trees were actually saying! But no. There was no point getting excited. The trees in Dorset had refused to respond to her gift in front of a scientist. The same was bound to happen here.

Eole took off his headphones. His face scrunched up and the colour gradually drained from it. He put his hands to his temples and didn't respond when she asked if he was all right. She'd better do this quickly.

She closed her eyes and concentrated on stroking the alder's trunk until she found the right place to lay her hands. Warmth filtered through its bark and her palms moulded its trunk. Usually, she waited while the tree's feelings permeated her – a kind of tuning-in – until she was vibrating at the same frequency as the tree. Then she would feel where it needed healing or how to shape it. This time, however, she asked it to express a single feeling.

Alders were quick trees: a feeling of speed and agility filled her.

"What you can hear and smell is quickness and lightness," she said to Eole.

There was no answer. She thanked the alder and opened her eyes. Eole was lying on the ground, a curled embryo, his hands covering his ears.

"Eole!" She crouched down. Had the trees detected the Tree Slayer inside him and punished him?

He squinted up at her. She retrieved his headphones, which were out of his reach, and put them onto his ears. He pressed them to his head with trembling hands, rolled over and shakily stood up.

"Are you OK?" she asked.

He stumbled along the track, away from the woods and towards the house. She followed.

"Eole? What happened?"

He rubbed his forehead. "There are too many voices, all shouting. And an acrid C3."

"C3?"

"It's from my classification of voice-smells. There aren't enough words to describe all of them." He looked at his watch. "We still have one minute and twenty seconds. Let's try a solitary tree."

"Forget about the five minutes. I can stay a little bit longer but I'm not sure it's a good idea. You look terrible."

He pressed a button on his watch and then pointed at her silver maple. "That one."

Rainbow felt a frisson of fear. One day, Mary might reappear. Or she may disappear completely. A few months ago, Rainbow would have been glad to see her disappear. Now, after Mary's support in the Pyrenees, she wasn't so sure she wanted to lose her. When they were in agreement, it was easy to be whole.

She stroked the silver maple's bark and let her hands rest just below the split. Eole took off his headphones and then scrunched up his face again.

"Can you hear it?" she asked.

"I can still hear all the voices shouting."

"Then come closer. You could put your ear against the bark."

"No."

"Why not? You'd hear the silver maple's voice on its own."

"I'm afraid it'll shout down my earhole. And it stinks. I don't want to stink of tree."

"Try," said Rainbow, biting back her retort that there was no better fragrance than that of trees. "You can always pull away if it's too loud."

He held his ear a few centimetres away from the trunk. "Quick! Hug it now," he said.

Rainbow closed her eyes and hugged. Mary seemed to expand in her mind, as if she were gathering strength from the tree and pushing the limit of their mental wall. Rainbow squeezed the wall back into place and concentrated on the silver maple's feelings. It was warm, comfortable and irresistibly hollow.

She became aware of Mary's yearning to melt into it. For the first time, she wondered if Mary was happy inside her. There was no reaction from Mary, other than this craving to enter the tree. Was Mary's body still stuck inside the silver maple? Could Mary rejoin it?

The maple's interior was as enticing as an empty bed when you're tired, as tempting as an open door into a cosy cottage when you've been travelling for days. It was … she tried to find a word to sum up its alluring comfort, a word she could give Eole. Yes, 'welcome'. The silver maple was emitting a feeling of welcome. She thanked it and opened her eyes.

Eole was vomiting at the foot of the tree, his headphones back on. She handed him a tissue and stood back from the repulsive smell.

"This is ridiculous. It's making you ill," she said.

"What feeling did you get?" he croaked.

"I think it was 'welcome'. But we can't carry on. It'll take a hundred years to understand their language and you'll be dead before we've got ten words."

He threw up again.

Rainbow heard a cry behind her. Alexandra was hurrying towards them.

"Mother alert," she whispered.

He sat back on his heels and wiped his face.

"Darling! I knew it! You're ill. You must come home so I can look after you properly."

He staggered to his feet. "I need to lie down," he said. "I can't face a car journey."

"It's a migraine. You haven't had one since Paris," said Alexandra. She pushed past Rainbow and led Eole back to the house.

Rainbow followed. Mum took them up to her bedroom so Eole could lie down in the coolness of the stone house. Rainbow fetched a bottle of water, took it upstairs and knocked on Mum's bedroom door. Alexandra snatched the bottle and closed the door in Rainbow's face.

🌿🌿🌿

Eole woke up to darkness. It was 1:14 a.m. His headache had passed and he was ravenous. Alexandra was stretched out on the bed beside him and Darwie lay in the corner of Jasmine's room on a blanket. Eole sat up. He was still dressed, except for his trainers.

Alexandra reached out to him. He whispered that he was going to the toilet and tiptoed out of the room.

Before going back to bed, he paused at the foot of the staircase leading to Rainbow's loft. A scratching noise came from Jasmine's room. He opened the door and Darwie nosed his way out. Eole picked up his trainers, told Darwie to lie down and crept up the staircase.

He knocked on Rainbow's door. There was no reply. He turned the handle and opened it a crack, noting how a sliver of moonlight made his hand glow white.

He whispered her name and heard her bed creak. He went and stood over her. She looked like a younger version of herself, her brown hair loose around her face. Before he could find a metaphor, her eyes opened. She stared at him, then cried out and bunched her sheet over her mouth.

"Jesus, Eole! What are you doing?"

"I'm looking at you. Shall we carry on?"

"Carry on what? It's the middle of the night."

He corrected her and then pointed out that they only had tonight to see if his idea was feasible. She argued, in a whisper, that they'd already seen it wasn't, and grumbled about having to get up at seven o'clock the next morning to meet Thierry. He told her his headache had gone and he wanted to make their treeopedia.

"You said my part in the mission was over," he added. "But maybe *this* is our real mission: to use my hearing and your understanding of trees to invent a device for translating the voices. Once we understand them, we can deduce where they come from and publish a scientific paper."

She blinked three times, then sighed and said she'd see

him in the kitchen.

He went downstairs with Darwie and made himself a cheese and ham sandwich from a stale baguette while he waited for her. He much preferred the commune at night, when everyone was in bed.

She looked a little more sparkly when she tiptoed into the kitchen, as if his mention of their mission had cheered her up, and they sneaked outside into a surprising brightness. The air was still, the sky clear and the moon almost full. Night-time here smelt of mist and pesticides as well as a mossy odour similar to Rainbow's own scent. She led him away from the woods and towards the vines, where there were fewer trees.

He listened to the voices before he put on his headphones. They were urgent whispers, rather than the aggressive shouting he'd suffered from earlier on, but they still jumbled together and made it impossible for him to isolate a single voice. Rainbow asked him if he was all right, which was pointless because of course he wasn't all right. He ignored the muted voices and concentrated on the sound of his and Rainbow's footsteps on the stony track.

An owl screeched. A kerfuffle in the hedge made them both jump, and then a fox streaked across their path. Rainbow stroked a tree that reflected the moonlight and explained that the silver birch's bark was made to reflect sunlight so that the birch didn't get too hot and dry out. Her face looked devilish in the shadows but in the light of the moon she resembled the Virgin Mary.

She stopped at a solitary evergreen oak tree and asked if he was ready to begin. He nodded, gritted his teeth and took off his headphones.

"Try hugging it," she said. Her own hands groped up and down its trunk and then she hugged it with her whole body.

Fighting his instinct to put his headphones back on, he reached out and touched the trunk with one palm.

The voice pain was no stronger.

He let his other palm rest against it. Still no pain: in fact, there was a little less pain, though it was still enough to make him nauseous. He put his arms around the trunk.

It was like opening the sluice gate at the Lac du Tech dam. The pain rushed from his head down through his arms and gushed into the tree, and the voices reduced to a burbling in the background.

From deep inside the tree came a single voice. He closed his eyes to concentrate better. It was the gravelly voice of an old man, but it was also a solo flute like the melody from Bach's Sonata in A minor. It was the smell of new grass shoots in spring and the texture of velvet water on skin. He filled his receptors with the multi-sensory pattern of the voice.

"Eole! Eole!" he heard Rainbow cry. Her voice was a thin strand compared to the complex voice coming through the tree.

He opened his eyes. "I don't want to let go. The pain has gone."

She clapped her hands and danced a sparkly kind of jig.

"I got a feeling of hope from the holm oak," she said. "Steadiness with hope sprouting all over it. Can you hear a voice?"

He fixed the voice pattern into his brain and matched it with the words 'hope' and 'steadiness'.

"OK, I've got it," he said.

She stopped dancing. "Aren't you going to write it down?"

"There aren't any words to write. Don't worry: it's safe in my head. Each time I hear that particular voice-smell I'll know it means 'hope'."

"So I don't get to see anything?"

"No."

Her sparkles dulled.

"What were you expecting to see?" he asked.

"I don't know. The phonetic spelling of the voices? Something that would help me understand them."

"But that's illogical. You can't hear or smell them. Even if I wrote down what I heard with its translation, you couldn't use it."

"I suppose not. So how will you make your device? How will I know what they're saying?"

"I don't know. I'm not at that stage of the experiment yet," he said. "Can I let go of the tree now?"

She folded her arms. "Do what you want."

"I want to carry on."

"Well, I'm going back to bed," she said.

He eased his arms away from the trunk. The other voices flooded back and the nausea returned. He retched.

"Just stop fighting them," said Rainbow.

It was like when Hestia told him to be normal: easy to say but difficult to define and therefore impossible to do. The voices weren't needling into Rainbow's brain, nagging her like a class of whining children. He held out for a few seconds, then gave up and put his headphones back on.

"I'm fine now," he said. "Please don't go. I need you."

She muttered something he couldn't hear properly, but stayed. They threaded through the woods, stopping every few metres to hug a tree together. Darwie followed them at a distance with his tail between his legs.

Rainbow's sparkles increased with each hug. She said the trees must understand his treeopedia idea because they each communicated a different feeling. Occasionally Eole sensed a pattern of voice-smells he'd experienced a few trees earlier, and he immediately knew what words Rainbow was going to give him. It was like a progress test. When two different species of tree expressed the same feeling, he could distinguish a part of the voice that was different, as if each tree had its own variant of a single melody.

After an hour, he asked if he could listen and guess before she checked, and a few times he guessed correctly. After another hour, the voices became more complicated.

He wanted to spend the rest of the night translating but Rainbow started to yawn. She laid her head against the trunk of the horse chestnut tree they'd just listened to, and told him it was time to get some sleep.

All the excitement of the past three hours together evaporated in the heat of his rising panic. She couldn't leave yet. He was just starting to appreciate the nuances within the voices.

"We must stay until we understand one hundred per cent," he said.

"Your treeopedia thing is interesting but it'll take years to understand a whole language. I need to get some sleep before I leave with Thierry tomorrow."

Eole wondered how old Thierry was and whether he would

be Rainbow's next boyfriend.

"I'm coming to the Pyrenees with Christophe in ten days' time," she added. "We'll carry on with your treeopedia then."

Eole had thought that the treeopedia mission would keep her beside him. If he couldn't persuade her with words, he would have to find another way. He might have to kidnap her and hold her hostage until she understood she was his *together*.

"Please stay," he said.

She yawned again. "One more tree, then bed."

CHAPTER 22

Under the moonlit sky, Eole followed Rainbow to the last tree. It had several trunks and Rainbow said it was an ancient yew tree. It taught him the collective noun for trees: a long, dusty, complex sound-smell that Eole had difficulty committing to memory.

He yawned. His brain was too tired to come up with a new plan to keep Rainbow beside him. He watched helplessly as she stroked the tree goodbye and turned towards Le Logis.

As he put on his headphones to follow her, there was a change of pitch in the babble of voices. A pungent odour like a rotten egg caught in his nasal receptors.

"Come on," said Rainbow. "It's almost dawn."

"Wait! Something's happening." He put his ear back to the yew's trunk. "Hug it again," he said.

She sighed and then put her hands back where they'd been. He watched her and listened, hugging too. She opened her eyes wide.

"It's changed," she whispered. "It's trying to communicate something, just like during your gale."

"Its voice has changed too. It's like the roar of the wind when you put your head out of a train window."

"I've had that feeling before," said Rainbow. "I can sense urgency."

"And I can hear the voice pattern we translated as 'one after another' earlier on."

Rainbow was hugging the yew tree hard. He copied her, closed his eyes and concentrated on a new, faint voice coming up from the tips of its roots. It was a single strand, totally different from the original voice – which implied that he was right and the voices spoke *through* the trees. This particular voice was misty, almost human, and contained the familiar smell he'd noticed when he first saw Rainbow. The voice spoke. A single word strained towards him, whipping and bending, until …

"Koad," he said.

Darwie howled. Eole opened his eyes. He'd never heard Darwie howl before. He held out a hand and Darwie slunk towards him and pressed himself hard against his legs. He started to tell Rainbow about Darwie, but stopped short. Rainbow's mouth was in an 'O' shape.

"Koad!" she said. "What do you know about Koad?"

"Nothing. I'm just repeating what the misty voice said. What is it?"

She narrowed her eyes at him, made a series of different facial expressions and then sighed. "I've no idea. Amrita said my other half would guide me to Koad."

"What's your other half?"

"I fear that *you* may be."

"No, I'm your soulmate."

"It's the same thing, Eole. Soulmate, other half, guide. You're supposed to lead me to Koad."

She didn't look very sparkly at the idea. He told her he didn't know what or where Koad was but, if it meant they could stay together, he'd look for it immediately. He added that he preferred 'soulmate' to 'other half', which was an illogical term because he was whole and Rainbow was double, given that she had Mary inside her brain too. He started to explain the details of his reasoning but she made the T-sign and asked if he'd heard any other words through the yew tree, which he hadn't. This total lack of mathematical logic on the part of Rainbow's Amrita didn't seem to bother Rainbow.

"The yew was definitely different this time around," she said. "It stood back and let something possess it, like when spirits speak through Aziz during his séances at the commune. It was a sign. It may have been Amrita, reminding me about Koad. You *must* know what Koad is. Think hard."

He'd never have forgotten such a strange word. He listened to the other voices around him while he thought. They weren't the jumble of noises he'd originally thought them to be. Each was communicating the patterns of 'Koad' and 'urgent' in its own way. It was the urgency that was making him sick.

He put his headphones on and walked a few steps one way. Then he walked the opposite way, lifting his headphones slightly away from his head so he could hear the voices without being overwhelmed by them. He turned right, backed up and turned left. He broke into a run, heading towards the commune, then stopped and listened again. Then he jogged back past Rainbow.

"What are you doing?" she asked.

It all made sense, like the pieces of a jigsaw: the voices, his special skill, Rainbow's talk about a mission, his role as her soulmate.

"This way," he said, pointing away from the commune.

"This way what?"

"The voices. I think they're telling us to go this way to reach Koad. Come with me and hug a tree. See if you get a feeling of confirmation."

Her face clouded with cumulonimbus. Her expressions shifted, as if she was having an internal conversation, and then her eyes narrowed.

"How do you know?" she said. "And how do *I* know you're telling the truth?"

He explained that the intensity of the voices was different according to which way he turned. When he turned away from the commune, towards the north, they were calmer and less urgent, whereas when he went towards the commune, they screeched 'Koad' at him in nauseating protest. It was clear. He just needed to be sure that he'd interpreted the meaning of intensity correctly and he could only do that if she helped him.

"This is it! Our *together* mission," he added. "We must follow the voices to Koad."

She swore, muttered something about Thierry, and then turned and walked back towards the commune.

❧

He followed her. Of course he followed her. Getting rid of him was like trying to pull chewing gum from her hair: the more she yanked at it, the tighter it clung.

It wasn't fair. Any doubt about Eole being her soulmate had been eradicated when he'd spoken the word 'Koad'. But he didn't know anything about it. Where was the enlightenment she'd hoped for? Of course she wanted to heal the last One Tree and save Amrita. But if Amrita expected her to give up her exciting future with Thierry for the mission, she could at least have given her the power to carry it out alone. Instead, she was supposed to follow in Eole's shadow: Eole, who could control the winds and hear the trees' voices but who didn't even care about them. She, Rainbow, was the trees' friend, not Eole.

If she went with him – having no idea of the distance, or whether it was a trap laid by the Tree Slayer – she would let Thierry down, once again. He'd warned her that he wouldn't take any more nonsense from her. If she left with Eole, Thierry would never forgive her.

A potion of frustration boiled inside her, releasing fumes of resistance: this was a plot for the Tree Slayer to kill her before she could heal the One Tree and restore Amrita; the true path lay with Thierry in Massane; Christophe would hate her going away with Eole; Alexandra would never let Eole go anywhere with her.

Perhaps Koad could wait until she returned from Massane. But Amrita had told her to hurry, and both Rainbow and Eole had understood the yew tree's message of urgency. Amrita had also told her to trust the trees.

Mary would want her to stay with Christophe. Rainbow tensed in preparation for her protest but she was silent. In fact, Rainbow hadn't felt anything from her since they'd hugged the silver maple. Was she still there or had she disappeared into the tree?

It wasn't the moment to wonder about Mary. This was a crisis point in her mission. It was obvious what she had to do, whether Mary liked it or not: she must follow Eole to Koad. Now the Tree Slayer knew her destination, she'd have to be really careful. There was no need to tell Eole about her task in Koad. The less information he passed to the Tree Slayer, the better.

Back at the commune, Eole followed her indoors.

"Get some sleep," she whispered to him when she reached the landing. "We have some tough work tomorrow to convince Alexandra."

He nodded and went into the bedroom. She climbed the stairs to the loft, wondering if he understood that she'd made her decision, or even that she had a decision to make.

A few hours later she hit her alarm clock and dragged open her eyes. The bag she'd packed for Massane sat beside her drawing desk.

Koad.

Her surge of excitement was dampened by the prospect of the tasks immediately ahead of her. She felt as if she were in prison and could see a forest of freedom laid out before her, but had to climb the barbed wire fence before she could reach the trees.

The first task was Thierry. It would be easy to ring him and say she was ill. She looked at herself in the mirror as she brushed her teeth. She'd feel worse in the long term if she lied. She left a note on the kitchen table telling Eole not to leave before she returned, and then drove to Thierry's house.

Thierry had always been understanding. He'd accepted her way of treating trees when no other tree surgeon would consider her applications and had forgiven her when she'd disappeared to the Val d'Azun for a week. He'd trained her and encouraged her and taken her into his life like a daughter.

Rainbow nodded when he reminded her of this. She nodded when he said he was disappointed in her. She sighed when he said she was throwing away her future and that voices from the trees sounded like hippie nonsense. And she dug her fingernails into her thighs when he told her that if she left, he'd be obliged to revoke his offer of sponsorship.

She apologised again and said goodbye. His disapproval hung over her. If Eole didn't lead her to Koad, she really would kill him. She slumped into the Mini and drove towards the motorbike shop. What was Christophe going to say?

A tall, blonde girl was walking up the street. Rainbow parked the car and watched her approach. It had to be Emilie. Rainbow sank down in the seat and tried to hide, which was impossible in a Mini, even for someone who was only five feet tall. Emilie looked up at the sky as she walked. There was the freshness of a little girl about her and she looked dreamy, smiling away at the clouds scudding across the sky. She was probably daydreaming about gears, engine oil and the greasy innards of motorbikes. Or, more likely, she was looking forward to spending the day with Christophe.

Rainbow should get out and face her. That's what Mary – wherever she was – would do.

Emilie passed the Mini without spotting her. Rainbow angled the rear-view mirror towards herself. She looked awful, with bags under her eyes and a spot welling right in the middle of one cheek. She sighed and smoothed down her boring brown hair.

Emilie didn't stop at the back door to the motorbike shop, but went around the corner towards Christophe's front door. Rainbow jumped out of the car and followed her.

Emilie rang Christophe's doorbell. Rainbow took a deep breath and walked up to the door. She managed a cool hello to Emilie and rang Christophe's bell too. Then she stepped up onto the doorstep so she was the same height as Emilie and fixed her eyes on the white plastic button with Christophe's name written under it in his childish handwriting. She had no idea how to start a conversation. It was much more difficult than approaching strangers in the Val d'Azun.

"You're Rainbow, aren't you?" said Emilie in a little-girl voice.

"Yes."

"I'm Emilie, Christophe's apprentice," she said with a smile. "I recognised you from the photo in Chris's wallet. He's always talking about you."

Rainbow smiled back. That had to be a good thing, didn't it?

The intercom clicked and Christophe's voice greeted them. He sounded sleepy.

"Just your wake-up buzz," said Emilie. "And Rainbow's here for you."

"Rainbow?" Christophe's voice brightened and he said he was on his way.

Emilie's smile disappeared. She no longer looked dreamy. "He's crazy about you. Don't hurt him, OK?"

How dare Emilie judge her? Of course she wouldn't hurt

him. Before Rainbow could think of a cutting retort, Emilie had gone. Where was sarcastic Mary when Rainbow needed her?

Christophe pulled open the door and swept her into a bear hug. She clung onto him. If only they could stay like this forever. Once she'd finished her mission, she would spend all the time in the world with him. She followed him upstairs, fed Apple and Acorn and, after putting it off for as long as possible, told him about her night-time research and Eole's conviction that he could lead her to Koad.

"What about Massane? How long would this trip to Koad take?"

"I don't know. Eole doesn't know."

He folded his arms. "I think it's a terrible idea. I know this Amrita thing is important to you, but you can't give up a career opportunity for something so vague. What would Thierry say if he knew you were thinking of letting him down again?"

She looked at her feet. She should have talked to Christophe first.

"I don't believe it! You've already told him!" He sat down, suddenly. "Don't I mean anything to you? I thought we were together, that we discussed stuff. We're supposed to be going on holiday at the end of next week and now you're heading off with another guy for God knows how long. How's that supposed to make me feel?"

"Don't be jealous –"

"Of course I'm jealous. I love you! But I'm not sure I understand you anymore."

"I love you too. I'm not going off with another guy, Chris. It's only Eole. There's nothing between us. Anyway, we'll probably be back in a couple of days. I'm the only one who can save Amrita and Domi says that if she dies, my own life is at risk."

"Domi? Huh. He knows nothing for real. Can't Koad wait until after our holiday?"

She shook her head. "I'm really sorry, but I have to do this now. I'll be back before next Friday."

Christophe stood up. "Fine. Do what you want." He opened his bedroom door.

"Chris! Please–"

"I'm getting ready for work. Have fun with Eole." He went into his bedroom and closed the door.

She sighed. There was nothing else she could do to reassure Christophe, not unless she changed her mind. A half-hearted kick of resistance came from Mary's side. So she *was* still there. Rainbow waited, expecting demands to go after Chris and make amends. But nothing more came from Mary. Rainbow picked up Acorn and nuzzled the kitten's soft fur, a double dose of despair overwhelming her. Mary couldn't be bothered to argue. She'd given up on Rainbow and it felt even worse than her former antagonism.

Rainbow waited for a few minutes, hoping Christophe would come out again and apologise for being moody, but he didn't. He'd given up on her too. She took one of the photos of them from the mirror frame and left.

Outside, Emilie was leaning against the wall and smoking. Perfect. All Rainbow needed was for Emilie to console Christophe while she was gone. Emilie called goodbye, but Rainbow pretended she hadn't heard. She didn't want Emilie to guess she'd argued with Christophe.

She kept her brimming eyes fixed on the ground and concentrated on the image Amrita had promised if she succeeded: of halcyon days, revelling, hand in hand, in the dappled sunlight of spring-green woodlands. It was Amrita's way of saying that if Rainbow succeeded, she would never be alone again: that Amrita would always be with her.

Eole was still here, of course, so she wasn't totally alone – though Eole's company didn't make up for Christophe or Mary. She must put all thoughts of them aside and complete the last part of her mission. Now she'd identified her other half and neutralised the Tree Slayer, only Koad remained.

CHAPTER 23

Eole's dream of an earthquake woke him on Thursday morning and he opened his eyes to find Alexandra shaking his shoulder. He pushed her hand off and rolled over.

"How do you feel?" she asked.

"Terrible," he mumbled. "Let me sleep."

Later, he was woken by whispers. He heard Alexandra say she was reluctant to wake him but had to get home for the goats and to take him to his doctor. She was talking to a woman – Eole wasn't sure which one because they all smelt of lavender – who intervened with little noises. Listening noises, Alexandra called them. But the rhythm of the conversation was too one-sided. The other woman should speak more, not just make noises. Alexandra's whispers continued, saying that even though he was more at ease here than she'd expected, she wouldn't be reassured until he was safely back in the valley.

He must have dozed off because he woke in the middle of a whispered sentence about Hestia, about Hestia's problem, about having to get back for her. He opened his eyes. The other woman was Jasmine.

"What's the matter with Hestia?" he asked.

"Darling! You're awake."

He repeated his question but Alexandra swept it away, saying Hestia was fine and wanted him to come home. He told her his headache was better, that he'd needed to catch up with his sleep because he'd been outside with Rainbow all night, and that now it was time for them to get back to work on the treeopedia, which meant he couldn't go back to the mountains with her but that he would ring Hestia this evening at six o'clock and he didn't need to see a doctor and now he must get up and have a shower so could they please leave him alone.

Alexandra and Jasmine exchanged a glance. Exchanged glances meant that the people knew something he didn't. He sat up.

"She hasn't left, has she? Rainbow?"

"She did, but she's back again," said Jasmine. "I'll go and tell her you're awake."

She left and Alexandra sat down on the edge of the double bed. "Listen, darling. I'm not happy about you staying here. They're completely scatty. Half of them seem to be drugged up to their eyeballs or in trances or something. All that black and purple make-up is unnatural. And those little ones, running wild! It's not a healthy environment. Goodness knows how the poor goats survive."

"It's OK. I'm not staying here."

Alexandra opened her mouth and closed it again, which meant she was confused.

"I mean I'm going on a mission," he said. "With Rainbow. That's why she's still here. She's waiting for me."

"A mission? No, darling. I'm sorry, but it's not possible. Definitely no mission. That's even worse than staying here. The only place you're going is home."

Her coaxing tone had changed into her steamroller voice. He'd heard it a lot at bedtime when he was younger and hadn't finished the book he was reading. She'd never understood that he needed to have the whole book in his head before he slept. If he didn't, his brain would turn in circles trying to fit the pieces together and his mind would end up inventing the missing parts. The following day, after finishing the book, he'd have difficulty pasting the information from the book over the top of the information his mind had created, and whenever he thought about the subject from the book he was never sure which was the proper information and which was the invented bit. Not knowing brought on *itch, shuffle and escape*.

She always got her way when she used her steamroller voice.

"Have your shower, and then we're leaving," she said.

There was a tap at the door and Rainbow asked if she could come in.

"Yes," said Eole, at the same time as Alexandra barked "No."

Rainbow opened the door and let in Darwie, who came and licked his hand. She looked sparkly around the edges and worried in the centre. She asked how he was, which didn't feel intrusive like when Alexandra had asked him, because behind her words she was actually asking if he still felt treesick and if he was ready to get back to work – and she was also showing that she hadn't changed her mind and was prepared for their mission. He was getting good at subtext. Hestia would be impressed.

Alexandra told Rainbow that Eole was as well as could

be expected and that they were leaving. Rainbow explained to Alexandra that she wanted to go away for a few days with him, and that she would look after him and make sure he rang home regularly. She added that he'd been fine so far with her, and that he hadn't had an episode since they'd been together because of a reiki technique she'd taught him.

That part was probably a mistake, because Alexandra's eyes went all squinty at the word 'reiki' and she broke the conversation rhythm by interrupting. Then she started to steamroll Rainbow.

Rainbow interrupted back, which was fair enough. She said, "I've given up my job and my boyfriend for this mission, so don't stop us now," and Alexandra said, "That's your problem. You should have consulted me first," and Rainbow argued back and Alexandra's voice got louder and Eole's feet started to itch and then Jasmine came in, and Rainbow talked about 'destiny' with Jasmine, who nodded and went away, which was lucky because Alexandra didn't like 'destiny' either and started talking about being in God's hands, and suddenly he was outside walking along the track with Darwie, but then Alexandra's lilac and Rainbow's woody-mossy scents got stronger and he started to run and he wished Hestia was in his brain with him because she would know how to hide, and then he saw the yew tree and he hugged it, and it felt good and he stopped thinking about Alexandra and Rainbow and listened to the music of the voice coming through the tree instead.

Although Rainbow wasn't fit, and had stopped to pick up Eole's headphones, she outran Alexandra. There was no sign of Eole. He would be sick again if she didn't find him soon. If only she could hear the trees' voices, they might tell her where he was. Maybe Eole could teach her to listen to them.

She reached the site of last night's treeopedia work and had just decided to ask a tree for help when she saw him. He was hugging the yew tree with Darwie at his feet. Of course: he wouldn't be sick as long as he concentrated on a single voice. She slowed down, puffing, and kicked through the undergrowth as she approached.

He opened his eyes. "You didn't need to make extra noise. I could smell you."

She grimaced. It would be disgusting to smell people. Her gift may not be so powerful but at least it didn't make her ill or force her to put up with vile odours.

She wiped the sweat off her forehead and handed him his headphones. He put them on and started expounding on how tree-hugging was even better for *itch, shuffle and escape* than her reiki roots trick. She made the T-sign.

"We've got to decide what to do," she said. "The others will be here in a minute. Alexandra will never let you go so the only solution is to sneak away. Are you happy to do that?"

"Yes."

"Sure?"

He nodded. "I want to stay with you and protect you one hundred per cent from the Tree Slayer and go on our *together* mission and find this Koad."

"Cool. So let's do it. We must be quick. Which way are the trees telling us to go?"

Eole held his headphones a little way from his ears and walked northwards through the wood. Darwie whined at his heels. Eole turned his head from side to side and then stopped at a birch tree and hugged it. Rainbow caught up with him, found the tree's communication spots and was overwhelmed by a sense of purpose, a sense of rightness and also a sense of a shady holloway path leading to the horizon.

"It feels like a long way. We'll have to borrow Mum's Mini," she said while Eole added the entry to his mental treeopedia.

"No. We must stay in contact with the trees. We have to walk."

"But it may be miles! I've got to be back next week for my holiday with Christophe."

He gave her one of his inscrutable looks. She sighed. At least the ground would be flatter here than in the mountains.

"OK, I suppose you're right," she said. "We'd better pack. We'll go the back way so we don't bump into Alexandra."

They followed a deer path through the woods, which took them to the front of the house. Nobody was outside. They were either at spiritual sessions indoors or had followed Alexandra along the track. She told Eole to pack his rucksack, then went indoors and tiptoed upstairs to her room. She stuffed her purse, minimal camping equipment, map, compass and sketch pad into her backpack. Although she tried to hurry, her movements were slow, as if Mary were physically manifesting her reluctance to leave. Rainbow hesitated over her tree book but it was too big and heavy to take. She picked up her walking boots, shouldered her rucksack and crept downstairs for food and water.

She tiptoed past Domi's consulting room and paused. Mary

didn't want her to go in. Rainbow lifted a heavy arm and tapped on the door.

Ignoring Mary's reticence, she briefed Domi on Eole's discovery, on her certainty that he was her other half and on their plan to find Koad.

He nodded and tapped his lips with the pen he was holding. "I knew you might leave with Eole. It was one of the futures Sandrine predicted for you. She shouldn't have told me but she doesn't understand confidentiality yet."

"One of the futures? What were the others?"

"You'll have to ask Sandrine," said Domi. He shuffled through a drawer, putting papers into a brown envelope.

"I don't have time to see her. Alexandra will be back any minute."

Domi stood up. "Then go with my blessing," he said. "It's not always reassuring to know what may happen. I'll deal with Alexandra, as long as you promise to keep in contact so she knows Eole is safe. This will be good for him. And for you. Destiny, remember?"

She thanked him and they kissed goodbye. "Take this," he said. "It may be useful."

She took his envelope, backed out of the room and filled up her rucksack with bread, cheese, salad and a bottle of water from the kitchen. When she glanced out of the window, she saw Alexandra approaching the commune from the track. She hurried to Eole's camp. Everything was packed and he was standing with his rucksack on, Darwie at his heels.

"Let's go," she said.

Chopin's Funeral March floated into her mind. Mary may have given up on her, but she still didn't want her to leave home.

PART III

WHOLE

CHAPTER 24

Eole and Darwie followed Rainbow to a hole in the hedge.

"This way. Quick," she said. She squeezed through the whippy hazel branches, her rucksack and Mary's resistance making her as slow as a tortoise.

Eole told Darwie to go through first, but he whined and cowered back. Eole raised his voice. Darwie whined again, then turned and streaked back towards Le Logis. Eole stared. Darwie had never disobeyed an order before.

"Come on, Eole, before they see us."

He whistled at Darwie, who ignored him.

"Let him go," said Rainbow. "He hates it when you use your gifts, anyway."

Eole pulled himself through the bushes and joined Rainbow on the other side. Darwie belonged with him but the poor dog hadn't seen a sheep for four days. He'd be happier at the farm, where he also belonged.

From the commune garden came the sound of Alexandra's voice. Eole put on his headphones and shut out the temptation to follow Darwie back to the mountains.

They crept along the length of the hedge and reached the birch tree in the woods behind the commune. Eole lifted his headphones from his ears and listened, then took the map and compass from Rainbow's rucksack pocket. The daytime voices were louder, perhaps because of the competition from the tractors in the vineyards, the birdcalls and the occasional small aircraft passing overhead. He could still hear the Koad pattern, and although the wind had risen and changed direction, he was relieved to note that the voices were still guiding him northwards and slightly west. If the voices were the wind talking through the trees to him, its message was consistent. But he mustn't analyse the origin of voices during the data collection stage of their treeopedia experiment: that could only come once he'd collected sufficient data.

Rainbow took off her rucksack and hugged the birch. Yesterday's feeling of purpose and distance was tinged with something new and she sensed a tender green shoot reaching up towards the sun. She told Eole to listen-smell, and they added 'enthusiastic' to his treeopedia. The birch was weak from an infestation of gall midges but she didn't have time to heal it.

"Which way now?" she asked.

Eole continued in the direction he'd taken before they'd packed. It was difficult to concentrate on the Koad strand in the voices. Sickness rose in his throat at the discordant interruptions. He reached out his hand for Darwie's muzzle, forgetting that Darwie had deserted him.

Rainbow noticed his face getting whiter as he turned this way and that. It would take them forever to find Koad if he threw up and then had to sleep for hours. She suggested he touch the trees as he passed and, when he did so, he said he felt better. She trailed her hands over the trunks too, remembering how Amrita had led her out of the gale-struck park. Soon, they would reach Koad and she would see Amrita again. She needed to think about the next stage of her mission, which involved saving the last One Tree so that Amrita would be restored. But Eole had no idea where Koad was. "Trust the trees," she muttered to herself. Although she suspected her destination was a special tree, like the François I oak, she mustn't make assumptions. She would trust the trees to tell her when the time was right.

At first it was pleasant in the shady woods, apart from the mosquito bites. But as she wandered along behind Eole, she started to get bored. Eole was busy listening to the trees while she traipsed after him with nothing to do. This was even worse than making his treeopedia: at least she played a part in that. Now, she was useless, just as her gift was useless compared to his.

They reached the edge of the wood without arriving at Koad. There was a strong headwind and a small road lay ahead. Two vineyards, separated by a row of small fruit trees, stretched beyond them. Eole took off his headphones and Rainbow looked around, wondering where the voices would send them.

"Are you sure we didn't miss Koad?" she asked.

Before Eole could tell her he was sure, he heard a car approach and smelt its fumes. It was a diesel.

"Quick! Hide," said Rainbow. She swung off her rucksack and crouched behind a clump of blackthorn.

Eole remained standing.

"It's OK. It isn't Alexandra," he said.

The car passed. Rainbow glared at him. "What if you'd been wrong and it *had* been her?"

"She would have seen us and stopped and then steamrolled me into getting into the car and going home and our mission to find Koad would have been over. But I wasn't wrong. Alexandra's car has a petrol engine."

He crossed the road, continuing the northwestward line the compass had shown from the start. The voices from the woods were a quiet chatter behind him and a sweet-smelling Koad call beckoned him through the vineyards. He reached the source of the call and found squashed, mouldering plums on the ground and ripe plums on a tree. A few green peaches hung from its neighbour. Rainbow reached out to pick the plums, but she was too small. She swore. He pulled down a branch so she could gather them, wondering what had made her cross, and they drank some water as they ate them.

"This had better be the right way," she said, wiping her mouth on her bare arm.

"It is. We must keep going to the copse over there. They'll tell us where to go afterwards."

A gust blew tendrils of Rainbow's hair into her mouth. She brushed them off and chastised the wind.

"Come on. We haven't got all day," she said.

She didn't wait for him, but leant forward into the wind and walked on.

Eole puzzled over her words, knowing they *had* got all day. Hestia was grumpy when she was tired, so maybe that was Rainbow's problem. He could help. He'd promised her he wouldn't use his special skill to make a gale again, but she hadn't forbidden him to use it. He stepped back from the tree, took a breath flavoured with conifer and pesticide and blew gently towards the copse.

Rainbow tripped forwards, her arms flailing in the suddenly still air. She regained her balance, turned around and saw Eole facing her. He stood like a singer, his lips pursed.

"Hey! You almost made me fall over."

He closed his mouth and looked down at his feet. She sighed. Amrita had told her to be patient.

"It's all right," she said to Eole. "Carry on blowing if you like. But next time warn me first, OK?"

Eole nodded. She still looked grumpy but, if he helped her whenever he could, as well as protecting her one hundred per cent so she didn't die on their mission, her sparkles would hopefully return.

They continued walking, Rainbow in front of him, and he pushed her gently along with his stream of air. Each time a car came, Rainbow told him to hide, which he did, even though he knew it wasn't Alexandra. Whenever they left a wood, the voices guided him from tree to tree – many of which, Rainbow pointed out, had been uprooted by his gale – until they reached the next copse or forest.

He studied the map regularly and marked the places they passed. During each break, he added more words to his treeopedia, and then Rainbow healed some damaged trees while he shaped clouds. It wasn't as satisfying as cloud art with Tintin in the mountains, because the clouds were further away. Tintin was further away too, but the mapopedia was still strong in Eole's mind. And now he had the treeopedia to work on. As the hours passed and he untangled the threads of the voices, he felt less sick.

At five o'clock Rainbow stopped at the far edge of a wood, shrugged off her rucksack and declared she was too tired to continue. The terrain was flatter than the mountains but their stopping and starting, coupled with the lack of sleep, made it a hundred times more exhausting.

Eole looked at his map. They were still two kilometres from a village. *Itch*. They couldn't stop walking. Not yet. Not until they found a telephone box. He reminded Rainbow that he'd promised to call Hestia, but Rainbow didn't understand the importance of six o'clock and lay spreadeagled on the dry grass, groaning. *Shuffle*.

He explained that Alexandra would be home by now and would have told Hestia he'd ring, and that Hestia would be waiting beside the phone, and that he had to check she was all right, and if he promised to do something at a certain time he had to do it, and—

Rainbow made the T-sign and sighed. "OK. We need to buy food and find somewhere to camp, anyway."

She'd only nibbled at the bread and cheese she'd taken from Le Logis kitchen, but Eole had already wolfed down everything, including the salad she'd brought for their evening meal. He ate even more than Christophe. She wondered whether Christophe was still angry with her and decided to ring him after Eole had spoken to Hestia.

She struggled to her sore feet. A massage would be bliss, but Eole was hardly going to touch her. He showed her the map and as she rubbed her shoulders she tried to visualise the way to the village.

"Why don't you just ask the trees to tell us the way?" she

said. "Since you're privy to their conversations."

"We haven't got time."

His gift was wasted on him. If she heard the trees' voices, she'd be deep in conversation with them by now – though of course Eole could hear them but not speak to them.

"If I speak to them and you listen, we'll find the village between us," she said.

She ran her hands over the trunk of a fir tree and found its communication spots. She emptied her mind and let its sap beat fill her, and then asked the way to the village. She understood nothing in reply, though she could feel the tree's parched thirst and its discomfort, its dreams of mountain mists and cool nights. She stroked it and opened her eyes, hoping Eole had caught some sound or smell he could follow.

He wasn't touching the tree. She let go of the trunk and looked around. He was a hundred metres away, his headphones back on, walking towards a road.

"Eole!" she yelled. It was maddening to have to rely on him.

He didn't turn around.

She swore and trudged after him.

CHAPTER 25

Eole waited for Rainbow on the outskirts of the village. She scowled at him as she took the lead and he followed her past the houses and into the centre, keeping his eyes fixed on a swinging strap on the back of her rucksack.

They arrived at a telephone box just before six o'clock. A single shop served as a bar, newsagent, tobacconist and supermarket. While Eole dumped his rucksack outside the telephone box, Rainbow went inside to buy some tins of ravioli and to ask if there was a campsite nearby.

Eole opened the telephone box door and discovered that the telephone didn't take coins. He had no phone card. *Itch*. It was five to six. His feet started to shuffle and he forced them to take him towards the shop rather than back the way they'd come. He hovered outside, looking through the window at Rainbow laughing with a woman at the counter. She hadn't laughed with him all day. He willed her to turn around and see him. Four minutes to six. Three minutes. He banged on the door.

Rainbow heard a thud, turned around and saw an agitated

Eole outside. She sighed. What was his problem now? He was even more demanding than the commune kids, and she was enjoying a much-needed social chat with the shopkeeper. She excused herself and opened the door. A trickle of sweat ran down the side of Eole's face. He shoved a twenty-franc note into her hand and asked her to buy him a phone card.

"Do it yourself," she said. That would teach him to ignore her suggestion to ask the trees for directions.

"I can't." Two minutes to six. "I don't know the shop or the shopkeeper, and I don't have time to work out what I would say and what she might say and what she might mean and how I would reply in each case and what I would do if she doesn't have the twenty-franc card and–"

She made the T-sign. "Jesus, Eole! It's not exactly hard." She went back inside.

One minute left. The shop door opened. He snatched one of the cards in her hand and raced over to the phone box. He had twenty seconds advance. He watched the numbers on his watch count down and then, three seconds before the hour, punched in Hestia's number.

Alexandra answered the phone. She didn't even wait for him to introduce himself, as she'd taught him to do, but ranted about being worried about him and angry about Rainbow's deceit. His brain listened, but in his mind he wondered how she had known it would be him on the phone and what she would have done if it had been someone else. Phoning was easy, if he closed his eyes, because there were no distractions. But it meant he had to concentrate hard to pick up extra signals in people's voices.

When she'd finished ranting she asked where he was.

Rainbow had warned him about this question, and he replied that he was safe and well but couldn't tell her and that he wanted to speak to Hestia because he didn't have much money and he couldn't give her his number or she may work out where he was. Alexandra started to make excuses about Hestia not feeling well, but then her voice faded out. There were some muffled bangs.

"Hey, big bro," said Hestia.

Eole smiled and smiled and then realised she couldn't see him smiling and he said, "Hey, little sis," and then his brain pointed out that she wasn't actually his little sister anymore and his mind unrolled all the unsettling thoughts tied to the word 'adopted' instead of listening to her.

When he caught up with her speech, she was telling him about how Alexandra had tried to set Darwie on Eole's tracks to find him but that he'd been useless and was now sitting looking sorry for himself in his basket. Her voice got gradually quieter and then she said that she missed him, and stopped talking. She didn't say 'over' like she normally did when it was his turn to speak on the phone, but he'd had so much conversation practice with Rainbow that he knew it was his turn. His mind projected an image of Darwie rounding up the sheep instead of sitting in his basket, which made him feel better, and he asked Hestia why Alexandra had said she was ill.

Hestia told him to wait a minute. Her voice started to judder, which meant she was walking. He heard a door slam, followed by the beeps that signalled the phone card was running out. Her voice was breathy in his ear.

"Actually, there's a bit of a situation here," she said.

This was Hestia's way of saying there was a big problem, because she was totally illogical with her choice of expressions. He opened his mouth to tell her to hurry up but she was already speaking again.

"Maman told me not to tell you, but she hasn't got a clue about important stuff. And Papa, well, he's Papa, so I can't talk to him. It's just that, well, I seem to be pregnant. Over."

An image of Dizzy with a swollen belly hanging down, bleating plaintively, came into Eole's mind. He couldn't match this picture with Hestia. There was a compatibility problem.

"Pregnant with a baby?" he said.

"Of course! What else would I be pregnant with? Eole? Are you still there? Over."

The beeps cut in again.

"Eole! Say something. I need to talk to someone who's not going to get all Catholic on me. Do you think I'm a slut? It was an accident. I think it happened at Caroline's party. Someone put vodka–"

The line went dead. The deadness of it filled his ear and he didn't know if he was relieved or frustrated that the phone units had all gone, and he didn't know if he should buy another card and call her back or not, and he didn't know if it was a good thing or a bad thing that Hestia was pregnant, but he did know that she was on her own with her parents and that even if he wasn't her brother, he was her brother and she needed him and Darwie missed him and he wasn't there. But Rainbow needed him too and he was here and it was complicated and his whole body felt as if it were going to split in two directions and he didn't know which part to jump into and he didn't know, he just didn't know.

Rainbow stuffed the ravioli tins into her rucksack outside the shop and was strapping a baguette to the top of it when she heard a bang from the telephone box. She saw Eole push open the cabin door, leaving the telephone handset swinging on the end of its cable.

"Eole?"

He walked away in a straight line along the middle of the road. She grabbed his rucksack, dropped it beside hers and asked the shopkeeper to look after them. Without waiting for an answer, she sprinted after Eole.

He stopped at the far end of the street, which was a T-junction, and stood in the centre of the road without turning either way.

She was nearly there. But a rumble of an engine was coming from around the corner ahead.

"Eole! Car!"

He didn't move.

"Eole! Get on the pavement!" she shouted.

There was no reaction from Eole. The driver wouldn't see him until it was too late. She would never reach him in time.

The car rounded the bend. She forced a final acceleration from her legs and pushed Eole towards the pavement. He stumbled and fell into the gutter. She tumbled over him and the car screeched to a stop.

She rolled onto her side, panting, and rubbed her knees.

Eole sat up and then stood. He looked around at the houses and street he'd never seen, and at the purple 2CV parked at an angle across the road. He turned over his hurting hands and smelt grit and blood on the palms, mixed with burnt rubber in the air. His head hurt but it was a thinking pain rather than a bruise. He asked Rainbow what had happened.

"I should be the one asking that question," she said.

An old man in flip-flops climbed out of the 2CV and asked them if they were all right. Rainbow reassured him. He apologised and helped her up before returning to his car and parking safely.

Rainbow turned back to Eole and asked what was going on but he refused to answer.

"Suit yourself," she said. He didn't even thank her for saving his life. The sooner they reached Koad and she could be rid of him, the better.

The driver returned, commented on how he'd never seen them in the village before, and asked if they were travellers needing a lift somewhere. The twinkle in his eyes as he said the word 'travellers' encouraged Rainbow to explain they were on a walking holiday and were looking for somewhere to camp. The shopkeeper had told her there were no campsites until the next town, which was too far to reach today.

"Come and camp at my farm. It's the least I can do after nearly running you over."

Rainbow didn't bother to consult Eole, who was staring at his feet. She accepted. The man, who introduced himself as Gabin, took them back to the shop for their rucksacks and then on to his farm a few kilometres away.

Eole was silent in the back seat the whole way. Gabin invited them to eat with him, and although Eole shook his head, Rainbow accepted. Why should she deprive herself of company just because Eole was locked in his head? They set up camp in silence and then Eole zipped himself inside his tent.

Rainbow looked at the solitary oak tree in the middle of their field and wondered if she should persuade Eole to talk to her. She asked him a few questions through the tent about his phone call but he didn't answer. If something was bothering him, he should tell her, not brood on his own.

She suddenly felt as solitary as the oak tree. Eole was sulking and she hadn't detected any feelings from her Mary side all day, not since Chopin's Funeral March. This wasn't how she'd envisaged finding Koad by her soulmate's side.

She hugged her loneliness into the oak tree's trunk, pushing imaginary roots into the ground between the real roots. She let the aches in her shoulders and the soreness in her feet flow down into the earth, and drew in the oak's reassurance. It seemed to hug her back. Thank goodness for trees. Humans were fickle but she could always trust a tree to be there when she needed it.

When she felt strong again, she washed in the cobwebby barn sink and then went indoors to help Gabin prepare their evening meal.

🌿🌿🌿

After serving dinner in his 1970s orange and yellow kitchen, Gabin wiped the waxed tablecloth and took one of many spiral-bound notebooks from a shelf. He'd been a traveller before settling down, alone, in his smallholding, and these were his travel logs.

Rainbow sat beside him, turned over the pages and studied the ink sketches and perfect French lettering. Each picture, though basic, was a story in itself, and she listened, fascinated, as he opened his other logbooks and described his trips to

Iceland, Indonesia and South America.

While Rainbow was stepping inside a groaning glacier in the Torres del Paine National Park and gazing at the bright blue ice above her, there was a bang outside the back door. Gabin stopped talking and hobbled towards it, bringing Rainbow back to France with a jolt. Had the shopkeeper told Alexandra where they were? She looked for a place to hide.

When Gabin opened the door, there was no one outside. He bent down with difficulty and picked up an empty plate from the doorstep. The noise must have been Eole: he'd refused to come and eat with them and she'd left his plate of duck breast and sauté potatoes outside his tent.

"He's rather shy, your young man."

"I'd better check he's all right." Rainbow took the plate from Gabin and washed it up, along with the other dishes. "Thanks for showing me your travel logs. They're beautiful."

Gabin stacked them carefully back on the shelf. "Are you keeping a record of your trip?"

"No. Ours is nothing like as exciting as yours."

"Well, I think you should, especially as you're an artist. It'll help make your surroundings more interesting as you walk. Then you can share your entries with the people who lodge you on the way. And when you're old, like me, you'll be able to look back and remember moments you'd forgotten."

Rainbow dried her hands. It was a good idea. She may only fill two pages of her sketch pad, but it would give her something to do while Eole pored over the map.

"Here, take this," Gabin said, and handed her an empty log book. "My travels stopped before I could use this one. If you ever come back this way, call in and tell me about your trip."

Rainbow thanked him and said goodnight. It was only when she'd shut the door behind her that she realised she'd forgotten to call Christophe. She'd find a phone box tomorrow – by which time he'd surely have calmed down.

It was cool and hardly dark, thanks to the moon. She rubbed her goose-pimply arms and walked around the corner of the barn towards the tents.

There was only one tent.

Eole had packed up and gone.

Rainbow gasped. Hestia and Alexandra would kill her. This was her fault. She had left him alone all evening, knowing something was wrong. Had she been secretly glad he was suffering? She must stop envying him for being able to hear the trees talking. He may be more powerful but he was hopeless alone. He relied on her for their decisions. And he was all she'd got.

She tossed Gabin's notebook into her tent, scrabbled around for her head torch and jogged down the drive. Her legs were stiff and she slowed down to a limping walk, looking left and right into the fields and clumps of trees.

Thierry had talked about trees helping each other to survive, calling forests 'symbiotic communities'. He'd also said she was too much of a loner and could learn from the way trees worked together. She and Eole were symbiotic, like two trees. They should be a team. What had she been thinking, letting him stew alone in his tent all evening? Her jealousy had blinded her to the danger of him getting upset. She had to find him before he raised a storm and allowed the Tree Slayer to kill the One Tree.

How long ago had he knocked on Gabin's kitchen door?

Surely not more than ten minutes? Any second now she would find him.

CHAPTER 26

Eole stumbled into a pot hole and fell over. Darkness on the plains was much harder to navigate than darkness in the mountains, and he wished he hadn't taken the short cut along the track. Maps should show the conditions of tracks rather than perfect lines that looked so easy to follow.

Ahead of him was a tunnel where tree branches met above the track. It was oppressive and smelt of leaf mould and brooding power. They'd found a passage like this earlier on and Rainbow had called it a 'holloway'. Her eyes had sparkled and, for some reason he couldn't fathom, she'd dropped her rucksack and done a row of untidy cartwheels down the centre. Then she'd had to go all the way back to pick up her rucksack, which had wasted time.

He took out his torch and carried on towards the holloway. He wished he was following Tintin, or that Darwie was by his side. Although the voices were a manageable whisper at night, he didn't like the dank smell of the close-knit community ahead. His headphones might be necessary.

The voices in the holloway trees were muttering to each

other like the chicken chatter in the battery house he'd once visited. He switched on his torch. Everything outside its circle immediately became darker and more menacing. He put on his headphones, leant forward into his rucksack straps and walked into the holloway.

The voices paused. He reached down for the comfort of Darwie's muzzle. But Darwie wasn't there. The sheep weren't there. Rainbow wasn't there either. He was truly alone with the trees: trees that had suffered from his gale. He suddenly wondered whether Rainbow's shining love for them protected him from their vengeance in the same way his special skill allowed him to protect Rainbow from the wind.

He quickened his pace. Guilt for the storm he'd created rose up inside him like nausea. He wished he'd thought of the consequences up on that Brittany hill. But he wasn't directly responsible. It was the Tree Slayer's fault for taking advantage of the low pressure he'd created.

He was nearly halfway through. The holloway pressed in on him from both sides and above. He broke into a lumbering run, shining his torch onto the stony track. In a few minutes he'd be out in the open and would be able to cut across the field to the safety of the road that led towards the train station.

Something moved to his right. He stopped and swung the torch towards it. Everything was still. Then a toad jumped. It was crossing the track, one slow hop at a time.

He pushed onwards, panting. The murmuring of the Koad pattern was louder. He tried to ignore the voices directing him back to Rainbow, but the soundwaves, imprisoned in the holloway, reverberated around him and hammered at his head. His headphones were useless here. The voices rose in intensity and another pattern came to the forefront. It was still Koad, but a new chord was harmonising with the main one. It was trying to attract his attention.

Curiosity overcame his pain. He leant against one of the holloway's bigger trunks, took off his headphones and pressed his ear to its bark while he caught his breath. The pattern corresponded to the feeling of 'solitary' that Rainbow had given him earlier that afternoon: 'solitary' or 'single' or the number 'one'. A different chord joined the Koad and One patterns. It was new, and he couldn't place it in his treeopedia, not without Rainbow to help him.

Another new chord jarred against the others. This one hurt. It grated on his teeth, like a fork scraping down a blackboard, sending spears through his brain. The voices were telling him to go back to Rainbow. It was no good: he had to get to Hestia. He tried to take a deep breath but the voices had thickened the air.

The new patterns screamed at him. He took his ear away and fumbled for his headphones. They dropped to the ground. The voices shrieked, jangling like the violins in *Psycho*. He slammed his hands to his ears. The torch fell onto a stone and cracked open, blinding him in darkness. He retched. He had to find his headphones. He bent down, his rucksack almost overbalancing him, and took a hand away from his ear to grope on the ground. He was sure they'd fallen right here. Why couldn't he find them? He changed hands and retched again. It was no good. He couldn't locate them. He knelt and pressed both hands to his ears. The voices were inside his head now. There was no escape. His head was throbbing. He couldn't breathe. He vomited: once, twice, three times.

He had to get out of the holloway and fill his lungs with clear air. Which way had he come from? He struggled to his feet. Stars burst in handfuls before his eyes. He staggered backwards, tripped and fell into oblivion.

🌱 🍃 🌱

Fifteen minutes. Twenty minutes, and Rainbow had still seen no sign of Eole. At least the night air was calm: but for how much longer, if he was upset? She doubled back along the road and jogged in the other direction.

She'd lost him.

She hurried back to the farm. There were no lights on in the house. She paused at the solitary oak and reached out to it. She might as well try, though she doubted it would tell her where Eole was.

In stark contrast to earlier on, the oak was agitated. Or maybe it was her own agitation she was transmitting. She turned off her torch, settled her mind and concentrated on the earth, the roots, the woody warmth of the bark.

The tree was definitely agitated. She pressed her need to find Eole through her hands, and the agitation increased. The tree was agitated about Eole. Could it detect that Eole was on the point of being taken over by the Tree Slayer? She willed an image to appear, to show her where he was.

Nothing happened. It wasn't a special tree like the François I oak.

There was no alternative: she had to get help. She rang Gabin's doorbell. He answered in his pyjamas and agreed to drive her. Wasting no time in getting dressed, he slid into his flip-flops and picked up his keys. They hurried outside and climbed into his 2CV.

"If he's heading to the station, he may have taken the track," said Gabin.

They advanced slowly, bouncing into ruts, and entered a holloway. The night air coming through the open windows cooled Rainbow as she peered into the darkness, searching for Eole's blond head.

A dark lump lay on the ground ahead. It wasn't moving.

The 2CV was too slow. She jumped out of the car and raced towards the shape. It was Eole. He was still breathing. She unclipped his rucksack.

Gabin joined her.

"Should we call an ambulance?" she asked him.

"Let's get him into the recovery position first."

They pushed him onto his side, away from the splashes of vomit. Gabin held his thumb over Eole's wrist pulse. His headphones were on the ground so Rainbow put them over his ears while Gabin counted.

"It's slow. Too slow," he said.

A sound came from Eole's mouth.

"Eole!" cried Rainbow.

His face, ghostly white, twisted in pain. He opened his eyes, pulled his hand from Gabin's grasp and put it over his ear, on top of the headphones.

"Hestia," he moaned.

"Let's get you into the car," said Gabin.

Rainbow said she'd help him up if Gabin could deal with his rucksack. Gabin hesitated, then picked it up and lugged it to the 2CV.

"Shall I help you sit up?" asked Rainbow.

Eole nodded, and Rainbow eased him into a sitting position. "I've got to see Hestia," he said.

"We'll call her from Gabin's phone," said Rainbow.

Gabin came back and tried to help her support Eole while he stood, but Eole shrugged him off and staggered to the car with a hand on Rainbow's shoulder. He slumped into the front seat.

"Can we shut the windows?" he asked Rainbow.

Rainbow closed them and Eole's shoulders relaxed. Gabin told him he needed to rest and that he should tell his young lady what was going on in his head instead of just upping and leaving.

"Tell him you're my soulmate, not my young lady," he said to Rainbow.

"Even more reason to confide in her," said Gabin.

Eole didn't reply.

Back at the farm, Gabin opened the barn door, pointed to a pile of loose hay and told Eole he could sleep there to save pitching his tent again.

"If I were you, I'd stay with him," Gabin muttered to Rainbow.

She thanked him and asked if they could borrow his phone the next day.

"Of course. As long as it's not a long-distance call. I'll be at market but I'll leave the kitchen door unlocked."

Rainbow thanked him again and he flip-flopped out of the barn.

❧ ❧ ❧

Eole sat on the hay and drank from the water bottle Rainbow passed him. The barn smelt almost like home. Now he was indoors the voices had stopped, but his head ached as if he'd had an episode. He wanted to sleep. He wanted to lie down on the hay and sleep and sleep and never have to make any decisions.

Rainbow was apologising for being jealous of his ability to hear the trees. She told him he was important and that she would never find Koad without him. If they didn't find Koad, their mission would fail. She, Amrita and perhaps he himself would die.

She wanted him to talk, so he told her about the phone call and then continued with the detail of his 'Hestia v. Rainbow' calculations and she didn't stop him with the T-sign, but she did make a hand-turning sign which meant he didn't have to go into all the calculation details, so he skipped them and told her about the holloway instead.

At the end of his speech she said it wasn't an either-or situation. He could call Hestia every day and talk to her, and yet still continue with the treeopedia, guide Rainbow to Koad and protect her one hundred per cent. He wished he'd talked to Rainbow straightaway and he wondered why it seemed so simple for her and yet so complicated for himself.

While he was wondering, she took out his sleeping bag, threw it onto the hay and made him get inside it, and then she got her own sleeping bag from her tent, and after that she switched off the barn light and settled down to sleep. He came to the end of his wondering and he concluded that being *together* with Rainbow was as good as being with Tintin and the sheep in the summer pastures, and that he'd like to carry on being her soulmate/guide/protector and he hoped their mission would last for a long, long time.

🌱 🌱 🌱

The next morning Rainbow's muscles had turned into concrete. She attempted to stretch in the hay, winced and then hobbled outside and packed while she waited for Eole to wake up. Domi's envelope was at the bottom of her rucksack. Inside, she found a wad of bank notes and a familiar sheaf of ancient papers, tied with a faded red ribbon. They were his mother's memoir notes on spiritualism and her experience of parallel worlds. Rainbow had read some of them last September, when Mary had arrived in Cognac, but she hadn't finished. Domi obviously thought she'd have time to read during her journey. She was thankful for the money but wished she'd left the memoir notes at home. She could hardly dump them to lighten her load.

Once Eole was up, she took him into the empty house to use the phone and then sat at the table to write and draw in her travel log. Christophe would be at work so she'd have to call him from a phone box later on.

Eole phoned Hestia and explained that his phone card units had run out yesterday. He told her he would call her every evening until he came home, and she interrupted and said it didn't matter if it wasn't exactly six o'clock. She understood about yesterday and said she felt better today and that she'd actually talked to Papa after Eole's call because she had to talk to someone – and Papa had listened, would you believe it? – and he'd made an appointment for her to talk to a doctor at the clinic. He wasn't fussing like Maman, and was actually taking her side in wanting an abortion. The only problem now was that Maman had resorted to muttering in Greek and buying candles and spending half the day at church with Père Laurent. Hestia even had to do the milking, which was disgusting and made her want to puke, but she was being mega-conciliatory.

Eole hadn't considered she might want an abortion. They didn't abort the sheep or goats when they were pregnant. If she had an abortion, would the problem go away, like one of her hangovers? In any case, it no longer sounded as if she needed him, which made him feel as airy as a cirrus cloud.

He ate the croissants and strawberry jam Grandad FlipFlop had left for them. It was difficult to imagine that life in Arras-en-Lavedan was carrying on without him. It would be the same if he and Rainbow failed their mission and died, which made him feel sad but also a little bit lighter, because if Patrick had talked to Hestia, then perhaps his burnout was over. Eole's former family seemed to be binding itself together perfectly well without him. If he was going to die, it made more sense to be with his soulmate than with a family that didn't belong to him anymore. And if he died, he would discover what happened after death, though of course he wouldn't be able to publish a scientific paper on his experience. He may even see Tintin again.

While Eole finished all the croissants and ate a whole baguette, Rainbow phoned Domi. She told him everything was fine, thanked him for the cash and brushed off his suggestion to finish reading his mother's memoir.

"Have you seen Christophe?" she asked.

Domi hesitated. "He popped in yesterday evening to see his mum."

Rainbow curled the twisted telephone cord around her

fingers. "How was he? Did he say anything about me?"

"No."

"Was he … alone?"

"No, he brought his apprentice friend."

Rainbow hung up. She tore a page from the travel log and started drawing with quick, heavy strokes. She'd known Emilie was a risk but she hadn't really thought Christophe would console himself with her, not after all he'd said about Emilie not feeling 'right' and about being in love with Rainbow. Well, he'd made his choice. There would be no romantic holiday together, after all. She'd put him back in her mental box and shut the lid. It no longer mattered if her mission took forever to accomplish.

She screwed up the page and started drawing on another.

Twenty minutes later, Eole was ready to leave. Rainbow stuck her thank-you caricature of Gabin in his 2CV onto his fridge and they locked up, slid the key under the stone and started walking.

"I hope we're not going via the holloway," said Eole.

"What do the trees say?" Rainbow studied Eole's white face and noticed the shadows under his eyes. Was this the effect of the Tree Slayer, devouring him from inside? She must look after him better.

Eole listened to the voices. He could hear a murmur from the holloway trees but it was too far away to understand if there was a Koad pattern or not. He had an idea, and warned Rainbow to shelter behind the barn. Then he faced the distant holloway and took in a deep breath. With it came the voices. He breathed out more gently, directing his face to the cloudless sky.

"We have to go through the holloway," he said. "Can I

walk behind you?"

Rainbow agreed. Last night she'd been too worried about Eole to pay any attention to the holloway, but now, as they approached it, she admired its shape. She imagined the roots intertwining under the earth, sharing secrets. It was magical. She could feel the power of it, drawing her in. It was inviting her to join its family, to interlace her arms with theirs and dig her toes into the earth beside them. She would sketch it in her travel log when they stopped for a break.

Inside, the light was dim. Eole looked around. The atmosphere had changed and the trees were no longer screaming at him, but the new chords were still there: chanting and urgent, harmonising with the Koad pattern like a family conversation around a dinner table. He showed Rainbow the tree he'd hugged the previous night.

They were in the middle of the tunnel. An oval of light at the far end reminded Rainbow that she mustn't stay too long: that, contrary to her growing desire to stay here forever, they must move onwards. She stroked the trunk of the ash tree Eole indicated. She didn't have to search for the usual secret places to communicate with it, because its whole bark was receptive. Her heart thumped. Perhaps the holloway was Koad, and this was the tree she had to save. She threw off her rucksack and hugged its trunk.

It was a mother tree, but it wasn't special like the François I and Drunken House oaks. She knew because it was filling her with emotion rather than using images and words. Yet its feelings were clear and forceful, as if it were almost a special tree.

It communicated 'family': a bonded family with internal

conflict, yet unified against outside forces. Without opening her eyes, she said "family" to Eole. The ash was strong. It was as if she were hugging all the holloway trees through this one. She longed to be part of their family. In response to her longing she sensed a ripple of acceptance, and then the ash's emotions stilled, as if it were taking a deep breath. She braced herself and told Eole something new was coming.

Eole brushed away an ant and pressed his ear to the trunk. The jarring *Psycho* violin sound from last night broke into the Koad pattern.

"Jesus! There's a forest of fear here," said Rainbow. "The trees are terrified."

Eole noted 'fear' in his treeopedia and continued listening, dreading a return of last night's pain. But nothing hurt, now he was with Rainbow. The Koad pattern crescendoed and he heard the strain of the chord Rainbow had already translated as One or Solitary.

"There's a little hope too," continued Rainbow. "Can you hear it?"

Eole could. It was the first word in his treeopedia.

"And now it's referring to you and me," she added.

Eole stocked the chord from last night in his treeopedia, a little disappointed that the voices were so illogical. 'He and Rainbow' should be two intertwined notes, one for him and one for Rainbow, but for some reason it was a single, pure note: one that warbled, hesitant like an untrained singer's voice at the end of a breath.

Rainbow fell silent. Something in the ash tree's feelings reminded her of the silvery mycelium network and of Amrita. Was it referring to the last One Tree? Was the One

Tree the last of the special mother trees, the sole survivor of the Tree Slayer's gale? As she formed these thoughts, the ash shuddered in agreement and fear. Rainbow already knew she had to save the One Tree, but she mustn't tell Eole and risk him passing the information onto the Tree Slayer. This, she would keep secret.

"Let's go," she said to Eole.

Eole was puzzled. "Why? The voices are still speaking. Now they're saying 'last', 'the One Tree,' and 'us'," he said. "There's hope in the last One Tree, and we're somehow linked to it."

"We need to get a move on," said Rainbow.

Eole hesitated. Normally, Rainbow was keen to hear what the trees said. Other chords, already stocked in his treeopedia, rose up through the tree.

"Wait!" he said. "Now the voices are saying 'follow' and 'save'. We must follow the voices to Koad and save the last One Tree, in which there's hope. I wonder what we must save it from – the Tree Slayer?"

"I don't know," she said. "Come on. It's time to go."

So much for keeping secrets from Eole. He knew everything now, which meant she'd lost her advantage over the Tree Slayer. How would it react? Would it force Eole to kill her? Or would it wait until they found the One Tree and then attack?

As soon as Eole found the One Tree she would have to gag him, which should stop him raising a gale. Then the One Tree would explain what she had to do in order to save it and restore Amrita's life force. Hopefully, once she'd done that, she could let Eole go again. She didn't want to think what else she might have to do to him.

She stroked the ash tree and bade it farewell. But the ash was irritated. She tried to calm her racing pulse and concentrate on the tree's emotions. It would be so much easier if she could hear its voice.

The ash disapproved because they were going too fast. They were wrong about there being hope in the One Tree. The hope was actually in her and Eole. But there wasn't much. She swallowed. Another feeling was building up.

Eole noticed a low vibration creeping over the warbling note, more of a disruption than a chord or a note. The vibration grew, overriding the Koad melody, and shook it apart. The Koad pattern distorted and disappeared.

"Rainbow! What's this one?"

Rainbow's voice came out as a croak. "That ... is death."

CHAPTER 27

For the first time since she'd learnt of her mission, Rainbow realised she might actually die.

She let go of the holloway ash tree and sat down. She'd known from the moment she heard Amrita's words that her life was at risk. But hearing it in a vision was one thing; having the trees remind her was quite another.

"The voices are warning us about death so that we can avoid it," said Eole, when Rainbow explained why she was sitting down. He told her that he was here to protect her from the Tree Slayer, so she needn't be afraid, and that the detail they'd gleaned was good because they now knew they had a particular tree to find and save. They could focus on this. "We all die, in any case," he added.

Tintin had died. Their sheep and goats died all the time. Hestia's baby was going to die before it was even born. Death was logical and the fact Rainbow was suddenly shocked was yet more proof of how being illogical was inferior to being logical.

"Come on," he said. "The voices are telling us to hurry."

She felt a heavy resistance to following him: Mary didn't want to die for Amrita. The chances of saving the One Tree in secret were slim, now that Eole, and therefore the Tree Slayer, knew what she was looking for. But her trust in Amrita had been rewarded so far. The One Tree was a spiritual tree and would advise her once she found it. She dragged herself to her feet.

Amrita had used her life force to heal the Rainbow-Mary split, and now it was RainbowMary's turn to heal Amrita. She wouldn't contemplate failing. Instead, she would focus on how being reunited with Amrita would bring her even closer to trees. She and Amrita were meant to be together, she was sure. That was her destiny, not death at the hands of the Tree Slayer. She had to continue. She wanted to continue.

To her surprise, no further resistance came from Mary. She seemed to accept Rainbow's decision, even if she didn't approve. Rainbow immediately felt more cheerful, and forced her aching legs to catch up with Eole.

🌿 🌿 🌿

They continued northwest for the rest of Friday. Whenever Eole heard new strains in the voice chords, he hugged the tree and added vocabulary to his treeopedia. It was far more interesting than Spanish and German lessons at school.

The treeopedia became more complex, allowing him to join the gaps between the words and ideas, and his ear developed more sensitivity. The odours associated with the voices didn't change much and he suspected their role was simply to catch his attention. Once he understood the main melody, he could concentrate on the sub-melodies and the sub-sub-melodies.

The more he understood, the less the voices jarred and hurt his head. They were like his five other senses, all jostling with new information whenever he changed environment. He'd learnt to control his five senses most of the time, and now he was learning to control the effect of the voices on his body. On Saturday he left his headphones in his pocket.

Rainbow stored her travel log and pencils in the front pocket of her rucksack. They kept her sane in her role as useless follower. Recording the disfigured trees they passed was soul-destroying, so she began to draw other details of their journey: the deer they surprised into leaping graceful arcs early on Saturday morning; the lookout rabbit thumping the dry earth and causing a scurry of white bobtails; the plop and ripple of frogs beside a river. Whenever she saw a particularly sick or damaged tree, she paused to heal or rebalance it while Eole lay back and exercised his lungs with cloud art. Then she urged him onwards. The longer they took, the weaker Amrita was becoming.

Eole liked sleeping in the wild, which they did every night after leaving Gabin. It was good practice for his ambition to live in Tintin's hut on the summer pastures with Rainbow. They washed in cold streams, foraged for free food and bought essential supplies from village shops. Then, on the fifth day of travelling, they stopped at a campsite. Eole argued that camping rough was better but Rainbow wanted to have a hot shower, wash her clothes and talk to people.

They'd almost reached the edge of Rainbow's map, so Eole asked her to buy one of the west of France. While she was at the village shops, he pitched both their tents and unrolled their sleeping mats and bags. Then he took out his multiverse book, as he'd done every evening, and tried not to superimpose Tintin's face on the pages. It was still impossible to concentrate and the words refused to transform into concepts. He gave up and went to the campsite phone box from where, at six o'clock, he rang Hestia.

Alexandra was always beside the phone when he rang, even though he told her his daily call was for Hestia. She tried to trick him into saying where he was, but he only answered her questions about whether he was drinking enough water and looking after his feet and eating balanced meals and sleeping properly. He spoke to Darwie too. Darwie whined and sometimes barked when he told him about the rabbits or sheep they'd seen. Eole's favourite part of the call was hearing Hestia's voice. She didn't bother saying 'over' at the end of her turn anymore because she said he'd mastered the art of conversation. He felt proud until she added "at long last".

"So, have you snogged her yet?" Hestia asked.

"Who?"

"Rainbow, you dork."

"No, and I don't intend to," he replied. He'd already told her that their relationship wasn't like hers with Mathieu Legrand.

"Well, maybe you should. Then you could get rid of one of your tents and your rucksacks would be lighter."

She was being logical, for once. He tucked away her suggestion and asked if she'd made an appointment to abort the baby yet. She went quiet and he had to repeat her name to make sure she was still there. When she said 'Yes', her voice had changed to the childish voice in the camcorder films from their Paris days.

"When is it?"

"Next week. The psychologist says I need to think about it, but I don't want to think. I just want to get it done and go back to the way things were before – though not with Papa. I want him to stay like this, always. He's been almost human. He took me to the library and we looked at some books together and now he's found a girl the same age as me in Lourdes who kept her baby and I think he's going to take me to see her, even though it's pointless. He says I need to consider both options so I can make an informed decision. It's like he's had a knock on the head or something. I wish Maman would get knocked on the head."

"Yes, me too. She keeps asking where I am."

"Where *are* you?"

He opened his mouth to reply. Then he remembered the times he'd seen Hestia and Alexandra in the kitchen, heads close together, laughing, and closed it again. Instead, he told her about the voices and the day's additions to his treeopedia, and she yawned and said she hoped Rainbow appreciated everything he was doing for her and would let him snog her at some point, and then she said she missed him and that it would be nice if he could come with her to the clinic next week and he didn't reply because he didn't want his mission to end that soon and he didn't want to have to make another decision, so he said he'd call her tomorrow and then hung up.

When Rainbow returned with the map and food, Eole said he had a suggestion to lighten their loads. Rainbow rubbed her sore shoulders. She'd already discarded a jumper, a pair of jeans and most of her toilet bag contents.

"Go on. I'm game. Anything to stop me feeling as stiff as a

hundred-year-old."

Eole leant towards her. She stepped back, so he held onto her shoulders to stop her escaping and kissed her on the mouth. A snog was longer than a kiss, but he didn't manage to hold his lips to hers for very long because she twisted out of his grip and pushed him backwards.

Her mouth was in an 'O' shape.

"Does that count as a snog?" he asked. "Because if it does, we can share my tent and leave yours here at the campsite and you can ask them to look after it and then pick it up on your way home, and I'll carry the poles and inner while you carry the pegs and outer, and that way our rucksacks will be lighter." He smiled at her, pleased with Hestia's idea.

Rainbow closed her mouth, still shocked. His kiss had been brusque, yet sweet. It hadn't occurred to her that he might want to develop their platonic friendship. She liked him but she didn't want more, even if Christophe *was* with Emilie now. She couldn't imagine ever wanting to kiss anyone other than Christophe. But she wasn't supposed to be thinking of him. He was in the box with Thierry.

"Let's get this straight, Eole. We're not girlfriend and boyfriend, which means we're not going to start kissing each other. And I'm not sleeping in your tent with you, even if it would make our loads lighter. OK?"

His smile faded and he nodded. She hadn't understood the snogging idea. But it was true that squeezing two people into a one-man tent would have made nights uncomfortable. She wasn't Darwie, though she was so small she'd only take up a little more room than him. And snogging wasn't as much fun as Hestia reported. He would tell Hestia that her plan was theoretically sound but impractical.

"Good. Here's your map," said Rainbow.

He laid it out on the grass in front of their tents and drew a line from Le Logis through their route to their current position. It was more or less straight. Using the side of his sleeping mat, he extended the line right to the edge of France. It finished beside the town of St Brieuc, on the northern coast of Brittany.

"I hope we don't have to walk that far. It'll take forever," said Rainbow.

"At our current rate it'll take twenty-two more days."

"That *is* forever."

Eole ran his finger along the pencilled line. They were almost at Fontenay-le-Comte. Most of the line ran through countryside, with the exception of Nantes. If they ended up having to cross the city, which would be stuffed full of people, he would breathe in deeply to bring the voices from forests on the far side towards him, then skirt it.

The map showed several forests after Nantes. One was called Paimpont.

Paimpont. The name sent an electrical impulse into his memory. It was the village where he'd been born. The word he'd hardly thought about since they'd left the Pyrenees flashed into his mind: ADOPTED.

He took a deep breath.

Rainbow flung out her arms to steady herself in the sudden gust. Eole's nostrils were flared. The old couple on the next pitch clung onto their sun hats.

"Eole! Stop!" cried Rainbow.

She watched his eyes come back into focus. He tipped

back his head and pursed his lips. She couldn't see any air, but the gentle puff of white cloud above them was sliced in two. And in two again. And again.

She had to stop him before the Tree Slayer took control.

"What's the matter? Talk to me," she said.

He clamped his mouth shut, grabbed his multiverse book and slid his sleeping mat inside his tent. Then he wriggled inside and zipped up the entrance.

She sighed. Was it a delayed reaction to her rejection of his kiss? She hoped she wouldn't have to pretend to be in love with him in order to stop him getting upset. She wasn't sure she could do it.

"I'm sorry if I've upset you," she said to his tent. "I didn't mean to. I really like you, but we don't need to kiss in order to be the best of friends. Please talk to me."

There was no reply.

"I'm going to eat sausage and chips at the bar and find some people to chat with," she said. "Why don't you come with me?"

There was still no answer from him. Could she safely leave him?

"Please don't disappear again," she said. "If you want to talk, come and get me or wait until I return. There's a packet of curry and rice here, if you don't want to be sociable. And don't forget your gale promise." She picked up her purse and travel log, and went to try the campsite chips.

Eole lay on his back, his eyes following a fly as it battered its head against the tent seams. His brain registered the fly while his mind pulled apart the jigsaw it had made of the mission with Rainbow. Had he misinterpreted everything? The voices seemed to be leading him in a direct line to Paimpont. They must want him to be reconciled with his biological family. His true family. The place he belonged. Perhaps Koad was a way of saying 'home' and Rainbow's mission with the One Tree was irrelevant.

His brain monitored the fly's attempts to escape, tracking its flight path with imaginary lines. It would be so much easier if he had just a brain and no mind. His mind confused everything, making muddy water of situations. His brain was cool and clear.

It was wrong to let his mind sidetrack him into a search for the place he belonged. He and Rainbow were on a mission together. They were soulmates. He had to protect and guide her so they could save the One Tree. If by chance the voices led them directly to Paimpont, well, that would just be a coincidence.

CHAPTER 28

Rainbow didn't like crowds but she welcomed the busy campsite bar after five days with such limited human contact. She was completing some sketches when a young woman dressed in hippie clothes asked if she could sit beside her. Rainbow accepted and learnt that Melanie Brown was English but lived in Brittany and was on holiday here in the Marais Poitevin.

Rainbow felt an affinity for the girl, perhaps because she reminded her of her commune family. She was a freelance journalist and nature lover and, when Rainbow showed her the travel log, she seemed enthralled by it. They talked about trees and biodiversity. The better Rainbow got to know her, the more impressed she became. They had so much in common. Could she be the English friend Sandrine had predicted she'd work with? This meeting was a sign. She could imagine saving forests alongside Melanie and learning from her enthusiastic efficiency.

She told Melanie about the commune and, after a couple of hours, it felt natural to mention her gift and explain that she and Eole were actually following the trees' voices. Melanie's attitude didn't change. She didn't look at her with sideways glances or move to another table. Rainbow wondered if she was being oversensitive about keeping her gift so secret.

When Melanie left to go to bed, she told Rainbow to keep up the travel log, adding that the journey would make a good feature in the nature magazine she edited. Rainbow considered inviting Melanie to join her and Eole, but decided she ought to keep her mission as quiet as possible. She took Melanie's business card, placed it carefully in her purse and said a reluctant goodbye.

The next morning Eole's strange mood had passed. Rainbow asked if he missed being with Darwie and his sheep in the mountains. He nodded. The map must have reminded him of home and Tintin. Remembering how much she'd ached after Michael's death, she wanted to hug Eole. But he'd hate that. When she'd missed Michael, she concentrated on dedicating herself to trees in his memory. And Mary's advice in the Pyrenees – to look forward to the future rather than dwelling on Christophe and the past – had really helped too. She suggested Eole should focus on the future and dedicate his scientific work to Tintin. He didn't make any comment, only looked up at the cloudy sky for a long time.

Over the next few days, she watched him closely but didn't see any more signs of his strange mood. She monitored the weather carefully too, dreading the arrival of a storm that the Tree Slayer might use to blow down the One Tree before she could arrive to protect it. Most days the sun shone; sometimes it was misty and occasionally it rained a little, but the air remained calm.

Every day she expected to arrive at Koad. And every evening she was disappointed when Eole announced cheerfully that they must continue the next day. They had a break on day thirteen – when they rang home and discovered they'd both passed their exams. They spent the afternoon lazing by a river south of Nantes and bought cakes to celebrate. Rainbow munched solidly through her chocolate éclair, trying to enjoy it and not think about Christophe, who would be on holiday in the Pyrenees right now, perhaps with Emilie. Eole couldn't celebrate properly because he kept thinking of Hestia, who would be going to the clinic in a few days without him. They were both glad to get back to their mission and put thoughts of home behind them.

On the eighteenth day they were soaked in a shower. Eole said they should stay in their wet clothes and keep the dry ones in their rucksacks. Rainbow sneezed and miserably agreed. Her nose was sore from blowing it and Eole's sniffing annoyed her.

Late that afternoon they reached a village, only to discover the shops were closed. She was exhausted. The idea of walking to the next village was too much, so she knocked on the doors of the few houses they passed to ask for food and shelter. Nobody answered. Then, in the middle of a dripping forest, she tripped and fell, hurting her ankle. She demanded that they stop for the night right there in a sodden glade beside a stream.

She crawled to an old sycamore tree and collapsed with her back against it. They ate some soggy biscuits and then Eole left to scavenge for wild food. Rainbow pulled off her boots and rubbed her aching ankle. She'd had enough. A tear slid down her cheek. Where the hell was this Koad? It had been a month since Amrita told her to 'go with haste'. They would never reach Koad in time to save the One Tree and Amrita. Even Mary couldn't be bothered to boost her. In fact, she'd hardly felt anything from Mary since her resistance in the holloway, when Rainbow realised she might die. Mary had lost interest in their mission.

The peeling bark on the sycamore's trunk made her back itch. It had been too wet to touch a tree all day. She hugged it and apologised for having wasted so much time. The last One Tree would no doubt have answered, but the sycamore said nothing. Instead, she had the sensation she was balanced on the boundary between life and death. She had to choose one way or the other. *Life, of course*, she thought.

Energy began to flow out from the trunk, through her arms and into her core. It was the rising sun after a dark night. It was like slipping into a warm bath when you were cold and hungry. Mingled with the restorative energy was hope. She must cling to her mission and keep going. She held on tight, drinking in everything the sycamore gave, and her eyelids grew heavy.

When Eole returned with a bunch of stinging nettles and some dandelion leaves for dinner, he found Rainbow asleep, hugging a tree like Hestia used to hug her teddy bear. He'd stopped calling Hestia every evening. When he'd called on results day and learnt he'd got the highest grades in his exams, she told him not to bother calling again since he was obviously more interested in celebrating his exams with Rainbow than coming home to support her. So he hadn't. But Rainbow said he should call anyway. He dithered over what to do and decided to leave it a week before he called again.

He lit the gas, fried the nettles and dandelion leaves and then let them stew in water. He and Rainbow would still be hungry after the meal, but he'd already spent a couple of days without eating a proper meal when he was in the mountains and he'd survived. They'd find a village the next day.

While Rainbow slept, he examined the broken clip on his rucksack. If he'd had access to Tintin's workshop, he could have fixed it easily. Instead, he'd collected discarded objects all day and puzzled over ways to combine them in order to mend the clip. Now, he took the clothes peg, paperclip, safety pin and string, and used his Swiss army knife to fashion a makeshift clip. It would last until they reached Koad. He suspected they were nearly there because the anticipation in the voices was rising. They were also only a three-day walk from Paimpont, but he wouldn't let his mind dwell on that.

Rainbow was still asleep. Dinner was ready and their tents pitched. There was nothing to do. He took out his multiverse book and looked at the cover. He must think of his future, as Rainbow had advised, and not dwell on the past with Tintin.

Science wasn't only his past: it was his future too. He'd told himself this every day since her suggestion, and each time her idea sat a little more comfortably in his mind. He opened the book and looked at the words.

They weren't just words, as they had been yesterday. They were individual windows, like in a train, and when he strung them together they took him away from the page and into the thoughts of the writer. The quantum physicist was talking to him. He had a direct link into the author's mind. He was reading again!

Late the next morning they stopped at a signpost. Rainbow listened to a hoopoe's hollow call while Eole unfolded his map and checked their position. She walked towards the sound and tried to locate the bird so she could draw it. Hoopoes were her and Eole's favourite bird – he had a nesting family in his garden – although the kingfisher they'd spotted at the river on their rest day had come a close second.

She'd almost finished Gabin's notebook. Her handwriting wasn't as neat as his but her drawings were more detailed. As they walked, she searched for themes. Her current fixation was with exposed roots and she thought some sketches were quite passable. Before that, she'd had a feather period, a flirtation with moss on rocks, a fungus fascination and a study of tree stumps.

The hoopoe remained hidden. She gave up and joined Eole at the signpost. A brown tourist sign, decorated with oak leaves in each corner, hung under the official road signs. In the centre were two opposing arrows, each with a forest name beside it. The one ahead was the *Forêt de Paimpont*.

"Cool! We've got another forest coming up," she said. It was much more pleasant walking in the shade than under the hot sun. "We may find Koad and the One Tree there."

Eole shrugged. It was the first time he'd seen the name Paimpont on a road sign. His mind stirred up muddy ideas and tried to mix *belonging* with their *together* mission. He needed his brain's calm control to keep the concepts separate.

Rainbow studied his face. He avoided looking at her directly, as if he were hiding something.

"Everything all right?" she asked.

He pointed at the sign and started walking towards Paimpont.

She tried to catch up but he strode ahead. There was no point pushing him. She didn't want to upset him and risk a gale. Apart from the moment after the kiss, he'd mastered his moods perfectly over the past weeks. He would tell her what was wrong when he was ready.

🌿 🍃 🌿

Eole counted down the seconds on his watch and then dialled Hestia's number.

"At last!" said Hestia. "I didn't mean it about not calling, you dork. Maman's been worried sick all week. It's lucky she's at church, otherwise she'd give you an earful."

Eole lingered on the sound of Hestia's voice before he analysed her words, because her voice made him feel warm and safe whereas her words made him feel guilty. He'd only done what she said.

"Rainbow should have told you to call," she continued. "Or is she too wrapped up in her precious trees to pay you any attention?"

"She did tell me."

"Oh, Eole! Never mind. So how's it going? Have you saved the planet and got your leg over yet?"

He blushed at the image her words presented him with and reminded her that their tents were too small. Then he looked back through his mental travel log – which was much more detailed than Rainbow's – and told Hestia the highlights of each day. When he'd finished, he asked if she and Patrick were back to normal.

"What do you mean, 'Patrick'? Come off it, Eole. I know they were out of order to keep your adoption a secret but he's still Papa. He's the one who brought you up. Well, tried to. That's far more important than the minor detail of blood. He was on my side for the abortion – which went fine, since you didn't ask – and even though it's over, he still comes and sits on my bed and asks me how I am."

"I'm sorry about your bab–"

"Don't say that word."

Eole was puzzled but Hestia was speaking again:

"So don't you dare call Papa 'Patrick' again. And before you ask, I don't want to hear 'Alexandra' either. Or 'Isabelle' instead of 'Aunt Isabelle'. OK?"

"OK. But it'll get complicated when I find my biological parents, because I'll have to call them Maman and Papa too."

"Because you're looking for them?" Hestia asked. Her voice had changed. It made him think of Scatty Cat skulking along the ground when he crept up on a bird.

"No. Paimpont's on our line, so if we stop there I might look. But it's a separate mission. I mustn't mix it up with our *together* mission."

"You're lucky. You've got two families instead of being stuck here in the back of beyond. You should go there and make enquiries about them. Who cares about Rainbow's weirdo tree stuff, anyway? She only thinks about herself. And trees are assassins. I reckon you should let Rainbow get on with her stuff and go and find your other parents. After all the help you've given her, she's done nothing in return."

Eole's feet started to itch. He rubbed them together and thought about roots. Rainbow was his soulmate. He had to guide and protect her.

His feet grew calm again and he told Hestia he'd ring her

the next day.

"I may not be here tomorrow. I'm going away for a few days," she said. "Ring me, in say, four days' time. On Friday, OK? See you soon."

He said goodbye and hung up.

Rainbow was sitting on the wall by the shops, eating one ice-cream and holding another. He started to tell her that she should have bought the second one after she'd finished the first one, because it would have melted by the time she was ready to eat it. Before he could finish, she made the T-sign, told him it was for him, not her, and put it in his hand.

He thanked her. Hestia was wrong. Rainbow had given him lots of things. He made a list in his head while he ate his ice-cream, and discovered that he owed her two more things than she owed him.

🌱 🌿 🌱

A day later they climbed a hill onto a plateau. Rainbow gasped at the huge forest stretched across the horizon. Although Eole had expected it, the extent of trees impressed him too.

'Koad', the voices told him.

'Brocéliande Forest', indicated a tourist sign.

"Maybe," he said.

"Maybe what?" Rainbow asked. The Brocéliande sign confused her because she'd assumed she was looking at Paimpont forest.

"According to Aunt Isabelle, Brocéliande is a mythical forest from the legends of King Arthur. It's supposed to be magical, with strange weather systems, and no one is truly sure of its location. I don't know whether Paimpont really is Brocéliande but the voices are telling me this is Koad."

"Woo hoo!" Rainbow dropped her rucksack and danced a jig. "Koad's a forest and we're nearly there. Come on, Eole! Aren't you glad?"

Eole stared at the forest. "No," he said.

"Cheer up! If Koad is Paimpont forest, Paimpont is Brocéliande and Brocéliande is magical, I bet we'll find the One Tree there. Tell me everything you know about Brocéliande."

He recounted Aunt Isabelle's stories and the references to Brocéliande in medieval texts for the rest of the day as they crossed the plateau and neared the forest. After weeks of passing trees maimed by Eole's gale, Rainbow was astonished to notice that there appeared to be no damage to Paimpont forest. She remembered the way the François I oak had sucked in the gale to prevent the other trees in the park from suffering. Amrita's last One Tree had to be inside the forest. It must be impressively powerful to have protected this huge area.

That evening, banks of cloud built on the horizon and when Rainbow and Eole rose, early the next morning, they were met by a wind that Eole described as 'westerly'. They walked down a steep hill and crossed a main road. On the far side, an ancient oak tree shaded the courtyard of a restaurant called Les Forges de Paimpont.

"Paimpont forest! Koad! We've arrived," said Rainbow. "And what a beautiful oak to greet us."

Eole massaged his earholes and then turned his head, listening in every direction. Something was wrong ahead of them. It was as if they were entering a black hole.

"What's the matter?" asked Rainbow.

"It's the voices. They've stopped."

CHAPTER 29

"What do you mean, 'the voices have stopped'?" asked Rainbow.

Eole covered his ears with his hands. The voices had accompanied him for weeks: he'd tuned into them and begun to vibrate along with them. Now, the lack of them made his ears scream. The silence was unbearable after the weeks of intimate symphonies.

"I can't hear them anymore. They're not saying 'Koad'. They're not saying anything."

Rainbow wondered whether the voices had stopped because they'd arrived at their destination. If so, the tree in front of them could be the One Tree.

Saying nothing of her hopes to Eole, she walked up to the ancient oak tree in the restaurant car park and stroked its mossy bark. Her hands settled and she opened herself to it. There was horror here: a history of axes and fire and men making metal. But there were no images or words. And no confirmation that they'd arrived at Koad. It wasn't the One Tree.

"The oak is communicating 'horror'," she said "Can

you hear it?"

Eole put his ear to the oak. There was no melody or voice or smell.

"No. Let's go into the forest," he said. He might hear the voices once trees surrounded him. And there would be more shelter from the coming storm.

They crossed a dyke that separated a lake from a low-lying village. On the far side, the forest was fenced. And silent. Eole glimpsed grand houses between the trees. He touched the wire fencing and read the 'Private' signs. He looked at the brambles and bracken, smelt groves of nettles and listened to the birds. Nothing indicated which way to go.

"Still no voices," he said.

They'd walked through dozens of private woods without coming across a single barrier, and now, the minute the voices stopped guiding him, he was lost. It was like the week of his arrival in the Pyrenees, when Paul Coutances and his friends had taken him on a walk and had suddenly disappeared, laughing, into the fog. Maybe his and Rainbow's *together* mission was over now he'd guided her to Koad. He wasn't ready for it to end.

Rainbow waded through the nettles to hug a row of trees along the fence. It was such a relief to find trees that were whole, undamaged by the Tree Slayer's gale.

"I can sense restraint, like tight wire cutting into a trunk and restricting its growth," she said. "I don't think they like the fence. Are you sure you can't hear it?"

Eole shook his head. For so many years he'd wished the voices would cease. Now they had, it felt like failure.

Rainbow sighed. They were so near and yet so far. A line

of dark clouds crept over the sun. To cap it all, it was going to rain. She walked to the biggest chequer tree she'd ever seen and sat down beneath it. She didn't have the heart to take out her sketch pad.

"What do we do now?" said Eole.

Rainbow chewed on a stalk of grass and considered. She'd planned to sneak away from Eole and the Tree Slayer as soon as they found the One Tree, but if he couldn't hear the voices, he was no more use as a guide. The danger he represented was greater than his value and there was no reason to stay with him any longer. Except that she couldn't leave him, not after the intimacy of their last month together.

"We'd better carry on until we get some kind of indication of where the One Tree is," she said. "I guess it'll be in the centre of the forest."

"But I can't guide you without the voices and the map doesn't show any paths in the forest so we'll get lost, and in any case how can we carry on if we don't know exactly where we're going?"

Rainbow glanced at Eole's feet and saw his right boot rubbing against his left.

"We *do* know where we're going," she said, quickly. "You're sure this forest is Koad?"

He nodded.

"So we're going to the One Tree."

Eole took his eyes from the safety of her face and dared a glance at the countryside around him. In the ringing silence, everything seemed suddenly foreign. He didn't know this place. There were no mountains, nothing to align himself with. What was he doing here? What was Rainbow doing here?

Without the voices, he couldn't be her guide. If he wasn't her guide, he wasn't her soulmate. If he wasn't her soulmate, who was he and where did he belong? He gripped the straps of his rucksack, holding tight so that he didn't fall off the world. He stared at the forest, at the road, at the verges. The forest, the road, the verges. They spiralled around him, getting closer. Forest, road, verges. Nothing made sense if he wasn't her soulmate.

His brain came to the rescue of his muddy mind. One thing made sense.

He let out the breath he'd unintentionally gathered in his lungs and pulled out the map. He put his finger on the spot where the road left the dyke and entered the forest. It continued directly to Paimpont.

"OK, Eole?" asked Rainbow. "We're going to find the One Tree. OK?"

She saw his right boot twitch, then it was stationary again and he nodded without looking at her. He was poring over the map. She'd thought for a minute that he was going to panic. She sighed and spat out her grass stalk.

"We just don't know how to get there yet," she added. "I could hug every tree until one responds, but it'd take forever."

"If we follow this road we'll reach Paimpont in a couple of kilometres," he said.

"What's the point of going into Paimpont? I doubt the One Tree will be in a village."

Eole didn't answer.

"Eole? Why do you want us to go into the village?" Rainbow asked slowly. "You've spent three weeks avoiding people and now you suddenly want us to go into a village full of them."

"It's logical."

"Is it? Explain."

"Well, we have a tree to find and save. That makes it a special tree, and special trees are generally old. People treat old trees as features and preserve them. So if there are old trees in Paimpont forest, we can assume that someone will know about them, especially if Paimpont is supposedly Brocéliande forest because the tourist industry will use anything it can to attract visitors and their money, like the cave in Lourdes where Bernadette Soubirous had a vision of the Virgin Mary and busloads of tourists visit Lourdes and line up outside the cave to be miraculously saved and buy water and stay in hotels and eat in restaurants—"

He saw Rainbow raise her hands to make the T-sign. He fast-forwarded to the end of his theory. "So if we go into Paimpont, we can find out where there's a special tree."

Rainbow smiled. "You're right. We can ask someone."

"Or look in a library."

"Whatever. Let's go!"

Eole followed her along the road through the trees. After a few minutes, when they were deeper inside the forest, he heard a susurrus of very faint voices. They were still there, but no longer talking to him. It was as if an orchestra had finished playing its symphony for the audience and the musicians were whispering to each other about where to go for a drink. He wished he could listen to a symphony right now, to immerse himself in music and identify which melodies came from which instruments.

In the bourg, a lake separated the houses from the forest. Paimpont was only a village, but it felt like a town to Rainbow after their weeks of walking in the countryside. According to the road signs, it had an abbey, a library, a campsite and a tourist office.

Eole wanted to find the library but Rainbow knew it would be quicker to ask in the tourist office. She left him and the rucksacks outside the abbey and entered the tourist information centre, where she was told that there were a handful of ancient trees, and that Hélène, the council office secretary, knew all about them. She also learnt that the forest covered twenty-two thousand acres and that they'd need to hire bicycles from Monique at Le Brécilien bar if they wanted to visit it. Rainbow bought a tourist map showing the forest tracks and then hired two bicycles and wheeled them back to Eole.

"I'm going to ask the secretary in the council office to mark the trees on the tourist map," she said to him. "Bring the rucksacks inside if it starts to rain."

Eole looked up. The sky was heavy with cumulonimbus but they hadn't charged enough to cause lightning yet. Storms were slow to arrive, here, unlike those in the mountains.

"I'll come in," he said.

"You don't have to."

He insisted, so they each locked up their bike and Rainbow led the way inside the abbey. She smiled at him as they opened a big wooden door into a corridor. It was good to see him taking a step to overcome his fear of strangers. She felt perfectly at ease with people now – as long as her dealings with them didn't touch on her gift.

"You'll be fine. Just take deep breaths," she said, and knocked at the secretary's door. "Not too deep, though."

Eole breathed in hundreds of years of monks' prayers and fixed his eyes on the broken strap on Rainbow's rucksack. She was with him. He could do it.

A female voice told them to come in.

The secretary smelt of fish, looked about one hundred years old, had artificial curly hair like a wig and wore a beige cardigan and a blouse decorated with blue flowers (species unidentifiable). She leant behind a counter, talking to a man about authorisation to take a group of children to Germany.

Eole placed his rucksack beside Rainbow's and they sat down to wait. It was always easier when he had time to size up a place before he had to interact, in the same way that stopping at a red traffic light in an unfamiliar town gave him time to read all the signs and analyse which road was the right one.

There was a bus timetable on the wall. His brain seized its reassuring lines of numbers and started to memorise them, the rhythm soothing the logical part of his head. But his devious mind – the part that dealt with incompatibilities and emotions – needed occupying too. Superimposition had helped his mind before Domi's hypnotism session, so he looked around the office and superimposed the interior of the council office at Arras-en-Lavedan over what he could see, hear and smell. The man became Monsieur Delage and the secretary became Mademoiselle Henri, which made him snigger because he couldn't imagine total babe Mademoiselle Henri with wrinkles, a perm and a beige cardigan.

While his mind was busy with Mademoiselle Henri's

appearance, his brain finished with the bus timetable and started to create a three-column question table. It contained his questions, Mademoiselle Henri's possible responses and his subsequent reactions in each case.

Before his brain could finish the table, Monsieur Delage left the office. Rainbow stood up and introduced them both to Mademoiselle Henri. Everything started to gallop along too quickly for Eole, including his heartbeat. Rainbow explained they were researching interesting trees for their art project. Mademoiselle Henri said she knew some amazing ones and Rainbow sparkled and took out her travel log and Mademoiselle Henri made exclamations like "Sublime!" and "Exquisite!" and Eole wondered how it was that he could actually hear the exclamation marks and he missed a bit of the conversation, and then Mademoiselle Henri started to write on the map and Rainbow asked him to come and look and he concentrated on the map and not on Mademoiselle Henri.

He noted the crosses and the names of the ten trees and memorised the circuit she recommended, and he realised he'd be able to guide Rainbow after all because she didn't understand maps and of course he was still her soulmate, and his question table faded from his brain and he relaxed his hold on his mind. He listened to Rainbow assuring Mademoiselle Henri that they would get permission from the owners for the private parts of the forest, and then he heard the full stop of her sentence.

His mind seized its chance.

"Rainbow," he said, "can you ask Mademoiselle Henri what the procedure is for finding my biological parents who lived here when I was born, please?"

And he'd actually said the words out loud and both Rainbow and Mademoiselle Henri were silent and the silence swelled into a huge bubble of confused air between them and he suspected his timing was wrong, as usual.

Rainbow stared at his blank face. Who was Mademoiselle Henri? Where had his question come from? She had no idea this was the village where he'd been born. What a coincidence that they'd arrived in the same ... She bit her lip. Was it a coincidence?

She'd trusted him. Blindly, Mary would say. Against her advice, Mary would say. Inside her, Mary's voice – or her own voice: she wasn't sure which side of the wall it came from – rebuked her for being so naïve.

She glowered at Eole and picked up the map and travel log. He'd manipulated the whole journey to find his biological parents. And now he wanted her to ask his questions for him! What a cheek! She couldn't even shout at him in case he got upset, raised a gale and allowed the Tree Slayer to kill the One Tree – if the One Tree really was here. If this really was Koad. How much of what he'd said was actually true? The trees hadn't confirmed the forest was Koad. She only had Eole's word to go by. Perhaps the reason for the lack of storm damage here was that Eole's gale had been directed south towards the Pyrenees, not to the west. And if he was capable of such a degree of manipulation, he may even have invented the voices. She should have listened to Mary's doubts in François I park, when he'd suddenly declared that the voices came from nature.

"Thanks for your help, Hélène," she said to the secretary. "As you just heard, Eole has some questions on a different theme, so I'll leave you both in privacy."

She knew what she had to do, though she didn't know if the idea came from her or Mary. She picked up her rucksack and left the room.

Eole felt sick. Why had he spoken those words? It wasn't what he'd planned. He'd meant to finish saving the One Tree before asking Rainbow to help him, not just blurt it all out like that. He started to follow Rainbow out of the office but she slammed the door in his face. At the same time, Mademoiselle Henri spoke:

"Don't be afraid, Eole. Come and talk to me. I know exactly what procedure you must follow because you're the second person to ask in two days."

His brain told him to stay and his mind said he might as well find out about his parents now because it would save having to come back and do the introduction bit again, and maybe this time he could perform because he'd learnt how to do conversations properly with Rainbow, and he could speak to Mademoiselle Henri because he knew her and she was gorgeous according to Paul Coutances, though he thought 'rhinoceros-like' was more accurate than 'gorgeous' – or 'total babe', which was Hestia's description of her.

He fixed his eyes on the back of the photo frame on the counter and started at the top of his brain's table of questions. Although Mademoiselle Henri didn't comply with the responses he'd devised for her in his table, she did tell him that he had to write to the *Service Adoption et Accès aux Données Personnelles* in Rennes, who would contact his biological parents and ask if they wanted to meet him and, if so, this would be organised by the social workers, and there was an association who could accompany him psychologically and it would take at least a fortnight.

All her information went into his mental notebook, although she insisted on writing it down along with the address. And then she stopped writing and stopped talking and when he looked at her rhinoceros face (though without a horn, obviously) she was staring at him and tapping her pen against her nose and he knew that if he said nothing and waited she would end up speaking, just like ~~Alexandra~~ – no, Hestia had forbidden him to say that – um, Maman-A, when she wanted to talk about something special he'd done and she was searching for the right way for the words to come out. And so he waited.

"The local newspapers covered a 'baby for adoption' story here about eighteen years ago," said Mademoiselle Henri. "I'm not saying it was you, and I can't tell you anything more, dear, but you might like to look at the archives upstairs in the library."

She gave him some paper and an envelope for his letter and then she wished him luck, and when he didn't move she said he could leave now and join his lovely girlfriend outside. He stood up and mumbled that she wasn't his girlfriend but his soulmate, and Mademoiselle Henri raised her eyebrows and then picked up her phone receiver and said goodbye to him while she tapped in a number, and so he shouldered his rucksack and when he glanced at her again, she was staring at him and her lips were moving, so he left the office.

He was surprised to see that he was in the abbey entrance and not in Arras-en-Lavedan. Rainbow had her back to him and was studying the town noticeboard. He was relieved to see she was still there, but she looked bristly like a hedgehog.

She would probably shout at him now, like Hestia did when he messed things up. She'd never shouted at him before. He didn't want her to shout at him.

He stood behind her and wondered whether it would make things better or worse to tell her that they didn't need the voices now they had the map of trees. They would find the One Tree and save it, and afterwards he would write his letter to find Maman-B and Papa-B.

"Murderers!" muttered Rainbow, reading a council notice. There was a project to cut down a part of Paimpont forest near a village called Argoad. They were going to build a golf course there and the tree slaughter was scheduled for this week.

A rustle made her jump. Eole stood close behind her with some papers in his hand.

"So," she said, folding her arms. "Have you found your biological parents?"

"Not yet. I've got to write to the authorities."

She studied him: he avoided her eyes but his feet weren't squirming and he wasn't drawing in a deep breath. It was safe to probe a little more: "What will you do if they don't want to meet you?"

"They *will* want to meet me. I'm not their responsibility now I'm eighteen so there's no logical reason why they'd refuse."

Rainbow nodded, pretending to agree with him. Gerard at the commune had been adopted. She remembered him saying how desperately he'd wanted to meet his real parents. But they hadn't wanted to meet him. He'd been gutted. And furious. Would Eole blow up a storm if he was rejected?

"Well, good luck," said Rainbow. "I hope it all works out

for you. I'm going home."

Eole thought he'd misheard, and then he wondered if she was giving up because she couldn't read the map. Whatever the reason, it didn't make sense.

"Why?" he said.

"I may be naïve, but I'm not stupid, Eole. You only pretended the voices were guiding you here so I would come and help you trace your parents–"

Eole made the T-sign but Rainbow ignored it: "I just wish you'd told me the truth," she said. "I'd have driven you here and we'd have wasted less time. I could have gone to Massane forest with Thierry and I needn't have lost Christophe to Emilie. But it's too late for regrets. We've done what you wanted and now I'm going to Rennes to catch a train home. I'm still counting on you to keep your gale promises. So this is goodbye."

Rainbow turned and left the abbey.

"No! Rainbow!"

She didn't stop, not even at their bikes. He did a double take: there was only one bike left. She was walking back through the village. He caught up with her.

"Your logic is all wrong!" he said. "I didn't invent the voices. They must have stopped because we've reached Koad and this is where the One Tree is, not in Massane, and you must stay with me because I can help you with the map, and it doesn't matter if you've lost Christophe because he's not your soulmate but I *am* your soulmate and it's a coincidence that Paimpont is on the line the voices have guided us along and I only planned to investigate my biological parents after we'd saved the One Tree but we were in the council office so it was logical to ask, and you can't go home yet because we haven't finished our *together* mission and I don't want you to die and I must protect you one hundred per cent and when I make a promise I always keep it."

"It's over, Eole. I'm going home. You'd better go home too. Remember to take your bike back first."

"You'll die if we don't save the One Tree. I don't want you to die."

This was much harder than she'd expected, but Mary was back in full force and wouldn't let her give in. Eole hadn't created a storm in the whole time they'd been together. She could trust him to keep his promises.

"I won't die: not if you keep your promises," she said. "The One Tree isn't here. I'm going home and so should you. Goodbye, Eole."

"I'm coming with you."

She marched along the road towards the cemetery. He was following her, of course, as she'd known he would. Her timing was perfect: the lunchtime bus was waiting at the bus stop, filling with passengers. She walked past. As the last passenger boarded, she doubled back and stepped onto it.

The doors closed behind her rucksack. The bus lurched into movement. She squeezed her eyes shut and imagined Eole standing, forlorn, his feet shuffling. Too bad. He deserved it. It would be safer for the One Tree if she found it on her own.

PART IV

BROKEN HALVES

CHAPTER 30

Eole watched Rainbow get onto the Rennes bus. He knew he wasn't as good at understanding people as he was at understanding sheep, but he could tell she was acting strangely. Her reasoning was illogical. Was she making an excuse?

Hestia had once made an excuse. She'd said she was going to revise at Caroline's house, which was illogical because she never did schoolwork on Friday nights. It was an excuse because instead of going to Caroline's, she'd run away from home. The police had found her in Paris, beaten up, three days later.

Had Rainbow given him an excuse so she could do something harmful? He had to find her.

He remembered from the council office timetable that the next bus was in an hour's time. He sat down in the wooden shelter to wait. Above him, the cumulonimbus clouds were almost fully charged and thunder started to rumble. Rainbow might not have realised they were storm clouds. It could be the Tree Slayer, lurking in the storm and preparing to kill her and the One Tree. It was the worst possible moment for them to be separated.

He watched cars pass. After half an hour a woman sat next to him. He stood up and waited behind the shelter, under some trees. The wind had risen and it started to rain in slow, heavy drops. He listened to the faint voices in the trees. They still weren't talking to him but at least his ears had adapted to the near-silence and the ringing pain had lessened.

A taxi approached. Perhaps he should call a taxi so he could get to Rennes before Rainbow: then he would intercept her at the train station instead of arriving an hour after her. He peered through the leaves to see if there was a telephone number on the car.

A girl was slouched low in the back seat. She looked like Rainbow.

It couldn't be Rainbow. She was in the Rennes bus.

He was sure it *was* her.

He lurched out from behind the trees but the taxi had driven out of sight. He had no idea which direction it had taken. *Itch.* What should he do now?

Rainbow hunkered down in her seat. Eole wasn't sitting at the bus stop and she didn't see him along the road either. He must have caught the bus just after hers, whatever time it had left. She hoped he would manage to catch a train on his own. She imagined him at Rennes train station, trying to avoid the rush of passengers, his feet shuffling.

No, she mustn't imagine that. Now she'd tricked him, she must finish her mission quickly so she could revive Amrita and learn about the secret side of trees from her. She had to find the One Tree. She no longer needed Eole and the voices because she had a map. She just hoped that the reason the voices had stopped wasn't because she was too late.

She still couldn't decide how much of what Eole had said was true. She'd concluded the trees' voices were genuine, and not his invention, because he'd heard the word 'Koad'. But could it have been the Tree Slayer telling him where to go? Perhaps the Tree Slayer already knew where the One Tree was. Perhaps it simply wanted to get Eole there alone and make him blow it down. In that case, she'd been right to trick Eole and send him as far away from Koad as possible. She'd thwarted the Tree Slayer.

As she got out of the taxi at the campsite, the clouds began hurling down rigid lines of rain and then hail. She sheltered in the toilet block, where a cleaner stopped mopping and said the storm looked violent.

Before long, branches started thrashing in the wind. A paper bag vomited its burger box and cup as it tumbled across the car park. Rainbow ran outside and laid her hands on the closest tree, a poplar, searching for signs of the Tree Slayer. There was the same wire-fence restraint she'd felt in all the Brocéliande trees and she couldn't detect any personal feelings at all. However, there was none of the fear she'd sensed during Eole's gale. It was a normal storm and not the Tree Slayer.

The storm didn't last long, despite the heavy black clouds.

"Wind's changed direction," said the cleaner.

Rainbow wondered if Eole had kept his promise and blown the storm away. It was impossible: he wouldn't have stayed here without her. He'd still be on the bus to Rennes.

She couldn't stop thinking about him as she pitched her tent in the far corner of the campsite. She should have accompanied him to the station and put him on a train before escaping. He wouldn't be able to buy a train ticket alone. He couldn't even go into a shop. How could she have been so cruel?

Mary insisted she stop thinking about Eole. She must concentrate on the One Tree. She'd do whatever it told her, which would probably mean healing and strengthening it so that it could withstand the worst tree-slaying storm. She'd watch over it and fill it with energy until Amrita appeared, restored to her full splendour. She and Amrita would become inseparable sisters, sharing tree secrets and healing swathes of woodland side by side. With Amrita beside her, she would be closer to trees than ever before. She mustn't fail like she'd failed the François I oak.

She took the tourist map out of her pocket and tried to find a correlation between the roads around her and the lines on the paper. It was useless. She'd relied on Eole much more than she'd believed. He was like a cumbersome winter coat: only when you took it off did you realise how cold the weather was. She would have to find another solution.

She walked to Le Brécilien bar, picked up her bike from where she'd hidden it behind a shed, and asked Monique for directions to the ancient trees.

"Apart from Druid Oak, they're not easy to find. Your best bet is to ask Serge from the Forest Friends group in Argoad to take you round them. Tell him I sent you. Here, use the bar phone."

Rainbow called Serge, who said he was too busy to help

students with art projects. She mentioned Monique's name and he discovered he did have a free slot, after all, tomorrow afternoon. It was amazing to see how talking to people could help achieve an objective. She would have to tell Eole – except that she'd probably never see him again. She wanted to put his name into the box with Christophe and Thierry, but she couldn't afford to forget him. He was her enemy now she was so close to the One Tree.

The rest of the day lay ahead of her, so she followed Monique's directions and cycled to Druid Oak. It was just past the small village of Argoad and didn't require permission to visit because it was on municipal land.

The partially hollow oak was tall but bent over like an old man. It was massive, with a twelve-metre circumference, and could easily lodge two people inside. Rumoured to be a thousand years old, according to Hélène in the council office, it grew on the edge of the forest. She ran her hands over its gnarled bark, awed by its age. Wrinkled swirls had grown over wounds that probably dated from medieval times. This had to be the One Tree, even if it wasn't central.

It was so old that she had difficulty finding a place to communicate with it. She concentrated on laying herself bare and letting her fingers ripple over its bark ridges. One place was slightly more receptive and she laid both her palms over it. The sap beat was slow. She invited it to speak to her.

There was no response other than a feeling of weariness, disillusion and a deep resignation. She detected 'being yet not-being', which could mean it was close to death, but there was nothing to suggest it was the One Tree. Disappointed, she gathered the little energy she could feel around her and sent it into the tree's heartwood, wishing it a peaceful slumber. There was no reaction. She felt sorry for it, in its kingly magnificence. She'd have served it willingly.

She made a few sketches in her travel log and then hugged the younger oaks growing nearby. They communicated nothing in particular either. The trees in this forest were distinctly aloof. She would no doubt understand the reason why when Serge took her to the One Tree tomorrow.

🌱 🍃 🌱

The plan Eole's brain proposed was good: he was going to stay in Brocéliande forest, find Rainbow and protect her while she attempted whatever harmful thing she'd planned to do.

His feet relaxed and he left the bus stop in the heavy rain. In a backstreet, he put down his rucksack, took in a steady, damp breath and filled his lungs. The air was salty around its extremities and heavy in oxygen from the thousands of acres of trees photosynthesising around him.

It was exhilarating to fill his lungs right up. Breathing in like this took him to a higher level, away from humans on earth and up to the nebulae in the sky. He felt powerful, a force to be reckoned with. This is how God would feel, if he existed (which he didn't). People and everyday life became insignificant as Eole rose above them and blended with something more elemental. His brain told him that it was because it lacked oxygen, and while he acknowledged this, it didn't stop his mind enjoying the experience of unity with the troposphere.

When he could take in no more air, he faced westwards and breathed gently out, pushing the wind and the cumulonimbus clouds away from Brocéliande and back towards the Atlantic Ocean. He didn't know where the taxi had taken Rainbow, but wherever it was, she would now be safe from the Tree Slayer.

Next, he focused on the tourist map he'd memorised. They'd already seen one of the ten trees – the Anatole Le Braz oak tree at Les Forges de Paimpont – so Rainbow wouldn't be there. If he went backwards around the circuit, his path and Rainbow's would cross.

He began by walking into Paimpont centre, where he picked up his bike from the abbey and strapped his rucksack onto the carrier. He was hungry. Starving hungry. He hesitated outside a small grocery shop and then cycled awkwardly on, his rucksack making pedalling difficult. He stopped and put his hand on a bakery door handle, but didn't manage to actually open it. He paused in front of an ice-cream seller. The man spoke to him before he'd prepared his words, so he turned around and cycled into the dripping forest.

He soon picked up the tantalising scent of plums. A fruit tree in a private garden dangled with dozens of them, as tempting as Eve's fateful apple. There was nobody around. Maman-A would be cross if he stole. She'd tell him that God could see him, even if *she* couldn't. But God didn't exist and Maman-A was nowhere near. He didn't know what Maman-B would think.

He climbed over the stone wall, filled his mouth and pockets with juicy plums and then topped up his water bottle from a tap. On the far side of the garden was an apple tree, though the fruit didn't smell ripe. He collected a dozen apples for dinner. He would share them with Rainbow when he found her.

Late that evening, when he reached the sixth tree, he still hadn't seen Rainbow or smelt her mossy-woody odour. This tree, Druid Oak, was the most venerable of those he'd seen so far, though Guillotin's Oak was a close contender. He took his rucksack into the woods nearby, pitched his tent in a glade far enough away from Druid Oak so that no visitors to the tree would notice him, and organised his bed for the night.

The ground had dried, so he went to sit under the mighty oak with his multiverse book. He put his ear against the trunk and listened. There was no voice inside.

It was comfortable under the tree. He stifled a childish urge to climb inside the wide mouth of the hollow trunk, yawned, and then plunged into the pleasure of reading. It was comforting to think that in a parallel universe, Tintin hadn't died. He might be in the mountains discussing multiverses with a parallel Eole right now.

❦

Back at the campsite, Rainbow ate her evening meal and then queued in the dark for the telephone. There were no other solo campers. In the Val d'Azun she'd hardly noticed she was alone, but after spending weeks with Eole – despite him hardly ever talking – the empty space around her seemed oppressive. She slotted her phone card into the machine. She wasn't going to phone Christophe. She would be resilient and just call Mum and Domi. She wouldn't even ask after him.

She dialled the commune number and recognised Sandrine's voice, which always reminded her of metal wind chimes.

"Hi Sandrine, it's me."

"Rainbow!"

Sandrine chattered about how she'd jumped five metres from a tree into the River Charente, and how she'd been snorkelling with Domi. When Rainbow asked to speak to him, Sandrine went quiet.

"Is he out?" Rainbow asked.

"No. I'll get him. Are you all right?"

"I'm fine. Why?"

"It's just that when I close my eyes and imagine you there, it's all dark and I can hear screaming."

"Don't worry. No one is screaming, but it *is* dark because it's night-time. Everything is fine."

Sandrine passed her to Domi. Rainbow told him she was in Paimpont forest, which Eole believed to be Koad, and explained that she and Eole had parted ways. She waited for a lecture on how she shouldn't have abandoned him, but Domi didn't comment. He didn't even seem surprised. Had he known since his session with Eole? Or was this something else Sandrine had predicted? Before she could ask, he changed the subject:

"How are things with Mary? Have you finished reading my mother's memoir?"

Rainbow had completely forgotten the wad of notes stuffed at the bottom of her rucksack. She explained that Mary had been quiet and had helped her stay resolute, which seemed to satisfy Domi. She added that she'd been too busy with her travel log to do any reading and then asked what he thought about her and Eole separating.

"I presume you ensured he was safe. You must trust your intuition and make your own decisions."

"Right. Anyway, how's everyone there?" asked Rainbow.

"Fine."

"Have you seen ... I mean, no visits from anyone?"

"Wait a minute. Jasmine's making signs at me." There was a pause, and then Domi said, "She wants to speak to you."

Rainbow listened to her mum talk about a new blues group of British ex-pats she'd found. She stared at the people outside the telephone box and made listening noises whenever Mum paused to take a drag of her cigarette. A queuing couple were holding hands and laughing together. Instead of making Rainbow feel close to her family, the phone call had only increased her sense of distance from them. She told Mum her units were running out and said goodbye.

She didn't take her phone card out of the slot. Christophe's number, which was tattooed onto her heart, flashed up in neon lights in her mind. She wanted to hear his voice and have news of Apple and Acorn. But she didn't want confirmation that he was with Emilie.

There was a bang on the window and the couple tapped their watches. She took out her phone card and let the two of them jigsaw into the telephone box.

CHAPTER 31

When Eole woke on Thursday morning, he was cradled in the roots of Druid Oak. His dreams of crying babies and multiverses of forested planets fell away from him like dewy cobwebs in the wind. He was cold, stiff and hungry, and it was raining – but his ears had adjusted to the lack of voices and no longer hurt at all. He couldn't even hear their whispers. It was a good start to the day.

He ate the rest of his apples and plums and collected some unripe hazelnuts. He should set up some traps for rabbits so he could eat properly. He needed wire, string and a stick, and would have to find their rabbit holes and leave traps there overnight. But if he left Druid Oak he'd miss Rainbow. There were still four trees to visit, all to the north east of Paimpont and a fair way from his cosy camp.

He lay on his elbows in his tent, sheltering from the drizzle, and staked out Druid Oak. A young couple came and walked around it, taking photos, and he had to avert his eyes when an old woman took off all her clothes and danced around it in the rain.

By lunchtime, there was still no sign of Rainbow. Perhaps she'd already checked Druid Oak, decided it wasn't the One Tree and moved on. Perhaps the One Tree was Arthur's Oak or Hindrés Oak, or the ash tree at Trudeau. Perhaps she was already there. He must move on. But first, there was something else he had to do.

He pulled some dead branches over his tent to camouflage it and then cycled slowly along a path that lay between the forest and a row of houses.

Several of the houses' rear gardens had sheds backing onto the path. He peered into each shed window. At the last house in the row he saw the tools and workbench he needed. He walked into the street at the front of the house. He was in the centre of Argoad and the mailbox had the name 'Cazenave' on it. He hid behind a hydrangea bush at the side of the house, where he could see the front and the back, and watched for an hour. It seemed to be empty. He climbed over the rear wall into the back garden. Several fir trees obscured the shed from the main house, which was ideal, but the shed was locked. He checked under the sodden doormat and inside the plant pots nearby, and then found the key under a garden gnome. He opened the shed door and went inside. It was exactly right.

Rainbow spent the wet morning walking around the lake in the village, hugging the biggest trees and trying to understand why the forest felt so restrained.

She talked to everyone she met, and learnt that most of the forest was private and had been planted to make charcoal for the forge ironworks. She'd lied to Eole when she told him she thought the One Tree was in Massane forest, but in fact it *was* more logical. Massane was far wilder than Paimpont. But Amrita had told her to trust the trees, and the trees' voices had brought her here. She just had to find which tree, out of the millions in the forest, was the One Tree. And then she could go home. She couldn't understand why home was pulling at her like this. The desire must come from Mary because the last thing she wanted was to go home and see Christophe and Emilie together.

An old lady with a walking stick seemed happy to stop for a rest, and told her that Brocéliande was part of an ancient forest called Brécilien, which used to cover the inland part of Brittany. She also told her that 'Koad' was the Breton word for 'forest' and 'wood'. It was more proof that Rainbow was in the right place.

After treating herself to a lunchtime *galette* pancake stuffed with ham, cheese and egg, she cycled to Argoad. The rain had eased off but the water on the road soaked her jeans and she was saddlesore from the previous day's cycling. It was a relief to arrive. She left her bike at the Forest Friends' office and met Serge, her guide.

He didn't want to see her travel log. Once he'd asked after Monique, he wasn't interested in her at all. She disliked him but he did know lots about the forest. He also had the authorisation to take groups to the privately owned trees, so she didn't have to waste time phoning the owners.

He drove a jeep to three stunning beech trees in turn. The first beauty was Roche-Plate Beech, supposedly the biggest tree in the forest. It had been struck by lightning many times, Serge told her, and when Rainbow hugged it she could feel illness and death, as she had with Druid Oak. Then came the majestic Traveller's Beech, whose wavy branches looked as if someone with the same gift as hers had been practising on it. Finally, they visited the creepy Ponthus Beech, whose branches reminded her of groping tentacles. Each beech tree was so magnificent that she was initially sure she'd found the One Tree. Each time, however, she was disappointed by the lack of communication from the tree.

Serge was enthusiastic about his environmental work in the forest, though he admitted that he didn't think his association would last long because the general public didn't care about the environment.

"You're wrong. Some people care," said Rainbow as she sketched Ponthus Beech. "Most people just don't think about trees and the role they play. They haven't been shown how important they are. If someone could show them, I bet the vast majority of people would fight for trees."

"You're still young and optimistic," he said. "You'll see, when you're older."

People over thirty were always so negative. "It's just a question of education," she replied.

Remembering how Thierry had stressed the importance of networking, she made conversation with Serge. She told him she was hoping to do an arboriculture course, if she could get sponsorship, and then asked him how he and his association would react if he saw proof that people could communicate spiritually with trees and shape their branches. He said they didn't sponsor students, and that Forest Friends were a scientific body, not a cult.

"It's already hard enough to get people interested in tree

welfare," he said. "If we start mixing science with mysticism, we're done for. You're right about education. We need to prove the importance of trees scientifically. That's the only thing that will convince people to take an interest in them and look after them."

She was right to pretend she was doing an art project and hide the spiritual side of her quest. Serge would scoff if she told him about Amrita and the One Tree. He certainly wouldn't help her.

She approached the remaining oak, beech and ash trees humbly, ready to bow to each. But none – even the ancient, stumpy Guillotin's Oak – responded to her touch with images and wisdom.

She stared out of the window at the hundreds of thousands of trees as Serge drove her back towards his office in Argoad. How would she ever find the One Tree? If she had to hug every single tree, she'd be a hundred years old before she found it. Was this what Amrita intended her destiny to be?

Perhaps she shouldn't have been so quick to ditch Eole. What if the Koad trees were waiting for her and Eole to prove their good intentions before speaking to them?

How stupid of her! If the precious last One Tree grew in Brocéliande, it was unlikely to publicise its existence, especially to the person who hosted the Tree Slayer. It would want to be sure they were honourable before revealing itself. She'd already noticed that the Brocéliande trees were restrained and didn't communicate their feelings. Was it the One Tree's influence? Now that the Tree Slayer had gone – and if she proved she was worthy of them – they might confide in her.

Serge's voice broke into Rainbow's thoughts: "This is the part of the forest the council is felling for the golf course," he said. "They should have started this week but the contractors only arrive tomorrow. They'll probably begin on Monday. Such a shame."

Rainbow looked to where he was pointing. "But isn't Druid Oak over there?"

"Sure is. They won't cut it down, though. They're going to keep it in the centre of the car park and make a feature of it. The oak is on its last legs, anyway."

"Why can't they make their stupid golf course in the fields?"

Serge parked beside the agency office. "The farmers won't have it. Anyway, I told you: nobody's interested in trees. Originally, the council bought the land to protect Druid Oak. But then Hugues Barateau – he's Argoad's mayor – persuaded the council to accept a company's proposal to build a golf course on it. The course will be good for the tourists who come here for the Arthurian legends. Our office is close by. We can offer them woodland activities and raise their environmental awareness."

"But you should be fighting for the trees!"

He pulled up the handbrake sharply. "Easy to say. Have you ever tried to fight a council's plans?"

"Well ... no."

Even as she said it, she could feel Mary nagging: Mary's best friend Trish had fought for trees. She'd lived in one with an ecologist group for six weeks and stopped a whole wood being felled. Rainbow had often felt Mary's yearnings for Trish. Now she was remembering Trish's laugh and she could smell the perfume that had filled her flat when Trish moved in with her temporarily. Trish would know what to do.

Rainbow shook herself, disorientated. These were Mary's memories, not hers.

"Take my word for it," said Serge. "You can't win. Money's more important to politicians than the planet."

"You should try, at least."

He gave her a long, condescending look. "We have. We did our best. If you're so upset about it, why don't *you* do something?"

Campaigning would be the perfect way to demonstrate her good intentions to the One Tree. If she managed to save this part of the forest, the One Tree might instruct its trees to communicate their feelings more freely. By hugging them, and through trial and error, she might eventually locate it. Fighting to save this part of the forest was the right thing to do. At the moment it was the only thing she could do.

"Right. I will."

He laughed. "Sure. And how will a slip of a girl persuade the Argoad council to change its plans where Forest Friends has failed? The contractors are on their way as we speak."

"I don't know yet."

If it were possible to enter Mary's parallel world, she would do so and ask Trish for advice. But it wasn't. Mary's arrival in Rainbow's world had been engineered by Amrita, who was too weak to help her now. Eole had read about merging paths in his multiverse book, but he was such a slow reader that he still hadn't finished the book when she'd left him. All *she* knew about parallel worlds was what she'd read in Domi's mother's memoir notes.

Was the answer in the part she hadn't read yet? Was that

why Domi had given her the memoir and nagged her to read it? She hadn't seen the brown envelope for days, and hoped it hadn't got wet in the bottom of her rucksack. She would check it as soon as she returned to her tent, even though she doubted it would help: the idea of popping into a different world was absurd. She must make a more plausible plan, since the contractors would start felling in four days'time.

"What do I need to know about the project?" she asked Serge.

He paused, jeep keys in his hand, and studied her face. "You're serious, aren't you?"

"You bet I am," she said.

"Then you'd better come into the office and see what you're up against."

She followed Serge indoors, imagining Druid Oak in the centre of a car park, surrounded by tarmac and isolated from the other trees. Thierry said trees survived better in forests because built-up areas were too warm at night. They needed the cool of other trees around them, not hot concrete. He'd also told her that the packed soil under tarmac stopped trees spreading their roots and receiving messages. Druid Oak would surely die more quickly in isolation.

She would prove her worth to the One Tree, wherever it may be, by launching herself into this campaign and saving the trees from being felled.

CHAPTER 32

Early on Thursday afternoon Eole finished in the Cazenave workshop. He'd made some rabbit traps, improvised a stand for his gas cooker and designed a belt to hold up his trousers, which had become loose.

He could have stayed in the workshop all afternoon and experimented with the electronic equipment and soldering iron, but he had to get back to his search for Rainbow. She'd have found the One Tree by now. It would be easy to spot her camp, even if it was more difficult to smell her woody-mossy odour here in the forest.

The photos on the workshop wall showed two adults and a teenage daughter, so he left a note addressed to the Cazenave family and one hundred francs for the materials he'd taken. Then he put the workshop key back under the gnome and set his rabbit traps by the burrows on the edge of the forest.

Since arriving in Brocéliande, his brain had found it easier to make plans. It was as if help came from something external. Was it the oxygen-rich air? In any case, it had cleared the muddy waters of his mind and was helping his brain make decisions. Hestia would be proud of him. At this rate, he'd even manage Toulouse university.

The sun came out and he ate two apples before cycling to Hindrés Oak. The tree was easy to find and much less impressive than Guillotin's Oak and Druid Oak. He looked up the straight trunk and into the high branches. It was tall, strong and special, like him. If he were a tree, he thought he might be this one. He put his arms around the trunk and laid his ear against it.

He could just make out a voice in its depths, but it was muffled, unlike the former rich music of the voices. He didn't know if his ears or the voices were the problem. He tried the other ear. It was the same. The voice was on the lower limit of the frequency he could hear, and when he let go of the tree, he could hear no voices at all.

Before he arrived in Koad the voices had been friendly and guided him. As soon as he'd reached Koad, they turned their backs on him. What had he done wrong? Had the Brittany voices recognised him as the source of the gale? He thought back to Tintin and that moment up on the hill when he'd begun blowing. He'd been filled with hate for the chestnut tree that had killed Tintin. Later, when he'd understood the extent of the damage the wind had caused, he'd been ... well, pleased. Proud, even.

The sweat on his back felt cold and clammy. How could he have been proud of such a terrible thing? Apart from hating assassin trees because of Tintin, he'd never really thought about them. They were simply there, like mountains, houses and streets. Even when he'd seen Rainbow shape branches, he'd only thought how good it was to find someone else with a secret special skill.

He stroked Hindrés Oak like he stroked Darwie. The bark wasn't soft but it was reassuring. It was solid and dependable. It was alive. Why shouldn't it have a voice?

Suddenly he knew that the voices weren't something speaking through the trees: they were the trees themselves. His mind knew it, even though it was totally unscientific because his brain didn't have any proof. A picture of Maman-A kneeling in church appeared to him. Maybe her irrational conviction that God existed felt like this.

He looked around the woods. Every tree now demanded his attention. Before, they'd been a mass of vegetation; now they were individuals, like people. They were a crowd of individuals with voices. He mustn't think of them as a crowd, or he'd get *itch, shuffle and escape* and never find his way out of the forest. They were a single entity, a symphony of different notes. That was better. They'd all spoken together, in harmony – and they'd spoken to him. To think he'd been able to hear and understand the trees' words! It seemed incredible, now he'd lost the power to do so.

He wanted to tell Rainbow. He had to find her.

He breathed in. There was a mossy-woody smell like Rainbow's personal odour, but it was richer, more concentrated, and probably came from the trees. He searched the surrounding undergrowth, looking for her tent.

He found nothing, which meant she wasn't here, which meant Hindrés Oak wasn't the One Tree. He picked up his bike and cycled towards the giant ash tree in Trudeau.

Inside the Forest Friends' office, a whole shelf had been allocated to fighting the golf course. Rainbow softened a little towards Serge. He'd spoken the truth when he said they'd done their best. She picked up a thick file. It was dusty.

"The decision was made months ago," said Serge.

She flicked through meeting minutes, reports on soil, flora and fauna, through designs of octagonal buildings and bird's eye views of car parks, golfing greens and fountains. Serge picked up a colourful plan of the club house and explained how it would use geothermal heating.

"We persuaded them to use solar panels too," he said proudly.

Rainbow closed the file and flicked through the next one: more meeting minutes. More reports. There were plenty of words but she couldn't find anything that mentioned the action they'd taken to save the trees. She didn't intend to waste time on the whole shelf of files. When she asked Serge which one held the details of their publicity campaign to defend the forest, he pulled a small folder and a handful of crumpled leaflets from the back of a drawer.

"On recycled paper, of course," he said.

It wasn't only the leaflet paper that was recycled. The slogan 'Save our Forest' had been recycled hundreds of times too, and the statistics listed below the title were uninspiring. The colours were dreary beiges and dark greens, as if the designer was already defeated. Rainbow sorted through the publicity documents in the folder and eventually found the words 'Protest Group' jotted on a piece of paper, with a name and address beside it: Druana Cazenave. It was an evocative first name, one that made her think of Celts, druids and oak trees – and she lived right here in Argoad, so it didn't matter that there was no telephone number. Rainbow could go and see her.

She continued to study the files of reports, noting all the negative effects the deforestation would have on the forest's biodiversity and asking Serge to explain the technical words. After an hour, she'd filled four pages with notes. She pocketed them and told Serge she was ready for the battle.

He glanced up from the forestry magazine he was reading and smirked. "Off you run, then," he said.

She'd been about to explain her plan to find Druana, who, she hoped, would help her get the protest group back together so they could demonstrate against the council. But it was obvious he didn't think she could achieve anything. She said goodbye and turned to leave.

"Hey!" he said. "Don't go doing anything stupid like chaining yourself to a tree or hijacking the contractors' equipment. We don't want any bad press. Talking of which, you might find this useful." He passed her a document and explained it contained their media contacts. "The local newspaper office will be closed now, but you can call from here tomorrow if you like."

She thanked him and accepted his offer to take away a file to study in her tent that evening. The information she'd gathered was important but the key to saving the forest was action. She needed Druana and her protestors.

🌿 🌿 🌿

Eole didn't find any sign of Rainbow at Trudeau either, so he knew by deduction that he would find her at the last tree in the circuit.

He didn't want to scare her and he needed to make sure she would listen to him and not fob him off with another excuse. As he cycled along the road under the trees, his brain planned how he would get her to listen. The most effective way would be to tie her up but he was sure Hestia wouldn't approve of that. Hestia was bound to find out: she always did. He would start by facing Rainbow and maybe holding onto her shoulders so she wouldn't turn away, like he'd done for the kiss. He'd only tie her up as a last resort.

He left his bike on the roadside and walked along the track to Gelée Beech. Rainbow wasn't hugging it, but she couldn't hug it all the time. She would be nearby, watching over it.

Her tent wasn't here. How could she possibly save the One Tree if she didn't sleep beside it? He turned in a slow circle, breathing in to see if he could distinguish her woody-mossy odour.

He couldn't.

He hadn't smelt it since she'd left him at the bus.

Was it really her he'd seen in the taxi?

If she wasn't here, he had no reason to be here. *Itch*. What was he doing? What was his plan?

He tried to put down roots but the trees' roots were taking up all the earth under his feet and there was no room. He hugged Gelée Beech. Without the voices there was no comfort. *Shuffle*. He had to move, but where? Where could he go? He belonged with Rainbow but he didn't know where she was, and he wanted to go home to Darwie but he was hundreds of miles from home and in any case he didn't belong there either. He breathed in and willed his brain to calm the long, panicky strings of thoughts in his mind. If he let go, his feet would take him away and lose him in the forest. He needed help.

A thought came to his rescue and nudged his brain into action. It reminded him that although Rainbow may have gone, he did have a secondary plan. He'd been born in Paimpont. This was his home. He belonged here, whether Rainbow was in the forest or not.

He let his breath escape upwards and watched it forge a fluttering path through the canopy of leaves, up to the cloudy sky. Yes. His secondary plan. He would stay and look up his biological family. Tomorrow he would go to the library, as Mademoiselle Henri had suggested. He hadn't been inside a library for weeks, hadn't smelt the fusty, friendly fragrance of plastic covers, carpets and ageing paper.

His feet calmed. First, he must plan tonight's meal. If his traps had worked, he might be able to eat rabbit stew. He walked back along the path towards his bike.

Footsteps were coming the other way. Rainbow?

He stopped walking and breathed in. It wasn't Rainbow. The smell was familiar, though. It was lilac, but without the goaty notes, and it felt like pointed knives but also like bedtime stories. For a second he was confused, suspended between past and present. His olfactory receptors were playing games with his brain. He stepped off the path and hid behind a leafy bush. It couldn't be Maman-A. She didn't know he was here.

It *was* Maman-A.

She continued walking towards him. His mind calculated probabilities and sought explanations as he watched her approach, and he settled for a ninety-five-per-cent chance that Rainbow had rung her.

He felt drawn to her. He could step out and surprise her and she would make a bleaty cry and the crease between her eyebrows would disappear and she'd smile and say "Thank you God for delivering my Eole safely," and make her love-hug sign, and then she'd take him back to her bed-and-breakfast because she had a passion for bed-and-breakfasts and was bound to be staying in one, and she'd order him a proper meal and let him close his eyes and guess what was on the plate before he ate it, and then she'd drive him home and Darwie would race out to meet him, his tail wagging so hard that it would look as if he was dancing, and they'd hike up to the summer pastures and check on Patou and the sheep, and he would lie back in the grass with his books and make cloud art and think about Tintin and science, and Hestia would stomp up and interrupt his thoughts and tell him off and then she would tease him and they'd laugh about something Papa-A had done and everything would be simple again.

Maman-A paused, as if she could sense him.

Yes, everything would be simple again, but only for a while, because then he would think about Rainbow instead of physics and meteorology, and every time there was a storm he'd counteract it and wonder about the Tree Slayer and the One Tree and he would never know whether Maman-B and Papa-B would have wanted him and whether he belonged better with them than with his adoptive parents in the mountains.

His brain told him to stay behind the bush. He would call Hestia tomorrow, as planned, and she would give him Maman-A's bed-and-breakfast address. Once he'd located his biological family, he would visit Maman-A and tell her all about them.

Maman-A walked on again.

His hands were shaking when he stepped onto the path. He didn't stop trembling until he was back at Druid Oak, dealing with the buck rabbit that had strangled itself in one of his traps.

🌿 🌿 🌿

Rainbow left Forest Friends and stopped a dog walker to ask for directions to the Cazenaves' house. He explained it was opposite the village bar, and she cycled along the street towards it.

She was armed with a file, her notes and a list of journalist contacts. It wasn't much, but it could be enough to fire up the locals if Druana was able to organise a meeting for tomorrow evening. That way, they'd have all weekend to prepare a strategy and would be ready to face the bulldozers on Monday.

She prepared a speech in her head as she pedalled. Of course, she wouldn't be making the speeches: that would be Druana's job. The idea of standing up in front of people and speaking made her feel sick, whereas Druana would be an experienced nature lover and activist, used to making rallying speeches. Rainbow would just give Druana her ideas. How inspiring it would be to work with someone else who loved trees enough to set up a protest group!

The last house in the row opposite the village bar had 'Cazenave' marked on its mailbox. She buzzed the bell at the front gate. The shutters were open but there was no answer. She buzzed it several more times, in vain. She looked up and down the empty street. The only movement came from someone inside the bar, which was also a brasserie and shop. She crossed the road.

The bar was big inside, with tables set for meals, but the only customer was an elderly man who was talking to the long-haired barman. Rainbow ordered a Coke and looked around. There were no 'Save Our Forest' leaflets on the advertisements board, so she asked the barman if she could leave one. He shrugged and told her he didn't have any spare drawing pins. She pinched some from the other adverts and asked if there had been any protests about the golf course.

"No point, is there? Not with Barateau heading up the council. Always gets what he wants, that one, doesn't he, Jacques?"

"Aye. Too right," said the old man. "Shame, though. All them strangers'll be looking in our front windows."

"Starting with those film stars tomorrow." The barman leant closer to the old man. "Did you hear they're invited to the festival? They've got some new environmental film coming out. There's talk of photo shoots and the like."

The old man harrumphed. "Can't be doing with showbiz," he said.

The two of them resumed their muttering. Rainbow took her drink outside onto the terrace, wondering if it would be worth watching the environmental film, and looked for a seat where she could keep a lookout on Druana's house. A collection of green and blue gas bottles chained together took up half the space. She sat beside them and filled in her travel log while she watched for Druana.

By dinner time, Druana still hadn't arrived. Rainbow hoped she hadn't gone on holiday. She decided to return the following morning, and cycled back to the campsite.

At the bottom of her rucksack she found the soggy memoir notes Domi had given her and spread them out to dry in her tent. Luckily, the ink hadn't run. She didn't want to risk damaging them further. She would read them as soon as they were dry – though now she had Druana, she didn't really need them anymore.

At least, she hoped she had Druana. If Druana wasn't back tomorrow, Rainbow would have to start campaigning on her own, without the help of an experienced leader. There wasn't much time left. Perhaps she should begin. She could ring Melanie Brown, the English journalist she'd met at the Marais Poitevin campsite. Melanie would surely want to protest about this project to massacre part of the magical forest of Brocéliande.

CHAPTER 33

On Friday morning, Eole woke to the sound of people talking beside Druid Oak. He unzipped his tent. It wasn't Rainbow. Of course it wasn't, he reminded himself: she'd left Brocéliande and now he had his secondary plan to carry out.

He washed in the stream and dressed. Today he had to go into Paimpont. Alone. His brain reminded him that although he had a demanding plan, he didn't have to think any further than the first part for the moment. It was like considering the ascent of Vignemale Mountain in separate, manageable stages instead of one difficult climb.

He cycled towards Paimpont. Cumulonimbus clouds were gathering in the sky, just like a couple of days ago, and the air was muggy. He'd have to monitor the weather while he was in the library: he must keep his promises.

There was a lot of activity on the road to Paimpont. A car with flashing orange lights came towards him and then a bulldozer on a flatbed lorry rattled past, blocking most of the road. A queue of cars followed the convoy and a couple of motorbikes zipped out onto his side of the road to overtake them. While he cycled, Eole concentrated on making a table of questions and possible responses for his contact with the librarian.

Unlike on Wednesday, the Paimpont streets were full of people. He put his hand in his pocket for his headphones. They weren't there. He hadn't needed them for so long that he'd forgotten to bring them. There was no time to go back to his tent, so he used his contingency method of staring at the ground and not engaging in eye contact with anyone.

The library was on the first floor of the abbey, above the secretary's office. He took a steadying breath, entered, and climbed the wooden staircase. A sign at the top told him it was closed today and wouldn't be open until tomorrow afternoon. While he stood on the landing, waiting for his brain to find an alternative plan, footsteps came towards him. There was a smell of fish and then Mademoiselle Henri appeared.

"Eole! Have you found your mum yet?"

He kept his eyes on his boots so he could visualise Mademoiselle Henri from Arras-en-Lavedan better, and shook his head. It was an illogical question because she'd said it would take a fortnight to get a reply to his letter, which he hadn't even written yet.

"Did you want to check the library archives?"

He nodded.

"It's closed, but I can let you in. I know you won't vandalise the books."

An empty library would be heaven (not that heaven existed). He waited for her to get the key and then followed her inside the series of little rooms. At the end she showed him some hand-bound books of newspaper cuttings about Paimpont.

She told him to pop into her office when he'd finished and then left him alone. He relaxed, sat down and pored over the books. Mademoiselle Henri had told him that the newspaper story about the baby dated from eighteen years ago. If the baby was him, the article would have been written after his birthday. He looked for cuttings from June 1978.

🍂🍃🍂

On Friday morning, Rainbow woke later than she'd intended. The memoir notes were still damp and, as she separated the pages, she saw the passage she'd read before about the danger of two parallel beings meeting. She remembered how she'd expected herself or Mary to be absorbed as soon as they'd touched hands – and when they hadn't, she'd discounted the authenticity of the memoir. But Mary *had* been absorbed, even though it hadn't happened immediately.

Rainbow read beyond the part where she stopped last year. Domi's mother had written about the after-effects of absorption and was emphatic that care must be taken when one personality was stronger than the other. "Rare are the cases where equilibrium is reached and true sharing achieved," Rainbow read. "Unless the need is dire, a mental separation is safer: otherwise the weaker personality can disappear altogether."

No wonder Domi had worried about Mary's personality taking over and suggested she construct a mental wall. Rainbow was relieved she'd kept the wall intact. Though, come to think of it, the original wall of solid bricks now felt more like a thin elastic membrane.

She tried to separate the page from the next one so she could read the following section, but when she peeled them apart the corner disintegrated into mush. She would read the rest later, when the paper was completely dry.

Walking to the campsite phone box, she compared the warning in the memoir notes with Amrita's words. Amrita had said she must recognise she was One with Mary, and Rainbow was pretty sure she'd done so by giving Mary more space and letting her make occasional decisions. Mary's recent lack of resistance was proof they'd learnt to accommodate each other. Amrita couldn't mean for her to step aside completely. The memoir was confirmation that if she did so, she would disappear.

She couldn't imagine Mary sharing. Mary would keep her strength to herself and force her desires on Rainbow. She would make Rainbow abandon Amrita and go home. The only time Mary had shared her strength was when they'd been in agreement. Rainbow decided she'd done what she needed to become whole. She wasn't going to sacrifice herself to Mary and risk letting down Amrita.

She called the newspaper office, holding the notes she'd made from Forest Friends' bulging files. An assistant journalist answered. Rainbow asked if she could speak to Olivier Montagne, Serge's contact.

"He's out this morning," said the boy.

"Can I speak to another journalist?"

"They're all out."

Rainbow told him it was important to warn readers that they were about to lose a part of their forest and precipitate the death of Druid Oak.

"Already done that story," said the boy. Rainbow could hear him chewing gum.

"Not from the point of view of the trees," she said. "I read your articles and none of them take the trees' side. I've got a whole lot of information about the biodiversity we're going to lose if they're cut down. And I want to gather supporters. Surely you've got a bit of space for a short piece?"

"I'll tell Olivier. But don't bank on it. Not today. We're expecting film stars in Paimpont."

Rainbow silently cursed the film stars and said she'd call again that afternoon, when the assistant thought Olivier might be back. Then she took Melanie Brown's card from her purse and rang her.

"Rainbow! How's your trip going?" asked Melanie.

Rainbow could hear the smile in her voice. She explained how they'd arrived at Brocéliande and told her about the golf course project.

"These councils," sighed Melanie. "They only think about making money in the short term so they're voted into office in the next round of elections. It's despicable. How's your travel log coming along?"

"I've almost filled the book. Listen, do you think you could do a feature on what's happening here?"

There was a pause. "I really feel for you, Rainbow. I know it's terrible, but this kind of thing is happening all over the country. All over the world, in fact. I wish I could help, but I need an angle. A 'people' angle. Readers need to identify with a person."

Rainbow remembered Trish telling her how her ecology

group had only caught the media's attention once they'd taken action, that it was the protestors who'd interested the public. No! Not telling *her*: telling *Mary*. She must keep that separation.

"What if I get a group of us to set up a camp in the trees? In Druid Oak?" she asked.

"Good for you. Do it."

"And you'd write something about us?"

"I don't know. It's not very original, is it? Listen, I have to get back to work. Let me know if you come up with an original idea. I'm only a ten-minute drive away. In fact, why don't you come and show me your travel log?"

Rainbow said she'd love to, and would get back to her, but she knew her voice lacked enthusiasm. Melanie repeated that she was busy and had to go.

Rainbow hung up. She didn't need journalists. All she needed was to convince the council to stop. She and the protest group would demonstrate outside the Argoad council office. They could pile dead branches in the street and stop the councillors getting in – or, better still, out. They could imprison them until that Barateau man agreed to listen.

She must gather the supporters, and for that she needed Druana.

❧ ❧ ❧

Eole scanned the article cuttings. There were reports on forestry groups, restored mills and the work of a local research centre. There were obituaries, election news, car accidents and open days. There was a photo of a baby.

There were no adults in the black-and-white photo, and the

baby could have been a girl or a boy. In a few seconds he would know his real name and the identities of his biological parents. He wiped his sweaty hands on his shorts and started to read.

It was a small article, a call for information from readers. A baby boy estimated at a few days old had been discovered at the foot of a tree in a village near Paimpont. He'd been wrapped in a silk-bordered cotton tablecloth embroidered with leaves, and was now at the nursery in Chantepie. The nursery wanted the mother to come forward because her health was in danger.

A ragged cloth with bumpy leaves and a silk edging.

Eole could remember the familiar smell of the cloth, in his Paris bed, scrunched up beside Pooh Bear. He remembered the way he'd rub the silk to fall asleep. He could see the green holly leaves, three in each corner, arranged around a red berry that tasted soapy. He could feel the threads of the fraying stitches in his fingers.

He'd been left to die. *Itch*.

His mother hadn't wanted him.

There would be no Maman-B or Papa-B.

He didn't belong with anyone. *Shuffle*.

He heard the chair fall over backwards and saw books scatter across the floor, but he couldn't stop because it wasn't him who was in control, and the sides of his vision were crawling inwards and the stairs tunnelled out in front of him, and he pushed away the flailing hands of fishy Mademoiselle Henri whose words flew at him like a murder of pecking crows and he was walking outside in the fresh air.

But something was wrong.

His ears hurt and Jesus Christ (who had perhaps existed, unlike God), his ears really, really hurt and something big was happening and his feet stopped and he clasped his hands to his ears and all he could hear was screaming and he thought it was himself but no, no, it was outside in the air like an orchestra taken over by the devil except that the devil didn't exist and the voices were screeching and twanging. And his brain latched onto the separate threads of the voices and understood the number '6000' and then '5999' and '5998', even though it wasn't exactly numbers he could hear, and he jumped on his bike and his feet pedalled to follow the counting, and by '1350' whatever was in charge of him knew where the voices were taking him and there was nothing else left for him to do because he didn't belong here or anywhere and so nothing had meaning anymore.

And when the not-exactly-numbers reached zero he recognised the tree and his brain told him what he had to do and his mind knew he'd promised Rainbow he'd never do it again but his brain didn't care about his promise. He dropped his bike behind a bush and took a long, deep breath.

CHAPTER 34

After her telephone calls and a mid-morning brunch, Rainbow cycled from Paimpont towards Druana's house in Argoad. She glanced up at the menacing sky from time to time, worried about the Tree Slayer.

On Wednesday, the storm had taken all morning to arrive. Today, the black clouds had arrived suddenly and a strong headwind channelled along the road, slowing her down. She was almost at walking pace, yet the treetops were only bowing gently, as if it were just a breeze. Somewhere in this forest, the One Tree must be sucking in the wind to protect its trees, just like the oak tree in François I park had done.

A gust blew through a fire gap in the trees and her bike swerved into the middle of the road. She fought to control it. If she'd kept Eole beside her, he'd have blown this storm back to where it had come from. But he'd promised to counteract any storms. Perhaps he lacked the strength from his home, hundreds of miles away in the Pyrenees – though his tree-slaying gale had ravaged the whole west of France, so this couldn't be the case. There was plenty of power in his lungs.

Was the wind coming from Eole? Perhaps he'd remained in Brocéliande, traced his biological parents and been rejected by them. No! He'd never have stayed here alone, and it would have taken far longer to find them. Or had the Tree Slayer sucked enough strength out of Eole to force him to unleash a gale?

Above her, the storm clouds darkened. Thunder rumbled and lightning flashed in the distance. She had to check if it was Eole. She dropped her bike on the verge and dashed to the nearest tree, a Douglas fir. It was trembling. She closed her eyes and concentrated.

The feeling of restraint had evaporated. Fear and death emanated from the panicking fir tree, just like the trees during the tree-slaying gale in Cognac.

Could it be Eole? There was one way to find out.

"Eoooooole! Stop!" she cried.

The howling wind paused, then continued.

It *was* him. He'd raised a storm and now the Tree Slayer would use it to destroy the One Tree.

What could she do? Without knowing the location of the One Tree, she couldn't go and help it fight the wind like she had done with the François I oak. She was powerless. She pressed herself to the fir tree and begged it to guide her to the One Tree.

There was no response, no other feeling than unrestrained fear and death. It was in too much of a panic to guide her anywhere. She hugged its neighbour and then the next tree along. Their response was identical.

She could do nothing to help. She was useless. She'd progressed no further in her mission since leaving Cognac.

If she'd vanquished the Tree Slayer by pushing Eole off the mountain, she'd have better protected the One Tree.

It was too late for regrets. The One Tree would die. She was about to fail her mission. What was the point in trying to campaign against the golf course?

She picked up her bike.

Whether the One Tree lived or died, it was wrong to cut down trees for a golf course. Her gift was less powerful than Eole's and she was the weaker half of her cohabitation with Mary. But she could still fight for the forest. It didn't require a powerful gift: only determination. Mary was determined. She and Mary had been the same person until they split, so shouldn't they have the same character traits? She could match Mary's determination. She could do this. Saving the Brocéliande trees would be the phoenix to rise from the ashes of her mission.

She straddled the bike and struggled onwards, standing on her pedals and forcing down each leg in turn to keep them moving. By the time she arrived in Argoad, the sparse raindrops had become a deluge.

The wind dropped as suddenly as it had started. Did this mean the Tree Slayer had succeeded and the One Tree was dead? Would the Tree Slayer come and kill her next? Amrita had said they would all perish if she failed. *Please let it be a false alert*, she willed.

Her tyres swished along the road and she squinted through the sheets of rain. Argoad was busier than yesterday. Cars were parked everywhere, including outside Druana's house, though there were no people in sight. They were probably in the bar, sheltering from the cloudburst. She stopped and pressed the bell at the Cazenaves' gate.

There was no answer. She rang again. Still no answer. Shivering, she dropped her bike, climbed over the gate and banged on the front door. Nobody replied.

She was drenched. And frozen. Opposite her, on the other side of the street, the windows of the bar were steamed up and she could make out the shapes of dozens of people. Warm, dry people. It didn't feel right to think of her comfort while the One Tree was dying somewhere in the forest. But if she didn't warm up, she'd shiver to death.

She dashed across the road, her teeth chattering.

It was lunchtime and the tables were full. Everyone seemed to know each other: the food must be really good for people to come all the way here to eat. She laced through the crowd to the bar and leant against it, rubbing her cold upper arms as she waited to order a hot chocolate. Her leaflet was still on the board. The men beside her were discussing the horse race they'd bet on, and she recognised Jacques from the day before. She wished the long-haired barman would hurry.

At last she caught his attention. He nodded at her, frothed the milk and served her drink. She took it and warmed her hands.

"Got caught in the rain, did you?" he said. "Can't complain about it, though. Bet you're glad it's brought the workmen to a stop."

"The workmen?"

"The foresters. You do know they arrived this morning, right?"

"What?" She clacked down her cup onto its saucer. Serge had said they'd begin on Monday.

"Yeah. No messing. Druid Oak will be first, so they say. Soon as the rain stops."

"No way! They're not supposed to cut it down! They agreed to keep it."

"That's what I thought too. Maybe Jacques got it wrong." He slapped down her change and turned to Jacques. "Eh, Jacqui! That old oak there. They told you they'd have it down?"

"Aye. Got the papers for it 'n' all. They wanted to give it the chop this morning, before anyone found out."

"I've got to do something," said Rainbow.

"Too late for that," said the barman.

There must be something she could do. She looked around for inspiration. She needed to divert them. Could she vandalise the workmen's machines? Pour water in the petrol tanks? Cause an explosion? Her eyes fell on the gas bottles she'd sat next to yesterday. There was one thing she could do.

"Can I have the key for the gas bottles?" she asked the barman.

"You want gas?" he asked, then chuckled. "Of course not. You want the chain."

"Yes. Please?"

He shook his head. "Crazy ecologists," he said. But he reached below the bar and then handed her the key. "I suppose I'll have to go and get it back when the police drag you off to prison."

"Maybe. Thanks loads." Rainbow grabbed the key and dashed outside into the rain. She couldn't help the One Tree but she would do her best for Druid Oak and the golf course trees.

Eole's mind was fuzzy from exhaustion.

He'd done it. This is what his special skill was for.

His mind felt blurred but his brain was clear and it was telling him what to do next, even though he hadn't planned any part of this sudden impulse since the screaming had started. He pushed his wet hair from his eyes and, after hiding his bike, marched along the forest path to Argoad. The screams had lessened into wails and the rain had almost ceased.

He stopped opposite the Bar des Sports. He had to find Rainbow. This part was going to be far more difficult than what he'd just done. There were lots of people inside. He hesitated. The door opened and a couple of men with cameras around their necks came out onto the terrace, holding out their palms and looking at the sky. They smelt of paper print. After lighting cigarettes, they huddled under the stripy awning of the bar beside some gas bottles.

He mustn't calculate tables of questions and responses. He would just cross the street and go into the bar without thinking what to do next, because whatever had taken over his brain would come up with the next instruction once he was inside.

He splashed through puddles and pushed open the bar door. A bell buzzed. The room was full of people but he didn't need to look at them or analyse their body odours or smell the coffee-chips-lasagne-cheese-red wine in the air. He just needed to look for the little cabin, probably next to the toilets, and if there wasn't a little cabin he would ask the barman for help, and the barman looked a bit like Jean Marlot in Arras-en-Lavedan and Jean was friendly despite his overgrown hair so even that would be OK: but look, he didn't need to speak because the little cabin was right at the far end of the bar and actually it was better that the bar was crowded because nobody noticed him walking across the room and getting out his phone card, and *yes* it was empty.

He pushed his card into the slot and tapped Rainbow's home number. When a girl's voice answered, he asked to speak to Rainbow. The girl said, "She's not here, Eole," and his mind wondered how the girl had known it was him and who at the commune had a voice like little bells, which made him forget the question he had to ask next, and the girl asked about Darwie and if he was happy now he was back with the sheep and he couldn't reply because he didn't know how Darwie was, and instead of answering her he said, "Where's Rainbow?"

And the girl said Rainbow was in Paimpont at the campsite, and then her voice changed and she said he must help Rainbow, and her words didn't come out in straight lines but were a tangle of 'death' and 'motorbikes' and 'darkness' and 'chains' and 'screaming', and as her voice scrambled out more words Eole felt overfull like the time he'd secretly eaten the whole quiz cake and had been sick, so he put his hand that wasn't holding the telephone receiver over his ear, and then he realised he didn't have to listen and he hung up.

He rested his forehead against the telephone unit on the wall. The voices in the bar rippled over him in little waves. After the stress of the telephone voice it was actually quite nice to hear people talking without them addressing him directly. It made him feel invisible, floating on a sea of words, and he felt light in his head but heavy in his body and it was good to relax for a moment while his brain calculated the quickest way to get to Rainbow at Paimpont campsite.

🌿 🌱 🌿

Rainbow cycled along the street, through the rain, desperately hoping she wasn't too late for Druid Oak. Mary resisted, making the cycling even more difficult. She wanted Rainbow to go home to safety, as far from the Tree Slayer as possible. Rainbow, furious at her stubbornness, swore at her.

At last, panting, she careered round the bend in the lane. Druid Oak was still standing. She couldn't fight the tree-slaying wind spirit to save the One Tree but she could fight humans and save this innocent oak and its neighbours.

Her wet brakes screeched and she stopped. A workmen's cabin, which hadn't been there yesterday, stood in the lay-by. Beyond it, facing Druid Oak, were a yellow bulldozer, a tractor and a trailer. The machinery was silent in the drizzle. She couldn't see any contractors or felled trees. She flung down her bike, heaved off her rucksack and tried the cabin door.

It was locked. All she had was a chain, a padlock and herself. It didn't seem much against the machines. In her imagination a heavy chain crossed and re-crossed her body, making twenty rounds of the trunk so that she was hardly visible beneath it. In reality, she'd be lucky if the chain went once around Druid Oak's circumference.

She hurried across the wet grass and laid the chain around the base of the tree. After five minutes of trying to grasp both ends, she realised it wasn't going to work. If Eole had been with her, he could have pulled it over the trunk's knots and it would have been long enough. But she was alone. She'd broken up their symbiotic team and she was weaker because of it. Thierry was right about teams being better than loners.

While she searched for another idea, the rain stopped and the sun came out. The workmen would soon be back. If she couldn't chain herself to the outside, perhaps she could climb inside. There was plenty of room, but Mary screamed that the contractors might not see her there before they started bulldozing. Anyway, there was no anchor for the chain. They would simply pull her out.

She reached for Druid Oak's communication spots, remembering how hard it had been to find them among the trunk's wrinkles. This time – perhaps because it realised she wanted to help it – the oak seemed a little more accessible. She relaxed and emptied her mind, concentrating on the slow sap-beat.

Hopelessness invaded her. It was the black of storm clouds, the emptiness of space, the rot of decomposing leaves. Death was coming for Druid Oak; darkness seeped up from its roots and through the undergrowth like a poisonous gas. The One Tree was dead. The tree spirit was dead and her demise spelt death for the whole forest. For all the forests in France. For all the trees in the world. And there was human death, too: a girl's death.

Rainbow disconnected herself from the tree's feelings. The girl was no doubt her, Rainbow, as Amrita had warned. She was too late. She'd failed. There was no point fighting. She let her hands fall to her side, leant against the tree and struggled to open her heavy eyelids. She would never see Amrita again. Her mission was over and she was going to die.

She felt as defeated as Druid Oak.

Druid Oak may be old and sad but its leaves were still growing. It was still producing acorns. She could at least try to help it, to lighten its consuming depression and give it hope. She had to succeed in one thing, even if she'd failed in her mission: especially as she'd failed in her mission.

She ran her hands over its ancient bark and summoned positive thoughts of comfort: carpets of green acorn shoots on a forest floor; the sun filtering through twigs; gentle rain tapping on leaves, trickling down branches and trunks and moistening the soil. She drew energy from the damp air around her and imagined it pouring through her hands into the tree's soul.

The tree refused to absorb her offering. Deep despair billowed from every fibre, repelling her efforts. She took a breath, ready to try again – then paused as a memory flashed into her mind: the beech tree in Dorset. When she'd forced it, she caused one of its branches to fall. It was wrong to insist.

She let her hands drop. The One Tree was dead, Amrita was dead, Druid Oak was dying and the Tree Slayer was probably coming to kill her. She wasn't even capable of chaining herself to a tree to save it.

She was a total failure.

CHAPTER 35

While Eole's brain calculated the probability of Rainbow being at the campsite, his mind listened to the bar chatter.

A voice mentioned Druid Oak. It came from a group of old men who were talking with the barman and discussing a girl who'd had a fatal accident at the tree.

He thought about Rainbow but the name they used wasn't hers – and, in any case, it had happened last week, before he and Rainbow arrived. He continued listening to the discussion about Druid Oak: why it was going to be cut down and what a shame it was after all these years, but how it was right to fell it after such an appalling accident, and that it was like those dogs that are friendly until the day they mutilate a child. Then the men talked about a druid who had hidden in the hollow tree to escape his enemies, which is where the tree's name came from. And then they talked about–

"You all right there, mate?"

Eole reminded himself that the barman resembled Jean Marlot in Arras-en-Lavedan, and nodded. He tuned back into the voices of the old men. They were discussing a baby.

Jean Marlot spoke again: "What can I get you to drink?"

"A baby?"

No! He hadn't meant to speak out loud. He looked at Jean Marlot, mortified. But Jean somehow understood that he wasn't trying to order a baby from the bar.

"Yeah. They found a baby there, years ago now, didn't they, Jacqui?" He turned to one of the old men, who smelt of stale sweat. "At Druid Oak," he continued. "That poor girl, though, falling to her death. It's a sad time for Argoad."

Eole's mind thought about the comfort of Druid Oak's roots on Wednesday night and how he'd dreamt of crying babies. He thought about the newspaper article and the baby abandoned at the foot of a tree. His two thoughts fitted together like Venn diagram sets.

He was the intersection.

"But this lot are more interested in those film stars," Jean Marlot added, nodding to the crowded tables. "That's journalists for you. I bet that's why you're here too, eh? To see the stars?"

Eole looked down at his feet.

"It's your lucky day, mate. The journalists reckon the stars'll do the photo shoots in this part of the forest, so you might want to hang around. Can't complain, eh, Jacqui? Good for business. We should have warned that ecologist girl, though."

"Ecologist girl?" asked stale sweat man. "The one what made off with your chain just now?"

Eole's brain stopped calculating campsite probabilities and his mind ceased its Venn diagram extrapolations. An ecologist girl and a chain. Druid Oak. Rainbow had told him a legend about a girl who'd chained herself to a tree: a human version of that Amrita she was always talking about.

"Yup," said Jean Marlot. "Clean forgot to tell her about the film stars, what with her panic about them chopping down Druid Oak. Anyway, what'll you be having, Golden Boy? Best get your order in before the journalists queue up to pay."

Eole didn't reply. He put his phone card back in his pocket and walked out of the bar. His brain had decided on the next part of its plan. All he had to do now was follow its instructions.

❧ ❧ ❧

The sound of a faraway engine jogged Rainbow out of the gloomy realisation that she'd failed in her mission. The contractors were coming back now that Eole's storm had passed. There was nothing she could do.

She staggered a few steps away from Druid Oak.

Her despondency lifted like a veil. It wouldn't help Druid Oak for her to fall under its spell of depression. She must try to talk to the contractors.

The first one arrived on a motorbike. She sat down on an exposed root and watched him park the red and black machine in the lay-by. He was alone: no doubt the boss, setting a good example. She pulled out her campaign notes and started to re-read them.

"Hey!"

The voice was wrong. She looked up.

"Chris! What–? How–?"

She took the hand he held out and stood up. Oh, the familiarity of his touch, the way his hand fitted hers so well. A sob rose in her throat and then his arms were around her and he was murmuring "Rainette, Rainette," and it felt so right.

She looked up into his face. "What are you doing here? I thought you were with Emilie."

"Emilie? I told you, she's not the girl I love."

"But Domi said you'd taken her to meet your mum at the commune. I presumed you changed your mind about her when I left."

He looked puzzled and then his expression cleared. "I took her for a reading. Nothing more." He smiled at her, his brown eyes warm and strong. "Domi said it was important to give you some space and let you do this. So I did."

"Oh!" She wasn't sure if she was pleased or angry with Domi. "So why did you come? I mean it's so cool to see you, but–?"

"Sandrine made a prediction about you. It sounded pretty grim so I thought I'd come and check it out. Domi told me you were in Paimpont. There's some kind of environmental festival there this afternoon and the streets are full of people talking about a film director who may be coming to Argoad today for photo shoots. I got chatting to some biker guys. They mentioned a girl who died here at Druid Oak and I thought I was too late, until they said her name. They told me about the golf course too. I immediately knew you'd be here. The woman at Le Brécilien bar gave me directions. They're really friendly round here."

"Hang on. A girl died here?"

"Yes. I think she was called Druana, or something strange like that. Druana Cazenave."

"Druana? I don't believe it! I was looking for her yesterday.

What happened?"

"Apparently she was climbing the tree barefoot when she slipped, fell and died," said Christophe. "Everyone's shocked because she was only eighteen."

Eighteen? Someone so young – even younger than herself – had organised a protest group? She wished Druana hadn't died, that she'd been able to meet her. They might have got on like sisters. Sadness for the girl she'd never known welled up inside her.

She wanted to tell Christophe about her connection with Druana. She wanted to ask about the details of Sandrine's prediction and find out whether he'd gone to the Pyrenees alone during his holiday. She wanted to ask after Apple and Acorn. But more engines broke the woodland peace and three cars pulled up.

Christophe bent down and picked up one end of the chain. "Let's get you attached," he said. "I presume that's what you want?"

Rainbow ignored the walled-in part of her mind that wanted to speed home to safety on the back of Christophe's motorbike.

"I do," she said.

🌿 🍃 🌿

Eole didn't bother looking up at the sky, which was normally his first reaction when he left a building. His storm had served its purpose and now he needed to reach Druid Oak and Rainbow as fast as he could. The road would be quicker than the path. He should have come to the bar by bike.

He urged his legs into a run. They were shaky and wanted to

slow down, but his brain wouldn't let him rest. He stumbled along the road, his brain chanting at him to hurry, hurry, hurry. It was louder than the trees' wailing laments.

A car overtook him. He thought about hitching a lift but knew he'd never manage it. The tree wasn't far away. In a few minutes he'd reach Rainbow.

🌿🍃🌿

Christophe closed the padlock and pocketed the key, then tightened the chain by yanking it over a knobble.

Rainbow held onto his hand. "I'm so glad you came, even though you didn't believe in Amrita's mission."

"I still don't know about Amrita. But I do know it's wrong to cut down so many trees for a golf course. This is important. This is real." He kissed her. "Anyway, your Amrita girl – the real one from India – did exactly this, didn't she? And she survived."

Rainbow hadn't told Christophe there were two versions to the legend's conclusion. In fact, she was starting to believe that Amrita had died – otherwise, the legend wouldn't have had such a strong impact. It was naïve to think Amrita had saved the tree and lived.

The contractors began to congregate outside the cabin. One of them had a chainsaw.

"Here we go," said Christophe. He kissed her once more and then sat on a log a few metres away.

This wasn't how Rainbow had imagined a protest. She'd thought there would be shouting and slogans, banners and excitement. She'd pictured herself beside a middle-aged Druana at the centre of an organised group of demonstrators wielding dead branches and forming a barrier between revving machines and the forest.

A woman in overalls and fluorescent jacket split away from the group of men. She came up to Rainbow and folded her arms.

"So, we have a protestor. Does the protestor speak?"

"Do I need to speak?" said Rainbow. "It's obvious that you shouldn't be felling trees, and certainly not this thousand-year-old oak."

"I agree. We shouldn't. And if we had the choice, we'd leave this old boy standing."

"You do have a choice. You can choose murder or … or mercy."

"It'll be euthanasia rather than murder. For the tree, not you. *You* are going to take the key out of your pocket and undo your padlock like the reasonable girl you appear to be. We're already four days late."

The woman turned around and whistled. The men by the cabin stopped talking, and she shouted a request for someone to bring the file. A young man hurried towards them.

The chain was cutting into Rainbow's waist. She wriggled to loosen it, but only made it worse. She stroked Druid Oak's trunk.

"Forget your papers," she said. "Come and hug the oak. Come and feel the life you want to destroy."

The woman riffled through her file. "Haven't got time for that kind of thing. Here, take a look at this tree surgeon's report. It clearly says the branches are a danger to the public."

Rainbow took the report and skimmed it. She didn't recognise the tree surgeon's name. Gripped by a sudden impulse, she dropped it on the damp ground, stamped on it and twisted her foot so that the paper ripped.

"Oi!" The woman pushed Rainbow's foot off the ruined document and retrieved it.

"The branches can be propped up," said Rainbow. "Instead of destroying Druid Oak, we should help it. We should work around it."

The woman wiped the report on her overalls.

"Look, we've got a job to do. If there'd been another alternative, the tree surgeon would have suggested it. Now, kindly unlock yourself and run along home."

"No."

Another car arrived. It was Serge's jeep. Rainbow felt a few centimetres taller.

"Here comes the man from the Forest Friends association," she said. "He'll stop you."

The woman snorted. "We'll see about that."

Serge jumped out of the jeep, ignoring the contractors, and paused when he saw Rainbow. He didn't greet the woman. A knot of triumph flared in Rainbow's heart. He looked resolute. There'd be enough room for him inside the chain if he loosened it from the knobble.

"Serge! They reckon they've got the right to cut down Druid Oak!" she shouted. "After their promise to keep it alive. Felling the forest is bad enough, but killing this ancient tree is a crime. They can't do it!"

Serge arrived and looked mournfully at the tree and then at Rainbow.

"Tell the contractors about your agreement with the council," she said.

"Right. Well. The thing is, Rainbow, there's really nothing we can do about Druid Oak. Madame Moulin" – he indicated the woman in overalls – "showed me the report this morning. I checked it out, spoke to the tree surgeon, discussed other possibilities to save the tree and even got him to quote me for the cost of branch props. But the mayor says it's too expensive. And it would be dangerous for the golfers. I'm sorry. We've got no choice."

"What? Of course there's a choice. I'll pay for the props."

"It's no go. The council won't have it," he said.

She could feel the prick of tears behind her eyelids. She mustn't cry. She looked away from Serge and the woman, up into the leafy branches of Druid Oak, and willed her tears to be re-absorbed.

"There is some good news, though," said Serge. "A local artist is going to make a sculpture out of the trunk."

"A sculpture? That's sick!" she said. "You're sick! Both of you."

She turned her head away as they exchanged glances. Through her blurred vision she saw Christophe stand up and face them. He asked if the local people were aware of the decision, and when Serge admitted that they weren't, he suggested they should be informed. She heard him talk about delaying the plan for Druid Oak until the rest of the area had been cleared, about giving them time to organise a fund to protect the tree and make it safe, about the trouble it would cause if they felled an ancient tree without consulting the environmental agency in the village of Concoret.

He carried on talking. Although Rainbow heard him, she couldn't concentrate. She was trying to blink away her tears so she could confirm what she thought she could see. Or, rather, *who* she could see striding towards her in a straight line.

PART V

ONE

CHAPTER 36

The Tree Slayer was coming for her.

"Chris! The key!" she said.

"What?" Christophe turned away from Serge and Madame Moulin, stepped close to her and took her hand. "Don't give up now. You can do this."

"Please. I'll explain. Just give me the key. Quick!"

"Why? What's the matter?"

"I'll explain–"

But Christophe spotted Eole. His eyes widened and then he looked hurt. He released her hand.

"You said he'd gone home. You told Domi you'd left him."

"I did leave him, I promise. The key, Chris. Please."

Christophe dropped the key in front of her, just out of reach of her feet. Then, without a word, he strode to his motorbike.

"Chris!" she pleaded. "Come back! I'll explain."

Christophe didn't turn around.

Eole's initial dismay at seeing Christophe with Rainbow turned to satisfaction. His task would be easier without Rainbow's boyfriend. The chain was perfect. It would hold her in place. The workmen even had a chainsaw, should it prove necessary.

He listened to Christophe's motorbike rev up and roar away, hoping the man and woman with Rainbow would leave too. But the man bent down and picked up the key. He gave it to Rainbow, saying, "Boyfriend trouble, eh?" – which was obvious because boyfriends were always trouble – and then he and the woman walked towards the workmen's hut. Rainbow was alone. Eole continued towards her and watched her stretch towards the padlock.

Rainbow glanced at Eole. He wasn't brandishing a weapon, though it would be easy for him to strangle her or grab the chainsaw – or just blow down the tree and her with it.

"Stop right there, Eole. Don't come any closer." She groped for the padlock with the tips of her fingers.

Eole stopped. But now she was reaching to fit the key into the padlock. His brain told him to act. He lunged forward and snatched the key.

"Give it back!" She tried to wriggle free but the chain was tight around her.

"No."

She stopped wriggling. He'd never disobeyed her before. Either he'd changed, or the Tree Slayer was in full control.

"OK, keep the key," she said. "You and the Tree Slayer may have killed the One Tree, but you won't kill me so easily. I only have to scream, and all those people will come rushing over."

Eole looked confused. Rainbow relaxed a tiny bit. He hadn't changed so much, after all. She needed to understand what the Tree Slayer intended so that she could help him fight it, but she must keep things simple.

"I know you broke your promise and blew up that storm earlier on," she said. "You've let the Tree Slayer take control of you and kill the One Tree, and now it's telling you to kill me. You've become the Tree Slayer."

Eole shook his head. It hurt, but he shook harder. No matter how hard he shook, the words stuck, like the blood-sucking tics behind Darwie's ears. He'd only done what his brain told him.

Rainbow watched as his feet begin to twitch. She could sense the battle in his head: the influence of the Tree Slayer against his conviction that he was her soulmate. She had to get him to speak so she could loosen the Tree Slayer's hold over him.

"So where's the One Tree?" she asked. "Tell me. It's your turn to talk."

"I'm not the Tree Slayer."

Even to him, it sounded wrong. He mustn't get sidetracked. He had a task to fulfil. Here she was, all bound up and unable to get away, and his mind was muddying his brain. His fingers touched the contours of the key. That's right, he had the key. The key to the trees. He must carry out the second part of his brain's plan.

He took a deep breath and began.

He explained how he'd understood that the voices really were the trees, and that although they still weren't talking to him, he heard them screaming when he came out of the library – where he'd discovered he was left to die at the foot of a tree when he was a baby. The trees were panicking because some foresters were about to kill them. He'd followed the screaming and found the workmen about to cut down Druid Oak and its neighbours, and he broke his promise and sucked in a gentle storm to prevent them, being careful not to hurt the trees, and it had worked!

He told her he thought she'd gone home, and that he'd hurried to the bar to phone her and tell her about the workmen and their machines because he couldn't keep a storm going forever and needed her help for a long-term solution. Then he learnt that the tree where he'd been abandoned was Druid Oak, which meant it was even more important for him to save it.

At the bar, crammed with journalists hoping to see some film stars, he'd heard that a girl had left to chain herself to Druid Oak. He deduced it was her and quickly came here to tell her all this. He didn't know how he'd get her to listen without her making another excuse and deserting him again, but luckily she was chained up so she had to listen to him, and he didn't even have to touch her or threaten her with the chainsaw. Now they were reunited, and as soon as the workmen obeyed Rainbow and went home, the trees would stop their wailing.

And then, because her mouth was in an 'O' shape and she still hadn't made the T-sign, he told her the Tree Slayer hadn't taken control of him, that his brain had simply developed a special skill in planning.

"The Tree Slayer doesn't take advantage of the wind I make," he said. "It didn't do so today and in fact I don't have any evidence of its existence. The gale last month was all my fault. It's cowardly to blame anyone else. I blew down those poor trees because I was angry with the chestnut tree, and now I'm really, really sorry. I did a bad thing. Tintin would have been cross with me."

Rainbow's mind was whirling from Eole's revelations.

"You could be right," she said, when she was sure Eole had finished. "Maybe Amrita called you the Tree Slayer because you killed all those trees in revenge for Tintin's death. By making you promise not to blow up another storm, we stopped you killing any more trees. And now you've come to value trees and regret what you did, the Tree Slayer in you is vanquished."

She hadn't vanquished the Tree Slayer: Eole had done it himself, though she had perhaps influenced him a bit. He had proven far more important in her quest than she'd ever imagined. She could never have done this alone – but he would never have done it alone either. They were good together. They were two halves that made a whole. Of course! Amrita had said she must learn to accept her other half – she didn't just mean Mary, she meant Eole too. Eole would argue that it was impossible to have two other halves. But Amrita was a tree spirit, not a mathematician.

"I was the Tree Slayer," said Eole. "But now I've found you and I'm going to make amends and help you find and save the One Tree, which will make me a Tree Saviour."

"I don't know about that," she said, all her delight at understanding Amrita's message disappearing. "The One Tree and Amrita are dead. I felt Druid Oak mourning them."

Eole shook his head. "I don't know exactly where the One Tree is, but it can't be dead. The trees are still wailing because it's in danger, which means it's probably in this condemned part of the forest. You must tell the workmen to go home so that we save my Druid Oak and the One Tree at the same time."

"You think it's still alive?" Had she misinterpreted Druid Oak's feelings? Were they the effect of the tree's depression rather than the reality? She couldn't reach its communication spots from where she was chained. She'd have to trust Eole, who was nodding in answer to her question.

She thought back to Amrita's message. Amrita hadn't actually said they must save the One Tree from the Tree Slayer – she just told Rainbow to rescue the last One Tree, without specifying what to rescue it from.

She knew Druid Oak wasn't the One Tree because it hadn't spoken to her in images and words. Maybe Eole was right: the One Tree was in the part of the forest destined to become the golf course and their mission was to save it from the contractors. Amrita hadn't told Rainbow to actually *find* the One Tree, just to rescue it. Perhaps she was never meant to find it.

Since they didn't know its exact location, they'd have to protect this part of the forest, or even the whole forest. It would be much more difficult than protecting one tree. It would be a lifetime's work. A destiny. At least, it *would* be a destiny if they could stop the golf course being built. For the moment, it didn't look as if they'd even overcome this first challenge.

"It's not quite that easy," she said to Eole. "I can't just tell the contractors to go home. They won't listen to my pleas to spare Druid Oak, let alone cancel their plans for the forest."

"But we have to stop them," said Eole. "We have to save the trees."

Rainbow's head started to throb. The mental wall between Mary and herself was stretched taut: Mary had an idea. But Rainbow could never carry it out. She wasn't as daring as Mary.

She'd managed to match Mary's determination so far because they'd been the same person until they were thirteen. But she needed more than determination to carry out Mary's idea. It would take nerve – and she lacked Mary's nerve. This particular character trait must have come as a result of Mary's experiences after their split. The difficulties Mary had faced had forged her personality and made her audacious. But Rainbow hadn't had the same experiences. She wasn't intrepid like Mary. She didn't have the same confidence. She'd never pull off Mary's idea.

Unless.

There was another way, though she risked losing her own personality. Was Mary offering this idea simply to escape her mental captivity? Would she share her strengths with Rainbow or simply enforce her desire to go home to safety? Did Rainbow dare lower her mental wall and let Mary in?

Domi had advised her to keep the wall, but his mother's memoir had said sharing *could* happen, even though the cases of reaching equilibrium were rare. The memoir had also mentioned dire need. Rainbow was in dire need of Mary's audacity. She thought back to Amrita's message about only being able to help if she were truly whole. Amrita had known this total integration would be necessary.

Rainbow's only hope of succeeding was to become One with Mary. She must trust Mary to share.

She took a deep breath, relaxed the mental wall and invited Mary in.

The desire to go home to Chris overpowered her. She clenched the chain. A flood of tumultuous feelings rushed through her, as if the act of fully accepting Mary was releasing ten months of frustration. An unfamiliar hard lump lodged inside her. Was this hate? There was also a certitude that the legendary Amrita had died in her attempt to save a tree. She searched desperately for something positive – the source of Mary's self-confidence – but there was too much turbulence to discern anything definite.

The rush of emotions calmed. It was a settling of water after the opening of a lock gate – and with it came the understanding that in one parallel world Amrita had lived, while in another she had died. The two versions of the legend could live in perfect harmony.

Did this mean she had become One?

There was no time to wonder whether she was truly RainbowMary. If she didn't act now, it would be too late.

"I have an idea," she said to Eole. "We must get the local people on our side. And for that, we need publicity. The media are already here, waiting for the film stars. Thanks to you and poor Druana, we now have an original 'people angle' to attract them."

She explained the details of her idea to Eole.

"I can't," he said.

"You've got to. It's our only chance," said Rainbow.

Eole freed her from the tree, accompanied by the contractors' applause and whistles. Then he hoisted her onto the lowest branch of Druid Oak and passed her the chain.

"Get down!" shouted Madame Moulin. "That branch is weak. There've been enough accidents here."

Rainbow swore at Madame Moulin and then grinned at the woman's shock. It was empowering not to care what people thought of her. "Now go," she said to Eole. "Quickly!"

🌱 🌿 🌱

Eole ran. Running was the easy bit, though he'd have preferred to walk slowly to give his brain more time to calculate the forthcoming task.

He'd never be able to do it. But he must do it. For Rainbow, for Druid Oak, which had been his protector when he was a baby, and for all the trees he'd hurt. He willed his brain to switch into planning mode again, to break Rainbow's objective into parts and only tell him what to do as each part came along.

His brain, busy making its table of questions and answers, didn't respond. If only Eole could control it, he'd avoid this unnecessary calculating. But how had he done it last time? When he'd come out of the library this morning, his new planning skill had self-activated. The screaming trees had forced every thought out of his head, other than following the counting voices.

He had let go.

He ignored his brain's calculations of possible dialogues and listened to the trees' wailing instead. The trick was to activate his senses and use them to turn his thoughts outward instead of inward. He studied the dark green leaves and needles of the trees beside the road, smelt the wet earth verges and concentrated on the hardness of the tarmac under the soles of his boots. As he arrived in Argoad's main street, a plan appeared in his mind, freshly presented by his brain and split into manageable parts.

The village was still full of cars. Now the sun was out, people were scattered over the street, leaning on car doors and smoking on the bar terrace. Some had cameras around their necks and others were wielding video equipment.

The sight of them chilled the sweat dripping down his back. *Don't calculate, just do it*, he told himself. He went into the bar and walked right up to the telephone in its cubicle at the far end of the bar without taking any notice of the barman's, "Hello, hello: Golden Boy's back."

The cubicle was empty. He took out Rainbow's card, dialled

the number and asked to speak to Melanie Brown. When he gave Rainbow's name, her voice went from frosty to tropical. And when he said the words 'people angle' and told her everything Rainbow had instructed him to say, she declared she'd be there right away (even though that was impossible). He put down the phone. There was no *itch, shuffle and escape*. He said thank you, not to God but to his brain, which was calm like Tintin and directive like Rainbow, but wasn't either of them. It was one hundred per cent himself.

He looked around the bar. The journalists had gathered outside under the awning or come back inside. Before he could start calculating, he activated the second part of his brain's plan: the most difficult.

"I've got a scoop," he said.

The man and woman closest to him paused, glanced at him, and then continued their conversation.

He looked up at the ceiling.

"I'VE. GOT. A. SCOOP!" he shouted.

Silence. Everyone in the bar was staring at him. It was a scene from a nightmare. He quickly looked down at his feet. They were moving, against his control. No! This wasn't part of the plan. They were taking him out of the door and onto the terrace and away from the nightmare. But this wasn't a nightmare. It was real. Rainbow needed him to tell the journalists. She believed he could do it, so he *could* do it.

He stopped on the pavement and turned around to face the bar. There was a bustle at the door and a tidal wave of people spilled onto the crowded terrace. Eole stepped back to keep his distance from them.

"What's the scoop?" "Who are you?" "Get on with it," they said.

He cleared his throat. "The council are about to cut down the trees."

A voice jeered that this was no scoop.

He mustn't listen to the individual voices. He just had to talk, even if he wasn't capable of the rousing speech Rainbow wanted him to make. He could only tell it as it was.

"The workmen are on the point of cutting down Druid Oak, which is a thousand years old, and the agreement was that it would stay but the council have broken the agreement, and Rainbow is chained to the tree to stop them but she can't do it on her own, and she wants you to go and film what's happening and tell everybody that it's a crime, and also I'm the baby who was abandoned at Druid Oak and because of me and the girl Druana who died there last week, Rainbow says it's a scoop and a people angle and you must come."

There was a silence. Then the journalists' voices rose in a babble and they weren't speaking, they were shouting, and some surged forward and grasped at him and pushed microphones in front of his face and he was confused because the next part of the plan was to take them back to Druid Oak, not to do media interviews outside the bar.

He pushed them away and let his feet go, and he was walking back down the road and he could hear footsteps behind him, and then he heard car engines start and then a motorbike overtook him and it was followed by a car, which stopped, and a rear door opened and his brain said this could be considered as an incidental sub-part of the plan and so he got into the car and now he was in a convoy of cars and motorbikes and someone was giggling and he realised it was him and that he'd done it.

CHAPTER 37

Chained to the lowest branch of Druid Oak, the key in her pocket, Rainbow tried to send the tree more energy. It was easier now her feet were off the ground, but Druid Oak still refused her help. It radiated gloom, death and the demise of the forest. Her hope started to seep away and she broke the connection. She must remain positive while she waited for Eole's return: she was One with Mary. She could do this, as long as she didn't think about Christophe's desertion. Chris was Mary's weak point and she missed him more than ever.

She began to sketch in her travel log. Below, Serge tried to persuade her to come down, while Madame Moulin threatened to get a ladder and pull her down.

Rainbow didn't look up from her page. "Bring the mayor and I'll consider it," she said.

Serge and Madame Moulin conferred and then Serge left in his jeep. Rainbow allowed herself a hard smile.

She was putting the finishing touches to her sketch of Christophe on his motorbike when she heard its engine. She looked up, her heart leaping in hope, and peered around the trunk. A car followed the motorbike, and then another. But the motorbike was green.

The rider dismounted. Car doors opened and men and women climbed out, some with cameras. Then she saw Eole. This must be the journalists. He'd succeeded!

She watched him walk in a straight line towards her. He didn't look particularly pleased with himself; but then, he wouldn't.

"Hey, good work, Eole!" she called down to him.

Eole felt fireworks of pride burst from him. He was sure everyone could see them. Would his elation cause spontaneous combustion? He didn't care if he burst into flame because he'd succeeded one hundred per cent on his own, which meant he was ready for Toulouse university. Hestia would be proud of him. Tintin would have been proud, too.

"Yes, it was good work," he agreed, and sat down on a tree root.

Rainbow skimmed her biodiversity notes while the journalists approached. Eole had done his bit. The rest of the campaign depended on her. She considered telling the journalists about her gift and the Koad mission, but the memory of Serge's words about keeping scientific stopped her.

The journalists started calling out questions. Before she could answer, another couple of vehicles pulled up and the journalists turned to look at them, no doubt hoping for film stars.

The first car was Serge's. A group of four people, one in a suit, got out of the second car.

"It's Hugues Barateau!" shouted a journalist.

Like a flock of flapping vultures, the journalists launched themselves at the mayor. Barateau picked his way across the drying grass towards Druid Oak, barking answers at the journalists' questions as he walked. Rainbow heard some questions about Druana, a few about the report on Druid Oak and lots about the film stars. There were none on the mayor's decision to build a golf course.

Madame Moulin came out of her cabin, followed by the contractors, and joined the mayor and his councillors at the foot of Druid Oak. Eole retreated. A surge of adrenaline pulsed through Rainbow. This was it.

"Now then, young lady," said Hugues Barateau. "You're impeding the course of a project which has been voted and accepted. Kindly undo that padlock and let everybody get back to work." He turned to Serge and snapped: "The ladder."

Rainbow could see the bald patch on the crown of the mayor's head. A few strands of hair were brushed over it. He obviously cared about his image.

"I'll happily come down," she said, "as soon as you promise to leave these woods alone and build your golf course in the fields."

"What a splendid idea. We hadn't considered that simple option during the planning meetings." His voice was sarcastic.

Several journalists tittered. The councillors laughed outright. Serge leant a ladder against her branch.

Rainbow ignored the mayor's sarcasm and argued her case for the forest. Barateau countered every point. Before, she would have given up after his first rebuff, but her new audacity strengthened with each snub. She was almost thriving on his disregard, surfing on her adrenaline. She gave answers she'd never have dared say before accepting Mary. This was herself, RainbowMary, speaking. To her delight, she discovered she could be ruthless and sarcastic, and was capable of using a whole new range of responses.

Barateau, however, was an expert. His whole career was based on turning other people's arguments around. Within a few minutes she realised the journalists and councillors considered her a spoilt brat.

It was impossible to change his mind.

He drew himself up for a final attack, his shoulders thrown back, index finger pointing at her, and paused. Cameras clicked.

"You say it's a disgrace to cut down a few trees, but who are you to argue? You don't even live here. The local population is satisfied. They're very much in favour of the golf course. It'll create new jobs and bring in more tourists. Now, I have more important things to do than waste my time with a petulant teenager."

He thanked the journalists for coming and told them to return to Paimpont, since the film crew had no intention of coming to Argoad.

Rainbow swore. He couldn't go yet! She hadn't finished with him. She would climb down and follow him until he listened to her. Actually, she would punch him. Hard.

"Hey! Barateau!" she shouted. "Most of the locals don't even *know* you're going to cut down Druid Oak! So much for democracy!"

He didn't bother to respond. Instead, he ordered Madame Moulin to climb the ladder and force her down.

She'd failed. But instead of wanting to curl up and die, she was angry. She contemplated throwing her bag down onto the mayor and knocking him over. She considered stretching a branch until it dropped on his head and killed him – except that he wasn't worth a twig of Druid Oak, let alone a branch. Instead, she spat on his bald patch as he strutted away.

More vehicles were approaching. Horns tooted and several journalists jogged down towards the road to get a clearer view. She peered around the trunk, wondering if the film crew had changed their minds, and gasped.

She had a full view of what was coming, unlike the people below her. A convoy of cars, motorbikes and vans took up the whole road. There were dozens of them. There were even some tractors at the back, with people hanging off the sides, their arms raised, fists clenched. Protestors! She didn't know where they'd come from. She didn't care.

"Check this out, Barateau!" she shouted. "Here come your *satisfied* local population."

The mayor said something to the councillor beside him and they hurried to their car.

Madame Moulin's face appeared at the top of the ladder. Rainbow controlled her urge to kick it. She was RainbowMary, not just Mary.

"Don't come any closer or I'll push you off," she said.

"That won't help your cause, young lady. Which is lost, in case you hadn't realised. I hope you've learnt a lesson today: idealism is for dreamers. Welcome to the real worl–" She clutched at the branch and yelped.

Rainbow looked down. Eole was standing at the foot of the tree, jiggling the ladder.

"It's OK, Eole. I can deal with her," she said. "Go and see what's happening on the road."

❧ ❦ ❧

Eole let go just before the woman crushed his fingers with her heavy boots. The area around the base of Druid Oak had emptied of journalists and he heard a crowd of voices chanting:

"Bar-ra-teau, au ca-chot!"

The people wanted the mayor to go to jail, which would be a good thing, though totally illogical unless he'd broken the law.

The mayor's car accelerated away from the lay-by, its brakes squealing at the corner. The horn blared. The people's voices increased to screams. The car reversed and manoeuvred through a three-point turn. Eole arrived just as it accelerated into the track beside him.

He jumped in front of it and spread his arms, like he did when herding a loose sheep back towards a hole in the fence. The car stopped, inches from him. Its horn blared again.

Eole stood his ground.

A journalist ran to the car and shoved a microphone through the passenger window, while another took photos.

"I think the locals have something to say to you, Monsieur Barateau," said the journalist.

Eole watched the mayor's tinted car windows slide closed. The photographer must have taken a good photo, because he smiled. Then the photographer and the journalist stood back from the mayor's car and looked towards the barrage. Any second now they would leave. Eole would be stuck here. He wouldn't be able to stop the mayor escaping *and* follow Rainbow's instruction.

He had an idea. He didn't stop to analyse where it came from, but walked around to the driver's door and opened it. The councillor looked up at him with the frightened eyes of a cornered marmot. Eole ignored the man, reached in and took the key from the ignition.

"Hey!" said the driver, and tried to grab it. He was too slow. Eole shut the door and pocketed the key.

"There's no messing with The Boy Who Came Back," said the journalist to the photographer. "Get a photo of him!"

Eole hurried towards the demonstrators. He needed to ask someone what was happening so he could report back to Rainbow.

He slowed down as he reached the corner. The vehicles had stopped in the road and doors were opening and slamming shut. People formed into a crowd and began to surge forward. He looked for the leader. Three men and a woman were at the front.

"Bar-ra-teau, au ca-chot!" came the cry.

He recognised one of the leaders.

"Bar-ra-teau, au ca-chot!"

The crowd swept towards him. It stank of sweat, red wine, beer and barbecued sausages. If he stayed where he was, he'd be swallowed up by it. But Rainbow needed him to warn her who was coming. He looked at the leader he recognised. If the boy had been alone, it would have been easy. Eole hesitated.

In a second it would be too late. He stepped forward.

"Out the way!" shouted a man.

Arms reached to push him aside. He stumbled backwards before they could touch him. The sea of faces surged past, heading towards Druid Oak and the mayor's car.

Eole stood, transfixed. Two of the faces at the back were familiar. Three, if you counted Darwie.

Maman-A and Hestia were following the protestors. Darwie saw him and yanked at his lead. Hestia let go and Darwie raced towards him, his hindquarters dancing from side to side with sweeping wags of his tail. Eole crouched down and hugged him, which made Darwie whimper and struggle to escape. Eole released him and settled for his usual light caress.

Hestia thumped him on his shoulder, which meant she was extra pleased to see him because it really hurt. He bumped fists with her and looked at Maman-A.

Maman, not Maman-A.

This was Maman.

How could he have intended to call anyone else 'Maman'? She stopped in front of him and traced the love-hug sign with her two hands. She kept making the sign, over and over again, tears running down her cheeks.

He didn't make the sign back. Instead, he reached out and touched her wrinkled hands: the hands she'd laid on his forehead when he was ill in bed.

She froze, like a Pyrenean chamois when it catches a threatening scent on the wind. His brain told him to do it and he didn't stop to think about which arm should go where and he didn't think about his lungs having all the air squeezed out of them or making Maman whimper like Darwie. He just put his arms around her and hugged her – and it didn't even hurt and she didn't whimper and he didn't feel trapped.

"Thank you God for delivering my Eole safely," she whispered.

Hestia cleared her throat and he let go of Maman. The word 'delivering' made him think of lambs, and lambs made him think of Hestia's baby, which he wasn't allowed to mention.

"I'm sorry I wasn't there for your abortion," he said.

She raised her chin and looked at the tops of the trees. He thought he could see tears in her eyes, but Hestia never cried. She probably had a speck of dust in them. Maman made the sign of a cross and Hestia rolled her eyes, which was exactly what she always did when Maman crossed herself.

"Papa's been great. You wait until you see him again," said Hestia. "So how are you? We thought you'd be here when we heard they were demonstrating for the trees. It wasn't Rainbow who fell off Druid Oak, was it?"

Rainbow! He'd forgotten his mission for Rainbow.

"No, that was some other girl," he said. "Rainbow's chained to it."

"Oh, good. I don't know why she bothers with trees, but still. Hats off and all that. It's a great party. Better than the boring B&B. Come on, let's get into the thick of it." She hurried after the crowd

Eole turned to go and report back to Rainbow.

"Eole! Don't you dare," said Maman. "Stand still so I can look at you properly."

Eole waited while she blew her nose. Then she told him off. She told him off for running away and for not eating properly and not keeping clean and not telephoning often enough, and Eole said nothing. He simply listened to the sound of her voice because it didn't feel like she was telling him off. She was doing the same thing as Patou when he came home after the summer in the mountains and sniffed every corner of the barn to refamiliarise himself with its contents. It felt right.

CHAPTER 38

Rainbow shifted her position on the branch so she could see the group marching around the corner towards her. Where had they all come from? She couldn't see Eole anywhere.

The journalists took photos, held out microphones and talked to the people at the edges of the crowd, which passed the contractors' cabin. Madame Moulin had disappeared inside, and now Rainbow saw someone throw a projectile at it. A yellow stain slid down the side, joined by red splodges: eggs and tomatoes.

The crowd continued towards the mayor's car, stationary on the track. Rainbow grinned. This was more like it. She wanted to join in. She wanted to open Barateau's car door and see globs of egg and tomato all over his face. She pulled the key from her pocket and slotted it into the padlock.

"Don't come down yet," came a voice from behind the tree. She jerked her head around. Could it be…?

"Chris!" The joy that electrified her was stronger than anything she'd ever felt for him before. "I thought you'd gone."

"I did go." He climbed up the ladder. "I went for a spin so I could think about you and Eole. I'm sorry. My reaction was out of order."

"That's OK. I didn't have time to explain—" started Rainbow. She was stopped by his kiss, which was quick but intense, as if he'd channelled all his love into one intimate second.

"You don't have to explain," he said. "I trust you. I should have trusted you from the beginning. Anyway, I stopped at the ecology festival in Paimpont."

"*You* brought all these people?"

"Not really. I told you the locals were great. They got me up onto the live music stage and I just mentioned the new authorisation to cut down Druid Oak. And the fact you were chained to it. Oh, and when I remembered they'd known Druana, and learnt that she'd protested about cutting down the trees, I said a few words about not letting her die for nothing."

"Wow! You should be a politician."

He laughed. "I was just lucky. The festival atmosphere had a lot to do with it. And the rumours about backhanders Barateau received from the golfing company. Let's hope the demonstrators' methods of persuasion work."

Rainbow looked past his shoulder. The protestors were yanking the mayor's car door handles and drumming on the roof.

"Things are getting out of hand," she said.

"I'll entice them over here," said Christophe. "Then you can talk to them."

"No! Wait."

Speaking to a huge crowd wasn't part of her plan. She didn't have any experience of soapbox politics. They wouldn't listen. Half of them looked drunk, anyway. She'd only planned to get the mayor here with the journalists and shame him into backing down. But it hadn't worked. What exactly could she say to the demonstrators? She and Druid Oak would end up covered in egg and tomatoes.

Christophe kissed her, whispered, "Courage!" and slid down the ladder.

She wanted to disappear into Druid Oak, like one of her bodies had done at the silver maple. She closed her eyes and imagined the wrinkled bark creeping over her arms, her legs and her back: absorbing her, like skin healing over a wound. It felt possible. She just had to press herself a little harder.

Eole couldn't see Hestia in the group and he wasn't prepared to get close enough to find her. He approached Druid Oak with Maman on one side and Darwie on the other, which was right. It felt like belonging, even though he wasn't at home.

"I'm going to give that young Rainbow a piece of my mind," said Maman.

Eole protested that Rainbow hadn't done anything wrong and that she was too busy saving the forest to have time to be told off.

Someone ran up behind them, breathing heavily. A smell of orange flower filled Eole's nose receptors and he saw a woman in her twenties, wearing ethnic genie trousers and a multi-coloured hippie smock. A faded blue scarf was wrapped around her head.

"Excuse me," she said. "I'm looking for Rainbow and Eole."

Before Eole could answer, Maman spoke: "Why? Who are you? What do you want with them?"

The woman introduced herself as Melanie Brown.

Eole told Maman that he'd phoned her, and while Maman looked at him with her eyebrows raised, blinking, he led Melanie towards Rainbow and explained what was happening.

🌹 🍃 🌹

Rainbow sensed she could disappear into Druid Oak's trunk, but she also knew she would regret her cowardice forever if she gave up now.

The lump of hate she'd felt inside her when she'd accepted Mary was harder than ever, which was strange, because although it was dense, it somehow comforted her. She concentrated on it, curious to know why it had become so hard. Was it trying to catch her attention? She visualised it in her mind's eye.

It wasn't a lump. It was a box. Whatever Mary had put inside it was as heavy as hate. Mary had more secrets. Until Rainbow opened the box and understood Mary completely, she still wasn't truly One.

Hoping it wasn't a kind of Pandora's box, she reached towards it with her mind and slowly opened it.

A purple mist swirled out and engulfed her. Carried within the mist particles was the conviction that she could do anything she set her mind to. It didn't matter what people thought. She was RainbowMary and if she decided to succeed, she would.

It wasn't just a box, it was a treasure chest – and its contents were the source of Mary's strength. Mary and her boxes! They were lifesavers.

She opened her eyes, ready to take on the world. A familiar figure was standing at the top of the ladder.

"So. This is the Tree of Life and Death," said Melanie.

"Is it?" Goose pimples rose on Rainbow's neck and arms.

"That's what the journos are calling it. I rang some colleagues and caught up on events, and Eole told me the rest. I think we can save the forest, thanks to poor Druana Cazenave and that cute Eole. And to Barateau's corruption. We need to get these local guys organised. Then we'll have a fab story to go with your travel log and your quest. I bet we'll get loads of pledges of support when the feature comes out. Is this your travel log? Can I have a quick look?"

Rainbow gave it to her and looked over Melanie's shoulder. The protestors were rocking the car, ignoring Christophe's shouts to gather under Druid Oak.

"We've got to get them over here," she said.

Melanie twisted round to look and then snapped the travel log shut.

"I'll deal with them."

She left Rainbow and elbowed her way through the people to the mayor's car, where she climbed onto the bonnet and then the roof.

"Listen to me, you lot. The mayor's not going anywhere. There's a girl in the tree, in case you hadn't noticed. She's ready to sacrifice her life so they don't cut it down. And she's got a great story for you. Come and hear how Druid Oak called her all the way from Cognac."

The protestors' faces turned towards Rainbow. She raised

an unsteady hand in acknowledgement. They must have latched onto the word 'Cognac' and thought there would be free drinks, because they traipsed across the grass and let Melanie organise them under the shade of Druid Oak.

Rainbow's heart crashed against her ribs, despite her conviction that she could do this. She needed to see a friendly face.

Eole was right below her, sitting cross-legged on the grass, his eyes fixed on her. Somehow, Darwie had arrived and his head was on Eole's lap, and Alexandra was beside him, sitting on her raincoat. Christophe was laughing with a girl. It was Hestia! Serge stood in the audience, talking to a journalist and showing him the flyer Druana had made. Even Madame Moulin had come out of her cabin – though Rainbow couldn't see the other contractors – and was standing behind everyone with her arms folded.

Rainbow and Eole were no longer a duet, as Eole liked to say. They were part of an orchestra. And she was supposed to conduct.

She felt sick.

She couldn't throw up. Not in front of everyone.

They were on her side. They all wanted the forest to remain intact, although Serge had made it clear that no one would appreciate anything spiritual. She had to be careful what she said. Melanie had caught their attention, but how could she follow it up without making her and Eole sound like weirdos? She, RainbowMary, would find a way, because she was One.

She cleared her throat and raised her hands.

The chattering below her stopped. In the sudden silence, the bulldozer engine roared into life.

"OK, so ... Hi there, folks. My name's Rainbow, and I'm not used to public speaking. I just wanted to say that I may be sitting here, in Druid Oak, but my protest isn't just for this tree. If I could, I'd be sitting in every condemned tree in this forest. Trees are important. They can't defend themselves from humans, so we have to do it for them. We mustn't let anyone fell any part of this magical forest of Brocéliande."

Some people clapped. There was even a cheer.

"Bar-ra-teau, au ca-chot!" chanted a voice.

A few heads turned to check on the revving bulldozer but nobody moved.

"What's this about cognac?" asked a woman.

"How did the tree call you?" said another.

Rainbow hesitated. The bulldozer edged towards Druid Oak, its caterpillar tracks crushing the wild flowers in its path. The tractor engine started.

She could ignore the hook Melanie had used to catch their attention. She could invent a story about a friend calling her to come and help, and in doing so hide the nature of her and Eole's gifts for understanding trees.

Or she could tell the truth.

Her gift defined her. Without it – without trees – she was nothing.

"It may be difficult to believe," she said, "but the forest called us. You see, I have a rapport with trees: I can understand their feelings. And my friend Eole – Druid Oak's baby – can hear them talking. Their voices guided us from Cognac to this amazing forest."

There was silence from the audience.

"Trees are far more developed than we realise. They

communicate with each other through their roots and by giving off chemical messages. In every forest there are special hub trees, or mother trees. They're ancient trees that protect and nurture all the trees around them. Science is just starting to prove this.

"But there's more. Some of these mother trees have a spiritual connection and they hold the history of all treekind. The trees refer to them as 'One Trees'.

"Brocéliande has a One Tree. More than that, Brocéliande holds the *last* One Tree. We don't know exactly where it is, or exactly what role it plays, but we do know we have to protect it, which means we must protect the whole forest. But we can't do it alone. We need your help."

Exclamations of wonder and a wave of chattering filled the air. People shouted out questions. Rainbow answered as many as she could, aware of the bulldozer creeping inexorably closer.

It reached the end of the branch she was sitting on.

The branch trembled. She stopped talking, mid-sentence.

Had the bulldozer touched it?

She laid her hands on the trunk. Druid Oak was shivering. She hugged it, but it was like hugging a rock: there was no reaction. The tree was too close to death.

A car door slammed. She glanced across the clearing to the track.

"The mayor!" she shouted, pointing at the figure running away.

Christophe and Hestia jumped up and ran after him. The journalists and a few members of the group followed them. Christophe caught the mayor's arm. The mayor shook off his jacket and escaped. Hestia launched herself into a rugby tackle and threw him to the ground.

Within seconds, the journalists had gathered around. Hestia sprang up, her fist raised in triumph. Hugues Barateau staggered to his feet and then brushed himself off with short, sharp strokes. The journalists brandished their microphones, cameras and notebooks.

A police siren sounded.

The branch shuddered. It was going to fall. She could unchain herself and save her life, or she could try to help it.

She threw herself along the branch and held it tight with her arms and legs.

Hold on, she breathed to it.

The chain cut into her back. She ignored it. Fibres twanged under her. It reminded her of another tree, another branch, another country. But this time it wasn't her fault. She closed her eyes and sent all her energy, all the energy around her, into the branch. Could she make amends? She begged it to hold on.

Gasps and shouts of 'Eole!' came from below the tree. The bulldozer horn blared.

Rainbow opened her eyes and saw Eole lying across the bulldozer's path, right below her branch. Alexandra tried to pull him up. Darwie dashed from left to right between the bulldozer and Eole, nipping at the caterpillar tracks.

The bulldozer stopped.

Rainbow willed Druid Oak to hold tight to its branch. Fibres strained and snapped. A series of images flashed before her eyes: flocks of people, gathered like sheep beneath her; an old man in a white tunic; a baby nestled in a bed of leaves inside the hollow trunk; a girl, falling through branches; herself, chained to the branch; a forest of withered trees without leaves; Amrita, lying down with her eyes closed, hands folded across her chest.

Druid Oak spoke one word.

Rainbow asked one question.

She received one answer.

"Eole!" she cried. "Move out the way!"

There was a blur of movement, a thunderous crack, rushing air. And then darkness.

CHAPTER 39

Rainbow woke up in a hospital bed. There was no pain. There was no empty space in her mind between falling with the branch and waking up in the hospital room. It wasn't like last time.

Voices chattered around her. She lingered on the familiarity of them and then opened her eyes. Her family were grouped at the end of her bed, their backs to her. Domi was asleep on the chair. Outside, it was dark. She wiggled her fingers and toes and shifted each joint. Good. Everything was stiff but she wasn't paralysed. She turned her head and saw another bed. It was empty.

"Eole?"

Although her voice was croaky, it was enough to bring a rush of faces and hands towards her. She blinked. They were all a bit wavy when they moved, and it was even worse when they all talked at once. She sipped from a glass Mum held out and tried to concentrate. There was something she needed to know.

Christophe took her hand in his. "Nice sense of drama," he

said. "But twice is enough."

She squeezed his fingers and closed her eyes. It was too complicated to look and listen at the same time. Is this what it was like for Eole? Eole. *That* was what she needed to know.

"Is Eole OK?" she asked.

"The doctors think so," said Domi's voice, after a pause. "You can go and see him a bit later."

She smiled but wasn't sure that her lips actually moved. They were so heavy.

🌱 🍃 🌱

The Lord's Prayer interrupted Eole's calculation of the nineteenth position in the Fibonacci sequence. He wished Père Laurent and the congregation would shut up and let him concentrate.

"Shhh," he said.

Miraculously, they went quiet – though of course it wasn't a miracle, because miracles were just a melodramatic way of referring to coincidences/events in the queue for scientific explanation. And now his own mind had interrupted his brain's calculation and he would have to start again from the beginning.

"Eole?" whispered Maman's voice.

He opened his eyes.

He closed them again.

It was all wrong. There was no churchy gloom, only a dim white blur. It felt like the middle of the night. And he must be half asleep because he hadn't even noticed that, instead of the usual musty stone and furniture polish, the room stank of disinfectant and blood. His head hurt and his ears were ringing. He opened one eye. Maman. Hestia. Where was Darwie?

He opened the other and looked around. It was dawn. He was in hospital. Darwie must be outside. Eole was the only patient in the room, which felt illogical. There should be someone else.

Rainbow.

His memory galloped across his brain like the mountain ponies when he teased them by raising a wind: Rainbow – the trees screaming – Maman – Druid Oak – the bulldozer – the branch crashing down and him rolling out of the way because Rainbow had told him to, but she hadn't told him soon enough and an offshoot of the branch had accelerated towards him and–

"What happened next?" he asked.

Maman and Hestia both started explaining at the same time. He felt sick at the thought of other people's hands putting him onto a stretcher and then taking him off and examining him and sticking needles in him. It was lucky he'd been unconscious. Even though he'd failed to protect Rainbow one hundred per cent from the bulldozer that had made the branch fall, she hadn't died. She was asleep in room 102.

"Can I see her?"

Maman told him he'd have to wait. She said that once the doctors had finished puzzling over the ear, nose and throat examinations and the X-rays of his lungs – and that they'd accepted he was exactly how God intended him to be – she was taking him home. She was going to feed him up and get him healthy again, since Rainbow hadn't looked after him properly. It was lucky God had been watching over him.

He yawned and fell asleep to the sound of her voice. When he woke up again the sun was at eleven o'clock and his room was empty.

🌹 🌿 🌹

Rainbow was properly awake this time. Mum helped her sit up.

"So what happened after the branch fell? Tell me they didn't cut down Druid Oak."

Domi, Mum and Christophe laughed. She couldn't see anything amusing.

There was a knock at the door. Domi opened it and revealed Eole standing in the same kind of thin overall as she was wearing. Domi told him to come in.

Eole looked at Rainbow, who nodded, so he came in and sat on the empty bed, as far from Christophe as he could get. Rainbow's mum – who looked like a witch, with all the dark make-up smeared around her eyes – passed him a wrap. He put it on the bed and answered Rainbow's question by saying he was fine, which was always the right (but illogical) answer.

"Christophe was just about to tell Rainbow what happened after you two were knocked out," said Domi.

Rainbow linked her fingers with Christophe's. "Go on, then," she said.

Christophe dragged his free hand through his hair. "Well, the contractor stopped the machine, jumped down from the cab and shouted at everybody not to move you in case you had spinal injuries. It didn't exactly make up for bulldozing the branch in the first place, but he handled things pretty well – otherwise the crowd would have dragged you both out from the debris. Luckily, the emergency services had just arrived, so the paramedics packed you up in the ambulance. The journalists went crazy, filming the action, recording their news reports and taking photos.

"The best bit was the mayor, though. He thought the police had come to protect him – but in fact they hustled him away to be questioned about allegations of corruption. Madame Moulin took charge once he'd gone. She told the contractors to pack up and leave, since they might not be paid for any work they did."

"So Druid Oak is OK, apart from the branch?"

"Yes," said Domi. "And given the reports on television last night, it doesn't look as if anyone will touch it for a long time." He paused. "So who's going to tell them?"

"Tell us what?" said Rainbow.

There was another knock on the door.

"That'll be Melanie," said Mum. She opened it and Melanie Brown staggered in, her arms full of newspapers.

"Ah, Druid's Baby and Tree Girl. Looking good," said Melanie. "Forget royalty. Forget film stars. You're the public's new heroes."

She dumped the newspapers on the end of Rainbow's bed, kissed her and waved at Eole.

"So, what are we going to call our association? We'll need a good name, as well as a bank vault for all the donations we've received."

Rainbow gasped. "You're kidding!"

Melanie chuckled and showed them the newspaper reports of the previous day's activities. She explained that she'd organised a telephone number for pledges. They were receiving donations for saving trees like Druid Oak all over France.

"Thierry sends his congratulations, by the way," said Christophe. "It sounds as if he's been calling all his contacts, telling them he knows you and can vouch for you. I guess he's had time to cool off over you letting him down."

"You're going to be a busy girl," said Melanie to Rainbow. "Oh, and a busy boy, if you want to do this too, Eole."

Eole watched them passing newspapers around and then looked out of the open window. He knew it was good news, because Rainbow was all sparkly. His brain told him he should be happy too, because he could continue to protect Brocéliande and the hidden One Tree, and keep Rainbow alive. But it would be official now. They'd have to meet people and tell them what they were doing. They'd have to report back on the trees they'd saved. It wouldn't just be two soulmates and the trees anymore. It would be a thing. A big thing, judging by the zeros on the sums of money the public had pledged.

Outside, the trees in the hospital grounds were probably whispering to each other. Now he had his treeopedia, he wanted to listen to the trees at home. A hoopoe called: *hoo-hoo-hoo, hoo-hoo-hoo*. He wondered how the hoopoe family in his garden were getting on.

"Eole?" said Melanie.

He turned back from the window. Their eyes were all on him. He looked down at his feet.

"I'm exhausted," said Rainbow. "Can you all go and get a coffee or something?" She squeezed Christophe's hand.

"Good idea," he said. "Come on, let's give them some peace."

Christophe shepherded Mum, Melanie and Domi towards the door. Rainbow told Eole to stay. Poor Eole. He looked pale and skinny. Alexandra must be furious about him losing so much weight. Rainbow had to tell him the news now, before Alexandra whisked him back to the mountains.

"It's OK, Eole. I know this association isn't your kind of thing, so you don't have to get involved if you don't want to. Our mission is over. We've saved the One Tree from being felled and now the association will continue to guard it."

She closed her eyes and let her memory linger over the last seconds before the branch fell, on the images Druid Oak had shown her.

Koad, it had said.

As she and the branch, chained together, had started to fall, she'd asked the one thing that mattered: *Are you the One Tree?*

I, Koad, am the last One, it had answered.

Rainbow opened her eyes and looked at Eole's blank face. "Druid Oak is the One Tree," she said to him. "Its tree name is Koad, which is the Breton word for forest and wood. We've saved it, Eole! Which means we've saved Amrita. Nobody is going to hurt Druid Oak after all that's happened – and with all that Melanie and I are going to do with our association. Isn't that the best news ever?"

Eole stared at her. They'd succeeded in their mission. He was no longer the Tree Slayer, but a Tree Saviour. He could go home with Maman and Hestia to where he belonged. He could return to his mountains, lie on his back in the purple heather with Darwie and make cloud art for the rest of the summer. He could study his multiverse book properly, now he could read again, without being distracted. He could even add an annexe to his mapopedia and include his own scientific findings, the ones he wouldn't discuss with Tintin. And he was sure he'd be able to actually enter Tintin's laboratory now, not just hover at the door, which meant he could begin a new project. All the platelets of events that had been drifting apart since his eighteenth birthday now fused together into a hot spurt of white light. He was going to combust. Happiness burst from every pore of his skin.

"Yes," he said.

Rainbow grinned. "You could show a bit more enthusiasm."

He smiled.

"That's better," said Rainbow. "There's just one more thing. It wasn't the bulldozer that made the branch fall."

"Yes, it was. I saw it."

"It only touched it lightly. That contractor knew what he was doing. The One Tree dropped its own branch, Eole. I know, because I was in tune with it at that moment."

Eole shrugged. It didn't matter how many branches the One Tree dropped. They'd saved it. And now Rainbow was out of danger and he could go home.

Outside, he heard a bark. He slid off the bed and hung his hands out of the window. Darwie raced across the lawn, followed by Hestia and then Maman.

"You're in Rainbow's room," said Hestia. "Got your leg over at last?"

Rainbow averted her eyes from Eole's bare bottom protruding from the hospital overall. She sat upright in her bed and flicked through her travel log, which Melanie had put on her bedside table. There was only one page left.

She picked up her pencil and started to sketch Koad, the

last One Tree. The minute she was discharged from hospital, she was going back to hug it properly. She would see its thousand-year story and restore its hope with her good news for the future of trees. And she would no doubt be reunited with Amrita, too. Amrita would fulfil her promise and from now onwards they'd spend halcyon days revelling, hand in hand, in the dappled sunlight of spring-green woodlands.

After hugging Koad, she would ride home with Christophe, cover Apple and Acorn with kisses and make amends with Thierry. She would learn to ride her motorbike, as she'd wanted to do since last September. And she and Melanie, using the funds from the amazing, tree-loving public, would make a success of their association.

She knew this was possible because she was RainbowMary and, if she wanted something enough, she had all the strength she needed to achieve it. Instead of helping one tree at a time, she'd find and protect all the ancient trees in France. With Amrita beside her, she'd discover and understand the spiritual side of trees and grow closer than ever to them.

Now *that* was pretty cool, as destinies went.

Rainbow's story continues in...

Tree Sacrifice (Book 3)

ABOUT THE AUTHOR

Although Harriet Springbett always wrote stories in her West Dorset home, she qualified and worked as an engineer. During a Raleigh International expedition in Chile she realised writing and discovering life were more important to her than her career. She moved to France, where she studied French at Pau University and then worked as a project manager, feature writer, translator and TEFL teacher. She now lives in Poitou-Charentes with her French partner and their teenage children.

Since her first literary success, aged 10, her short stories and poetry have been published in literary journals and placed in writing competitions, including a shortlisting in the renowned Bath Short Story Award. She leads writing workshops, has judged the Segora international short story competition and blogs about being a writer in France at https://harrietspringbett.wordpress.com.

ACKNOWLEDGEMENTS

Firstly, I would like to thank Françoise Gourvès from the Maison des Arts in Arras-en-Lavedan. I met her while admiring an art exhibition there, and she invited me to be a writer in residence at the arts centre so that I could carry out further research for *Tree Slayer*. Arras-en-Lavedan is renowned for its local artists and has an outdoor art circuit as well as the permanent and temporary exhibitions in the Maison des Arts.

While on my residency, I had help from lots of lovely local people, including farmers Pascal and Dominique Gainza and their sheep, goats, and sheepdog Dora. Special thanks to Karine and her team from the bistro-bookshop 'Le Kairn' in Arras-en-Lavedan, who hosted me for talks about *Tree Magic*, answered my questions and fed me delicious dishes. More about my discoveries in the Pyrenees can be found in my blog on https://harrietspringbett.wordpress.com.

Please note that while I use Arras-en-Lavedan as a setting in *Tree Slayer*, Eole's farm, the campsite and the summer pastures are invented from different landscapes around the

Val d'Azun. All the characters are invented too, of course.

Thanks also to the people who helped my Brocéliande research by remembering the 1996 version of Paimpont, especially Valérie from Le Brécilien bar and Laurent Goolaerts at the library. Benoît at the CPIE environmental agency in Concoret and Marc Magels from the Arthurian Centre gave me information on the ancient trees in Brocéliande, while Concoret's mayor was kind enough to show me photos of Guillotin's Oak from twenty-two years ago. I hasten to add that I invented all the Brocéliande characters, Druid Oak and the village of Argoad with its bar, environmental agency and mayor – many thanks to author Suzie Tullet for suggesting I do this.

My character-building was enriched by Juliette Henry, Nicolas Gilouard and Cedric Mauger, for which I thank them wholeheartedly. Many thanks to Jackie Maude, my reiki master, for all she's taught me. And as ever, I must thank my early readers, Darylle Hardy, Rachel Richards and Melanie More, for their time and diplomatic honesty.

Despite their good advice, there was still plenty of work for my editor at Impress Books, Julian Webb. Many thanks to him for his valuable suggestions, which have helped develop my writing skills. The whole team at Impress Books are a pleasure to work with, and I'd particularly like to thank Sarah Sleath, my *Tree Magic* publicist. She helped me get to grips with the scary world of book marketing and, at YALC 2017, introduced me to the friendly book bloggers from #SundayYA.

Talking of books, several authors have been key in inspiring me: Peter Wohlleben, with *The Hidden Life of Trees*; Henriette Walter and Pierre Avenas for *La Majestueuse Histoire du Nom des Arbres*, a French book about the origins of tree names; and the wonderful Robert Macfarlane and the late Roger Deakin for their nature writing. I'd also like to acknowledge all the other people who write, tweet and talk about the importance of trees and the environment. Although *Tree Slayer* is set in 1996, I have used tree communication research published in recent years.

I'd like to say a general thank you to all book bloggers for taking their precious time to read and review books. Personal thanks go to my writing colleagues for shared pains and pleasures, and to my friends and family for their continued support and interest. They were the ones who consoled me when the real Hurricane Martin blew across southwest France in December 1999, destroying six out of ten trees in Cognac's François I park.

And finally I must thank *you* and my other readers for reading, reviewing and writing me the most delightful and moving messages. I hope you found *Tree Slayer* a satisfying sequel to *Tree Magic*.